A SIP OF MAGIC

KATE SWANSEA

A SIP OF MAGIC

KATE SWANSEA

Cover Art: Karen Dimmick / ArcaneCovers.com

To see five crows is a bad omen, for it is a sign that the fates are conspiring against us. It is a warning to be cautious, for even the wisest of witches cannot escape the grasp of destiny.
—The Albright Family Grimoire

CHAPTER I
SERENA

They say that if you squint your eyes just right, you can read your fortune in the tea leaves at the bottom of an empty teacup. Life, death, prosperity, calamity, it's all in there if you know how to interpret the scattered remnants of the dregs.

But when Serena cast a lingering gaze into her nearly empty teacup the day she arrived in Pembrooke, she felt a wave of awe and horror pass through her.

Not your everyday tea-drinker, Serena understood the leafy hieroglyphs like an artist understands her canvas. To her, each hint of a symbol was a secret message, a whispered prophecy, woven in the magic-imbued leaves.

And right then, strange patterns were shifting and dancing in the sepia liquid at the bottom of her cup. Like a seer lost in the depths of a crystal ball, Serena zeroed in on an ominous shape that was forming, dissolving, and reforming in the tea puddle.

Frowning down at the cup, her immediate reaction was to quietly mutter, "Well, fuck."

Just one or two more sips would drain the cup and allow the image to settle.

A shiver of reverence and dread passed through her. But symbols were tricky. They could be misread, misunderstood, miscalculated. Serena toyed with the handle, unwilling to take the final sips, as she pondered what the cryptic message would be.

She'd been in Pembrooke for exactly thirty-five minutes and this was the last thing she wanted to see. The seaside town was quaint, gorgeous, idyllic—exactly the sanctuary she had been looking for when she had fled sun-baked Arizona. Pembrooke had beckoned to her like a siren's song from the moment she noticed the ad for the retail space. So, for fate to turn its capricious hand against her now, after her difficult move to this Oregon haven, would be nothing short of infuriating.

Her thoughts were interrupted by a bloodcurdling sneeze.

Across the expanse of worn oak that formed their table, Clara Summers, her new landlady, dabbed at her eyes.

"Bless you," Serena said, flashing her most sympathetic smile.

"Excuse me. Oh goodness, my allergies are so terrible this time of the year."

They were sitting in the ochre-toned shell of what was once a bustling café. The empty room breathed echoes of a past life, scuffed wooden floors and the aged brick of the walls bearing testament to laughter, conversation, and countless shared meals. A patchwork of mismatched chairs surrounded the old oak table at which they sat, where Serena's thin fingers cradled a nearly empty cup of black tea.

"And of course the farmer's market is every Saturday morning in the school parking lot," Clara said, picking up right where she'd left off before the sneeze. "You can walk to it from here." As Clara's words swirled around the room, a lingering tension hung between them. Serena noticed the slight quiver in Clara's voice, the hesitations before she spoke. For Serena, this was not unusual; she had long grown accustomed to the fear and wariness that often accompanied her interactions with humans.

"Witch," they would occasionally mutter when they thought she couldn't hear them. She'd gotten much better at hiding her powers over the years, but somehow they just seemed to sense something was a little off about her.

The landlady paused again to sneeze into the crook of her elbow, before fishing a handkerchief out of her purse.

Three more sneezes followed, each more theatrically explosive than the last. Clara sat at the center of the storm, eyes watering and nose wrinkled as if a great battle was being waged beneath her sternly pinched face. Each successive sneeze sounded less like a dainty sniffle and more like a startled goose honking in alarm. Her eyes, now crimson and accusing, darted frantically between Serena and the handkerchief clutched desperately in her hand. Clara attempted to regain her composure with a vigorous blow into the cloth, which ended in a sound remarkably similar to a trumpet's call to arms. Serena had to bite her lip to keep from laughing at the spectacle, though a traitorous giggle did escape, only to be drowned in the cacophony of Clara's symphony of sneezes.

"Drink the tea. It will help." Serena slid the still full cup and saucer closer to the woman.

Lifting the cup to her lips, Clara's reddened eyes bounced around the room, occasionally resting on Serena, a touch of wary curiosity glinting in her gaze. After swallowing several sips, her eyes narrowed. "Did you say you're planning on making this old cafe into a teahouse?"

"Yes, that's the plan," Serena affirmed with a small smile,

her voice resonant in the expansive emptiness. She glanced over her shoulder to admire the dusty space. "Yes, I've been brewing teas and herbal remedies for ten years and I'm ready to have a proper teahouse."

The place was perfect. Wide, arched windows lined an entire wall. They allowed sunlight to cascade through, casting warm, gentle shadows on the stripped wooden floors that sprawled beneath. The play of light and shadow imbued the open room with an almost ethereal charm, a whisper of a promise of future warmth and comfort. A singular bricked wall stood in stark contrast, a robust testament to the building's resilient past, its red tones mellowed by age but still vibrant, drawing the eye and invigorating the senses. Nestled towards the back, a secluded kitchen waited in anticipation of home-made breads to be baked, and fragrant spells to be conjured.

The kitchen was bordered by a wooden staircase. The stairs, worn but sturdy, curved upwards to a concealed second floor, a private space soon to be her personal sanctuary. Hers and Kita's. She glanced out the window at her car before returning her attention to Clara.

"I figure the counter would make an excellent tea bar. And the rest of the dining space will be filled with chairs and small loveseats grouped around tables. And there will be pastries in display cabinets beneath the bar. And of course the teas...I'd like to display them on shelves behind the bar in pretty glass jars."

Clara's thin eyebrows arched upwards as she took another sip from her teacup, the corners of her mouth twitching appreciatively. "Well, I must admit, this tea is certainly good. Exceptional even."

"Thank you, Clara." Serena smiled. Funny how her landlady had not yet noticed that her sneezing fits had already stopped, her breathing less congested now.

Curiosity piqued, Clara's eyes moved from the electric kettle on the dusty counter to the glass teapot, and the accompanying cups and saucers, all carefully arranged on the worn wooden table next to the empty cardboard box. "You always travel with all this?" Clara gestured towards the brewing paraphernalia, her tone carrying a hint of bemusement.

"At least with a kettle," Serena replied with a grin. "The rest I can get by without. But I've kept everything in reach since I left Sedona."

"Your people back in Arizona then?" Clara prodded.

"Nah," Serena said shaking her head. "It's just Grace—my mother—and right now she's either in South Dakota or Philadelphia. Just flip a coin and you may be right," Serena said with a small shrug and an uneasy laugh.

"Oh," Clara said with a small chuckle, but she didn't look very amused. "And no special someone either—pretty girl like you?"

Serena shook her head again. But there had been a man back in Sedona. He had filled her life with music and poetry in the hot evenings of the painted desert. But she couldn't see herself sticking around in Sedona, as beautiful as the red rocks were, and as amazing as the spiritual energy in town had been.

Nope, it had been time to move on again.

Men, like the seasons, had a tendency to disappoint, Serena mused. They had a knack for ending things in the cruellest of ways. Tracing it back ten years, she could pinpoint her first heartbreak. Eighteen, young, dumb, and hopelessly in love with a drummer. She'd taken a leap of faith, dropping out of college and coming home for him, only to find him packing up to tour with the band. And no longer interested in a serious relationship, after begging her to come join him only the month before. Her dreams had disintegrated like a sandcastle hit by a wave, forcing her to piece together a new life from the ruins.

Grace, never a fan of any of her boyfriends, was gallivanting around the country on yet another whimsical journey when it happened. Grandma Bess, still alive at the time, was on her farm in Vermont. So, Serena was left alone to pick up the pieces and venture forth. The beginning of her nomadic existence.

There had been a few more romances after that, a cavalcade of promises and pretenses. But each tale was simply a new chapter in the same sorrowful saga. So, Serena learned to protect herself, not to expect much from these fleeting connections. She became the first to leave, the first to break free, preserving her heart from the anguish of abandonment.

The man in Sedona had been tempting, though. His amazing melodies had serenaded her under the starlit desert sky, his guitar strings plucked at her soul. Occasionally his verses had echoed through her mind on the road these past few days, a sweet residue of what could have been. But in the end, it was always better to be the one who said goodbye.

"Well, there are quite a few local delights here in Pembrooke to keep you busy." Clara's voice startled her from her thoughts. "The Labyrinth is a brew pub that is popular with young folks such as yourself. It seems to fancy itself on par with the Belgian monasteries, but my husband does say their pale ale is excellent, anyway. Then we have Borealis, which is very good, although Chef Paul insists on serving frog legs, sea urchins and stinky cheese on occasion. Personally, I've never understood the fascination, but to each their own."

Serena nodded, carefully sipping her tea while mentally cataloging the places.

"Then there's Kurt's Natural Market," Clara continued. "A shop filled with all manner of leafy, organic things. I swear half of them aren't even edible. But then again, you might be the type to find such curiosities intriguing." She pursed her lips at the assortment of herbs next to the kettle on the counter.

"I'll keep that in mind," Serena chimed in, her attention diverted back to the leaves swirling in her cup. The conversation's normalcy was a comforting distraction, but Serena found her gaze drawn back into the hypnotic heart of her nearly drained teacup. The remnants of the tea leaves were conspiring in the remaining drops, forming a dark, swirling canvas of foreboding patterns. They danced and twisted beneath the surface, clamoring for her attention, ready to divulge a prophecy she wasn't sure she was ready to see.

Clara's words seemed to ripple and refract, lost in the shadows of the emerging omens before she grew silent. A long moment passed, fraught with anticipation and dread, before Serena finally broke the spell.

Feeling a strange mix of unease and anticipation, Serena lifted her gaze and blurted, "So, is there anything else I should know about Pembrooke? Any festivals?"

"No, no festivals, I'm afraid." Clara's smile faded. "Haven't had any for the past five years."

"Five years? Why is that?"

The landlady's gaze shifted as she toyed with the brooch at her collar. "They got cancelled." She paused for a moment, her eyes flicking up to meet Serena's.

"Why?"

Dropping her gaze to the table, Clara sighed. "Five years ago, something happened here... Something quite terrible."

Serena leaned forward, intrigued and concerned. "Did it happen during a festival?"

Clara gazed out the window, her mouth set in a grim line. "Ah, that's a tale for another time. We do have our stories, like any other place. Secrets and tragedies, they're part of the fabric of any town. But Pembrooke is a lovely town, Serena, that's all you need to worry about now."

Serena glanced down at her cup. "But sometimes, understanding the past can help navigate the future." She tried to keep her voice casual, not wanting to spook the older woman.

"Just an unfortunate event," Clara mumbled, avoiding Serena's inquiring gaze. "It's best we focus on the future, Serena," she responded firmly, effectively closing the conversation as she stood to leave.

Baffled yet intrigued, Serena could only nod.

A knobby hand slid a ring holding two keys across the table. "Rent's due by the fifth. Feel free to make the space yours," she said. "Within reason, of course. Check with me before doing anything drastic."

"Thank you, Clara. I will," Serena assured her as she walked the landlady to the door.

"There's a law firm just across the street there, if you need any legal advice," Clara said, pausing in the doorway. She pointed to a one-story gray building. "Jared Westergard works there. Local boy, went off to the big city for law school. Could've made it anywhere with his brains and looks, but he chose to come back home, surprisingly."

As Clara stepped outside, her gaze fell on the large timber wolf hanging its head out of the window of Serena's old car. Kita was getting antsy and Serena was feeling guilty for keeping her in the car as long as she had. She had thought she'd be just running inside to pick up the key, but after hearing Clara's sneezing, Serena knew she needed to brew the woman some tea to calm her allergies.

Clara frowned. "You're sure a big dog like that will be all right, cooped up in that little upstairs apartment?" Serena got a sense she asked more out of annoyance than concern. The pet deposit she'd paid upfront could only cover so much, she supposed.

She didn't bother correcting Clara that Kita was really a wolf. It was better that people didn't know. After all, she hadn't chosen to keep a wolf as a pet; rather, the wolf had chosen her.

"She'll be fine, thanks. I make sure she gets plenty of exercise."

"Hmm. Well, just make sure she doesn't disturb anyone. And you'll need to keep her on a lead; we have a leash law in Onyx County." She flashed Kita another sour glance before nodding to Serena and moving to take her leave. "Welcome to Pembrooke, Miss Albright."

With a nod and a wave, Serena watched Clara waddle to her old Cadillac sedan. As the landlady drove away, Serena pulled open the passenger door of her car to unleash her little beast.

"Come on Kita, let me show you our new home."

Kita bounded inside with Serena trailing behind. As the wolf ran around, sniffing in all the soon-to-be teahouse's nooks and corners, Serena moved to clear off the lone table. Clara had finished all of her tea, and Serena surmised she'd be good as new for at least a week, based on the spell and the ingredients Serena had selected.

As Serena reached for her own teacup, she paused. Then, lifting the cup to her lips, she downed the remaining tea in one gulp. Carefully inverting the cup to empty the remaining drops onto the saucer, she turned the cup clockwise three times, then righted it once more to inspect the contents.

The leafy remnants at the bottom of her drained cup clung together, forming a distinct pattern, shadows of the unspoken that left her breath hitched in her throat.

Five crows.

Stark and unmistakable against the pale porcelain, the shapes of five birds stared back at her.

If Grandma Bess were alive, she would have nodded vigorously and given her best I-told-you-so face. "You don't just go hopping about from place to place, girl. Find yourself a house and stay put. It's safer that way." Then she would have muttered to herself about "those trials" and gone back to chopping herbs or stirring whatever concoction she had heating over the fire.

Grandma Bess had never approved of Grace's lifestyle or the way Serena had emulated it once she grew up. Her grandmother had also given Serena the only notion she'd ever had of what home was. Her orderly little farmhouse was always adorned with cinnamon scented rowan and oak branches twisted into wreaths and brooms and frames, and all matter of homey decor. And the house was always filled with the scent of baking bread or apple tarts, made with fruit from her own grove.

A palpable heaviness settled in Serena's chest as she peered closer at the cup, her heart thundering a primal drumbeat in her ears.

It was a somber message, a harbinger that sent an icy shiver slithering down her spine. It carried a warning, a sign of something that dared not speak its name. Grandma Bess had spoken several times of the five crow omen.

"If you ever see it, Serena, pay attention to anything new that comes into your life. Figure out what it is quick as you can, 'cause by goddess, something is coming for you."

With a sigh, Serena glanced around. The echo of the dark sign seemed to linger in the soon-to-be teahouse, reverberating through the empty space. As she carried the cups to the sink, the residue of magic clung to the silence, coloring her new beginnings with an uninvited shade of uncertainty.

CHAPTER 2
SERENA

Serena took a centering breath and dumped the soggy tea leaves into a garbage bag. She would keep her eyes open for possible threats, but there was no time to stew over the meaning of the dark reading now. Besides, readings only told what was *likely* to happen; nothing was ever set in stone.

Kita trotted around, sneezing as she passed through a spider web. Streams of early afternoon light poured in from the street as Serena toured the space again, absorbing the cozy kitchen, the wood staircase that ran up to the second floor living quarters, and the second-floor balcony just *begging* for a small garden of flower pots and herbs.

"What do you think, girl? Needs a coat of paint, obviously, but it's... nice, don't you think?"

Kita simply yawned in response, warmed from resting in the car for much of the morning and made lazy by the calming quiet. She certainly looked the part of a majestic, regal beast, her charcoal grey fur plush against her large, sturdy body. But in reality, Kita often reminded Serena more of a spoiled lapdog than a wild wolf.

When Serena first found her, paw caught in a bear trap in the woods of northern Minnesota, she'd been worried that Kita wouldn't adjust to civilization long enough for Serena to nurse her back to health back at the cabin. But even after she was fully healed, Kita had refused to return to the wilderness, refused to leave Serena's side. Serena quickly realized Kita could understand what she was saying to her, too, and that's when Serena knew she had found her familiar.

That seemed like ages ago now, as she watched Kita sniff at the thick carpet in Serena's soon-to-be bedroom and then deftly maneuver the unfamiliar stairs.

As Serena descended, the soles of her favorite brown leather boots scraping against the wood steps, she surveyed what would become her teashop, just beyond the kitchen doorway. She could almost see the tables, arranged just so. Customers from all over town, sipping tea, talking, *healing*. She grinned, the anticipation of satisfaction nearly as good as the real thing.

It was perfect.

Blowing out a long breath, Serena shook the travel-numbness from her limbs. No time to waste. Yanking the front door open, she plucked a large, smooth stone from the barren plot of dirt out front and propped the front door open. That spot was clearly intended to be a small garden area, fit for a handful of small bushes or a smattering of pretty blossoms. Serena didn't have to spare much thought on her plans for the space.

The town of Pembrooke was in a word, quaint. Perched at land's end on a wide cliff, it was a beautiful coastal town with buildings that looked like they were stolen from a nineteenth century New England village. In between the buildings, the vast blue Pacific Ocean peeked through like a sparkling gem, its waves crashing one hundred feet below.

As she led Kita outside, Serena anxiously scanned the street for any passers-by. Luckily, it appeared to be a slow morning. She saw a young dark-haired woman walking into a building across the street, but she didn't pay Serena or Kita any attention.

A smattering of roadside flowers caught her attention. Pink, fluffy blossoms that rose in a delicate point.

"Do you see those?" Serena prodded, glancing over to Kita with a slight smile. "That's astilbe. Good for inflammation, nausea, and menstrual cramps." The wolf sniffed at the blooms but then got distracted by a nearby squirrel.

Patience. That was what these flowers symbolized. *Good things come to those who wait.*

The leash stashed in the glove compartment of her car hadn't seen much use since she'd initially bought it, but Serena wasn't keen on getting fined for something so trivial, even if she knew that in Kita's case it wasn't necessary. Once Serena had proven herself to be worthy of the wolf's trust, Kita was surprisingly obedient and well-mannered. Overly curious maybe, but she almost never did anything outright destructive. Keeping her on a leash felt like an insult, somehow. Less than she deserved. Well, at least she'd finally be getting her money's worth.

"Forgive me," Serena cooed as she clipped on the lead. "But rules are rules. Usually, anyway." Kita bristled slightly at the restraint, but she behaved herself, nonetheless. Serena made a mental note to reward her with treats once they were finished unpacking.

Serena tilted her head in thought, looking up at the building's rust-colored brick exterior. It was old but it wasn't dilapidated; she only saw one broken window. The walls all looked stable and sturdy, and the trim, leaded windows, and brick façade were beautiful. Grace would call it "historic". It had a certain charm to it, but it undeniably needed some TLC. She glanced this way and that, assuring herself that she wasn't being watched by any pedestrians or nosy shopkeepers.

The brick was cool against her hand when she reached out, the surface not yet warmed by the May sun. She inhaled through her nose, closed her eyes, and whispered a few words. Thick, emerald leaves quickly spread along the wall, her palm their epicenter, as they curled over the brick and stretched up to the second floor.

Ivy was one of her favorites. Beneficial for coughs, sunburns, lice. Handy to have around, but mainly she enjoyed it for its aesthetics, the way it provided life and color to otherwise plain buildings. Besides, ivy was always one of the first steps of her settling in process. It was a small charm, a touch of her magic to make the place her own, even if temporarily.

"Much better, don't you think?" she asked Kita, stepping back to admire her handiwork. Kita brushed against her legs in approval. Serena laughed, patting her soft head before turning her attention to the barren plot in front of the shop.

With a few whispered words, she called forth a cluster of Queen Anne's Lace to grow and bloom in the vacant garden, spreading until it bumped the stone border. Yes, she felt confident that it would be able to find sanctuary here. At least for a while. A while was all she ever asked for.

Serena took a few steps backward with a look of self-satisfaction. Spreading out her hands, she gestured to the space just beneath what would be her bedroom window. "And we can put the sign right there, in big, fancy lettering. Oh! And we could make a private dining space that can be rented for parties there, in that little room in the corner," she suggested, peering through the large window.

Making her way to the car, she beamed up at the building teeming with potential, and blindly grabbed for the car's back seat handle.

The moving van would be there later in the afternoon, carrying with it her larger furniture. For the moment, she was saddled with the odd, floating outcasts. Books but no bookshelf, pillows and sheets with no bed to place them upon, cheerful knick-knacks that were pleasant enough to look at but were left without a home. For a few hours, anyway.

The box nearest to her was filled with books, deceptively heavy for its size. She wrapped her arms around it, stumbling when she hefted the awkward load. At that moment Kita barked, startled by some unseen disturbance. Serena lost her grip, yelping in warning when the box slipped from her grasp. She instinctively jumped away from it before it could crush her toes, and found herself crashing into a solid presence at her back.

"Oof!" a low voice exclaimed, and she whirled around to face it.

"Oh," she said.

Tall. A good handful of inches taller than Serena, even in her heeled boots. As Serena's eyes trailed upwards, the man before her stood out immediately, not just because of his height, but also because of the sheer force of his presence. He was striking, with a razor-edged jawline and deep-set, hazel eyes that seemed to pierce through her. His dark hair, caught somewhere between the orderliness of straight and the wild abandon of curly, cascaded in loose waves, resting just at the nape of his neck. His crisp white dress shirt was well-tailored to his toned torso and unbuttoned at the top, as if he found the act of dressing up somewhat stifling.

There was another thing, too. Witches had an uncanny talent for recognizing their own kind, an innate sense that buzzed like a silent whisper when another magic-bearer was near. The man had that air about him—an underlying power that he carried effortlessly, but one that was palpably intense. His eyes seemed to dance with an inner storm, revealing depths of knowledge and capability that were both intriguing and threatening. While his physical allure was undeniable, it was this raw, magical potency that made Serena feel an unfamiliar anxiety, an edginess that treaded the line between fascination and fear.

"Sorry," she stammered. "I didn't see you—" Serena tried to step backward, but her spinning, combined with Kita's unfamiliarity with being on a leash, had left the pair tangled.

She huffed, heat and anxiety creeping up her neck in a cocktail of embarrassment and frustration. "Kita, stay! She's— I'm sorry, she's never like this."

Slowly, carefully, she maneuvered the man and herself out of the tangled leash, immediately crouching to begin gathering her fallen things. She grimaced, picking up a volume that had landed a bit harshly. Serena felt an odd pang of sympathy for the book, its pages curled and crushed against the pavement. Gently, she smoothed them into place and closed the cover before returning it to the box.

The man smiled politely before kneeling beside her. With furrowed brows, he dusted some dirt off of a leather-bound journal and turned it over in his hands. He opened it, thumbing through the pages, and Serena immediately snatched it from his hands. The moment it was back in her grasp, a wave of embarrassment overtook her. She felt ashamed of her rudeness, yet deeply annoyed that he would look through her journal despite being a total stranger. "I'm sorry," she mumbled halfheartedly, placing it in the box.

"You've mentioned that," he said.

Serena blew out a sharp breath. Her first day in this town

was not going as she'd hoped. "You shouldn't just rifle through people's things, that's all."

To her surprise, he continued collecting the books, despite her attitude. "I didn't see a title; I was just curious."

"It doesn't have a title," she answered shortly. "It's just notes. Research."

"*Your* research?"

She nodded.

"What sort of research is it?"

"Botany, mainly. Medicine. A bit of floriography sprinkled in," she said.

"Sounds like quite the page turner," he deadpanned.

Powerful or not, if there was one thing Serena couldn't tolerate, it was arrogance. She glared over at him, sending daggers into his studious hazel eyes. "I'm sorry I can't offer something more entertaining."

"No? You seem plenty interesting to me."

Pausing, Serena narrowed her eyes. Was that... a come-on? "Well, I'm a brewer, not a librarian," she shot back, partially just to see what he would do next.

She moved to lift the box, then was surprised when the man hefted it into his own arms with ease. Initially alarmed at the idea of this strange warlock handling her things, she surrendered a breath later and gestured for him to bring the box inside.

"A brewer?" he echoed, stooping slightly to pass under the threshold. "Beer or coffee?"

"Teas."

"That's a shame."

She frowned. "Why do you say that?" She asked, trailing after him as he carried the box into the kitchen.

"I work at Westergard and Ross, in the building across the

street. I thought that if you were brewing coffee, I might finally have somewhere to stop in before work."

"Hmph." Serena glanced out the window at the simple grey building across the street—the law office. "And if I served beer?"

"Then I'd come in after, naturally."

She couldn't help herself; she smiled. "Well, I make a lot of different teas, you know. There's bound to be *something* in here that catches your eye."

The man set the box down with another soft grunt, then looked her up and down as if signaling that *she'd* caught his eye. She realized a moment too late that she straightened her posture in response, as if she was trying to impress. The corner of his mouth quirked upwards. "I bet you're good at brewing up all sorts of things. For now, I'll settle for the crap in the break room, thanks."

Serena nodded in acquiescence. "Suit yourself. And thank you, for the help."

He smiled down at her, all white teeth and lightly tanned skin. "What else are neighbors for?"

"Maybe my past neighbors weren't up to Pembrooke standards," she replied, offering her hand. "I'm Serena, by the way."

As his calloused hand met hers, a spark of surprise jumped across their contact. Her gaze flickered down to the grip, then back up to him. His eyes held a glint of amusement, a smirk playing on his lips that told her he'd felt it, too.

"Jared Westergard," he said, his deep voice carrying an undercurrent of something she wasn't sure she wanted to decipher just yet. His eyes ran over her in a subtle sweep, scrutinizing her just as much as she was him.

She glanced again at the sign in front of the law office

across the street. *Westergard and Ross.* So he was one of the owners.

Stepping back, she felt a flush creeping up her neck and warming her cheeks. "So," she started, lifting a brow, "Prosecution or defense?"

"Civil. Land disputes, contracts, business, estate planning, that sort of thing."

"Contracts. Yes, I can see how those would be much more thrilling to read than my botanical notes."

He smirked at her clapback. "Sure it's dry," he replied, his eyes never straying from her. "But someone has to do it." The quiet confidence, the intensity of his gaze, and the subtle play of his muscles beneath his shirt was unnerving.

To distract herself, Serena slipped into old habits. She looked him up and down, scanning for signs of stress, fatigue, depression. "Well, if you ever need to unwind, come over for a cup."

"Hot tea for the soul?" His brows rose slightly at her proposition, before he began to make his way to the door.

"You could say that. I'm aiming to be a bit of a cure-all. Whatever ails you, we'll have a brew to fix it."

He paused, turning to narrow his eyes in barely-concealed suspicion. "Well, I'll keep that in mind, once it opens."

"And the first one's on the house," she offered, holding the door for him. "Consider it payment for giving me such an... eventful welcome."

CHAPTER 3
JARED

J ared froze in the threshold, eyeing the new ivy covering
the storefront. Next he turned his attention to the
woman's SUV. Built for rural terrains, it was painted a
cheerful robin's egg blue. No sign of a moving van, either.
"You certainly travel light."

"You learn to," she replied airily. "Makes moving easier."

He looked at her over his shoulder, flashing a smirk. "A
traveling tea brewer then. How whimsical."

"Oh, sure," she replied, resting her hip on the door frame
with a lazy grin. "Whimsy to spare. Didn't you notice my
faithful canine companion?"

Jared huffed. "Tough not to when she's holding me hostage
in the street. I hope you're planning on keeping her upstairs—
I'd hate to see you get sued because some wolf fur ended up in
someone's teacup."

Her eyelid twitched, just slightly. *Touchy, touchy.* He
wondered if she was this defensive about everything, or if he'd
somehow managed to stumble his way over both of her sore
spots.

"She'll be fine. Thanks."

He shoved his hands into his pockets, awkwardly observing the building's exterior, the shallow pothole in the center of Bailey Street, his office window well within sight of the empty shop, along with its new proprietor. He should really be going. There was nothing keeping him here, and he was running late. The new associate he was supervising might think he didn't take his work seriously, and she struck him as the type to walk all over him if she thought she could.

And this woman—no doubt a witch—clearly didn't want his help. Didn't need it, either, judging by the way the toned muscles in her arms shifted when she moved, fully on display past the straps of a canary yellow tank top. They'd already gotten off on the wrong foot together, and if she was moving in just across the street, then the chances of avoiding her were slim to none. Best to cut his losses and keep his distance, for now. Maybe start fresh another day.

So, he was a bit surprised with himself when he took a breath, squared his shoulders, and said, "Well, no time to waste. Let's get started on the rest of it."

"What are you talking about?" Serena's voice trailed after him as he strode over to her car. Sultry and velvety, like she belonged in a bar somewhere classy, crooning Lana Del Rey numbers for tips.

Jared opened the back car door, grabbing a small box labeled 'flatware' in crooked, swirly script. "We can knock this out much faster together." He gestured to her dusty boots, and to the large dog—make that a wolf—she still had in tow. "And to be honest, it didn't seem like you were getting very far on your own."

When he glanced up to face her, she appeared irritated. Hands on her hips, staring him down like he'd insulted her mother. It might have been intimidating, if she wasn't struggling to look up at him without squinting into the morning sun. The rays caught her gold-streaked hair where it hung in her face, lending it an angelic affectation. Pretty, in a way.

"Something the matter?" he asked, moving up the sidewalk.

She huffed in annoyance. "I guess it would save me some time," she grumbled, opening the other door to lift another box.

"Oh please, no need to thank me," he said.

"Try not to break any plates and maybe I'll start thanking you again," she said with a brisk tone.

"So," he said, moving to brave a journey up the narrow stairs in the back of the shop. "Where was the last location of this whimsical, traveling tea shop?"

"Nowhere," she replied. "This is my first try at having a proper storefront."

Jared huffed at that, chancing a look over his shoulder at her. "So you're using the people of Pembrooke as your guinea pigs, effectively."

"Not exactly. I've sold teas before. It was just out of my garage at my last place in Arizona."

"Classy."

"Well, I would've said it had a... rustic sort of charm," she argued.

He chuckled then took a moment to observe the upstairs apartment as he moved through it. It was quaint, cozy. Small. She lived alone, then. "Well, I won't claim it to be 'rustic', but I hope you'll find Pembrooke to be charming enough for you."

She tilted her head. "Are you charmed by it?"

He paused, surprised by her question. "Maybe for the first twenty years," he said with a tight smile. "Novelty doesn't last forever, I'm afraid. But it's home." Truth was, nothing felt like home anymore. Not for the past five years, anyway.

Slowly but surely, the pile of boxes dwindled, the two of them toting them up the groaning, wooden steps and into various empty rooms. Serena had a look of quiet satisfaction on her face, pride blooming as the loft space filled with books, clothes, knick-knacks. By the last trip out, she was positively glowing, the spread of her lips narrowing striking, green eyes.

She retrieved a small, open box from the passenger's seat floorboard, gently cradling it in her arms like something precious. As he followed her for one final trek into the soon-to-be teahouse, he peered over her shoulder curiously. Mason jars, all carefully labeled. Seeds, soil, dried herbs, and blossoms.

He bit back a groan. *Oh, come on.* Couldn't he have one moment's peace? "You said you're into botany?" he asked, gently testing the waters.

Serena smiled down at the supplies in her arms, a dimple forming on her right cheek. "Mm-hmm. Have been since I was little. And look at me now—I get to play with plants all day. My childhood self would be so proud."

Jared nodded along, feigning nonchalance. "You know, a lot of people ascribe value to different plants, beyond any aesthetic or uh... culinary value."

She nodded in mild interest at that. "Sure. The upper class has been practicing floriography since the Middle Ages. Assigning meanings and symbols to nature, using plants to communicate when discretion was needed. Secret messages. You could start a war by just sending a few carefully chosen blossoms. Or a love affair..."

He shifted awkwardly and rubbed the back of his neck. He wasn't looking forward to broaching this subject. Something told him that this wouldn't end very pleasantly. "Well, I don't know much about symbolism, but I do know a thing or two about... witchcraft."

Serena chuckled. It didn't ring quite as warmly as it had before. "Right, right. As in double, double, toil and trouble?"

"Serena."

She glanced up, the abrupt change in his tone evidently grabbing her attention. She furrowed her brows, frowning up at him from beneath a curtain of long lashes. "Yes?"

He plucked a jar of dried purple flowers from the box, holding it up and shaking it slightly as he spoke. "This," he said, "is vervain. Very popular in magical circles for warding away malicious energy."

Serena had the nerve to *actually* roll her eyes at that. "It also serves as a potent anti-anxiety agent."

Jared scoffed. He didn't buy it for a moment, but then again something in the twitch of Serena's lip told him that she didn't think he would. "Anti-anxiety? Don't most teas have calming effects?"

The innocent shrug she offered in response was nearly insulting. Like she thought this was just a game and, worse still, she thought she was winning.

"They do, generally. But some people require a more... targeted remedy."

He smirked, selecting another small jar like it was a piece on a chessboard. Another move to counter hers, to level the playing field or even gain an advantage. "Henbane, Serena? You expect me to believe you cultivate *henbane* as part of your pet passion?"

"Is it that unheard of?"

"Henbane is inedible. Poisonous, even. The only reason you would risk having it in your home is if you were using it for magical purposes."

He was expecting her to bristle at that. To roll her eyes again and tell him to mind his own business. Instead, she gave a small nod of respect and flashed a wicked smile.

"To serve poison in a drink is the mark of genuine civility. It is the act of a true lady, who knows how to hide the taste of death behind the veil of pleasure," she said.

Checkmate.

"You admit to brewing magical poisons?"

"No, I admit to nothing of the kind! It is the amount of leaf that I use that tips the scale from medicine to deadly poison." She pointed to the jar of henbane. "I drop one pinch of that into your oolong tea and I soothe your toothache or earache. I drop in three pinches and you drop dead at my feet."

Jared felt his mouth drop open.

"Oh, come on! It's the same as any medicine you buy at the pharmacy," she added, crossing her arms. "But I'm a healer. Not a killer."

"Yet you say only a fine line separates the two." He crossed his arms and studied her. "Look, I'm sure you're not planning to brew poisons, but magical teas are also out of the question."

She gave him a sidelong glance. "Where'd you learn so much about magical plants, anyway?"

Jared responded with a spread of his arms, a casual display of false modesty. "It's what I do."

"You encounter a lot of henbane as a civil attorney?"

"No," he replied. "But I do encounter it as a member of the Pacific Northwest Magic Council."

Now she gave him the reaction he'd been anticipating. She outright groaned at him, snatching something from his hand for the second time that morning. "Seriously? You're a Lens?"

"Keeping a watchful eye on the magical community," he recited, much to her apparent disgust. "I take it you aren't too fond of us?"

"Watchful eye," she repeated sarcastically. "Unblinking is more like it. I had a run-in with one of your colleagues in the Adirondacks Branch, three summers ago. He nearly ruined my reputation on the basis of some trumped up charge that wasn't even my fault."

He cleared his throat, attempting to adopt a more professional air. "Well, I can't speak for them, but I assure you, I'm only ever exactly as strict as I deem necessary. I'm sure they gave you plenty of leeway out East, but there isn't a very big magical population in Onyx County—only a few dozen practicing in Pembrooke, and fewer in certain other towns closer to Portland. The witches here keep a low profile, and it's better for everyone if we keep it that way."

"A low profile, how?" Serena crossed her arms.

"Just two main rules you gotta follow if you want to stay in Pembrooke. One, no public magic. And two, no covens. So as long as *this*," he took the box of jars from the small kitchen counter and moved to set them on the balcony, "doesn't wind up in your teahouse, we shouldn't have a problem."

Serena laughed, but he had trouble locating any actual humor in the situation. "You're kidding, right? It's tea, not poison. It isn't hurting anyone."

"You say that now. What about when you're found out by a human? You think they'll laugh it off when they know they've been enchanted?"

"I'm not going to be found out!" Her voice climbed with her irritation. Kita was in the kitchen now, evidently put on the defensive by her owner's exasperation. She circled Serena's legs, weaving around the dark denim of her jeans. "Herbal medicine has been used for thousands of years in the human world; they don't know that the plants they're consuming also have magical properties! If someone comes in complaining of back pain and I tell them I have a tea with anti-inflammatory properties, their first assumption when they wake up feeling better won't be that I've cast a spell on them!"

She was coaxing his harder edges to the surface now,

and he could hear it in his voice. "If I allowed you to operate unchecked, I would be putting every witch in Pembrooke, myself included, at risk. Surely you can understand that."

"Sounds to me like you're just paranoid. This shop is going to be good for your community. Just give me a chance to get started and you'll see."

"I think I'd prefer to stop this problem before it can start, truth be told."

She paused, eyeing Jared as he rested his hands on his hips and regarded her. Serena set her jaw, fists clenching and releasing almost rhythmically. "You can't stop me from healing people."

"If you wanted to heal people, maybe you should've gone to medical school."

"Is that why you went to law school, then?" she spat with a scowl. "To get innocent people in trouble?"

Jared sent her his most passive aggressive smile. "You aren't in trouble. Yet."

She stalked off to begin unpacking a box of baking supplies. "Welcome to Pembrooke, indeed," she muttered. "I'm sure you remember where the door is, Mr. Westergard."

He dragged a weary hand down his face. "Look, I really do have your best interest in mind here, Serena. I don't want to see anyone get hurt, that's all."

She frowned at him. "Is there something looking to hurt me here?"

His mouth turned sour and he quickly looked away. "All I'm trying to say is that small towns like this one aren't always as quaint and harmless as they seem and, if you rock the boat, you might find that the people here aren't too keen on getting hit by rogue waves."

Serena narrowed her eyes. Challenging him. "Thanks for

the tip," she said, her voice cold as iron and twice as hard. "I'll keep that in mind."

He took her ire as a signal to leave well enough alone, for now. Though he suspected that she wouldn't be likely to heed his advice. "It was nice meeting you, Serena...?"

"Albright. And *really*, the pleasure was all mine."

CHAPTER 4
SERENA

The following days were a blur. An altogether not unpleasant, largely chaotic sort of blur, the likes of which Serena hadn't experienced since she was a teen and accidentally infused her tea with cannabis instead of mugwort.

Her newborn teahouse was a veritable revolving door of vendors, deliveries, and supplies. She'd deep cleaned every speck of grime before carefully inspecting each appliance in the kitchen. To her surprise, most of it was perfectly workable, though she would have to invest in a new standing mixer since her old one broke in the move. A part of her suspected that a certain lawyer was at fault for that, though she had no proof to support her belief. Still, at least she wouldn't have to *fully* exhaust her savings.

As was to be expected in a town of Pembrooke's size, she was treated to a steady parade of looky-loos. Townsfolk poking their noses in the door or peering through the windows, curious about the new establishment. She was quick to tell onlookers that they would have their answers soon enough, and sent them off with a wink and a grin and a promise that the grand opening would be well worth the suspense.

It was thrilling, seeing it come together. Fulfilling in a way she hadn't even thought to hope for. Setting up a more professional storefront had been mainly an act of opportunity, since working from her home suited her lifestyle much better. Putting time and effort, not to mention money, implied a certain level of permanence. The putting down of roots. The prospect of stability had always seemed unappealing to her, and yet setting up shop here felt... good. A much needed change of pace, she supposed, after so many years of floating on the breeze.

There was just one prominent dark cloud on her proverbial horizon. A tall, insufferable cloud with an attitude problem and too much confidence for his own good. At least he wore it well enough. Not that Serena would ever say as much to his face. She had more than a sneaking suspicion that Jared Westergard, attorney-at-law and member of the Pacific Northwest Magic Council, was the reason for her dark tea reading.

If she wasn't careful, she could find herself entangled in a formal investigation by the council. *Those damn Lenses.*

Jared had taken to spying on her. Perhaps 'spying' was a strong word. The two of them worked directly across the street from one another, and the curtains hadn't arrived yet, so it wasn't as if she could expect him to look away every time he was outside. He had as much of a right to casually—or not so casually, as the case may be—observe his surroundings, just as Serena did. It wasn't worth getting irritated over.

Why was it so difficult for him to just mind his own business? Must he insist upon standing on the front step of his building, sipping his coffee from a paper cup, whenever he had a break? She'd thought about confronting him one day, challenging him to come in and say something if he found her daily actions so interesting. But then, just as she'd been bracing herself to march over, she had the misfortune of making eye contact with the man.

Jared had seen her watching him, watching her. And he'd taken two fingers to his forehead, giving her a cheeky salute and smiling smugly as though *she* was the one who'd been caught in the act. She avoided even the shortest glance in the front window's direction for *days* after that.

And of course this line of intrusive behavior had been exacerbated when a certain civil attorney just *happened* to be passing by just as she received a rather large shipment of dried lotus—excellent for confidence, and with a unique flavor, too —and stopped his commute just to peer disapprovingly over the vendor's shoulder. She'd flashed him a smile, though it may be more accurate to say she bore her teeth in his direction, and he'd gone on his way. But she'd been left with the bitter feeling that his role as a nuisance would only become more prominent as the days went on.

He was a poison, she reasoned. All Jared Westergard had to do was exist in her orbit and she would find herself unable to focus on anything else. She caught herself, on more than one occasion, looking out her bedroom window first thing in the morning, seeing that dreary little office across the way, and spending her entire morning shower muttering to herself. Petty, passive aggressive little comments that were really quite unlike her. She blamed him for this, naturally. For polluting her air. She could only hope it didn't work its way into the tea.

But today Serena was decidedly *not* thinking about him. She absolutely refused to let him ruin this day for her. She'd been sketching the teahouse floor plans for days as she awaited the shipment, planning and re-planning the seating layout in the front area nearly every night.

She propped the front door open, eager as the delivery men

parked their truck outside. Most of the dining tables and counter stools would be arriving soon. Wrought iron tables with reclaimed wood tops, and tall, elegant barstools with lavender cushions.

Today, though, she was receiving something a bit... special. They'd initially been something of an impulse purchase, but the more she'd looked at their listing online, the more she'd grown to love these pieces. There was something pleasantly eccentric about them, which led her to believe that they wouldn't be found anywhere else in the area. It would make the teahouse all the more special. The low sale price had sealed the deal.

A sharp cawing sound drew her attention to the sky. A group of birds swooped past her head, their black silhouettes sharp against the sky, before settling on a tree branch across the street. Their beady eyes bore into her, then flitted to the delivery men, observing with unsettling intent. Ice prickled her skin.

Five crows.

She took a deep breath, redirecting her attention back to the workers, but not before noting that the tree the birds had chosen was Jared's. If she hadn't been sure before, now she was even more convinced that Jared was somehow tied to the bad omen.

That lawyer will be my undoing.

Forcing a smile, she stood outside the door as the delivery men carefully toted several deep purple, velvet loveseats into the building. They were even more luxurious in person, with dark wooden frames and plush cushions, draped in the soft, decadent material. And they were already bringing about their intended effect—a small crowd had gathered along the street to catch an eyeful of the fascinating furniture being hauled into the teahouse. Serena could hear a small chorus of murmurings, interest thoroughly piqued.

"Purple velvet," someone muttered.

"Enjoy the tease," she said, smirking over her shoulder at the crowd. "Won't be long now until we're open for business."

"Tasteless."

She gave her full attention to the speaker, a woman who looked to be in her late thirties, with short dark hair. "I'm sorry?"

The woman met her eyes. "I said your little establishment is wildly tasteless! This is a wholesome community. *Children* use this street. And I, for one, don't think that the children of Pembrooke should have to be forcibly exposed to your... depravity!"

It felt remarkably similar to being slapped across the face. "Depravity?" Serena echoed, brows furrowing in confusion. "Ma'am, I don't know what you've heard, but this is a business focused on healing its customers—"

"I'm sure," she scoffed. "Your clients must leave feeling very *healthy*, hmm?"

"I... I'm not sure what you're implying?"

"People are talking about this place all over town," another woman supplied. "One of those so-called 'massage parlors'. Well, no one in Pembrooke is interested in *unwinding* with you, missy."

Serena opened her mouth to argue, but found herself at a momentary loss.

"Don't try to deny it," the first woman insisted. "Not when you're dragging in all that... that brothel furniture!"

The outburst had garnered further talk from the crowd, most of it less than complimentary. For a moment, Serena had no recourse but to scan the faces before her, dumbfounded by how such an outrageous rumor would even come about, let alone gain traction.

Then she saw *him*.

Rage rose like bile in her throat. Jared was standing outside his building, paper cup in hand as usual. When she looked his way, he waved, and it was too far away to be certain, but she swore she saw him wink.

Her face went red in the blink of an eye, flushed with a near uncontrollable ire. Her hands began to move rhythmically, tightening into fists before releasing, again and again. She closed her eyes, took a quick, harsh breath.

"Ladies," she managed, her teeth gritted. "I'm not sure what you've heard, or who you heard it from, but this establishment is just an ordinary teahouse. Pastries and hot beverages. Nothing untoward."

This placated a few members of the group, but Serena still detected a few dismissive huffs and one "we'll see about that," within the chatter. She sighed, fully deflated from her once high spirits.

"Excuse me? Um, Miss?"

Serena turned to see a young, vibrant-looking woman with a mane of tousled auburn hair. The woman smiled reassuringly when she caught Serena's eyes. "Don't worry about them," she said, stepping closer. "People in this town can sometimes have trouble adjusting to new things. They'll come around."

"Well, thank you. It's nice to hear a vote of confidence for a change. I was starting to worry I'd missed the memo on some important piece of Oregon etiquette."

The woman held out a pale hand, fingers just peeking out from the stretched sleeve of a periwinkle cardigan. "I'm Lily," she said. "It's nice to meet you."

"Nice to meet you, too. Lily is such a beautiful name. Did

you know that lilies are toxic to cats? Certain breeds are beneficial for the heart in humans, though—lilies, that is, not cats."

Lily flashed an awkward smile, and Serena felt herself
blushing again.

"I mean—I'm sorry. I just have medicinal teas on the brain
these days. I think I need a good long nap. And I'm Serena."

She sighed with cautious relief when Lily laughed, hoping
that the woman was laughing *with* her and not *at* her. "Wow,
you really know a lot about flowers for a brothel owner," Lily
said, following her statement with a playful wink.

Serena chuckled. "Funniest thing about my massage parlor
is we have way too many teacups and way too few massage
tables. Must've been a mix-up with the delivery men."

"Maybe you should pivot," Lily suggested. "Just give up
and sell teas instead."

Serena glanced a final time at the disquieted group, casting
a rueful eye towards Jared's building, then leaned close to Lily
and spoke low. "Would you like to come in for a cup?"

Lily arched a brow. "Before the grand opening? I'd be
honored."

The two women went inside, leaving the small crowd on
the street. Serena led Lily up the stairs, already speaking as she
went. "I hope you don't mind sitting up in my home kitchen
for your free sample," she tossed over her shoulder. "The
teahouse is in a bit of a... transitional phase at the moment."

"As long as I'm not intruding."

When they reached the top of the steps, Serena made an
exaggerated show of inviting her into the tiny apartment
kitchen with a wide sweep of her arm. Lily chuckled, pulling
up a stool as Serena filled her kettle with water. Kita made her
presence known, trotting up to nose at the stranger's legs.

Lily reached down to scratch the wolf behind the ears as
she spoke. "So, what brings you to Pembrooke? Did you wake

up one morning and think to yourself 'If only my life wasn't quite so exciting'?"

"I hope you aren't implying this town is boring, when I have a genuine angry mob on my doorstep."

Lily shrugged. "You've seen one angry mob, you've seen them all."

Grinning, Serena opened her tea cabinet, rummaging through dozens of jarred and labeled herbs and flowers. "I've been everywhere else, I was bound to end up in Pembrooke, eventually." She sniffed a jar of dried clover before wrinkling her nose and setting it aside. "What about you, what do you do around here, beyond saving people from street hecklers?"

"I actually run the Tinker's Trinket, the antique oddities shop next door. I've been meaning to pop in and say hi for days now, but you've seemed so busy every time I've seen you."

"Well, I hope being next to my depraved establishment doesn't ruin business for you."

Lily shook her head, smiling down at the tabletop. "Where did a rumor like that even come from?"

"I can think of a few places," Serena said.

"Really? You've been in town for less than a month. How could someone already have it out for you?"

She rolled her eyes. "Just some busybody lawyer at that firm across the street. I ran into him the day I moved in. Let's just say we didn't hit it off."

"The one over there?" Lily asked, gesturing toward the living room window. When Serena nodded, she frowned. "Which lawyer?"

"Tall, dark, and insufferable."

Lily cocked her head. "You think Jared Westergard started a catty rumor about you?"

"If he didn't, then I don't know who did."

She narrowed her eyes, mouth twisting. "I don't know, that doesn't really sound like him. He's not usually so immature."

"Maybe I bring out the worst in him."

Lily waved the comment away, leaning back in her chair. "I wouldn't worry about it. He's even given me some trouble in the past, and we've known each other for years now. He means well, he's just a bit uptight these days."

Serena set Lily's tea in front of her—yellow rosewater and peach for improved friendship and good luck—and sat down across from her. "Trouble?" she echoed. "What sort of trouble?"

Lily stirred her tea a bit anxiously, staring down at the swirling liquid. "Nothing, really. I own the Tinker's Trinket with my partner, Emela. She's... sensitive, especially around people. And sometimes, when she gets overwhelmed..." She trailed off, frowning. "Anyway, he was worried we'd attract unwanted attention. I told him I'd keep an eye on Emela, and he hasn't really bothered us much since then. He definitely never tried to sabotage our shop, though. He's a lot more passive than that with us. Just, you know, keeping a watchful eye."

Serena blinked. *Watchful eye?* "He tried to get you in trouble with the Lenses?"

Lily grinned and clapped her hands. "I knew it! Another witch in Pembrooke. I think that brings us up to forty-five, now. So, that's why Jared is giving you so many problems; he thinks you're going to serve magical teas to your customers, doesn't he?"

She rubbed her thumbs across the pads of her fingers, grimacing slightly. "Not exactly," she said. "He *knows* I'm going to serve them."

The other woman's jaw dropped. "You're insane."

"You think so? Try the tea, tell me if I seem insane."

Lily looked down at the cup with fresh interest. "What's in it? Do I want to know?"

"All good things, I swear. Try it."

Sniffing the drink, Lily slowly brought the chipped yellow mug to her lips. "It's good," she said after a moment, taking another sip. "Fruity, floral. They won't suspect a thing from taste alone. Might even chalk it up to the placebo effect." She narrowed her eyes in concentration, searching. "The magic's subtle, too, when it's infused. I barely feel it, and I know what I'm looking for. Are you sure this is even potent enough to work?"

Serena nodded. "I've run plenty of tests. Every member of my coven back in Arizona swears by my remedies. It'll work; the people of Pembrooke will be healthy as horses. If that nosy Lens across the street can learn to mind his own business, at least."

Lily ran her finger around the rim of her mug. "You must've really pissed him off for him to sabotage you like that."

"It's not my fault that he expected me to be a pushover!" she argued, taking a seat across from Lily. "You should have seen him. He thought that he could just waltz up to me, flash that pretty smile of his, and I'd roll right over."

"He's got a pretty smile now, does he?"

Serena froze. "Did I say that?" At Lily's answering laugh, she groaned, glaring at the ceiling. "Well, yes, he does. You've seen him, you know that."

Lily smirked. "He's handsome all right. Not exactly my type —I've got a boyfriend, so I try not to look—but I'm starting to get the sense he's yours."

"Sure, if he kept his mouth shut. He's like a thorny rose. Not bad to look at, but I wouldn't want to handle one."

"I'm surprised he even bothered with the pretty smile

routine, honestly. I don't think I've seen him smile for anyone since his wife died a few years back."

Anger wilted somewhat, Serena's heart gave space for a measure of sympathy to bloom. "His wife died? Oh. That's a shame."

Lily nodded, cradling the teacup in both hands. "About five years ago. And Jared, he was never really the same, after. I mean, he's always been a little bit practical, but it's like he doesn't even know how to *breathe* anymore, you know? Like a switch in his head got stuck, and he can't seem to turn it off. Now all I ever see him do is work."

Serena sighed, regarding the wood grain on her kitchen table. She respected his strength, to persevere through his loss. Still, it didn't excuse his behavior in her eyes. "Well, I'm glad I encouraged him to do something fun, since he certainly found today's fiasco *very* amusing."

"Hey, he might've done you a favor," she countered. "I mean, there's no such thing as bad publicity, right? People are going to be coming from all over Onyx County to see you now."

She snorted. "Sure, sure. 'Honey, let's go to that teahouse with the *depraved* velvet sofas'."

Lily grinned. "You should make the sofas a part of your branding. In for a penny, in for a pound, right?"

"Hmm. The Velvet Teahouse," she mused, a smile rising to her face. "You know, I actually like the sound of that."

"Well, when The Velvet Teahouse does finally have its grand opening, Enzo and I will be there cheering you on."

"Enzo?"

"My boyfriend. Though my type unfortunately seems to be tall, dark, and chronically absent."

"Where is he?"

"He travels a lot for work with this new job he took. He's going to be in Singapore for the next few months."

"Oh, that is tough, Lily. Well, absence makes the heart grow fonder, they say." She slid Lily's empty teacup toward her and flipped it upside down on its saucer.

"Right. *They* say a lot of things, don't they?" Lily flashed a wan smile then glanced down at Serena who was rotating the cup on the saucer. "What are you doing?"

"Let's see what the tea leaves have to say." Picking up the cup, she glanced inside at the soggy leaves clinging to the bottom.

"Ooh. You're also a tassomancer. I guess that makes sense. What does it say?"

Serena's eyes narrowed, her gaze fixed on the patterns the tea leaves had formed. Her fingers traced the edges of the cup, and she tilted it slightly, letting the shadows play across the shapes.

"You're on a path filled with creativity and fulfillment," she began, her voice soft and contemplative. "The twists and turns in the leaves show a journey filled with personal growth. And there are strong connections to two people you love." She looked up, meeting Lily's expectant eyes. "But here, near the rim of the cup, the leaves cluster and tangle. That usually indicates a challenge or obstacle. Not in your business. This is in your personal life, relationships."

Lily leaned forward, her eyes flicking to the cup. "What kind of obstacle? Does it involve Enzo?"

Serena's gaze returned to the cup, her brow furrowed. "It's hard to say for certain. The tea leaves speak in symbols, not specifics. But the way they're gathered here, close to a symbol that might represent travel or distance... it could be connected to Enzo's absence. And there's a... false presence hanging over you both. Someone or something that will cause you pain."

"False presence?" Lily looked away, her mind seeming to toy with thoughts of what this could mean.

"Just remember the leaves show possibilities, not certainties. They reflect the energies around you at this moment, but you always have the power to shape your own future."

Lily nodded. "I know. Enzo and I, we'll get through whatever it is, I'm sure."

"I think you will," Serena said with a nod.

Lily grinned, standing. "I should probably get back to the shop. "But just a warning: be careful with Jared Westergard. It's his job to keep all the witches in Pembrooke in line. Most are scared to death of him. Just stay under the radar and he's harmless. Even the magic council can be sidestepped. But Jared... sometimes I think he may be involved with... something else."

"What do you mean?"

Lily shook her head. "I'm not sure. He's kind of a secretive guy, but I've seen some things over the years that have made me nervous. I didn't really notice until after Willow died. But looking back, it was always there. Anyway, Jared knows some pretty scary-looking people, if you know what I mean."

"Oh. Okay, thanks for the warning."

"Just watch your step with him. Thanks for the tea and the reading, Serena. And like I said, don't let those jerks out there bring you down. You're going to do great."

BUT THE NEXT DAY, SERENA DID SOMETHING *NOT* SO GREAT. IN THE softened glow of early afternoon, she, against her better judgment, succumbed to an impish whim, in spite of Lily's warnings to be careful with Jared.

Kurt's Natural Market was an old-world gem tucked away on the town's southern edge, its wooden floors worn down by generations of local patrons. The air inside smelled of earthy roots and freshly baked bread. Serena's wicker basket was heavy with the tang of ripe blueberries and the zesty promise of lemons, ingredients for a summer cake she envisaged baking that evening. The hum of the teahouse preparations and her burgeoning friendships buoyed her spirits.

But then, a slight chill clouded her warmth. She felt the weight of eyes upon her. Glancing subtly, she identified two elderly men with furrowed brows whispering furtively as they openly watched her with pointed fingers, their gazes riddled with judgment. The audacity of one, his thin, silvered eyebrows arched dramatically, made her fingers curl tight around the wicker handle.

Serena approached the checkout, where a bubbly, curly-haired girl, no older than sixteen, chattered away with customers, revealing braces as she laughed. Pembrooke, she had quickly realized, was a well of whispers where secrets seldom remained submerged.

Attempting nonchalance, Serena unloaded her groceries as she remarked, "This lovely store could do with a touch more security, don't you think? Perhaps a camera or two. Especially after that unfortunate incident with the lawyer."

The young cashier looked up, her clear eyes clouded with confusion. "What do you mean?"

Serena leaned in slightly, her voice conspiratorial, "Well, rumor has it that Jared Westergard was spotted shoplifting at the hardware store."

The girl's eyes widened. "Why would Jared Westergard steal from Abe's Hardware?"

With feigned innocence, Serena replied, "*Allegedly* stole. I wouldn't know, of course. But it may have something to do with the financial mismanagement charges he's been under investigation for. And, you know, how they froze his bank accounts. Of course it's all still under investigation. But one does wonder if this establishment could be his very next temptation."

The murmurs behind her grew louder. The woman behind her in line huffed, "Such a pillar of justice he claims to be, and yet here he is, stealing from good folks and breaking laws himself."

"A total hypocrite."

Paying and collecting her belongings, Serena replied with an enigmatic smile, "At the end of the day, it's really none of my business, though." As she exited, the bell chimed softly, leaving behind a store abuzz with her artfully spun tale. She knew that by sundown, this delicious morsel of misinformation would be on every pair of lips in Pembrooke.

CHAPTER 5
JARED

J ared was feeling very pleased with himself lately. He hadn't been completely sold on the idea when he'd started that rumor about Serena Albright's teahouse. He'd been worried that it might generate too much interest, albeit negative, and on the whole prove to be counterproductive. Seeing her on the curb that day though—red in the face and staring daggers at him—he'd been certain that it was an excellent idea, after all.

Still, Serena seemed to be infuriatingly unflappable, bouncing back from the embarrassment within the day. She'd even fashioned a gimmicky shop title from the affair, the garish purple sign taunting him every time he'd hazard a glance out his office window.

Until today. Today, he was in higher spirits. Because today was the grand opening of The Velvet Teahouse.

And not a single person had so much as peeked their head inside.

No one new, anyway. Lily Hart had stopped in that morning, purchasing two cups of tea to go. Ostensibly one for herself and one for her business partner, Emela. Aside from that though, the "Grand Opening" had been a monumental failure.

It was best for everyone, that's what Serena didn't understand. This town needed an openly practicing witch like Jared needed a hole in his head. He had everyone's safety in mind, Serena's included.

The council would want to hear about these magical teas, would insist on hauling her in for a lengthy investigation. And yet, he was loathe to report her to the council members just yet. He'd done some digging and found out that her last run in with the Lens out East had been related to selling some anti-wrinkle cream in a few fancy boutiques in upstate New York. Apparently they'd worked *too* well and attracted far too much attention. Her venture had ended in a council investigation.

If Jared instigated another council investigation, it would be her second. And with the council's strict "Three Strikes" policy, he didn't want to be the one to bring her one step closer to being locked up in a penarcanium. Careless was the only way to describe this woman. It would be better for her if he could just get her to walk away from this ridiculous teahouse venture and move on.

But she seemed to be settling in and even making friends. Honestly, it worried him how close she and Lily were becoming. Jared himself hadn't spoken much with Lily in years, and rarely on anything more than a strictly professional level. She had always been more a friend of Willow's than his, after all. Since Willow's death, he'd avoided Lily more than anyone else. Too many memories.

But Lily was a good person; he knew her well enough to say that with confidence. Bright and kind, with a good head on her shoulders. And she'd taken in Emela—that walking house of cards—out of the goodness of her heart, when she'd stumbled her way into town. But seeing Lily get involved with a loose canon like Serena? It spelled disaster, and he seemed to be the only one who could read it.

So, yes. He was pleased that The Velvet Teahouse was failing. Even if the pretty owner seemed nothing short of crushed. Even if the next day he'd waved at her through the window, and those big green eyes of hers looked like they'd been crying. Even if he'd grown to find her endless optimism somewhat endearing.

Very pleased.

CHAPTER 6
SERENA

T wo customers.

The Velvet Teahouse had been open for three days, and that was what she had to show for it. Two. Lily, and a man who worked at the hair salon next door. It felt like it was only a matter of days before the shop would have to shut down. She could almost hear the buzzards circling overhead. If things kept up the way they were, she was finished. It wouldn't have been the fastest she'd breezed through a town. Hell, she might even be able to get her deposit back on the building. But shutting things down now stuck like a seed in her teeth. It was a matter of pride, now. Rolling over so soon would be an admittance of defeat.

So Serena got up early, washed her hair, made herself two eggs over easy with a piece of toast, rolled up her sleeves, and marched straight down to the teahouse kitchen.

Reaching up to the topmost shelf, Serena's fingers brushed against a collection of half a dozen sparkling jars, each meticulously labeled and neatly arranged. She carefully pulled down the one marked 'Lavender Extract', a concoction she had painstakingly prepared from fresh blossoms, distilled to perfection over several days. Her fingers traced the cool surface of the glass as she brought it down, releasing the faint floral scent even before the lid was opened.

Serena laid the ingredients neatly on her countertop: finely milled almond flour, crystalline cane sugar, egg whites, confectioners' sugar as light as snow, fresh lemons, honey, and a pinch of cream of tartar.

After adding a dash of the homemade lavender extract to her meringue, the heavenly aroma instantly wafted up to blend seamlessly with the tangy smell of freshly grated lemon zest. She whisked to a smooth, frothy consistency before folding in the almond flour and sugar to create a thick, glossy batter. With a steady hand, she piped out a dozen dollops onto a baking sheet lined with parchment paper. Each round was identical, adorning the pan like tiny purple moons.

Once out of the oven and cooled, she sandwiched the shells with a bright and citrusy lemon buttercream, the tantalizing filling seeping out from the edges. As she completed the final macaron, she took a step back, admiring the vibrant, purple delicacies lined up on her counter.

After arranging the cookies on a tray, she took up a post on the sidewalk, her apron catching the light breeze and flapping against the legs of her skirt. Wiping her hands on her apron, Serena glanced up at the empty teahouse. She wouldn't take this lying down. One piece of unflattering gossip would not be the thing that sunk her. And she certainly wasn't letting Jared Westergard have the last laugh.

Looking up and down the street, she locked eyes with the first pedestrian she saw. The man ducked his head down, quickly walking past. That was fine. There would be more. A minute later an older couple approached, hand in hand. She put on her best winning smile.

"Excuse me? Hi, would you—"

He held up a hand. "We're happy with our church, thanks."

She looked across the street. The grey brick of the law office seemed to be mocking her. She set her jaw.

"Free cookies!" she called, as loud as she could muster. "Free cookies here, courtesy of The Velvet Teahouse!"

A young boy on a skateboard passed by, slowing down just enough to pluck one from the plate without a word. Maybe Jared had been right about the town lacking charm.

"Enjoy!" she called after him. "And, please consider visiting the Velvet—Hey!"

A door behind her swung open, creaking on uneven hinges. "Serena? What are you doing? I heard screaming—" Lily cut herself off, distracted by the plate in her hand. "Are those macarons? Can I have one?"

Serena smiled, despite her dampened spirits. "Sure. *Bon appétit!*"

The other woman hummed her approval after the first mouthful. "That's so good! What flavor is that?"

"Lavender lemon. Freshly baked."

"And they're so pretty. You made these yourself?" Lily raised her brows. "You're going to be terrible for my health, I swear. I almost hope the Lenses do shut you down, for the sake of my waistline."

Serena waved her off. "You look great."

"You noticed?" she quipped, grabbing another cookie. "I'm going to give one of these to Emela, okay? She's got a major sweet tooth. Plus, she's skin and bones."

Serena cast a curious look in the direction of the antique shop, but she couldn't see anyone inside. "Am I ever going to meet this mysterious partner of yours? Or do I have to believe she exists based on good faith alone?"

"She's real!" Lily insisted. "She's just... not great with new things yet. You'll meet her soon, I'm sure."

Serena nodded. "Sure, whenever she's ready. Tell her that I hope she enjoys the cookie."

"Noted. So, is there a reason you're peddling desserts on the side of the road instead of working?"

"I *am* working! The teahouse is dead, and I'm trying to drum up a little business."

"Well, this should definitely help. Because these?" She gestured to the half-eaten cookie. "Are fabulous."

"Thanks, Lily."

"My birthday's in August," she sung over her shoulder as she made her way inside. "Just saying!"

Serena spent the bulk of her morning passing out samples, though most passersby didn't stay to learn the actual name or nature of the establishment. Still, she hoped it would help in the long run.

As Serena divvied out her last remaining macaron, she became momentarily distracted by movement across the street. A tall man, with close cropped blond hair and wearing a gray trench coat, was ambling along the sidewalk. Of course there was nothing unusual about a man walking, but something about him caught her attention anyway. He moved with an otherworldly grace, his long limbs casting eerie shadows on the sunlit pavement. Something exuded from him. Strength? Power? Magic? It was something definitely not native to Pembrooke and made her uneasy.

Walking back to her empty teashop, Serena lingered in the threshold and glanced back.

Across the street, the blond man approached Jared, who was now standing outside his office. They shook hands, but there was something weird about the way they did it. Each man grasped the shoulder of the other man with his free hand.

It looked too formal, ritualistic even. With a quick glance around, Jared's eyes grazed over hers before the two men retreated into the stoic facade of his office building.

Lily's warning came to mind. Hadn't she said that Jared was known to associate with unusual people? The man in the trench coat was definitely not a Lens, and was definitely strange. So who was he?

With a sigh, Serena retreated into her shop. What did it matter who Jared was entertaining? She felt like an utter failure. Not one customer had entered the teahouse. If she couldn't make a go of the teahouse, then she'd be leaving Pembrooke within a couple of months anyway.

When the bell over the door finally did chime, just after five o'clock, it was such an unfamiliar sound that it actually startled her.

"Oh, sorry!" A thin man stood, looking around the empty shop. "Are you open?"

"Yes!" She squeaked, posture jumping to attention. "I mean, yes, we're open. Please, come in."

He nodded to her, taking in the room before sidling up to the counter. He was young, couldn't have been more than twenty-two, with a mop of dark hair falling in his eyes. "You've got really great light in here, you know," he said. "I noticed it through the windows. Interesting design choice, not having curtains."

Serena sighed, hoping her bitterness wasn't too apparent. She'd all but given up on those curtains ever actually arriving. "It's better in the evenings than in the morning," she replied.

"I was wondering...would it be all right with you if I sketched in here?"

Serena couldn't disguise her slight disappointment. Of course, he was only here for the ambiance. "Oh, well, I guess that would be—"

"I would buy drinks, the whole time I'm here," he bargained. "I'm not looking to loiter or anything. It's just that I'm an artist, and this looks like a perfect spot to set up in the afternoons. You know, people watch, sketch the other customers, have some tea. Only if that's okay with you, of course."

She certainly wouldn't say no to the business, or the company. "Well, I won't promise you that there will be many customers to study, but you're welcome to have a drink and sit for as long as you want."

He tilted his head. "Well... you have interesting features. I could draw you, until more people come in."

She beamed at him. "Okay, yes, that would absolutely be okay! Just take whichever spot has the best view, and I can get something started for you."

"Sure. How about the... 'Soothing Spirit Infusion'. I'm Aaron, by the way." He raised his arm, flicking his wrist a few times before extending his hand. When she asked him why he did that, he replied, "Repetitive strain injury. Too much drawing, I'm afraid."

"Say no more. I've got just the thing for you."

As the late afternoon light slipped through the kitchen windows, Serena set about her task. In her hands was a plump, knobby ginger root, which she peeled to expose the fragrant, fibrous interior. With a few quick flicks of her wrist, she sliced the peeled ginger into thin slivers. Its spicy scent began to fill the room, mingling with the soft, earthy aroma of chamomile and sage hanging from the wooden rack on the wall.

Reaching for a pinch of vibrant orange turmeric, she ground it into a fine powder, adding a sprig of fresh mint. The earthy undertone of the turmeric danced with the zesty ginger as Serena tossed them into the infuser basket of a delicate glass teapot painted with verdant green leaves.

Then, Serena turned her attention to the green tea. Carefully, she selected a handful of the dried, curled leaves, holding them above the teapot. Closing her eyes, she began to whisper a spell, her voice hardly more than a breeze brushing against the surface of a calm lake. As the words slipped from her lips, a soft, warm glow began to radiate from her fingers, enveloping the tea leaves, which she dropped one by one into the infuser. A barely perceptible glow spread to the ginger and turmeric as her magic flowed. Serena slowly poured hot water into the teapot, allowing the magical ingredients to steep and blend together, transforming the simple brew into a powerful elixir imbued with her healing intent.

After a moment, the warm glow faded, leaving behind the simple beauty of the tea leaves, ginger, and turmeric. She removed the infuser and carried the steaming pot to Aaron, along with a teacup plated with a lavender lemon macaron.

His eyes lit up with gratitude as he inhaled the aroma of the tea.

"Ginger and turmeric are good for pain and inflammation," she explained with a small smile. Of course she'd neglected to explain that it was her whispered magic, more so than the ginger, that was the most potent ingredient in his beverage.

WHEN AARON RETURNED THE FOLLOWING DAY, HE WIGGLED HIS fingers in the air as he grinned. "You're a miracle worker," he said as he presented her with a finished portrait of herself, much to her delight, and begged her to brew more of the ginger tea.

On day five, Serena had eight customers. By day seven, over a dozen. Slowly but surely, word seemed to get around about the teahouse, positive buzz this time. She was still worried about being able to keep the lights on next month, but the business was finally bouncing back from its disastrous grand opening.

She expected Jared to come in any day to threaten to have her shut down, but he didn't make an appearance. In fact, she once saw him across the way during his lunch break, and he'd actually not frowned at her. It was odd, because he had to know what she was doing. Some of her teas weren't particularly potent, but many were, and the sheer quantity of remedies being made each day would surely alert her dealings to every witch within miles. Still, she figured it was a matter of time before he blew in through her door to cause trouble again.

The artist, Aaron, took up a table near the front window five days out of the week, sketching customers, pedestrians, the plants outside.

So it went. Several ladies came in seeking relief for menstrual cramps. Kathleen from the hair salon next door was nursing a nasty cold. The girl who checked her groceries at Kurt's market was complaining about acne. Any issues her customers suffered from, Serena would cure them with a cup and a smile.

And some of the customers who stopped in were witches, Serena soon discovered. She was getting better at sensing them in an instant. Like the beautiful tawny-skinned Hailey who stopped in seeking a remedy for the flu. With mischievous golden eyes, she studied Serena and then the jars of dried herbs behind the counter.

"I've heard you make amazing remedies," she said with a raspy, strained voice, her hand fluttering to her throat. "Some even say they are *blessed*."

Serena met her eyes, understanding her meaning. "Goddess-blessed" was a term witches used to describe magic. So, here was another witch in Pembrooke. Serena scanned the woman, from her thick dark curls to the tips of her pointed boots. "Fatigue, sore throat, headache, fever, and cough? That about sum it up?"

When Hailey gave a slow, respectful nod, Serena turned and made short work of concocting a steaming to-go cup full of a potent flu remedy she had developed herself. Elderberry, echinacea, cinnamon, lemon, honey, and a few whispered words. Hailey inhaled the steam and smiled. "I'll be seeing you soon, Serena," she said as she gave her a knowing look and sauntered to the door.

She'd barely been open for five minutes on Monday morning when she heard the bell chime. "Just a second!" she called, bending to pull a tray of fresh blueberry muffins from the oven.

"Take your time, dear! We're patient people."

Serena smiled when she took her place behind the counter. Two new faces: a middle-aged woman and a little girl with her hair tied in long dark braids. "Well, good morning, ladies! Stopping in for a pick-me-up before we head off for school?"

"We sure are," the older woman replied. "When my son mentioned this shop, I just knew we had to come in and see it for ourselves!"

"Well, thanks to your son for the free advertising," she quipped, gesturing to the chalkboard behind her, listing the names of her curing teas, as well as the various flowers, herbs, and fruits she had on hand. "Anything in particular that strikes your fancy?"

"Well," she looked down at the little girl, then back to Serena. "What do you recommend for someone who hasn't been to a tea shop before?"

"That would depend. What sorts of things does this mystery person like?"

"Hmmm," the woman hummed in exaggerated deliberation, and the girl piped up, looking to Serena with an expression that seemed endearingly serious.

"I like sweet things. And fruit. Do you have a fruity tea?"

Serena grinned. "Do we? We've got tons! Let's see: how would you feel about..." She rummaged about behind the counter, double-checking her stock. "Cherry and pomegranate?"

"Mmm. Make that two," the older woman said. "And are those blueberry muffins?"

"Yes, ma'am, they are. Should I set a couple aside for you?"

The woman nodded. "Oh, I think you definitely should."

Serena chuckled. "We've got fresh baked goods every day, so you'll have to come back and see what we have another day, too. Who knows, I might be persuaded to whip up something special for you."

"So is it 'we', or 'I'?"

She blinked. Had she been saying 'we'? "Oh it's just me."

The woman whistled low. "Lot of work for just one woman. Maybe you should try to hire one of the students at the high school for a summer job, once school lets out. You might actually get some free time."

Serena just laughed. "I don't even know what I'd *do* with free time if I had it, she confessed. "I'm just focused on the shop, for now. But I'll keep that in mind, thanks."

The three of them chatted idly as they drank, breaking up the monotony of the rainy morning. Something about the little girl's oddly studious behavior struck Serena as unspeakably adorable. Like a learned habit that she didn't fully understand. Something she picked up at home, Serena reckoned, but it put a smile on her face. When the pair paid for their drinks, Serena gave them a paper to-go bag. "Two muffins, on the house," she said. "Providing that you stop in again soon, that is." They were quick to agree.

Over the following weeks, the two became near daily visitors to the teahouse. Usually in the mornings, but occasionally in the afternoons instead. Serena loved talking with nearly all of her customers, but the two of them had become the highlight of Serena's day. Judith was recently retired and had lived in Pembrooke since she was a child. Her pride and joy was her granddaughter, Zoe, and Serena could see why. Zoe was bright, friendly, and very inquisitive, often excitedly asking Serena about her life and the different teas she made. Judith occasionally gave Serena baking tips and recipes, having baked for her son and now her granddaughter throughout their lives. Serena had even taken to baking strawberry cookies three times a week, first thing in the morning, so that Zoe could bring a few to school to share with her friends.

In what felt like no time at all, The Velvet Teahouse had a vibrant group of regulars. Aaron made portraits for Lily, Judith, and Zoe, even offering to sketch Lily's elusive partner, if she ever decided to come outside. Serena and Aaron had even come to a mutually beneficial business arrangement. Customers who purchased teas had the option to have their portraits done, for a small fee, of course.

Occasionally Hailey, an artist herself, would sketch with Aaron, when she had a rare day off from her job at the upscale restaurant, Borealis. And sometimes Hailey would bring along her friend Alice— another new witch in town who had moved from New York City. Serena and Alice would compare notes on their favorite restaurants in New York, or play argue about the best places to pick up bagels or pizza.

Her life shifted from a calm to a whirlwind nearly overnight, and before she knew it, she had nearly forgotten about her fear of failure, or the Lenses, or being found out. The Velvet Teahouse was thriving, finally, and word about Serena's teas was spreading. A few customers had even come in with a list of ailments rather than drink orders, apparently having heard that her teas were "super remedies". She'd just shrugged, and smiled, and told them it was just good old fashioned herbal healing. It wasn't a lie, after all; it just wasn't the whole truth.

And what her customers didn't know wouldn't hurt them.

THAT EVENING, AS SERENA WIPED DOWN THE COUNTERS AFTER HER last customer left, the whisper of footsteps beyond the front door pricked her ears, a little intrusion on her solitude. She cast a quick glance at the old clock, which, with its hands nearing the day's end, was hinting at time's ebb. With the intention to gently turn the latecomer away or perhaps serve a simple brew, she waited for the door to swing open.

Yet, the door remained closed. The footsteps were replaced with a distinctive creak, a sound that immediately drew her attention to the window. A ghostly face appeared, pressing against the glass, eyeing her. Just as swiftly as it had appeared, it vanished back into the depths of the night.

A shiver rippled through her, and her gaze darted over to Kita, who was snoozing without a care by the door. "Quite the watchful guardian you are," she tossed a jesting barb at the oblivious wolf, her tone laced with affectionate sarcasm. Kita cracked open an eye and then shifted position and fell back asleep. With a final survey of her domain, Serena crossed the cozy dining room, securing the front door with a sturdy click, the mysterious visitor's image fading in her mind as the lock slid home.

CHAPTER 7
SERENA

"And you're sure this isn't going to wipe my brain?" Lily asked, for the ninth—no, tenth—time in the past ten minutes. She lowered her chin onto the counter as she stared at the dark blue concoction bubbling away in a small cauldron on the burner like she was worried it would rise up and bite her. She glanced over at her friend, Charlotte, another witch, who worked at the local coffee shop. Charlotte was watching Serena's bubbling brew with wide, brown eyes.

"Well, the good news is that if it does wipe your brain, you won't know the difference," Serena said.

To her credit, Lily did manage a laugh at that, but it didn't disguise her obvious nerves. Charlotte, who had taken a lot of chemistry classes in college, appeared less disturbed but more skeptical.

"This is tea?" Charlotte said.

"It doesn't even smell *edible*. I don't think this is supposed to be a drink, Rena," Lily said.

Serena shook her head. "Andromeda oil is extracted from the uropygial glands of Australian Andromeda Birds. It's rare, but it's natural and perfectly safe." She poured a small teacup full of the blue concoction and slid it toward Lily and Charlotte. "This is enough to wipe the past twenty minutes from your brain. So, smell but don't taste."

Lily wrinkled her nose. "It doesn't smell natural. Smells like..." she sniffed the air. "Dry erase markers."

Serena chuckled, stirring the cup with an amused glint in her eyes. "You know, the first time I made this, I was trying to create a tea for pain relief. But I wound up creating a tea that made me forget I even made it."

"You mean you brewed it, tasted it, and then just promptly forgot about it?" Charlotte said.

"Yep," Serena affirmed, wielding her stirring spoon with an air of theatricality. "I devoted an entire day to brewing and tasting and, by evening, I had no idea why I was standing in front of this blue bubbling mess in the cauldron. And I even forgot my own recipe. I was a hot mess."

"As fate would have it," she resumed, her eyes twinkling, "my friend popped by just then. I told him a funny joke about a garden gnome and a broomstick and he had a good laugh. But then, when he sampled the brew, his expression went blank, and he asked me, in all seriousness, 'What was that funny story you were about to tell me?' It was then that it finally dawned on me that I had unwittingly birthed Amnesia Tea."

Lily, though still a bit apprehensive, was now smirking. "I can't believe you accidentally created a memory-wiping potion. That sounds like something out of a sci-fi film."

"Yeah, but don't worry. Today's recipe is the latest iteration, tweaked to ensure it eases anxiety without the memory swiping side effect. Or at least, that's the plan."

Serena held up two vibrant green leaves and a sprig of small purple flowers and whispered an incantation. With a flourish, she dropped the herbs into the cauldron and it instantly gave off a plume of fragrant steam, prompting both of them to cough and wave their hands around. The brew transformed from a deep, starry-night blue color to a soothing shade of periwinkle.

Lily peeked over the edge of the cauldron with a hesitant expression on her face. She tentatively sniffed the air, her eyes widening in surprise. "That actually smells...not half-bad," she admitted, a hint of intrigue making her almost forget her earlier anxiety.

"Like oranges," Charlotte said.

Serena ladled three cups of the periwinkle colored tea and took a sip, sliding the other cups toward her friends.

"Let's hope you remembered the correct version, Rena," Lily quipped, succumbing to nervous laughter.

"Well, if we're lucky, this could end up being Relaxation Tea, or maybe Forget-Your-Worries Tea. If we're not so lucky... well, let's hope you weren't too attached to your name."

The shop door chimed and Serena glanced up. As a man swaggered in, she rolled her eyes. "Not again," she muttered.

Lily glanced over her shoulder. "What's Colin doing in here?" Lily said with a note of concern. He sashayed over to Serena, his grin as oily as the pomade in his hair. "Serena, darling," he crooned, "I must say you're looking enchanting as ever."

"A little early for whiskey, isn't it, Colin?" Lily said.

Colin ignored Lily as he sank into a counter stool.

"Colin," Serena said coolly, "I don't think I serve anything you'd be interested in."

"But I come bearing gifts, my sweet." He winked, presenting a wilted bouquet of daisies he'd likely picked from the roadside.

"Colin, you need to leave," Lily said.

But Colin, undeterred by their cold reception, ignored Lily

and scooted his stool closer. His gaze landed on the teacup containing the dark blue tea. "Free sample, Serena? Don't mind if I do."

Before Serena could protest, he had tipped the cup and taken a gulp of the Amnesia Tea. His expression quickly went blank. His eyes darted around the room, confusion coloring his features, like he had just woken from a dream and was unsure of his surroundings. Serena and Lily exchanged shocked glances.

"Umm...Colin," Serena began, seizing the opportunity, "You were just leaving, don't you remember? There's a meeting you can't miss. At... Town Hall."

Colin, still looking puzzled, nodded slowly. "Oh, yeah. I almost forgot." He got up and stumbled out of the shop, a dazed expression still on his face.

After the door closed behind him, Serena, Charlotte, and Lily shared a look and then burst into nervous chuckles.

"Is he gonna be okay?" Charlotte said.

"Yeah, it was only strong enough to make him forget the past twenty minutes or so. He'll be fine." Serena sighed.

Lily tried to lighten the mood, her smile cheeky as she joked, "You know, Rena, maybe we should bottle that tea as 'Pest Repellent.'"

CHAPTER 8
JARED

"Magic."

That's the word he'd heard someone saying at the pharmacy last night. Some clueless teenager complaining to her friend about her hair being dry and bleach-damaged. And then she'd said it.

"You should see if that lady who runs The Velvet Teahouse has something for healthy hair. My mom went in there last week and mentioned that working late shifts had been like, terrible for her insomnia. She drank the tea the lady gave her, and the same night she got a full eight hours."

Jared had nearly dropped his wallet.

"Seriously?"

The girl nodded. "I'm telling you, the tea there is like *magic.*"

Magic. Just like magic.

He'd been furious. He'd held off on reporting Serena to the council, initially. Hoping that she'd heeded his warning and was attempting to maintain a low profile. Evidently not. He had to deal with this before someone got hurt.

So, before work on Friday, Jared marched straight into that damned teahouse, ready to give that woman a piece of his mind.

And found his own mother there. With his daughter.

"Zoe?"

She smiled and waved, her gappy grin almost fooling him into thinking everything was okay. "Hi dad! Are you here to get a cup of tea before work? It's good for you, you know."

His whiplash left him reeling for a moment. "What on Earth are you two doing here?"

"Oh, grandma's been bringing me here before school! She said that it would be good for me to try new things, and to support a new store, and Miss Rena is really nice to us!"

His mother nodded along, looking quite pleased with herself. "Thank you for the recommendation, sweetie. Have you tried the chocolate croissants here? They're to die for! The first time Serena made them, her pastry wasn't quite flaky enough, but I told her how I usually do it. She's got the hang of it now."

He glanced around the building. Serena was nowhere to be seen. She must have been back in the kitchen. He lowered his voice to an accusatory hiss. "I wasn't recommending it! I told you this place was suspicious!"

"Suspicious is a step up from boring, in my book," she replied with a mirthful smile. "I wanted to see this little rebel for myself. But between you and me, she doesn't seem so tough."

Jared groaned, running a hand along his face in exasperation. "We'll talk about this later. Z, get to school."

"But Serena's making my special cookies!"

He felt a territorial sort of rage well within him, his blood turning cold. She wouldn't. Would she? She was already feeding humans enchanted teas on a daily basis, who's to say she wouldn't give magically enhanced baked goods to a child? "What makes them so special?" he asked slowly.

Just then, Serena came striding into the room with a platter of pink cookies, looking altogether like she'd never seen a finer morning. Her cheerfulness disappeared in an instant when she locked eyes with Jared.

"What brings you in this morning?" she asked, trying to feign pleasantry.

"I'll ask the questions," he gritted out. "What are you giving her? Did you put something in those?"

"Calm down," Zoe said. "They're just—"

"I said get to school!"

"Hey!" Serena interrupted. "You can't talk to her like that!"

"I can talk to her however I want; she's my daughter!"

Serena's eyes went wide at that. She turned to the girl, giving her a forced-looking smile. "Zoe, you should probably get going. I'll see you tomorrow, okay? Tea's on the house today."

Zoe followed Jared's mother out of the shop, clinging to her pink school bag. When the two of them were alone, Serena held the plate out to him. He glared at her.

"They're just strawberry," she said. "Try one, if you don't believe me. Nothing magical about them, I promise."

He sighed, frowning around at the shop. "I came in here to give you another warning."

"Of course you did."

"And I come in to find that you've got my *family* involved in this?"

She blew out a frustrated breath. "You make it sound like I've gotten them involved in a crime."

Suddenly, the space between them seemed to diminish. He took a step closer, his height magnified, and the proximity forced Serena to tilt her head up. Her fiery gaze met his. The soft scent of lilac and rain emanated from her, a heady blend that felt incongruent with the intense scene playing out. For a split second, the amber undertones in her eyes captivated him, drawing him in. He swallowed hard, trying to quell his reaction.

"Enchanting humans without their consent *is* a crime," he growled.

She took a defensive step back, but not far enough to break the unexpected intimate atmosphere. "I don't know why you're so insistent about ruining this business when I'm not hurting anyone! The council really doesn't have bigger problems? I haven't done a thing to you."

"Sure, aside from telling everyone in town that I'm a thief."

She smirked, a hint of humor in her eyes, which only intensified their allure. "Right, because you're so clearly above petty gossip."

"I was trying to protect you!"

"You were *trying* to sabotage me!"

"What do you want me to do?! You won't listen to reason!"

Her emerald eyes held a look of challenge. "Then rat me out to the Lenses! Tell them you think I'm using magic on my customers. Go ahead!"

He took another step, bringing their bodies closer than before. Their faces were now inches apart, their breaths mingling. A surge of warmth spread through him, unexpectedly intense, as he caught a fleeting glimpse of vulnerability in Serena's eyes. "Is it so wrong that I didn't want you to get into trouble? You're really going to vilify me for spreading some stupid rumors instead of turning you in to the council?"

Serena huffed, crossed her arms, blew a strand of highlighted hair from her face. "You know, a lot of people assume that control freaks like you are only so uptight because they get off on it. That they like the power. But do you know what I think, Jared? I think you want to control me because I scare you."

The woman was taunting him now. Something shifted in him. He set his jaw, staring her down with pure ire. She arched a brow.

"Admit it. You're *afraid*," she said.

All at once, every pipe in The Velvet Teahouse groaned. Serena flinched at the sound, looking around the building in horror. In the kitchen and in Serena's loft, he heard the telltale disastrous sound of jars bursting. She stared at him, eyes wide.

"What did you do?"

He swallowed uncomfortably. He hadn't intended to do that, not really. He'd only wanted to freeze the jugs of water in her refrigerator, maybe any tea she had brewing in the back. But oh, Serena was so *vexing!* She brought out a side of him that was unfamiliar, impulsive, unpleasant. If he wasn't careful, she'd end up corrupting him.

"I should go."

"What did you *do*?!"

As she bolted upstairs to investigate the damage, Jared made for the door, flipping the sign out front to "closed" on his way.

CHAPTER 9
SERENA

Broken pitchers and jugs.

Not just burst containers, containers that had burst because all of the liquid in said containers was *frozen solid*. Frozen water in the refrigerator and in Kita's bowl. Frozen milk, frozen extracts in the pantry, frozen *toilet*.

Her hands clenched into fists. Released. Clenched again. Some prophet of ethical magic use he was. He'd frozen every drop of water in her home and in her shop, and then just run off.

She couldn't call her maintenance men. It was June, what reason could she possibly give them for all of the water in her pipes being frozen? The frozen pipes in her building weren't a problem, yet, but she knew that the moment everything thawed, her home could be a disaster, if one of the pipes had burst.

Not bad, Westergard. Game on.

She moved all of her valuables out of the room and set up buckets, just in case. As soon as the state of the water was no longer suspicious, she would call Clara. Maybe that would be quick enough to avoid any major damage. For now, though, she waited. She couldn't exactly open the store until the effects of Jared's spell faded and the water finally thawed, anyway.

Well, now she had her morning free.

JUDITH HAD TOLD SERENA ONCE THAT THE VELVET TEAHOUSE JUST looked like it belonged to her. The furniture, the ambiance, even the scent inside, all of it suited her personality. A reflection of her character, built from brick and velvet and a few dozen plants. And laughter, soft laughter that seemed to linger in the air, absorbed by velvet. Serena wasn't sure if she saw what Judith saw, in the teahouse or in herself, but she often considered that sentiment and whether it held any truth.

If Judith's hypothesis that shops matched their owner's personalities were true, then Lily Hart was decidedly *not* the person Serena believed her to be.

The Tinker's Trinket was dark. Even on rare sunny afternoons, the tinted windows out front kept much light from filtering in. It always took a good minute or two for Serena's eyes to adjust to the change. Cramped, too. There was scarcely enough room to walk among the large shelves and display cases, and Serena constantly worried about bumping into something and sending merchandise flying.

And what a collection of merchandise it was. The usual fare for a secondhand shop, in part. Vintage silver jewelry and chipped antique teacups and unwanted paintings. Further back, though, closer to the counter Lily manned, were the true points of interest for Serena. Centuries-old medical equipment. Frightening dark tinctures floating in crystalline vials. Flowers and animal parts, preserved in jars of formaldehyde.

Tinker's Trinket was a place where magic felt tangible, where history seemed to breathe, and where Serena usually felt like she was one step away from uncovering something extraordinary or terrifying, or both.

The jewel in the Tinker's Trinket's proverbial crown, according to Lily, was the chest filled nearly to the brim with salvaged old photographs. Where and how she got her hands on such things, Serena wasn't sure she wanted to know. But they had pored over them together one rainy afternoon, Lily excitedly showing them to her by the handful and cooing over faces that were surely long dead.

But old photographs were not what Serena was looking for as she meandered through the crowded aisles.

"*Bonjour*, beautiful!" Lily called from the back of the store, chipper as could be, despite the macabre surroundings. She waved a pale hand adorned with numerous rings as she walked forward with a beautiful young woman with silky dark brown hair, who was carrying a small box of books. "Serena, this is Zara, she works at the library. Every once in a while I get in a special book or two that need to be kept somewhere safe— away from mundane eyes, if you know what I mean. Zara oversees a special collection for us."

"Oh," Serena said, flashing a knowing smile at the new witch. "Nice to meet you, Zara."

"Nice to finally meet you, too, Serena. I've heard a lot about your teas, and I definitely plan to visit you soon," Zara said.

"Anytime! I look forward to it," Serena said as the brunette witch exited the shop with what looked like two grimoires.

"So what brings you in?" Lily said, as Serena picked up an antique bell from a table.

"I'll never understand what you see in all this stuff," she said with a smile, gesturing at the shelves. And yet, today she felt a peculiar pull, a whisper from the shadows, urging her to explore deeper. The shop seemed to almost beckon her into its dark embrace.

"What can I say, I have a soft spot for the strange."

"I guess that explains why you hang around the teahouse," Serena mused, ambling around the shop. "All these little pieces of people's lives. It just seems so... sad."

"Not to the people who love it," she replied. "To me, they are snapshots of the past. The only way we can go back in time and get a taste of a bygone era."

"You make it sound almost romantic." Serena picked up a silver antique hair brush and ran her fingers across the yellowed bristles.

"I think it is. Anyway, no one in Pembrooke loves this stuff more than me."

Serena chuckled. "Except Emela, I'm guessing. Since she spends all her time in here."

Lily shook her head. "Emela's office is upstairs. She handles the Trinket's finances, writes poetry in her down time. She's working on a book, actually. Beautiful stuff, I'll send you a copy, if it ever gets published."

"She doesn't share your affinity for the old and forgotten, then?"

Lily shrugged. "Eh. She's more of a behind-the-scenes girl," she said. "Fantastic at accounting and marketing, though." She rounded the counter, shaking out her loose auburn waves. "So, what are we in the market for?"

"I've got my morning open, courtesy of one Mr. Westergard. Thought I might as well treat myself to a new decoration, and to your company."

Lily blinked at that. "Wait, he shut down the shop?"

"Not quite," she sighed. "Just indulging his habit of annoying me and wasting my time."

"Still?"

Nodding, she fingered a display of several taxidermied mice as she began to explain Jared's latest offense.

Lily blew out a harsh breath. "I'll say this, Rena, I don't know if what's going on between you two is going to end in a wedding or a funeral, but either way, I'll be the best dressed person there."

Serena snorted. Just then, her eyes landed on a twelve-inch bronze statuette of a kingfisher bird. "Hello, gorgeous," she muttered, reaching out to trace its metal wing.

"Hm? Oh! That little guy's a steal. It'll make you look like you have town spirit, too. Pembrooke is full of kingfishers. He'd look so cute in the teahouse, too. Maybe on the counter beside the register?"

Serena smiled, picking it up and testing its weight in her hand. "What do you think? Is he strange enough?"

Lily shook her head. "No, not by half. But he suits you just fine."

SERENA FROWNED UP AT THE DRAB GREY BUILDING THAT HOUSED Westergard and Ross. She could see Jared through his office window, pushing his dark curls back from his face with a weary expression as he sipped the dreadful break room coffee from a chipped white mug. She stood still, watching him stab at his laptop like the keyboard had insulted him, until he finally stood and left the room. That signaled her time to strike.

Pressing her palms against the gray concrete, Serena closed her eyes and muttered a few lines. The vines crept up the wall, slithering their way in through his cracked window. He may grow to regret letting some fresh air in, but that wasn't her problem. The vines curled around his office: under his desk, along the floor, over the ceiling. Their tendrils stilled around the door frame, lying in wait.

When Jared returned and shut the door behind him, he had

just enough time to take in the state of his office before the vines tangled in a thick, verdant knot across the center of his closed door. He would be trapped inside until he could cut through all the vines, or she chose to release him. Unless he grew bold and decided to jump out the window, that was.

With a smirk, Serena turned and strode back across the street. She would let him out when the water in the teahouse thawed.

CHAPTER 10
SERENA

In the end, Jared's little stunt didn't set her back very far. A little water damage in her kitchen ceiling, a lot of mopping, a morning of inconveniences. But overall, life in The Velvet Teahouse continued as usual. More so than she expected, in fact.

"And your dad is *definitely* okay with you being here?" Serena asked Zoe, for what must've been the tenth time later that afternoon.

"Grandma says it's fine, and that dad is *overreacting*."

"Maybe," she said. "But I still wouldn't feel right about letting you disobey him. I mean, he's still your dad."

"And I'm his mother," Judith countered. "If I tell him to relax and let his daughter have a cookie, he listens."

She tried to take that in stride. "All right, if you say so. But if he comes in here yelling at me for serving you, I'm throwing both of you under the bus." She handed them a small paper bag.

Judith chuckled. "At least you had the courtesy to warn

me." With a wave, she and Zoe headed for the door, exchanging a few words with a tall, well-dressed woman with a dark-haired bun who had just entered the teahouse.

She flashed a weak smile as she reached the counter. "Hi there. Is it true that you serve herbal remedy teas?" she asked. "*Blessed* teas?"

Serena smiled at the insinuation, settling across the counter from the new witch. "We sure do. Tell me the problem, I'll pick your poison."

The woman huffed. "Stress."

Serena nodded, snapping her fingers. "Easy. Coming right up," she said, and moved to rummage through her ingredient stock.

"Thanks. I'm going to need it."

"Yeah?" she prodded over her shoulder. "What's stressing you out?"

"Work. I'm an attorney at Westergard and Ross across the street."

"My condolences," Serena said with a snort. I know one of the lawyers practicing there. Word of advice: Don't tell him you stopped in here."

The woman gave Serena a curious look when she returned to the counter. "Something I should know?" she asked.

"It's nothing, really. He and I just... don't exactly see eye to eye."

"Let me guess. Jared? He can be a bit...difficult sometimes. He wasn't always like this. Just for the past few years, anyway."

"Yeah, ever since his wife died, I heard."

"Well, she didn't just die. She was murdered."

Serena froze. "Goddess above. You can't be serious." Had she misjudged Jared? Grief could certainly make people act in unpredictable ways.

"I wish I weren't. And they never caught the guy. Willow was an *amazing* person. Good friend of my sister's, actually. The whole town was devastated."

Serena paused and turned to the woman. "Did it happen during a festival, by chance?"

"How'd you know?" Just then the woman's phone buzzed. "Oh wait, I have to take this."

Serena finished the stress brew, pouring it carefully into a cheerful to-go cup as the woman discussed what sounded like work related business with her caller. Serena pondered what Jared and Zoe had both been through over the past five years. The little girl she was growing fond of was growing up motherless. Thank goodness they had Judith.

As the woman reached for the cup, she pulled her phone away from her mouth and said, "Well, until Jared gets better drinks in the break room, I'm sure I'll be seeing you again soon."

"Come by on your lunch break," Serena suggested. "You can have your portrait done!"

The lawyer chuckled. "I might take you up on that. I'm Rowan, by the way. Since it sounds like I may be making regular visits."

Serena smiled. "Looking forward to it, Rowan."

A FEW NIGHTS LATER, WHEN SERENA WAS PREPARING TO CLOSE UP shop, she glanced up to see the same long, pale face peering through the window. She started for a second, reaching for the walking stick she had propped against the mantel.

But this time, the door creaked open and a willowy woman slid into the teahouse like a wisp of smoke, finding a place for herself at the deserted counter. Her hair, long and as pale as moonlight, cascaded around her, creating a veil that almost succeeded in obscuring her features from Serena's prying eyes.

"Oh! We are just about to close for the night. Is there something quick I can make you?" Serena said.

When the woman responded, her tone was flat and lifeless. "Yes, could you please make me a tea?"

The woman's demeanor had Serena's protective instincts buzzing. She eased her way down the counter. "Are you okay?" she asked softly.

The woman tugged at the sleeves of her sweater. "Been better. Hoping one of your famous teas might help me."

"Sure," she said, moving to lock the door behind them.

"I know that you usually close at six, but I just—" she let out a long sigh. "I could really use some help right now." The woman eyed the locked door several times, her leg twitching with nervous energy.

"It's okay. You're safe here. Whatever it is, I'll do my best to help you."

The woman shook her head, suddenly angry. "No, no, that's just it. I'm not safe here. I'm not safe anywhere, and I'm so tired, and I just—" she stopped abruptly, wrapping her arms tightly around herself and took a deep breath. Her next words were a quiet plea. "I just want it all to stop."

"I'll try," Serena insisted. "Depending on what it is, I'm not sure if I can—"

"You can!" She blurted. "Use your magic. Lily told me that you were a witch. That you had a spell, one that could fix me."

Serena froze. "You... you're Emela. You're Lily's business partner?"

Emela nodded, rubbing at her upper arms.

"Does she know that you're here? Do you need me to call her for you?"

Emela shook her head with vigor. "No, no. She doesn't know; she thinks I'm out at an appointment." A small, sad little smile quirked at her mouth. "I prefer evening appointments. Fewer people on the streets. But I skipped my appointment, this week. I wanted to come here instead. Because I... well, like I said, I think you can help me."

"But what exactly is wrong?" Serena said.

She watched the other woman take a long, slow breath before taking a seat at the stool next to her.

"I lived through the Bosnian War," Emela said. Before we moved to the States. I was very, very young, but I remember things...the sounds of constant shelling, visions of terrible things being done... Horrific images seared into my brain."

Serena's heart dropped, settling deep in the pit of her stomach. "Oh my god. Emela, that's awful."

"It was, yes. I mean, I was okay. My family, we were okay—that is to say, we all survived and everything. But I don't think I was the same afterward. I mean, who would be?"

"What are you experiencing now, if you don't mind me asking?"

Her mouth twitched. "I have good days and bad days. On bad days, I get flashbacks," she replied, voice lifting at the end, like it was a question. "And I'm very sensitive to loud noises. Not annoying, or a burden, just... sensitive. Mostly I feel irritable, angry even. It can be hard, for me...being around other people. And if I get overwhelmed, well, that can be... can be problematic, in some regards."

Serena opened her mouth to ask for clarification when Emela slid a stray teacup into the center of the table. A second later, Serena heard a cracking sound and a small pile of powder sat where the cup had been. Pulverized into thousands of tiny pieces.

Emela's a deconstructionist. And a moody one at that.

"The council told Lily that they were worried I'd have an episode and destroy the shop. We tried to tell them that I've never hurt anyone with my magic, but you know how they are."

Serena nodded, already mentally cataloging all of the plants she had in the back. "Well, I'd be happy to brew you a tea. I've got tons of agents for anxiety, some more intense than others. And I can try something for the flashbacks, but it might take a few tries for me to get it right. I've never actually treated something like this before, I have to warn you. Supplement with something for appetite, insomnia—"

Emela held up a hand. "No, you don't understand," she insisted. "I don't want you to give me remedies for my *symptoms,* I want you to cure the *illness.*"

Serena faltered. "I'm not sure if I could do something like that."

"You can!" Emela insisted, leaning closer over the table. "All you need to do is give me the new tea you've been working on. Lily told me all about it. That would wipe my memory, and then I'll be better."

She balked. "Wipe your memory?" she echoed. "You... you want me to give you Amnesia Tea?"

"Yes! Just make me forget. Erase all the memories I have of those early days. You can do that, can't you?"

"I..." Serena swallowed, trying to find her footing. "Technically I *could,* yes. But I'm really not sure that's the best solution."

Emela reached across the table, then, taking both of Serena's hands in her own. "But I've tried everything. I've seen therapists, and I've gone to support groups, taken medications. I've tried every coping mechanism there is, and I can't..." She looked down at the counter and shuddered. "I just want my life back. Please."

Serena's mind reeled. She felt like her brain had been replaced by a hall of mirrors, leaving her disoriented. Erase a tangle of memories that substantial? Could she *do* something like that? With something inconsequential, she'd done it safely in every trial, but Emela's trauma was a life-defining experience. The memories had been there for more than twenty years and colored loads of the other memories that followed.

If Serena was somehow able to magically remove anything related to the war memories with surgical precision, Emela's mind could be left filled with Swiss cheese holes. What if removing the memories drove her mad? Or changed her on a fundamental level? Serena wouldn't be able to live with herself. It was too risky.

Emela was pleading. Helpless and hopeless with nowhere to turn. Could she really send her away?

Another knock sounded. Both witches flinched, staring at each other.

"Rena?" Lily's voice was muffled through the door but it was unmistakable. "You okay? I was closing up for the night and noticed your lights were still on."

Serena looked to the door, then back to Emela. Lily knocked again. "Rena?"

To her surprise, Emela stood and opened the door. Lily's eyes widened when she saw her friend, who had begun pacing, in the empty teahouse.

"Emela? What are you doing here? I thought you went to your appointment."

"I'm not going anymore," she insisted. "I'm done with therapy."

"Why?" Lily's gaze turned on Serena. "Are you making a tea for her? Is that it?"

Serena sighed. "Lily—"

"Serena is going to erase my memory," Emela interrupted, hands tugging at the edges of her sweater. "So that I can move on."

The look in Lily's eyes made Serena's heart twist painfully. "You weren't going to test the Amnesia Tea on her, were you?"

Serena found herself wishing that she were a witch who specialized in illusions, so she could disappear.

"Serena?"

"No. Yes. I mean, she asked me to, but I don't think it would be very wise at this point."

"I don't care!" Emela insisted, voice rising. "I'm tired of nothing getting better, Lily. I'm tired of feeling held back by something that wasn't my fault. Is it so wrong that I want it to just disappear?"

"And what if *you* disappear right along with it?!"

Emela froze in place. "What?"

Lily's short heels clicked on the hardwood as she approached, her hands tender where they gripped her shoulders. "Emela, your trauma doesn't have to define you, but yes, it *did* change you.."

"But what if I don't want what it changed me into?" she argued. "Someone who's either scared or angry all the time? What if I don't want to keep the parts of me that came from what happened?"

"You don't know what parts those are! You never can, not really."

Emela set her jaw, shrugging Lily's hands away. "I don't want any of it, then. I don't care if I'm a completely different person without it, I want it gone. Don't you understand that I've been suffering for over twenty years now? Just when do you think it's going to get better?"

"You can help, right, Rena?" Lily said." Something for nightmares, or anxiety, or..."

Serena let out a breath she hadn't even realized she was holding, nodding enthusiastically. "Yes. Absolutely, anything you need for symptom management, Emela, I'll brew it for you. Just send Lily in, if you want, rain or shine, and I'll give it to you on the house. Or you could come in yourself, maybe? The teahouse isn't too busy in the early afternoons, and I'd love to get to know you better."

"And if it doesn't help?" Emela said.

"Then we can move on to the Amnesia Tea."

Emela eyed her for a moment before nodding. "I guess that sounds fair."

"I have something in mind already," Serena said, scurrying behind the counter. A few minutes later she slid a tall, lidded paper cup across the counter.

"Thank you. For the tea, and for listening." She glanced up at Serena, a weak smile softening her sharp features as she picked up the cup. "I should probably get going, but... I'll see you soon?"

Serena smiled back. "Come back tomorrow morning."

EMELA'S TREATMENT BECAME A FACET OF SERENA'S ROUTINE, FROM there on out: an anxiety remedy first thing in the morning; a sleep aid just before closing, which Emela would immediately deposit into a thermos to be kept warm until nightfall.

The following Friday, Emela stepped into The Velvet Teahouse, asking if she and Lily could stop by and hang out after closing time, much to Serena's surprise. How could she refuse?

Emela opened up as her anxiety began to lessen. The treatments seemed to be helping. That evening she lit up when Lily spoke, laughing along as her best friend excitedly recounted stories from their past. It was endearing, but it also made Serena realize how alone she herself felt. Yes, Lily and now Emela had quickly become dear friends of hers, but she still felt as though she was on the outside looking in.

No one knew Serena the way that Emela and Lily knew each other. She'd never given anyone the opportunity. Always gone in a flash, before anyone could manage to learn her favorite flower, or what pizza toppings she liked, or what movies she liked to watch when she was sad. Hazards of the lifestyle, she supposed. Still, she couldn't help but look at Lily and Emela, and feel a bit jealous of their friendship.

"You feeling okay? You look a little gloomy."

Serena looked up at Rowan with a somewhat weary smile the following morning. "Just a little tired, I guess."

"I heard they make teas for that," Rowan quipped. Her smile turned to a smirk. "Or does the magic not work on you?"

"I try not to self-medicate," she muttered.

Rowan looked to either side of the near-empty shop, then leaned close. "You know, my sister Sophia and I, we work with crystals on the side. I could bring you one, if you like. Tiger's Eye fire-etched with my magic, maybe? Put a little pep in your step?"

Serena's eyes flickered around the room. "You work for a Lens," she said. "Is this a setup or something?"

Rowan chuckled. "I'm just trying to network. You've lived in lots of places around the country, right? You don't think it's odd that there's not a single coven in all of Onyx County?"

She simply shrugged, though she did find it odd. "Thanks to your boss, I guess." It had been a shock, how different the culture within the witch community was here. "Though we've practically started one," she mused. "There's four witches that come in here on a regular basis."

"You know, Litha is the day after tomorrow. We should all meet up to celebrate," Rowan insisted, in only a half-teasing tone. "Make it official."

Serena had barely had time to think about the summer solstice or how she would celebrate the sabbat this year. Ordinarily she would spend time lots of time outdoors, bathing in lakes, meditating in the sun, transferring the special solar energy to a few favorite plants, communing with Sulis or Freya. And of course, rituals and feasts with whichever coven she might be associated with at the time. Rowan was probably joking, but the more Serena thought about it, the more exciting it seemed to celebrate midsummer with her new friends.

"Here?"

As Rowan nodded, Serena laughed. "A witches' gathering right across the street from a Lens. What could possibly go wrong?"

LITHA DAWNED IN A BLAZE OF GOLDEN GLORY, PAINTING THE SKY WITH hues of orange, pink, and red as the sun began its ascent on the longest day of the year.

The world seemed to pause for a moment, wrapped in a luminescent embrace as nature acknowledged the sun's apex in the cycle of the year. Trees stood tall and proud, their leaves shimmering in the early light, and flowers opened their petals wide to drink in the warmth. Birds sang a harmonious chorus, welcoming the day with joyous melody, while the gentle rustle of the wind whispered ancient blessings through the fields and forests.

Around a hastily constructed stone circle, a group of five witches gathered briefly in secret, their faces illuminated by the radiant dawn, their hearts connected by the powerful energy of the solstice. Dressed in flowing dresses, they raised their arms in unison, invoking the deities of the sun, calling upon the spirits of the land, and celebrating the dance of light and life. The air seemed to hum with magic and promise on a day of celebration, reflection, and connection. A day where the mundane met the divine, and the Earth itself seemed to sing a song of abundance and gratitude.

Later that evening, the same five witches met up again in the closed teahouse.

"Lily, would you help me set up?" Serena said.

"Sure, love. What did you have in mind?"

Chewing on her lower lip, Serena surveyed the empty shop. The small, windowless room in the corner caught her attention. It was more private and intimate. Plucking a tall, whimsical, wingback chair from a table, she began to pull it across the floor, the sound a soft scrape that echoed in the silence. "How about," she grunted, "a bunch of these, around a circular table in that secluded room?"

The suggestion hung in the air, resonating with something more profound, a hint of destiny, perhaps. Lily's eyes met Serena's, and something unspoken passed between them, an understanding that this was more than a simple gathering.

It was a beginning.

Lily nodded. "Sure, sounds smart. Oh, but please don't drag that, you'll scuff the hardwood. Here, let me."

And the next moment, five wingback chairs and a round wooden table rose inches off the ground, floating with ease into the spare room. Serena sighed with relief. "I am never moving to a town that doesn't have a resident air witch again."

Lily chuckled. "Glad to hear you love me for my personality, Rena."

"Oh good goddess!" Emela said. "I thought we all agreed that as long as we don't use our magic then we are not technically breaking any rules if we meet up."

"It's still light out, love; no one can see in. And no one is even outside. If there aren't any witnesses, did it really happen?" Lily said.

"Besides, this corner room has no windows." Crossing her arms, Serena observed the little room. Five tall, ornate candles floated in from where they previously sat on the front counter, settling in the center of the table. The room seemed to pulse with the promise of secrets soon to be shared. A coven to be born.

Rowan strode into the room at that moment, gently lighting the candles with the flick of her finger to cast the room in a warm glow. "What do you think?"

"I like it," Hailey said, coming in behind her. "It looks... regal. Like thrones around the round table."

"The Pembrooke Witches: Queens of Onyx County," Lily mused with a snort.

"Not Queens," Serena corrected. "How about Goddesses of the Pacific Northwest?"

"Yeah. At least it's humble," Emela chuckled.

Hailey smiled, taking a seat at the table. "And this is The Goddess Corner. Not a bad name for a meeting place."

"The Goddess Corner. Official meeting space of The Velvet Teahouse Witches," Serena murmured.

"Well, it does sound very official," Hailey said with a nod.

"Or very ostentatious," Rowan said.

"I think it's an excellent beginning," Lily said, sitting down beside her.

"All we need now is wine," Rowan said, pulling two bottles from a bag on the floor.

"And snacks," Emela added, bringing in a tray of cheese and fruit and setting it on the table.

Serena pulled up the chair nearest to the door, looking around at her friends with a grin. "Five witches walk into an empty teahouse. What's the punchline?"

CHAPTER 11
JARED

J ared had never been so tired. He felt like he'd been tired
for years now, and no amount of rest actually brought
him any relief. Stress could pile on and fall away, and he
always felt run ragged. Always another case, always some
matter of business with the council, always something with
Zoe. He was grateful for his mother's help—he never would
have survived past Zoe's first year of elementary school
without it. But parenthood was still draining. Rewarding, of
course, but draining.

On top of the usual whirlwind of responsibilities, he'd now
been saddled with an exhausting client. A simple matter of
dividing possessions in a divorce that had devolved into a
poorly written soap opera before his eyes. And now he was up
to his neck in printed copies of text logs from their phones and
about a decade's worth of "he-said-she-said's" from five
different members of their family. He was irritable, he was
underpaid, and worst of all he was working very late.

Tonight was Litha, which meant his mother had prepared
a feast for the midsummer sabbat. A feast he was in no mood

to consume. It was getting dark on the longest damn day of the year and he was still at work, he noted with a sigh. Lighting a candle, he said a silent prayer to Freyr before standing to leave.

As he locked the office door, he noticed that the lights were still on in The Velvet Teahouse. He'd been so crushed by mundane, everyday inconveniences that he'd barely paid any mind to the much more exceptional annoyance just across the street. It was almost refreshing. He hadn't seen so much as a glimpse of Serena Albright's face since the day she'd trapped him in his office. *That* had been quite the affair. Had to hack his way through the vines with a fountain pen and a staple remover. Though he supposed he deserved it after potentially damaging her shop and apartment. Not his proudest moment, but if she would only stop being so stubborn and actually *listen* to him.

In his own defense, he had gone back to the teahouse to check on any damage he had done. Serena had been gone, but she'd left the door unlocked. He'd gone inside, unfrozen the pipes, and checked for leaks. He'd even repaired the one cracked pipe he'd discovered. Cleaned up everything afterward, as good as new.

And there she was now. Practically bouncing as she made her way from a side room in the teahouse to the dining room. He watched as she removed some food items from a display case and set them on a platter, and before he knew it, he was crossing the street.

Maybe he could try talking to her again. After all, it seemed that in the eyes of everyone else in Pembrooke, Serena was a very welcome piece of the community. Bright, inviting, exceedingly warm. Pretty, too. If prettiness was the sort of thing one were looking for, that was. She could surely have a thriving business built on her skill and her charisma alone, without putting anyone at risk with magic. If he could just convince her of that fact.

He'd managed to keep the town safe for years with his rules and careful monitoring. And now she was threatening to unravel everything with her foolish recklessness.

Another woman appeared in the room, following Serena to the counter to marvel at what looked like large cinnamon rolls. Then, three more. Lily Hart, along with her partner, whom Jared doubted he would've recognized were it not for her proximity to the redhead. Those two being there after hours, he could understand. Lily had been frequenting the teahouse, nearly every day, in fact. It made sense that she and Serena had become friends. And Emela likely hoped to kindle a friendship of her own, which was a pleasant surprise to Jared because he could count the number of times he'd seen that woman leave their shop on his hands.

The third one was Hailey, the waitress from Borealis. The fourth one, however, was his own associate, Rowan. And something about them all congregating in the teahouse after closing time made a wave of dread pass over him.

Witches, all five of them.

Lily Hart specialized in air and gravity; Rowan, pyromancy. Hailey could manipulate emotions. Emela was a deconstructionist. And Serena, was the verdant, blooming thorn in his proverbial side. Five witches in Pembrooke, all under one roof. Practically a coven.

Five witches gathering on the summer solstice.

His fist rapped on the door before he could gather his thoughts, unsure what exactly he wanted to say, but unable to keep himself from speaking anyway. Why, why couldn't this girl just keep her head down? Why was it so impossible for her to simply go about her business, live life, hover beneath the radar? Couldn't she see that she was putting everyone in danger, putting *herself* in danger? He tried to take a breath, to be reasonable.

Jared's knuckles pounded on the door again, his frustration growing.

All of his reason seemed to leave him the moment she opened the door. He was momentarily arrested by the soft green of her eyes, so vibrant against her pale skin, accentuated by those dark, feathery lashes. A pang of something he couldn't quite define jolted through him, making the edges of his anger blur, if only for a beat. The words he'd come armed with seemed to hang in the balance of that split second.

Serena's prior cheer vanished, her lips drew into a thin scowl as she glared up at him through her lashes, a garland of woven daisies atop her hair. The door was barely open, blocking him from what he knew was happening inside. "What do you want?"

"You should really invest in some curtains before you have any more witches' gatherings," he snarked in return, nodding toward the nearest window. "I can see what you're doing. So can everyone else in Pembrooke, not that you seem to care."

She lifted her brows, eyes wide in feigned shock. "Thank you so much for the warning," she said. "I don't know what I would do if someone caught me spending time with my friends in my off hours. You don't think it'll end up in the papers, do you?"

His lips curled into a mocking smile. "Don't patronize me, Miss Albright."

"I've finally lost my first name privileges, then?"

"You can't start a coven," he said, shaking a finger at her. "Not here. Not in my town."

Her face was cold as stone. She crossed her arms, leaning on the door frame as she arched an eyebrow at him. "*Your* town?" Her lips twisted into a scowl. "I'm not afraid of you, Mr. Westergard."

He leaned closer and practically growled at her. "I'm not who you should be afraid of. There are far worse things than me out here watching. Now, if you don't disband, I *will* report you to the council. I've been lenient with you until now, but I won't stand for a coven operating here."

She smiled cruelly, eyes blazing with fury. "I don't believe you."

Jared tilted his head in an approximation of curiosity. "Do you enjoy being difficult, Miss Albright?"

"Excuse me?"

"Antagonizing me. Flaunting your blatant disregard for the rules and the safety of others. Belittling and discounting me at every turn. Do you gain some satisfaction from that? Is this fun for you?"

Serena floundered for a moment, a rosy tint rising on her cheeks. After a few seconds, she finally managed to say, "I think you should be going, Mr. Westergard."

"So you can keep ignoring every warning I give you?"

"No, so you leave before I tell you that you're a calloused, self-important, pompous ass! Someone who would rather I hide myself away than actually help people!"

In the blink of an eye, his anger shifted from molten to frozen. It made him feel unnaturally still. Placid but volatile, like a half-frozen lake not trustworthy to walk over. "When I'm finished with you, Ms. Albright, you will *never* work anywhere in Onyx County again."

And for once, it actually seemed to frighten her. He could see it in her eyes. He wanted to enjoy that feeling, scaring her. But mostly he just felt tired, even more so than before.

Jared turned to leave, refusing to look back.

THE HOUSE WAS UNCHARACTERISTICALLY STILL WHEN JARED ARRIVED home. A garland of fresh flowers adorned the dining table and enticing smells wafted out of the kitchen. But there was no sign of Zoe or his mother.

"Where have you been?" His mom appeared just as he was about to sit down.

Dragging a hand down his face, Jared muttered, "Same place as always. What's that saying about all work and no play?" He leaned in to kiss her cheek. "Happy Litha, mom."

"Blessed Litha," she murmured in return. "Jared?"

When he looked his mother in the eyes, he felt the color drain from his face. She was despondent, and the mere sight sent a tendril of fear crawling up his spine. "What happened?"

All she had to say were two words to send him crashing to earth. The two words he dreaded, had been dreading for eight years, and would continue to dread for the rest of his life.

"It's Zoe."

It was like being punched in the gut. He felt the ground swoop underfoot, his universe reorienting itself around a new axis. The house was quiet, he realized. He felt sure that his mother could hear his heart, until it went still.

"Is she okay?"

She shrugged. "She's got a high fever, had to be sent home from school. I've been looking after her all afternoon. Didn't you listen to my voicemails?"

He patted at his pockets. Did he even bring his phone to work today? "I haven't really had time," he admitted lamely wondering why she couldn't adapt to text messages instead. Those he noticed. "Thank you, Ma, for picking her up."

"Of course."

He sighed heavily. "So, is she asleep?"

"She'll probably be out for a few hours. I gave her some medicine earlier, supposed to make you drowsy."

"Good. That's... that's good." *Willow, I wish you were here. I'm trying. I'm trying so hard for her.*

She smiled reassuringly, placed a hand on his shoulder, squeezed. "She's going to be fine," she said, but the fear hadn't left her eyes. For the second time that night, Jared found himself wishing that he could take that fear away as he raced up the steps to check on his daughter.

CHAPTER 12
SERENA

T he next two days started normal. Serena wasn't awakened by angry Lenses at her door, ready to run her out of town. There hadn't been a plague of locusts called upon her apartment. Kita didn't even roll over until Serena was out of the shower both mornings. Whatever reckoning Jared had promised was evidently not scheduled until at least later in the week.

The tea shop was slower than usual, which gave her ample time to consider the midsummer celebration. Had she gone too far? True, Jared was infuriating, but she didn't really think that he was a bad person. Misguided, maybe. Acting like a bit of a prick, but with his heart in the right place. And she'd taken him past the edge of rivalry, that night. She could see as much in his eyes. He was incensed. Serena had never seen him like that before. She'd expected to be pleased with herself, when she pushed back at him like that. She was anything but.

More than once she caught herself looking out the front window, out to the little office across the street. She could go over there, with a peace offering of some kind. A blackberry loaf? Something about him told Serena that he liked black-berries.

It was her pride, more than anything else, that welded her in place. She wasn't at fault. She wasn't *sorry*, not really. Not for healing people with her teas, and certainly not for hosting a gathering on Litha. She couldn't apologize, not if she wasn't truly sorry.

That didn't mean it felt any better to see him so unhappy.

When the bell in the door frame rang and Judith stepped into the teahouse, Serena's face lit up. "Judith! Come in, I was worried when I didn't see you before school yesterday and this morning." She froze when she saw the look on the older woman's face. "Is everything okay?"

"No, it's not, Serena. I need your help."

It wasn't even something she needed to consider. "Say the word, whatever you need."

Judith stepped close to the counter, speaking low. "I need you to help Zoe. Please."

"Zoe? What happened, is she sick or hurt?" Serena's heart started to race with anxiety in seconds.

"She started feeling ill two days ago. I thought it might just be the flu, but her fever is so high and she's barely conscious. The doctor came by and doesn't seem to know what to do with her. I'm worried for her, Serena. Could you come see her? Try to heal her?"

"Jared said that he was okay with this?" she asked with a frown. "Last I heard, he was pretty adamant that I not use magic on Zoe."

Judith shook her head dismissively. "He's too stubborn for his own good. He's worried sick over her, and I know you can help."

Serena faltered, but Judith reached out and took her hand. She looked Serena in the eyes. "At least come see her. Please?"

She swallowed, regarding their hands. "Let me close the shop."

The Westergard home was a few blocks away. Stately and well-maintained, with a wrought iron fence and a small swing set out back. She braced herself when Judith led her through the threshold, not quite sure what to expect, but undeniably waiting for something unpleasant to happen. The other shoe to drop, perhaps.

"What took you so long?" Jared's voice rang down the hall. He poked his head out of a door, then sighed as he shook his head. "Ma, what have you done?"

"I brought someone who could help," Judith said.

"You told me you were going to the pharmacy."

She pulled a small bag from her purse, holding it up. "I *did* go to the pharmacy. And then I stopped at the teahouse."

Jared plucked the bag from his mother's hand. "Fantastic, thank you. Now see Miss Albright to the door, please."

"Look, I'm only here because I care about Zoe," Serena asserted. "I'm not sure if I can help her, but I'd like to try."

He placed his hands on his hips, looking to the tile floor as if for advice.

"At least let me take a look at her," she bargained. "I can tell you what I'd recommend."

Jared let out a weary sigh. "Fine. Go ahead. Upstairs, second door on the left."

CURLED UNDER A THIN BLANKET AND PROPPED UP ON A MOUNTAIN OF pillows, Zoe slept fitfully in her bed. She was a bit small for her age, but she looked especially frail now. A wet cloth rested on her forehead, her cheeks flushed and sweat-damp.

"She's been in and out of consciousness since yesterday," Judith said, as Serena observed. "Can't stand, can't eat. It came on out of nowhere, too. The doctor doesn't seem to know what it is."

Serena sat on the bed and reached out with a gentle hand, pushing back the thick, dark hair plastered to Zoe's forehead. "Elderflower, to start," she muttered. "Yarrow. Echinacea. Thistle and peppermint, too, for her appetite. It would probably take multiple doses to heal her, though. Couple days, I'd wager. But I believe I can do it."

"In exchange for...?"

She jumped at the proximity of his voice, startling again when she turned to find Jared looming just over her shoulder. He was frowning down at Zoe where she slept, like a lion watching over its cub.

"What?"

"What will you want in return?" he clarified. "For treating her?"

"Nothing," she replied, slightly offended. "Like I said, I care about Zoe. She's a sweet kid, I won't let her suffer when I can help." She smiled up at him, trying to offer him some kindness. "I'll treat her for free, if you'll let me."

He sighed. "Serena—"

"I know that you don't trust me," she blurted, rubbing her fingers as she spoke. "I know that you and I don't really see eye to eye. I know. But this is more important to me than any bad blood between us. Don't you feel the same way?"

Jared regarded her, then Zoe. "All right. If you're certain you can help her, I won't stop you."

"Well, thank the goddess," Judith muttered from the hallway.

"Good." Serena stood, took a centering breath. After rolling her shoulders she cracked her knuckles. "Now, show me the kitchen."

CHAPTER 13
SERENA

Brushed metal bowls. Clean, clinical white counter tops. No tea kettle, which made her glad she'd brought one from home. For everything else, she would make do.

Serena tied her hair back, looking over the various leaves, roots and seeds like she was a general addressing her troops. She'd brought far too many, but she'd been in such a panic when she packed her supplies. She would already be preparing the brews in an unfamiliar location, the home of a Lens—the lion's den—and the last thing she needed was to suddenly realize she'd forgotten a crucial ingredient.

It didn't help that she'd become acutely aware of a hostile presence over her shoulder, watching her from the kitchen doorway.

"Can I help you?" she asked, not bothering to look up.

His footsteps echoed on the hardwood. "I was just wondering the same thing." Jared filled the small space with an energy that lifted the hairs on her arms. He was wearing a snugly fitted T-shirt and jeans this evening. She was so accustomed to seeing him in dress shirts and blazers that the sight of his well-defined, bare arms was an unwelcome surprise.

"You want to help?" She hesitated in surprise for a moment before relenting. "Fine. Do you have a mortar and pestle?"

"I'm afraid not." His hazel eyes creased with apparent worry.

"There's one in my bag. You can use it."

He reached for the bag, and Serena instinctively wanted to slap his hands away. Tell him to mind his own business. Chalk it up to old habits dying hard.

"So, what am I crushing?" he asked, hefting the pestle in his hand as if testing its weight. His rugged features were drawn with concern, and beneath the tousled hair were the dark circles of a sleepless night. But the worry lines and the tiredness couldn't hide his attractiveness. Even in his disarray, he looked unnervingly handsome.

"The echinacea seeds. I'll prep the yarrow and elderflower in the meantime."

He smirked. "You got it, Boss."

Serena tried to focus on the herbs in front of her. But as much as she wanted to dismiss Jared as an irritating thorn in her side, the sight of him in his kitchen stirred something unexpected within her. She knew she needed to stay on guard, but for the first time, she was tempted to ease her defenses a little.

They fell into a small silence after that. Shared, private. It was oddly companionable, working side by side on a simple task. When Jared was finished, she added the seeds to the kettle, leaving it to brew. She busied herself with tidying up her supplies, not yet willing to disturb their newfound peace. While she was still furious with him, she didn't enjoy being at odds with him. It was just difficult *not* to be.

It was Jared who broke the silence in the end. "So," he said, trying rather bravely to adopt an air of casualness. "Which came first, your plant-based magic, or the fascination with botany?"

She glanced up sharply. "Both, I guess. I've always loved nature: chasing lizards, getting dirty, picking wildflowers. I discovered pretty early that I could make new flowers bloom, to take the place of the ones I picked. It wasn't until I started honing my magic that I started actually researching plants, though. Learning which plants could help me in certain ways. I was pretty immature and selfish at first. I knew what spells and which herbs to use to get people to do what I wanted. And my mother, she was..." Serena trailed off, remembering herself. "Sorry, I'm talking too much, aren't I?"

"I asked."

"You don't have to." It came out more rudely than she intended. But she didn't want Jared to feel obligated to strike up small talk with her after their volatile history.

"Look, Serena. What do you say we call a truce? I appreciate your coming over today trying to help, and right now you're a guest in my home. I figure we can set aside our differences for Zoe's sake."

She nodded. *For Zoe.*

"So, you were saying? About your mother?"

"Well...Grace was really into ascribing meanings to things. Astrology, crystals, floriography. So, I learned a lot about symbology from her."

"Is she a witch, too?"

Serena nodded. "Psychometrist. She can heal with her hands, and also sense things about an object's past when she holds it. Pretty different than my powers. Hard for her to teach me. But honestly, I think Grace handled our magical differences better than she handled buying my first bra."

Jared laughed at that. She couldn't remember ever hearing

him laugh before. It was warm and rough, like worn leather boots, and she liked the sound of it. "I'm sure she was a good mom."

"She did her best."

"Yeah." Jared leaned back against the counter, sighing at the ceiling. "I hope Zoe gives me the same grace, when she's old enough to have some perspective."

"I'm sure she thinks you're a good dad," Serena said, sliding the ground echinacea seeds toward her.

"Maybe. I don't know, I worry sometimes that I'm making the wrong choices. She seems happy enough, but I catch myself staying up at night. Just thinking to myself. Do I spend too much time at work? Am I smothering her? Does she feel like I don't understand her? Hell, am I *trying* to understand her?" He dragged a hand down his cheek and Serena found herself surprised at his candor.

"And my mom, you know, she's trying her best, too," he continued. "And I'm grateful to her. I don't think I could do it without her, but I still sometimes feel like I'm doing it all alone. It's a lot to take on."

Before she could reply, he forced a tight smile, attempting to clear the air. "But hey, look who's talking up a storm now."

A thread of sympathy wove its way through her heart, but Serena struggled with how much she wanted to open up. She whispered a short spell as she threw all the ingredients into the infuser basket and poured in the hot water.

"If it makes you feel better, Zoe has never complained to me about you before. So, I think that's a good sign." Serena placed the lid on the teapot and waited for the tea to steep.

"Thanks." His smile turned softer at that and Serena felt like something cold and hard was starting to thaw between them.

"But then again, she's only eight. Just wait until she turns thirteen. That's when the real fun begins," Serena deadpanned.

Jared glanced up in alarm, but then allowed a small, uneasy smile to spread across his face.

"So, what about you?" she asked, trying to will away the tension that brewed in the room. "You mentioned before that you were able to recognize a few magical plants. How did a water witch become so well-acquainted with plant-based magic?"

Jared shrugged. "Let's just say that before law school I used to work outdoors a lot–logging, firefighting, you name it. I did a lot of aimless exploration, to be honest."

"Aimless exploration?" She echoed. "Well, I guess that's how almost everything starts." She was intrigued by his answer. Jared Westergard seemed anything but aimless.

"It's also where it ends for some people. More of a hobby that I grew out of than a proper passion, I suppose. You learn a lot about yourself when you become a parent. You have to prioritize how you spend your time." He glanced sidelong at her. "But I bet you know all about prioritizing time, don't you? Running that shop all by yourself has to take up a lot of your time."

"I do find myself missing when I had more free time," she agreed. "Still, I guess it's always good to learn more about yourself. Finding out where your priorities lie."

"And where do your priorities lie?" he prodded. "Helping people, laws and common sense be damned? Sounds like you have a savior complex to me."

She was about to give a sharp retort, but then paused to consider his words. Was there some truth to them? Sometimes she didn't know what motivated her to do the things she did. "And what if I said that I'm not sure what my priorities are yet?" Serena said. "Does that make me immature?"

Stepping back, Jared leaned against the counter. "Humble, I think, is the word that I would use," he replied after a moment. "Too many people claim to be so sure that they know exactly what they want out of life. Part of me wishes I could be afforded that luxury. Figuring things out, I mean. I feel like I need to know everything now, these days."

"It's exhausting," she agreed.

Jared sighed. "My parents always just seemed like they had it all figured out, you know? Even when I was a kid and they weren't even thirty yet—my age, man, I'm getting old. I just feel like I should have it together by now. Or at least I should *seem* like I do."

"I don't think that's very realistic," she countered. "There isn't a permanent state of being, after all. You're always going to be undergoing some kind of transition. I don't know if 'having it together' exists. At least not the way you're defining it."

"Maybe," he shrugged. "I guess I always needed to feel like there's a finish line somewhere."

Serena removed the infuser basket, filling one cup before pouring the remainder into a thermos. Gesturing to the still steaming mug, she said, "You'll need to let this cool down for about five minutes. Make sure she drinks it all. I'll leave the rest with you in this thermos. Give her a cup every six hours. This bag has the dried tea. Steep a tablespoon in hot water for five minutes when you need more. I'll be back in a couple days with more tea. If her condition worsens, give me a call."

"Thank you. Listen. It's... It's very compassionate, what you're doing for her. I hope you know that isn't lost on me."

"Like I said, I'm happy to do it. For Zoe." Serena let the statement hang in the air for a moment of awkward silence before saying, "Well, I guess I'll leave you to—"

"Would you like to stay for dinner?"

She blinked. "What?"

"I'm grateful that you're treating Zoe, but I wouldn't feel right about it if I didn't at least offer you a hot meal for your trouble."

She hesitated, glancing around the room as if for a sign. "I'm not sure."

"Come on. It might not exactly be Michelin Star material, but I'll make up for it with sparkling conversation."

Serena thought it over. Twenty-four hours ago, the idea of sharing dinner with Jared Westergard would have sounded like a fate worse than death. But now?

"What are you having?"

He looked pleased with that answer. "Well, Zoe will be having your tea and chicken noodle soup, and you and I will be dining on... well, whatever I can throw together with the stuff in my fridge, I guess." Jared lifted a hand to rub at the back of his neck, looking almost sheepish. I haven't had time to go grocery shopping in a while."

Despite herself, she smiled. Crayon drawings on the fridge. Mismatched coffee cups. Hazel eyes that were starting to grow on her. "'Whatever' sounds good. Count me in."

"Whatever" turned out to be a decent, if cobbled together stir fry. She'd had worse. She'd had *better,* but she'd had worse. She and Jared sat at the dining room table together. They ate, they made pleasant but stilted conversation. It didn't escape her that his attention seemed divided, his eyes flicking down toward the hallway where Zoe was sleeping.

"She's going to be fine," she assured him after a while. "The treatment might take a couple of days to take effect, but she'll be right as rain before you know it."

"I guess I can just be a little over protective," he confessed with a slight sigh. "It's just hard not to worry. Feels like anything could happen, especially with all the magic that's in our family."

"Do you think her magic is going to present soon?" Serena asked.

"I would be shocked if it didn't. Her mother was a witch, too."

Her mouth twisted. "Lily told me about your wife's passing. It's terrible, I'm so sorry."

He nodded. "She and Lily were friends, way back when. Ran in a lot of the same circles. Willow was an air witch, same as Lily, so they had that in common."

"Jared? You don't have to answer, but... what happened to her, if you don't mind me asking?"

Jared took a slow breath as a dark cloud passed over his features. "It was about five, almost six years ago, now. Willow was running the Fall Festival in Pembrooke and had to drive up into the mountains to Oxport, to buy some supplies. It started raining, so the roads were slippery. Then right in front of her, this car just swerves and runs some poor fool right off the road. They flip, and by the end of it, the driver's pinned underneath the car.

"Willow, she was the sort of person who would never just let another person suffer. Not if she could do anything about it. Kind of like you, I guess." He held up his hands in a helpless sort of gesture. "There was someone who needed help, and she could offer it. What else could she do? She pulled over, she held out her hands. Lifted the car off of the driver before it could kill him."

"That's incredible," Serena said. "She sounds like she was a very noble person."

"She was," he confirmed. "Bravest person I ever knew, had a heart like a lion. It was what I always admired most about her. I have a tendency to get stuck in my own head, from time to time. But Willow? When she saw that man was in danger, she didn't even think, you know? She just acted. Fearless, even though maybe she should have been more cautious." He shook his head. "She probably never stopped to look around, never stopped to see if she was being watched. But someone *was* there, they saw her lift the car and..." He trailed off.

She frowned in confusion. "What, someone ratted her out to the Lenses for saving someone's life?"

"Not the council, no. Serena. Remember when I told you there are far worse things watching and waiting out there? Ever heard of the Brotherhood?"

She searched her memory, eyes narrowed. "Maybe in passing, but I've never known anyone who was affiliated or anything. Is it a religious order?"

"Witch hunters. They're a cult," he said. "Got started in the Middle Ages. Disappeared for a while after the witch trials, but reemerged in the 1800s. Spread to the States, and slowly across the country, and new chapters cropped up almost everywhere, including in Oregon. Real puritanical bastards, they hate witches with a passion.

"The magic council has been watching them for decades, but didn't realize what they were capable of. Preaching bigoted rhetoric is one thing, but outright violence? Why would they even consider it?" His tone turned grave as he spoke. "The council laughed them off, more or less. Figured at first that they would keep to themselves, maybe even fizzle out on their own. But over time they started to become aggressive, violent. That day of the accident, one of them saw Willow. A week later, I went out of town. The members tracked her down, came to our house..."

Serena was stricken. She'd heard of those sorts of cults before. They were not just organizations with extremist mission statements, but outright witch hunters. There were rumors of one starting in northern Arizona before she skipped town, but she hadn't necessarily believed it. After all, cults of that nature hadn't publicly operated in centuries. "Zoe... was she...?"

"She was at my mother's house when it happened, thank god. I used to have nightmares about scenarios where she wasn't, though. Even more of versions where I hadn't gone away, where I was there when Willow needed me. Still do, sometimes. But no, Willow was busy helping with the festival, and so my mom was spending lots of time taking care of Zoe."

Serena shook her head, struggling to process the rush of emotions she felt. "I can't believe you stayed in Pembrooke," she said at last.

Jared shrugged. "It's my home, I can't leave. My mom's lived in this town her whole life; I couldn't just abandon her here and hope that she didn't get hurt. But that's when I decided to join the council. Now I do what I can from the inside. Stand up for our community, take witches' cases pro bono, when I can. Keep an eye on the Brotherhood, in case it ever looks like they're poking their noses around Pembrooke again."

"The council, they didn't do anything about what happened to Willow?"

"They investigated in secret. Watched them. Tried to dig up solid evidence they were connected to the crime. The only eyewitness who saw them together was too scared to come forward to the authorities. He wasn't a very reliable witness, either. So in the end, there wasn't much they could do without taking it into our own hands or revealing who we were to the Brotherhood. The council decided to operate in the interest of the greater good, like always. Didn't matter to them that I became a member. Didn't matter that most of them had known Willow and me for years. More important things at stake, and all that."

He gazed at the candle on the table. "Look, I'm sorry for what I did, the other day. With your pipes and everything. But I meant what I said the day we met. This area isn't as nice as it seems on the surface. I don't want you to get in trouble, but there are worse things than the Lenses lurking in Onyx County."

"I'm sorry, too," she confessed. "For trapping you in your office."

Jared chuckled. "You kidding? Hacking my way out of there was the most fun I've had in months. Good stress relief, too."

Eyes wide, Serena studied Jared. "Be careful," she teased. "Talk like that, and I might be tempted to grow a garden outside your office. That sad little stack of bricks could use a pop of color."

He glanced back up, studying her with an expression she couldn't quite read. "Yeah," he finally said. "I think it could."

KITA WAS EAGER AS THEY WALKED, TUGGING AT THE LEAD IN SERENA'S hand all the while. She didn't even seem to be in a rush to get anywhere in particular, she just wanted to *go*. Restless energy, she reckoned, although Serena hadn't been slacking on exercising with her. As the two of them half-ran along empty sidewalks, the streetlamps buzzing overhead, Serena found herself thinking about the time she'd spent in Pembrooke.

She had never envisioned herself long term in a place like this. Sure, she was a social person, liked making friends and so forth. She sometimes entertained the idea that the covens she'd interacted with throughout her life were still active, still together. It brought her comfort, thinking that those social circles were still out there, even if she wasn't a part of them any longer.

The moments when she felt happiest were when The Velvet Teahouse first opened for the day. Serena had always been a morning person, but now, more than ever, she relished in rising with the sun, scarfing down breakfast and racing down the stairs to get started. Lily and Emela would sneak in as soon as the teahouse opened, before any other customers arrived. They'd have Emela's first dose of enchanted tea, pastries for the two of them, maybe something for Lily, to put the proverbial pep in her step. Not that Lily ever needed that, since her step was plenty peppy to begin with.

Then along would come Zoe and Judith, and Serena got to send Zoe off to school with a smile, and Judith would unfailingly remark on how pretty Serena looked that day. Next was Rowan, off to slave away at Westergard and Ross for another day, but not without a little rosemary infusion for focus. Serena would look out the window and, like clockwork, there was Jared Westergard. Still stubbornly drinking that terrible coffee from the office break room and pretending not to look in through her front window. Maybe he would catch her eye, maybe he would wave. Maybe on a good day she would wave back. Later in the day Aaron would arrive, and sometimes Hailey, too.

And it was... nice. In this quiet, simple sort of way. New. To just wake up, do her job, have a little time left over. It made her happy, in a way that felt so simple but so true. Like something that could maybe last this time.

As she wound her way back around to her own sleepy street, she paused by the building across from her teahouse. Peered up at the darkened window that she knew led to Jared's office. She found herself picturing him, the day that he'd frozen her pipes. How he'd had to fight his way through her vines, likely furious. She smiled. He really wasn't so terrible to be around. When he wasn't choosing to be entirely insufferable, at least. And she'd gotten a glimpse of his true colors, last night. Warm, kind. Heart in the right place, even if he was a bit misguided, just as she'd thought when they met. Smart, too. Ridiculously good-looking.

She groaned. It wouldn't do to think like that, and she knew it. Jared was too... stagnant, for her to entertain those thoughts. He'd lived in the same town his entire life, for god's sake. He had a family, and an office job, and *stability*. Historically, Serena didn't do well with any of those things. It wasn't worth the investment, even just in the back of her mind.

Serena unlocked the door of the teahouse, sighing to herself. It wouldn't work out. No use spending time on it.

No distractions.

"Hey there," a voice said.

She jumped, dropping Kita's lead as the wolf began to growl. When she turned, she saw a man outside the Tinker's Trinket, stumbling toward her. *Drunk.*

"You're that girl with the magical remedy teas, aren't you?" Colin slurred. "Se-reeeena."

She faltered. "Sorry, but we don't open until—"

The next moment, Colin was seizing her by the waist, pinning her arms to her sides. Kita barked and snarled. He wrenched the door open, shoving her inside as he kicked the wolf. Serena crashed against a table, the force knocking over two of the neighboring chairs and, when she looked up, he was locking the front door. She could hear Kita barking just outside. Colin turned toward her with a menacing smile.

"Now what can you make me that has a little kick to it?"

CHAPTER 14
JARED

J ared stood near the counter, waiting for the old copper kettle to start whistling. The teas weren't so difficult to prepare, now that Serena had left him with the needed equipment and ingredients. It was kind of her, not only offering her services, but teaching him to help Zoe on his own. Perhaps she thought that he would dislike relying on her if she had to prepare each remedy. Truth be told, he almost wished she'd kept them to herself. If only so he had an excuse to see her again.

He'd grown almost embarrassingly accustomed to having her around. Seeing her across the way, morning sun catching her hair through the windows. Sitting in his office and peeking outside, looking at the facade of The Velvet Teahouse and picturing her hard at work, with flour and dried leaves dusting her apron, flashing that contagious little smile at everyone who passed through.

As little as he liked to admit it, he'd noticed the effect she'd had on the community. He needn't look any further than his own doorway to see that.

Emela Maric actually going out. Making friends. He never thought he'd see the day, and Lily seemed over the moon about it.

Aaron Abercrombie was actually making money, for the first time in months. Poor kid had been scrimping and saving since he moved to Onyx County. Fresh out of art school, waxing poetic about the area and how much natural beauty it boasted. Now that he was posted up in The Velvet Teahouse, he was not only drawing again but he seemed *inspired*. He made enough from tourists to afford groceries between larger commission pieces, and Rowan had shown Jared photos of his latest paintings on her phone a few days ago, asking if they could commission one for the office.

Her influence had invaded his own home, even. His mother, who'd been complaining for months about feeling listless and bored in her retirement, had suddenly reignited her passion for baking. His kitchen was filled near bursting with exotic breads, unique cookies, and delicately decorated cakes. This recent fervor, he inferred from listening to his mother recount their conversations, was Serena's handiwork.

But no one seemed to delight in Serena Albright's presence quite like his daughter. Zoe didn't always warm up to others. People sometimes found her impolite, or even off-putting. She was simply misunderstood, in Jared's eyes. Blunt because she was honest, chatty because she was passionate, inquisitive, but not to a fault. Serena seemed to share his own view. As a result, Zoe was now a veritable expert on teas, in addition to the thousand other subjects that she loved to study.

The people of Pembrooke were better off with Serena Albright around, not just physically but emotionally, too. Her effortless charm seemed to put everyone on Bailey Street into a slightly better, more inviting mood. Himself included.

Maybe the cheerfulness could be chalked up to all the new

KATE SWANSEA

flowers in the area. To the yellow tulips, sitting pretty in a vase at Zoe's bedside. To the ivy and Queen Anne's Lace outside The Velvet Teahouse. To the little white blossoms that had clung to the vines in his office, which he'd contemplated salvaging after his escape. He hadn't, in the end, but he'd thought about it. To the roses and begonias that mysteriously popped up in places they'd never been before, all up and down Bailey Street.

But she was still breaking all the rules, wasn't she? Carefully laid rules that had kept the witches of Pembrooke safe for the last few years. *His* rules.

And yet, she had done so much to help the town. Maybe if he just kept his distance, he could continue to turn a blind eye to what she was doing, to allow her spirit to infect the town.

She was opening up something inside him, too, he feared. Serena was as bright as the sun and as alluring as the moon. And a growing part of him wanted to be a part of her orbit. But he had a young daughter to raise, a law practice to run, and a council to serve.

A council she was actively defying.

No, he had too many responsibilities now. He couldn't afford to chase after impractical love. Especially when he still felt haunted by Willow's memory. Yes, it was better to keep his distance from Serena Albright.

He was interrupted from his thoughts by the sound of scratching at his front door. When he opened it to investigate, he was met with an unexpected but familiar face. Serena Albright's wolf, staring up at him from his front step. She appeared agitated as she paced back and forth. He sighed, searching his memory for the animal's name.

"Kita?"

She barked at him in response. He frowned, stepping out the door to search for some sign of Serena. Nothing. "Did you... come here on your own?"

Another bark. It was then that Jared noticed the leash dragging across his porch, as if Serena had been walking her and gotten separated from Kita somehow.

He knelt in front of Kita, brows furrowed. Sure, he'll try talking to a wolf. Why not? "Did Serena send you here?"

At this, Kita took hold of his pant leg, tugging him outside with all her might. He felt a frantic sort of fear roll down his spine. Without another thought, he grabbed his car keys and headed outside, freshly prepared tea still cooling on the counter in his kitchen.

WHEN HE PARKED OUTSIDE OF THE VELVET TEAHOUSE, KITA LEAPT out of the car, running to the teahouse door and growling loudly. He looked in through the window, and what he saw through the glass made his heart stop.

One of the tables was overturned, shattered glass littering the floor. There was a man inside. Colin, the town drunk. He had Serena cornered against the front counter, her wrists pinned to the wood. Serena was kicking, furious as she struggled with all of her strength, snarling in his face. There was a cut on her cheek. A thin trickle of blood blazed a trail along her freckled face.

Jared yanked on the knob. Locked. Of course. His heart was racing. He felt each second ticking by with blood-curdling finality. Kita pawed at the door, barking.

Serena was still struggling, and the man slammed her against the counter. Madness, that's what this was. What sort of reckless lunatic assaults some poor woman in full view of the street? If you're going to attack someone, at least don't do it behind a wall covered in curtainless windows.

Windows.

He reared back and elbowed the glass panel nearest to the

door handle, looking away as the window shattered into the shop, a few pieces landing at his feet. Jared reached through the opening, his wrists brushing against shards of glass as his fingertips fumbled for the lock. With a desperate lunge, the lock clicked out of position, and he immediately threw the door open, ready to attack.

A stupefied look on his face, Colin stood awkwardly facing the door as Kita rushed inside and made a beeline for him. Serena pushed her assailant away and a thicket of briars wove itself around Colin's ankles. They crawled up the man's body, looping around his arms and restraining him with ease, even as Kita's teeth latched onto his ankle. He yelped in pain, pulling at the vines like a madman until they began to tear.

A volley of sharp knives sailed across the room, some cutting through the vines, and others sinking into Colin's clothing. In seconds, he was pinned against the wall by ten blades impaling his shirt and pants.

Serena glanced at her now empty knife stand and then over at Jared with seeming disbelief. Jared had inadvertently revealed another of his powers, but he'd reacted instinctively.

Striding forward, he approached Colin, not taking his eyes off the lunatic, even as he asked Serena if she was okay.

"Yeah," she said in a shaky voice.

Colin was struggling against his bonds, and gazing up at Jared with terror. And defiance. The little shit deserved to have his face smashed in. No, he deserved far worse.

A knife appeared next to Colin's face, spinning in place in the air, inches from his cheek. A blade awaiting its final command from Jared, who was studying Colin's wriggling body as he contemplated where he wanted to shove the first knife.

"Jared." An angelic voice pulled him from his dark thoughts. Serena had her hand on his arm, her grip gentle yet firm. "Don't." The single word was a plea wrapped in unspoken understanding.

His jaw was set, teeth clenched so tightly that it seemed they might shatter under the pressure. His fury was a tangible force, one he was unsure he could rein in. The floating knife quivered in the air, mirroring Jared's conflicting emotions. Then, as if heeding Serena's plea, it began to lose its momentum, spinning slower and slower before it clattered harmlessly to the floor.

Jared looked at her, still trying to control the beast that sought retribution.

"You're okay," he said, his voice barely a whisper, as if he was trying to convince himself rather than her. He shook his head, turning away from Colin, who was still pinned like a butterfly against the wall.

Colin's desperate wheezing filled the room, his fear palpable. But as Serena looked at him pinned to the wall, she didn't look satisfied. Instead, a flash of pity crossed her face, as if she wondered how Colin ended up like this. And why he had targeted her.

She released her grip on Jared's arm, moving instead to place her hand on his chest. "Let's call the police," she suggested. "They'll handle him."

Jared met her gaze with disbelief for a moment before he acquiesced to her request. "Okay," he agreed with no small amount of reluctance, pulling out his phone to make the call. He cast one last glance at Colin, a stark warning lingering in his gaze. "They better get here soon."

As he placed the call, he watched Serena take a labored breath, rolling her shoulders. Her lower lip was split, and she reached up to wipe the blood from her mouth. She comforted Kita, easing the wolf back into a more relaxed stance. For a moment, Serena's eyes locked on her restrained attacker, her face hard and fiery. Then she looked up to Jared, and her wounded mouth broke further around the strain of a crooked smile.

"Look who's got the savior complex now," she said as he hung up the phone.

"You sure you're okay?" he said.

She shrugged, looking down at the red patches blooming around her wrists. They'd be black bruises by morning, he suspected. "I've been worse," she mumbled.

Jared approached the man now tangled in thorns. "You know this guy, Serena?"

She shrugged. "Not really. He's been in the shop once before. Do you?"

"Unfortunately, yes." He crossed his arms, glaring at the man. "Colin Parker here has a bit of a bad reputation in town. Slapped around your last girlfriend, didn't you?"

The man sneered at him through unfocused eyes and he could smell whiskey on his breath. "I'm not telling y'all nothing."

Jared grabbed him by the lapels, shaking him slightly. He couldn't remember the last time he'd been so angry. True, Serena drove him mad, but she didn't deserve this. She spent her days serving tea and healing people. Including Jared's daughter. There was no reason for her to be anyone's target.

"You think you're tough, is that it?" He all but growled, shaking the man again for emphasis. "Hm? Trying to prove that you're strong by assaulting an innocent woman?"

"I just came in here for a drink, man. That's all."

Blood boiling, Jared snarled. Who the hell did this guy think he was? Jared should—well, he *shouldn't*, but oh god, he wanted to. A surge of protective energy washed over him. Seeing Serena like this, bloody and furious, it enraged him.

He forced himself to take a step back. With a staggering

amount of effort, he willed his fists to unfurl where they gripped the other man's jacket. He needed this man out of his sight, before he lost his carefully cultivated control.

Jared watched the assailant like a hawk until the cops arrived. When their cars appeared, Serena withdrew her briars and Jared the knives, to avoid suspicion. Jared immediately grabbed Colin by the arms, holding them firmly behind his back until the police could restrain the man themselves.

When Serena told the police that she didn't want to press charges, Jared balked at her, but she'd been insistent.

"He's just drunk," Serena said.

"Well, we'll still be taking him to the station overnight for public intoxication," the officer said.

Jared watched them start to escort Colin away, and found his proverbial hackles raising without his permission. "Hey, listen to me."

As Colin turned, Jared drew closer, speaking in low tones so only the man could hear. "You better get your ass out of Pembrooke, and don't even think about coming back. If I catch a whiff of you in my town, I'll rain down on you like the goddamn apocalypse, got it? This lady so much as spots your ugly mug walking down the street, I'll be on you before you can blink."

Colin's eyes widened, but he didn't reply, and Jared watched him leave, itching with unresolved anger.

"Are *you* all right?" Serena said after they left. She kneeled to upright a fallen chair. "I think I can hear my ice boiling."

He tried to shake himself, willing the tension out of his shoulders as he rushed over to pick up the overturned table. "Pretty sure I'm the one who's meant to be asking you that."

"I'm fine. I'm tougher than I look."

Jared frowned, stepping closer. "You're bleeding," he

observed, daring to tuck a strand of now wild hair behind her ear.

"I've got bandages upstairs," she replied with a wan smile. "It's really not a big deal." She walked behind the counter and pulled out a corked bottle of wine and two glasses.

"Why did you let him go?"

Serena sighed, regarding the remains of the broken window. "I was thinking about what you said earlier, about being careful with humans. He suspected, even before I used magic on him, that I was a witch. But I resisted wrapping him up in vines for as long as I could. If he got arrested it might make the papers, and then whatever he decided to say might start rumors." She shrugged and poured the glasses half-full. "I don't know, it didn't seem like it was worth the trouble." She brought the glasses over and sat down at the table, gesturing for Jared to sit as well.

"I could've worked out something with the council. Maybe. I would have tried." Jared slouched into the chair.

"Like I said, I don't think he was worth it. He was drunk. Probably won't even remember much tomorrow."

He tried to take that in stride. Every inch of him was screaming to put that man behind bars, though, since he couldn't kill him. He was surprised with himself, to be honest. Surprised by how deeply he'd become invested in Serena's well being.

"How did you know?" Serena said.

"Kita told me," he said, nodding at the wolf who had curled up next to his feet.

"Kita ran to find you?"

Jared nodded and scratched the wolf on the neck. "She was clearly distraught and dragging her leash on the ground. I knew something bad must be happening."

Serena glanced down at Kita in surprise and then what

looked like gratitude. "Well, well. You have redeemed yourself, Kita. You can have your old job as guard dog back."

The wolf looked up and yawned before settling back down and closing her eyes.

"But you're taking the fall if my landlady yells at me for that window, you know," Serena said, half-smiling up at Jared. The mischief in her eyes set him at ease. Serena Albright: Unshakable, indestructible, indescribable.

"That's the second time it's been broken since I started renting the place," she added.

He smiled back at her. "I'll pay for a replacement, how about that?"

"Such a gentleman. You know what? I might take you up on that."

Jared nodded and took a long drink. She paused and he knew what was coming next.

"That was quite a party trick you pulled... with my knives," she said softly.

He shrugged. "Yeah. I may be... more than what I seem."

"More than just a water witch, you mean?"

He leaned back in the chair, feeling the soft velvet against the back of his head. "Yeah, something like that. My people are Norwegian. We have an ancient, rare form of Norse magic passed down from one of my ancestors." There were other things that he wanted to tell her, but now just didn't seem like the right time. She'd just been attacked and their focus should be on her, not him.

She nodded, seeming to respect his reluctance to say more. "Thank you, by the way. For coming."

"I'm just glad I was nearby and could help." He finished his wine and slid the goblet toward the center of the table. "Besides, Kita wasn't going to take no for an answer."

He stalled. He had no reason to stay any longer, and yet the idea of leaving her alone chafed at him. She may not be a damsel in distress, but something about her made him *want* to protect her, even if she didn't need it. To keep her from harm's way, and take care of her the way she was always taking care of others. Who was making sure that Serena was healthy and happy, while the rest of the community thrived? It certainly wasn't Jared.

But maybe it could be.

"Serena?"

She looked up at him, her green eyes shining in the low light. "Yeah?"

Jared licked his lips. "I'm really glad you're okay."

Her gaze flicked back down to the floor, but she smiled. "Yeah, I'm fine. One of the hazards of being a woman, I guess."

"Well, it shouldn't be." He was getting angry again and needed to calm down. "Are you sure you'll be all right on your own, after all that?"

"They just hauled Colin away, so I'd say I'm safe for now." Serena's brows drew together in a tight frown. "What are you suggesting, exactly?"

"Nothing!" he said, perhaps a bit too quickly. "Nothing. I was just going to tell you that you can call me, if you get nervous. I don't mind."

She breathed out a weak laugh. "Kita usually helps me feel safe, but I appreciate the offer."

"Before I leave, I'd like to board up that shattered window," Jared offered, his tone softer than before.

Serena looked up, a hint of grateful surprise in her eyes. His pulse quickened. "That... that would be appreciated, Jared. I have a few wooden crates stored in the back that you might be able to use," she said, directing him with a subtle gesture of her hand. "And the toolbox is just inside the storeroom," she added.

As he moved to gather the required materials, Serena began the task of sweeping up the shattered pieces of glass that littered the floor. The shop was quiet, save for the gentle whisper of her broom's bristles against the wooden floorboards.

Jared worked quietly and efficiently, his focus fixated on his task. Yet his thoughts were a sea of jumbled emotions. Willow's doe eyes flashed through his mind, along with her beautiful crooked smile. He remembered the broken glass on his living room floor from *that* day. The glass was scattered on the teahouse floor in much the same way when he flung open the door and raced inside, the broken bits crunching beneath his soles.

An uneasy silence hung in the air between them, each lost in their thoughts and the tension simmering beneath the surface.

After hammering the final nail, Jared broke the silence, his voice rough. "Well, I should let you rest, Serena. It's late; it's been a long day, and I'm sure you're exhausted." He avoided her gaze, his own attention riveted to the window.

Serena was behind the counter now. She paused her sweeping, a sharp nod betraying her surprise at his perceptiveness. "Yes, rest sounds good right now. I'll stop by to check on Zoe tomorrow." Then, after a brief hesitation, she added, "And, Jared, thank you. For your... help today."

Jared finally met her gaze, his eyes softening. His gaze strayed momentarily to her lips, stained a vibrant red from the wine. "Anytime, Serena," he said. His eyes held hers for a moment longer than they should have, the silence once again descending around them, heavy with the weight of unspoken words.

CHAPTER 15

SERENA

Serena decided to close the teahouse early the following day, after the text from Jared arrived.

The morning had started normal enough with knocks on the teahouse door downstairs shortly before the shop was supposed to open. Emela was there for her daily dose. Serena welcomed her inside, assuring her that the broken window was no cause for concern. As the two of them waited for her brew to steep, another knock sounded. She was fully expecting to find an impatient customer, but was surprised to find Rowan there instead.

"Are you okay?" Rowan asked the moment the door opened. "Jared told me you got attacked last night. Something about a crazy drunk?"

Emela blinked at that, giving Serena a shocked expression. "Is that what happened to your cheek? I noticed the cut, but I wasn't sure if I should say anything."

"I heard about someone being arrested for assault last night," Rowan noted. "I have a buddy who's a cop. He said that this guy, Colin Parker, tried to attack someone but the victim didn't press charges. Was that you?"

"Yeah, that was me."

"Colin? Lily said he came in harassing you the other day," Emela said. Serena nodded.

"Did he break your window?" Rowan prodded with a nod at the door.

Serena blew a lock of hair from her face. "No, but he did smash one of my tables. The window was broken by a Jared Westergard, trying to play the white knight."

Rowan breathed out a joyless laugh. "I believe it, with the way he's stalking around the office today. I've never seen him so pissed."

"Really?"

She nodded. "I came in this morning and I thought that he was about to tell me I was fired. I asked him what was up and he went on a tirade about how you got attacked."

"A tirade?" Serena repeated. "Was he really that upset?"

"Yeah. Said he was going to run the guy out of town. He was furious, Serena. I didn't even know it was possible to get him that riled up."

Emela frowned. "Wait. I thought you two couldn't stand each other?"

"Well, Mister Westergard certainly seems to have changed his tune this week," Rowan said.

Caught off guard, Serena quickly rolled her eyes, though she couldn't quite keep the smile from touching her lips. She hoped the heat that crept up her cheeks wasn't too conspicuous. "It's not like that," she began, a defensive tone to her voice. "We've been spending time together lately because his daughter, Zoe, got sick a few days ago, and I've been helping him with her treatment."

"That's why I haven't seen Judith and Zoe coming in for tea. Is she okay?"

"I don't really know. Jared's been giving her the brews on his own for the last couple of days. I'm planning on going to check on her today, though."

That piqued Emela's interest. "Jared Westergard is using enchanted teas on his daughter? Am I the only one to find this ironic?"

Serena shrugged. "He's a good dad; he wants her to get better."

"Well, just be careful, okay?" Rowan said. "I don't like the idea of you being on your own, after what happened yesterday."

Just as Serena was about to respond, her phone buzzed. She glanced down at the screen and her brows furrowed at the text message displayed. "Apparently, Jared shares your concerns, Rowan. He's planning on taking a half-day from work and wants to discuss something with me."

Rowan raised her brows. "Really?"

"No, wait..." Serena's voice trailed off, the color draining from her face as she stared at the follow-up message. Her heart began to pound against her chest. "Oh, no."

"Serena? What's wrong?" Rowan asked, the teasing gone from her voice.

"It's Zoe," Serena murmured, the words barely above a whisper. "Her condition has worsened. They've admitted her to the hospital."

"Strange..."

"What is it?"

Serena frowned to herself, her hand resting on Zoe's

clammy skin. "Her condition was improving up until this morning, you said?"

Jared nodded. "It seemed like it, anyway. Her temperature was going down. She was sleeping more soundly." Standing constant as a royal guard, Jared stared down at Zoe in the propped up hospital bed.

"And now she's worse," Serena muttered, mainly to herself. "And all the lab tests came back negative?"

"No. The infectious disease tests from earlier came back negative," a tired voice in the corner of the hospital room said. Judith was slouched in an armchair, rubbing her eyes from her short nap. "But right now, liver and kidney tests are abnormal, along with white blood cell levels and, what else did they say, Jared? Low blood pH?"

Jared nodded. "They say it's indicative of a toxin. She most likely ate something poisonous. We still haven't figured out what, though."

For a long, terrible moment, Serena wondered if she had been the one to feed Zoe the toxin, through one of her brews. She mentally reviewed every ingredient, every combination she had concocted. No, they were all perfectly safe. Then she began to wonder if Jared or Judith suspected her teas. If they did, they gave no indication. And they still wanted her help. Even Jared, who had been suspicious of her magic from the beginning, seemed to trust her with his daughter's life.

"It would help to know what we were dealing with," Serena sighed. "Did she spend time outdoors before she got sick? Did she get bitten by something? Did she eat something strange that she found outside?"

Jared turned to look at his mother. Judith nodded. "She had a playdate at the park the afternoon before."

Serena glanced up at Jared. "What was she wearing that day?"

Jared flashed a hopeless shrug at his mother.

"Her favorite jeans with the light blue tee-shirt. Oh, and her red jacket."

"Can I see the clothing? I may be able to detect plant fibers on them, if they haven't been washed yet."

"Check her hamper," Judith said with a wave. "I'll stay here with her."

Twenty minutes later Jared and Serena stood in the hall outside Zoe's bedroom. Jared strode inside and Serena followed, sinking onto Zoe's empty, made bed.

Jared dug through Zoe's hamper and pulled out a pair of jeans, and a long sleeved tee. He tossed Serena the outfit and then yanked a red jacket from a hook on her wall. He began digging through the pockets of Zoe's jacket as Serena visually inspected the clothing for traces of plant matter. She sniffed the shirt and checked the pants pockets.

"Serena." Jared dangled a plastic baggie in front of him a minute later. "Take a look."

Serena took the baggie and inspected the contents. Seven small-capped gray mushroom with long gray-green stalks lay at the bottom. Serena sucked in the air.

"Is this what I think it is?" Jared said.

"Devil Cap Mushrooms," she breathed. "Highly toxic. What I've given her so far has slowed the toxins, but hasn't really knocked them out yet."

Jared pulled out his phone and typed a furious text message, presumably to his mother.

"What do we do now?" he said, looking up information on the mushroom on various websites.

"I need to think..."

"It says there isn't an antidote for this toxin. Mostly just supportive measures for the liver and kidney functions. You don't know of anything that might help?" His voice was calm, but she could see the worry in his eyes.

Serena stood and huffed in frustration. "I can think of *some* things, but I'm somewhat limited as to what supplies I have access to." She began pacing around the room. "In a perfect world, there are plenty of things that I could give her. Gracemouth Trumpets, Icelandic Jesebelle, Serenity Fungus. If I could get my hands on some Promise Mushrooms—"

"Serenity Fungus?" Jared repeated.

"Yes, it's a very rare subspecies of mushroom that only grows in waterfall basins. And if I could actually *find* some, then I'm sure it would cure her, but unless you have some secret riches hidden away, it's way too expensive and way too rare for me to get."

He tilted his head. "White fungus that clings to the rock face?"

"Yes?"

"Flat caps, with a lot of frilled dangling tendrils? Kind of looks like a cluster of stalactites?"

"That's the one." She cocked her head at him. "Why?"

"But can't you just... grow some with your magic? I mean, I've seen firsthand how effective you are with vines."

"Those were *plants*; everything I can grow is a plant." She gave a helpless shrug. "I can't grow fungi. No mushrooms. Different biological kingdom."

He set off down the hall with purpose. "I know where to get Serenity Fungus."

She blinked, trailing after him. "You do? Where?"

"It grows under the waterfall outside town, in the Weeping Woods. I can show you."

"Serenity Fungus grows in *Pembrooke*? You're serious?"

"Unless there's a lookalike that can also grow in those

conditions. I'll call Ma and let her know, and then we can go now and harvest some."

Heart racing with renewed hope, she followed Jared toward the primary bedroom in a daze. This could provide a real, true cure for Zoe. She was practically giddy with excitement. She stilled in the threshold of his bedroom, watching as he prepared for their impromptu journey. He fished a worn pack from his closet, checking its contents: rope, flashlight, and a small leather bound journal.

Jared reached to unbutton his shirt, making quick work of it, before yanking it off and grabbing a shirt more suited for the outdoors.

"Do you need to go back to your place? Get any supplies?"

She watched him pull the shirt over his head, the fabric draping over his toned chest, and Serena felt heat creep into her cheeks.

"Serena?"

She coughed. "Um, if you have a spare mason jar, then I can just use that. I'm good."

He nodded to himself. "Good. I might pack a couple, in case you see anything else that might be useful."

"Thanks." The word came out almost as a sigh, and she could feel the blush deepening on her face.

He smiled then, his eyes crinkling at the corners, and something in his expression tugged at her. "No problem."

THE WEEPING WOODS, OFFICIALLY KNOWN AS DAKRYA FOREST, WAS A vast, verdant area that sprawled across the heart of Onyx County. It was famous for its lush greenery, its high population of kingfisher birds, and most prominently, the two waterfalls that book-ended the forest. Aristerá Mati, or Left Eye Falls, was easily accessible, a tourist attraction just near the forest's entrance. Dexi Mati, Right Eye Falls, was slightly more difficult to visit. The hike was challenging for a novice outdoorsman, and it took the better part of an afternoon to reach the waterfall. Jared assured her that he'd seen Serenity Fungus growing in the Right Eye Basin, even if there was no evidence of them in the Left Eye, and the two set out to forage. As she stumbled in places along the rough path behind Jared, Serena was glad he had insisted she stop at home to change into more suitable clothing and hiking shoes.

Much of their trek was quiet. The two of them shared a companionable silence, lost in thought, taking in the scenery. Overhead, birds tittered away excitedly, and underfoot a multitude of lizards and toads crossed their path. After a while, they reached a small river. With a welcoming hand, Jared offered to guide her across. She laughed, but obliged when she realized just how slick the smooth stepping stones were.

Jared expertly navigated through the woods, stepping over fallen logs and sidestepping brambles with a grace that made Serena feel clumsy in comparison. The sunlight streamed through the canopy, casting his features into sharp relief. She felt annoyed when she found herself distracted by the way his biceps flexed under his shirt as he held back a particularly persistent branch.

"So what kind of lawyer moonlights as a forest ranger?"

"The kind who finds 'objection' and 'overruled' losing its appeal to the sound of the wind through the trees." His playful tone took the edge off his serious expression.

Serena let out a surprised laugh. "Well, that's one way to escape the courtrooms. So, you're saying you'd rather be 'exploring exhibits' out here than inside?"

"Absolutely. The trees are a lot less argumentative."

"And here I thought your attraction to the law was all about arguments."

"Nah," he chuckled, leading her deeper into the forest. "It's about balance. And in my case, balance means swapping the courtroom for the great outdoors whenever I get a chance. I grew up near woods like these. My uncle used to take my cousin Liam and me hiking almost every weekend."

As Jared's smile softened at the memory, she realized his familiarity with the forest wasn't just practical knowledge; it was a connection to his past.

"I can see the appeal. It's peaceful out here."

He glanced sidelong at her. "It is, isn't it? A good place for brewing thoughts, I'd imagine."

"Not just a pretty face, you're witty, too."

"Well, I guess I'm steeped in the habit," he deadpanned.

Rolling her eyes at his terrible tea jokes, she shook her head. "I should really bring Kita out here," she mused, glancing up at the tall fir trees surrounding them. "I'd have to check her for ticks after, but she'd love it."

"Down to earth girl like you? I'm surprised you haven't mapped out every meter of this place already."

"I haven't really had much time for exploring," she said with a small sigh. "Going to your place to check on Zoe is the only time I've left Bailey Street for something other than running errands in weeks."

"Really?"

She quirked a brow. "Have you ever passed the shop and *not* seen me inside?"

"No, but I thought I might just be getting lucky."

Serena opened her mouth to laugh but the look on his face made her realize he wasn't joking. Jared Westergard, her arch nemesis, the man who wanted nothing more than to drive her and her teahouse out of town was now hinting that he enjoyed seeing her around?

She cleared her throat. "Not quite. Just keeping busy, that's all."

"Still, you should really take some time to experience the area. There's more to see around here than you'd think."

Sure, there were a lot of places she wanted to go. The dunes, the sea caves, the lighthouse at Cape Meares, the tide pools. And just in Pembrooke there was Baker Beach, the cute little art museum, and the French restaurant, Borealis, where her friend Hailey worked. But she was just so busy. And even if Serena had the time, they were the kinds of places best enjoyed with someone else.

"Tall talk from the man who told me that he abandoned his love of exploration in favor of four beige walls," she said.

"Okay, first of all, they are *off-white*."

Serena snorted. When she glanced at him, he was smiling at her. It was cute the way his eyes crinkled up when he grinned.

"Second, I've had an entire lifetime to poke my nose around Pembrooke," Jared continued.

"Yeah. I envy you that."

"Yeah?"

She nodded. "Grace was a travel nurse. Made good money, but we had to move every few months or so. I didn't really mind at the time, but... I don't know, looking back on it, I feel like I missed out on a lot of things. When I set out on my own, I didn't even know *how* to settle down, if I'd wanted to."

Their eyes met, Jared's soft and sympathetic.

"Living in Pembrooke is the first time I've ever really felt like I was part of a community, you know?" she continued. "Sometimes I remember that I've only been here for a couple of months, and I feel stunned, because it feels like I've already lived here for years. Like Lily and Emela and Hailey have been my friends forever. I can't imagine how it must feel to have roots as deep as yours."

He shook his head. "Well, I hate to burst your bubble, but it's really not as blissful as you might imagine."

"No?"

"Living in the same tiny town your entire life?" he said, his voice betraying that he thought the distastefulness of it should be obvious. "I mean, aside from a few years in California for law school, of course. Everyone in Pembrooke knows me, or knew me, or *thinks* that they know me. And I'm grateful to this place, really. I don't even know if I *could* move away now. But sometimes I resent how rooted I am."

Serena frowned at the underbrush. "I'm beginning to think that there are worse things in the world than familiarity."

"Maybe," he conceded. As they walked, the back of his hand brushed her own. She expected him to pull away. When he didn't, she drifted to the side, putting more space between them.

"Part of me has always dreamed that Zoe's going to grow up to see the world. Do all the things that I never got to do."

"You still could see the world, you know. Maybe not move away, but you could travel."

Jared tipped his head back, regarding the slightly overcast sky. "I don't even know where I would start. You've seen it all, right? Where would you recommend?"

"All the world? Hardly. Most of the states, yes. I guess it depends on what you're looking for."

The sound of rushing water had been steadily growing as they walked, and Jared responded by pointing towards a nearby hill. "Today I'm looking for Serenity Fungus," he said. "Come on, the Basin's down here."

. . .

"Incredible."

"If you say so," Jared said, half-shouting over the water. "Hard for me to think of a mushroom as being particularly awe-inspiring, though."

He was standing behind Serena, redirecting the flow of the waterfall so that she could more easily harvest the fungus. It was pearlescent, shimmering slightly in the jar.

Holding up the jar when she stood, she approached him with a victorious glint in her eyes. "This fungus is *incredibly* rare. You can't just buy it in a store; you have to know someone who just *happens* to have located a cluster. You can't even cultivate this mushroom. It has to grow naturally for ideal magical potency."

The way he looked at her gave her pause. Fond, with a lopsided little smile on his face. He looked more relaxed out here. Calm. Loose. Happy, even.

"What are you smiling at?" she teased.

He cleared his throat, his gaze dropping to the mushrooms. "Nothing. I was just thinking. You know, if you're so mesmerized by these, I should take you to Prometheus Cave when Zoe's better."

Serena lifted her brows. "Sounds intriguing."

"It is. It's half-flooded, so it's dangerous to visit, but in the summertime it fills with these bioluminescent plankton. If you go out near the cliffs at night, you can literally see it *glowing*."

Her eyes lit up. "That sounds amazing! You'd really take me?"

"Sure. Easier to get there with a water witch on your side."

Serena gave him a look of false shock. "Using your powers in public just for fun? What would the council say?"

He smirked. "Something tells me that my secret would be safe with you."

"Of course. You think I'd sell out a friend?"

Something in his expression shifted abruptly and he appeared to mull that over.

She gave his shoulder a playful push, urging him back along the path. "Stop avoiding your neighbor like the plague, and then we'll talk, hmm?"

He held a hand to his chest, as if offended. "Avoiding my neighbors? I'll have you know that I get my hair cut every six weeks at O'Malley's."

Serena grinned, picturing the salon and barber shop next door, and fell into step with him. This time when their hands brushed, she glanced over and noticed Jared smiling to himself. She kept her hand just where it was.

CHAPTER 16
SERENA

"Listen, Serena, I don't want to insult your expertise or anything but... are you *sure* this is edible?"

Serena narrowed her eyes at him, swirling the pale, cloudy liquid with a teaspoon. It glistened, just as the Serenity Fungus had and, after letting the mushrooms dry out for an hour, it smelled... well, "earthy" may be too complimentary.

"Taste it if you don't believe me."

Jared gave her a dubious look, then reached out for the mug. She immediately smacked his hand. "Don't actually drink it!" she scolded. "She needs to drink all of it for peak effectiveness. Every single drop, is that clear?"

He made a show out of rubbing his hand, casting her an unconvincing glare. "Has anyone ever told you that you have terrible manners?"

"And yet you never seem to learn your lesson."

The smile that formed quickly fell from Jared's face as he regarded the tea, a deep crease forming between his thick brows.

"Hey." She brought a hand to Jared's shoulder, squeezing reassuringly. "This is going to work, okay?"

Jared just blew out a long breath, casting his eyes to the ceiling.

"Serenity Fungus is practically a cure-all with the right spell, Jared. It would heal her of almost anything. She's already doing better, this is just to get her over the last hump." Her hand fell, and she set to rubbing the pads of her fingers again. "I would tell you to trust me, but I know that's asking a lot of you, given our history, so..."

"I do trust you."

She blinked. "Really?"

Her mouth went dry when Jared turned to look down at her. She hadn't realized how close they'd been standing, before, but they were only a handful of inches apart. Her breath caught in her throat.

"Yeah," he said, his gaze flitting over her features. "You're a good person, Serena. I trust you."

Serena's pulse quickened. "Well... thank you. That means a lot."

He shrugged it off. "Of course. I mean, you trust me, don't you?"

She froze. She knew that the correct thing to say in this situation was "yes", regardless of whether it was true or not. The question hung in the air, echoing in the silence of the room. It caught Serena off guard, gripping her heart like a cold, frosty hand.

Trust. It was such a small word, yet packed with a weight so immense that she felt her breath hitch in her chest.

Trust wasn't something Serena doled out easily. Trust could be a dangerous thing, a treacherous road leading to the heartache she'd experienced once too often.

Her eyes avoided his, those intense hazels that had

somehow started to feel familiar, welcoming even. But trust him? Jared Westergard, her grumpy yet oddly endearing neighbor who had previously pledged to close down her teahouse because she used magic. Yet here he was, not just tolerating, but even participating in her magic, and for his daughter no less.

She realized then that she liked Jared. His gruff exterior had begun to soften around her, revealing glimpses of a man with a heart as fierce and protective as a warrior's. A man who had raced to her rescue when she was attacked in her own teahouse. They had become friends, unlikely allies in the healing of his little girl. But trust? Trust was another layer, another depth she wasn't sure she was ready to explore.

The silence stretched a touch too long, the suspended moment echoing louder than any words. Jared's face changed slightly, a shadow of disappointment flickering across his eyes before he masked it with a slight smile.

"Um.. sorry," she murmured. "I know I didn't say what you wanted to hear." Sure, Jared had protected her against Colin. But he had also spread malicious rumors about her shop, threatened to close her down, and frozen all her water. She knew he was a good man, but she'd have to reconcile those instances along with everything else.

He shook his head. "It's fine. Understandable in the circumstances, and I prefer your honesty. Maybe someday."

Abruptly, he cleared his throat and clapped his hands together. "Well, I should probably get back to the hospital and give Z her, uh... mushroom water." He wrinkled his nose. "Can you at least put some honey in it or something?"

"Which one of us is the healer?"

He held up his hands in mock defense. "Whatever you say, Doctor Albright," he mumbled, tightening the lid on the thermos before heading for the garage.

"Thank you, Nurse Westergard," she called out, following him to the car.

"I'm going to ignore that!"

WHEN THEY REACHED THE HOSPITAL, ZOE LAY STILL AND PEACEFUL, A small beacon of innocence in the starkness of the sterile room. Jared and Judith gently roused her enough to coax her into swallowing the tonic. Serena stood back, her heart pounding against her ribcage as she watched the scene unfold from an isolated corner.

A silent vigil began, forty minutes suspended in a shared hope and the strength of a family's love. Jared and Judith, pillars on either side of Zoe, clasped her tiny hands like lifelines, their eyes, mirrors of desperation and determination, never leaving her face.

Time seemed to stretch and warp, the room falling into a poignant hush, interrupted only by the rhythmic beep of the heart monitor and the soft rustle of the hospital sheets. As the minutes passed, Serena noticed a subtle shift: the pallor of Zoe's face began to be replaced by a rosy blush, a sign of life returning, warming the cold dread that had settled in the room.

Slowly, as if emerging from a deep, troubled dream, Zoe's eyes fluttered open. Her gaze, clear and bright, found her father's tear-brimmed eyes. A beaming grin spread across her face, lighting up the room with her innocent joy.

"Daddy!" The single word pierced the heavy silence, sounding sweeter than any music.

"I'm here, pumpkin. I'm here," Jared assured her, his voice a deep murmur layered with raw emotion.

The girl's eyes scanned the room before she wrinkled her nose. "This is a very *interesting* room, Daddy. But I like my room much better. Can we go home now?" Zoe's voice, soft and sweet, carried a note of strength that had everyone holding their breath.

Across the room, Serena caught the twinkle in Jared's eyes, bright and teary under the harsh hospital lights. A ripple of wet laughter, shaky yet warm, escaped his lips as Judith joined in with a hearty chuckle. "Yes, sweetheart, we will be going home soon," he managed to say, his voice thick with relief and joy. They both leaned over Zoe, enclosing her in a sweet embrace.

Serena felt a lump in her throat, a strange mix of relief and unspoken fear. She swiped at her eyes, the corners of which had started to sting with unshed tears. In the quiet anonymity of her corner, she turned, her heart echoing with the poignant scene she had just witnessed, and silently slipped out the door, leaving behind a scene of love rekindled and hope reborn.

CHAPTER 17

JARED

The cliffs on the outskirts of Oxport, just an hour and some change north of Pembrooke, were famously steep and unforgiving. Harsh limestone, made cruel by eons of erosion, promised an unpleasant end to anyone who might lose their footing too near the edge. As Jared drove, the headlights lonely beacons to guide their way, he struggled to keep his gaze steady. The roads here were temperamental, winding with the contours of the cliff face. He'd taken this path many times before, knew it demanded his full attention, and yet from time to time he found himself getting distracted.

Serena's features were soft in the ambient light of the dark interior. Her long hair framed her face, the faint blue glow from his dashboard catching the tip of her nose, the swell of her cupid's bow, the planes of her cheekbones. Carved from moonlight and shadow, she scanned the landscape from the passenger seat next to him.

"Is that it, over there?"

He followed her outstretched finger, looking to a blue-green halo of light that shone just beneath the surface of the water. "Yeah, that's it. Prometheus Cave is right in the middle of it."

She leaned forward in her seat. "I can't believe you can see it glow from this far off! It's amazing."

Jared chuckled. "Wait until you see the inside."

Zoe had been home for a week and was doing well. It was time to fulfill his promise to Serena now.

And there was something else. A discussion he needed to have with her, but one which filled him with existential dread. He'd been so grateful for what Serena had done for Zoe. So caught up in the good she was doing for the town that he had forgotten about the flip side, the dangers. He had been deluding himself, really.

It had taken a visit from one of the council members the day before that had snapped him back to reality. Joe Fiori had slipped into his office on the pretense of council business. But the real reason for his visit became painfully obvious within a few moments. After staring out the window at the teahouse, he turned to Jared.

"New place opened up, I see," Joe had said.

"Yeah."

"People are talking about it all the way in Oxport, you know. Saying the drinks are like little miracles, if you can believe it."

"Is that right?"

"Thought I should come and check them out myself if they're so damn amazing. You know, I have a bum knee that's bothered me for years. Wondering if she could fix me up with something."

Jared had glared up at him and the understanding that passed between them was very clear. Joe was warning him. Threatening him, even. They had beef, he and Joe, and he knew Joe would do anything to get back at Jared. He was toying with him now.

"But I gotta get back into town." Joe shrugged. "The girlfriend's waiting on me. Dinner plans tonight and such. But maybe I'll come back and try it out another time. Drinks gotta be good from what I hear. Wouldn't it be funny if they really were magic, eh, Jared? A magic teahouse right across the street from a council member." He chuckled. "The council would never believe it, huh?"

Jared had gone cold at his words. He knew how much trouble Joe could make for him and how much Joe was itching for payback.

That was when Jared realized that the teahouse needed to go. Or at least Serena needed to just brew regular, non-magical teas. She could still make a living with tea and baked goods. Hell, even more if she'd just add coffee to the menu. But how could he convince Serena? The woman was maddeningly stubborn. He needed to try to reason with her, though, before things got really bad. He'd start tonight at the cave.

THE TIDE WAS ADVANCING AND THE CAVE WAS A FAIR DISTANCE FROM the shore. Serena stood at the edge of the waves, the toes of her sandals just kissing the water each time it crested. Her hair blew in the salty breeze.

"It's not so far," she said, observing it with a contagious level of interest.

"If you aren't a strong swimmer, it is. Used to be a pretty popular spot to explore, since it's only half-submerged. It isn't hard to get in there and poke your head around. It's getting back out that's the hard part. If you aren't careful, the current can slam you into the cliff."

"You don't seem too worried," she teased, and Jared grinned.

"I'm not."

He took a deep breath, focusing his thoughts on the water and pushing it out of the way. A narrow passage to the sea floor opened up, just wide enough for them to walk through. It took considerable effort to maintain, but his self-control was better than most.

Usually.

"What are you smiling at?" he asked, nearly losing his hold on the water, altogether.

Serena just laughed, her bright smile catching the moonlight. "It's just that no one's ever parted the sea for me before, that's all. Do you do this for all the witches you meet?"

Somewhere in the back of his mind, he was aware that it was a joke. That she expected him to laugh it off, to roll his eyes and tell her not to get used to it. "No," he said. "No, just you."

Her smile fell, her eyes flickering around his face for just a moment. And then the next second she was grabbing his hand, pulling him forward. "Come on, you can't hold it open all night, can you?"

Jared followed, naturally. He privately suspected he would've followed even if the spell hadn't held. Just walked out to sea, trailing behind her.

They made quick work of the path, Jared removing most of the water from the cave and sealing them behind a wall of seawater. In the dim light, an unearthly glow painted the water and walls, its shimmering dance casting fleeting constellations on the rock around them. Scattered puddles dotted the cave floor, every movement within the water a symphony of sapphire and jade, swirls of cosmic illumination, faint and vivid by turns. Serena was giggling like a child in a candy shop, staring wide-eyed at the cave walls. The turquoise glow of the algae cast her in a near alien light.

"I've never seen anything like this before," she said, and though her voice was soft, it seemed to echo against the rock. She reached out, fingertips brushing the leaves of an aquatic plant, glowing where the algae had overtaken it. "It's mystifying."

"I was hoping you'd like it."

She smiled over her shoulder at him. "I should send some pictures to Aaron. See if he could paint it."

"Maybe. I don't know if it could live up to the real thing, though."

"Have you ever seen a moonflower before?" she asked, glancing back. "Their petals are so reflective that, at night, it almost looks like they're glowing."

He lifted his brows. "I'd like to see that. Maybe you should grow some outside the teahouse. Like a natural nightlight."

"Oh, no. I love the flowers that are already outside too much to change them."

"Yeah? Those little white ones? Z always says they look like lace parasols."

Serena laughed softly. "They do. They're called Queen Anne's Lace, in some parts of the country. Or just Wild Carrot Flowers, but that's not quite as romantic."

"Any particular reason why you like them so much?"

She nodded, kneeling down to observe the cave floor. "The first flower I ever manifested with my powers was a Queen Anne's Lace blossom. I must have been seven or eight years old. My mom and I had just moved to a new town, this tiny place in Georgia, and the kids were... not so keen on having a new classmate."

Jared stepped closer, watching as her brows furrowed. "I was so sick of feeling like I never *fit* anywhere. I got off the school bus and ran out into the woods near our apartment building, and I curled up in a ball and just cried until I tired myself out. And when I opened my eyes, there it was. A tiny white flower at my feet."

Her fingers traced the ground as if she were outlining the bloom.

"There's an old wives' tale about Queen Anne's Lace, you know," she said, her voice wobbling slightly. "They say it's a sign of sanctuary. That anywhere it grows is bound to be a safe haven, for anyone in need. Every time I move somewhere new, I always grow a patch. Just in case anyone out there is looking for somewhere to go." She glanced up, suddenly looking embarrassed. "I'm sorry."

"Don't be," he said, moving to sit on the ground next to her. "That's beautiful."

She tried to laugh him off. It struck him a bit too much like a sob. "It's silly. I guess they just... make me feel safe." He watched a shadow flit across her face, a fleeting memory or sorrow.

"I think I could have used some of your Queen Anne's Lace when Willow passed," Jared said. "I was lost for a long time. Like being caught in a never-ending storm, without the faintest light to guide me."

Gazing up from beneath a fringe of long lashes, her eyes connected with his just then, and a wordless understanding passed between them.

"I can't imagine how difficult that was for you. I haven't had someone that close to me die before. My father's gone, but I never knew him. I don't have any memories."

He studied her for a moment. "You've experienced your own losses and pain, Serena. Your eyes tell me you've known grief, too." Jared shifted his weight to lean against the cave wall, in a spot that was bare of algae. "But hey, we didn't come her to talk about sadness and death."

"Why didn't you turn me in to the council?"

He glanced over in surprise. In the silence that followed, with the stars of the sea painting them in ephemeral hues, Jared pondered her question.

"What makes you think I still won't?" he said.

"And you wonder why I don't trust you."

He smirked. "You make a fair point. The truth is, you've done more good for Pembrooke in two months than I've seen the council do in thirty years. You're one of those rare people you come across only once or twice in a lifetime. The kind of person that genuinely makes the world a better place. And that is something I would defend and protect to my dying breath."

A long, slow exhalation came from Serena. He didn't bother to look up, doubted she believed his words. But it didn't matter; it was the truth, even if he just realized it in that moment.

"So you're not just some mindless, pretty bureaucrat after all, are you?" she said. "I have to admit you really had me convinced that you were just a pompous ass who cared more about arbitrary rules than about real people. But I'm starting to see there's more than meets the eye. There are definitely deeper layers to you, Jared Westergard."

"Hmm. Serena?"

"Yes?"

"Do you really think I'm pretty?"

Lifting her brows, she swatted his arm before they both burst into laughter.

Still smiling, Jared leaned against the wall and took a breath. "I'm glad you've been letting me show you around, Serena."

"Yeah, really?" Serena scooted back and leaned against the wall next to him.

He turned to face her, the cave wall pressing against his back and the top of his head. In the surreal realm of twinkling lights and shadowy stone, the distance between them seemed to contract and stretch like the ebb and flow of the sea. They gravitated closer, as if some silent force drew them together.

"Yeah, really. I've been living here so long, everything has more or less lost its luster. I'm jaded, I think. Stopped being able to see the forest..."

A stray droplet from above landed on Serena's cheek, and Jared, almost instinctively, reached out to brush it away. As she raised her hand at the same time, their fingers touched, electric and hesitant, both seemingly aware of the palpable energy between them. She gazed up at him with those endless, green eyes.

"You see so much life in this place. Everywhere you go, you see value, meaning, beauty. It's just been nice to see things through your eyes," he confessed, her breath hitting his cheek.

"Jared..."

He paused but her eyes were half-closed, her head angled up toward him. Before he realized what he was doing, he dipped his head, brushing his lips over hers.

Honey and peaches drifted through his mind as he tasted her softness.

Serena's eyes were closed when he pulled back and, as she opened them, they seemed impossibly brighter. He traced the outline of her jaw with his thumb, then his fingers trailed down her neck to the curve where it met her shoulder.

He brought his lips back to hers and kissed her again, more deeply, feeling her hands enmesh in the hair at the nape of his neck.

"This is insane," Serena murmured.

"Why?" His lips glided along her jaw

"Just last week we were at each other's throats."

His mouth traced a meandering path down to her neck, his

tongue flicking over the delicate skin of her throat. "Still am," he mumbled. "I have to admit I like being at your throat."

"Mmm. Maybe I could get used to you there, too."

As his hand slid down her side, his thumb glided over the contour of her breast. He was dimly aware that he was supposed to be having a serious conversation about closing the teahouse or changing its menu, and that he was failing miserably. All that seemed to matter to him in that moment was Serena and how beautiful she looked in the eerie light, how nice she smelled—like honeysuckle—and how good she felt in his hands. He wanted more.

A cold wetness soaked into his ankle, ripping him from her touch. He pulled away and observed how the puddles on the floor were beginning to overflow.

"High tide is moving in," he said, reluctantly standing. "I need to get you back." He was already tiring, keeping the water at bay. Once the tide rolled in, it would become too difficult and too dangerous to stay in the sea cave. He extended his hand to Serena, who grabbed on and pulled herself up alongside him.

He wished they could stay longer, wished he could kiss every inch of her in that cave with its haunting glow and echoed whispers. His eyes lingered over her for a moment. Her snug jeans, her loosely buttoned top, the way she almost seemed to be blushing as he let his eyes roam freely.

Something knocked into his legs and he stumbled backward. A small shrub dotted with delicate flowers sprang from the cave floor. He was sure it hadn't been there before.

"I'm so sorry!" she squeaked, immediately stepping back. "I didn't mean to do that, it was an accident. I—wow, I haven't grown anything by mistake since I was in high school. That's... embarrassing. I'm sorry."

Jared laughed, musing over the spontaneously created plant. "It's okay," he said. "They're pretty."

On a whim, he plucked one of the flowers and drew near to her once more. He tucked the blossom behind her ear, nestled in her honey-highlighted locks.

Yes. Very pretty.

He wanted to kiss her again, but she was frowning down at the bush, mouth twisted.

"I've ruined the ecosystem," she lamented. "Hopefully it'll just wash up on the shore tonight. It will make for some very confusing driftwood, come morning, but at least we won't have to worry about it forming any roots."

He smiled softly, endeared with the way she'd become so invested in the well-being of these plants. "No, we wouldn't want that."

When they left the cave and reentered the natural light of the beach, he could finally make out the flower's actual color. Soft pink, just like her lips.

CHAPTER 18
SERENA

T he following morning was slow. Serena figured that Rowan must have had a late start to her day, and even Lily and Emela had made themselves oddly scarce. That was the way of things, though. If everyone else was busy, The Velvet Teahouse was not. Her business fed on leisure. Serena, as it turned out, did not. The idleness of her hands was disquieting, after the constant revolving door of activity. Oh, Hecate help her, was she becoming a workaholic?

That would be rich. Just as her counterpart across the way was finally loosening up, *she was* becoming the uptight one. Serena tucked a strand of hair behind her ear, thoughts drifting to the night before. It was... nice, spending time with Jared. At least when he wasn't trying to destroy her business and she wasn't accidentally getting so swept away that she manifested camellia bushes at his feet.

Pink camellias, really? So embarrassing. Still, he hadn't seemed to find it particularly off putting.

Then there was the kiss. Sweet goddess, how she had melted in his arms. And the feel of his lips against her. She closed her eyes, imagining what could have happened if the tide hadn't started to fill the sea cave.

With a sigh, Serena grabbed a broom and marched out to the porch. This would not do. Daydreaming about Jared was a waste of time. Whatever had happened between them had been a mistake. They had merely gotten caught up in the moment. Now that Zoe was doing better, they could get on with things.

Zoe. She was another wrinkle in Serena's entanglement with Jared. Getting involved with Jared would mean getting involved with Zoe; they were a package deal. And Serena was hardly the best candidate to be a mother figure to a little girl. She'd hardly been raised properly herself. No, Zoe deserved far better than anything Serena could provide. The idea of anything happening between her and Jared was absurd. It had been just a kiss, and now it was time to move on.

The rhythmic swish of the broom was almost hypnotic, the world around Serena receding as she lost herself in the meditation of motion. But as she made her way towards the end of the porch, a shimmer out of place snagged her attention, a crude drawing on one of the bricks. Setting the broom down, she walked toward the design at the end of the building. Painted in white, its form at first appeared ambiguous, perhaps the creation of a child's wandering hand. But as she drew nearer, it began to take on a more familiar shape. Was it...a crow?

Heart quickening, her fingers traced over the picture. The image was rudimentary, yet the implications weighed heavy on her. The memory of the tea reading with its five crow symbols loomed over her like a storm cloud. An unsettling feeling knotted in her stomach. She swiped her fingers over the drawing, but it wouldn't wipe away. Whether this was a child's artwork or a marking of some sort, she couldn't be sure.

But she was reasonably certain it hadn't been there the day before.

She took a step back, scanning the rest of the walls for any other oddities, half-expecting to find more. Nothing. Only that singular crow, crudely drawn but with intention. How strange it was that it found a home on her teahouse's wall.

A whisper of a memory surfaced: of old stories, tales told by Grandma Bess about omens and symbols. Crows had always been carriers of messages from beyond, omens of change or warnings from the universe. Was this the universe trying to tell her something? Or was this just the playful work of one of the Pembrooke children? Or something—or someone —worse?

Suddenly, she heard footsteps behind her. Turning, she saw Hailey approach, her expression one of mild curiosity as she noted Serena's focused attention on the wall. "What are you looking at?" she asked.

"Do you think this looks like a crow?" Serena motioned toward the drawing.

Hailey took a moment, studying the drawing as she neared. Her face darkened slightly. "It does," she murmured. "Though it's pretty amateurish. Probably some kid drew it."

"That's kinda what I was thinking," Serena replied, her voice laced with a mix of worry and confusion. "But with my recent tea reading..."

Hailey took a step closer. "What tea reading?"

After Serena explained, she felt a jolt of fear that passed as quickly as it had come. She glanced at Hailey, knowing it had come from her. Hailey's emotions were contagious, but she usually tried to channel them into her art instead of spreading them to others. Once in a while they slipped, though, and she had to quickly reel them back in.

"And so, you think this is another sign?" Hailey said.

"Maybe." Serena exhaled. "But a sign of what?"

"Has anything else happened?"

"No. I thought at first that Jared was the reason behind my dark tea reading. All the sabotaging he was doing, you know. But now..." Serena shook her head. "We're on good terms now. And he would never do something like this."

"Did you ask him?"

Widening her eyes, Serena shook her head quickly. "No way. I just got him to back off the teahouse. I wouldn't want to give him another reason to try to shut me down." She glanced over at Hailey, to try to change the subject. "You look like you could use some pomegranate and violet tea. Splash of China berry."

Spinning on her heel, she returned to the shop with Hailey trailing behind. She needed to keep busy so she wouldn't make herself crazy with her anxious thoughts. She busied herself with preparing Hailey's takeout cup and then focused on that morning's muffins, quickly whipping up the batter.

With school letting out, she anticipated getting busier during the day. Maybe she should consider hiring an assistant. Take Judith's advice and find someone to bake, take orders, and wash dishes. It would certainly give her more free time.

It might be difficult to find any teenagers who could bake well enough, but then again she never would've been able to bake *half* as well without Judith's help. Maybe she would be willing to help her train a new hire. Then, Serena would have more time to spend doing whatever she pleased. Spending that time with whomever she liked. Maybe she could talk Jared into having a picnic with her, by the beach...

The bell above the door was merciful enough to put her out of her misery before her thoughts could begin to spiral. Thank goddess, the last thing she needed was another excuse to think of Jared Westergard.

"Hey."

The moisture left her mouth all at once. She smiled up at Jared. "Hi. Are you finally making the switch to tea?"

He chuckled. "Not quite. Actually, I just had a message to deliver."

"A message? Good news, I hope."

"Very. Zoe's back in school full time now. And she told me to thank you. For making her better."

Serena beamed at that. "Well, you can tell her that seeing her in my shop again will have made it well worth it."

"Worth getting dragged out to the woods with me?"

"More or less." She gave him a look of fond annoyance.

"I still wish you'd let me pay you," he said.

"I'm still waiting on that new window to come in. Maybe throw some silk curtains in, while you're at it?" she joked.

"Have dinner with me."

She nearly fumbled her mixing bowl. "I'm sorry?"

"You've been here for months and you haven't so much as sampled the local nightlife," he argued. "My buddy Royce runs a brew pub, on the North side of town. I can take you there. He's even got pool tables and darts. Could be fun, right?"

In less than two weeks, Jared had gone from being the sort of man whom she would sooner spit on than smile at, to being someone she was now considering going out to dinner with. Yet even as she glanced up at those gorgeous eyes, a part of her still wondered if he had some sort of devious ulterior motive.

"When?"

"Well, are you busy tonight?"

Tonight? As in, about ten hours from now, after the shop closes? *That* tonight? Goddess, how quickly could she shave her legs?

"Tonight sounds... good. Sure."

156

He grinned, and Serena pretended that she wasn't on the verge of panic. "Good. I'll meet you here, say seven-thirty?"

Seven-thirty. She figured she could clean up in ninety minutes. "Okay. Yeah."

SHE WAS STILL FIGHTING WITH HER HAIR WHEN HE KNOCKED ON THE front door. It usually didn't take her long to get ready for things, but she had failed to consider the fact that she hadn't had an occasion to dress up since she moved. Which naturally meant that most of her shoes were still in a cardboard box that had been shoved to the back of her closet. After dumping out the entire box, she had settled on a pair of strappy heels. Paired with the mid-length green sundress she wore, and the Tiger's Eye pendant from Rowan hanging around her neck, she felt almost fashionable. Feminine and pretty in an effortless sort of way. Maybe.

But she'd been fussing with her hair for an embarrassing amount of time by now. Buns and braids and in a dozen different styles, all promptly torn down until she very nearly wanted to just shave her head and be done with it. In the end, she gave up and just combed her fingers through the loose waves as they spilled over her shoulders, and sighed.

Jared knocked again. Why was she so concerned, anyway? He'd clearly thought she was easy enough on the eyes at the beach last night, hadn't he? Staring at her with that gleam in his eyes as he oh-so-gently placed that blushing little camellia...

She unfurled her palm. Before she could second guess it, she let a pale pink blossom sprout from her open hand. She nestled it in her hair, pinning it in place before taking a deep breath and racing down the stairs.

Standing on the porch of the teahouse, Jared looked like

one of the marble gods Serena had seen in museums: captivating yet elusive, seductive in a slightly unsettling manner. She was acutely aware of how his intense gaze swept over her, the way his eyes caressed her face and wrapped around her curves.

He blinked before evidently finding his voice. "Wow," he breathed, and Serena suppressed a satisfied smile. He cleared his throat, searching for his composure. "I mean, you look great."

Her smile bloomed without her permission. "Thank you. So do you."

Serena held out an arm, smirking when he took it. "Go on then," she teased. "Show me the very best that Pembrooke has to offer."

"Of course. Only the best," he assured her, and they set off down the street.

CHAPTER 19
SERENA

The Labyrinth, contrary to its name, opened up before Serena with a surprising elegance that felt hip and homey at the same time. It was a harmonious fusion of metal and wood, with concrete floors and high ceilings that were criss-crossed with exposed pipes. Each booth, carved meticulously from seasoned wood, was shadowed by the imposing presence of metal barrels, a juxtaposition that was both comforting and unexpected. Towards the rear, a time-worn wooden staircase led to the second floor, a lofted space filled with plush seating and the soft clicks of pool balls. The centerpiece, the bar, stretched in a graceful half-moon curve, showcasing a parade of craft beers that spoke of ancient recipes and modern innovations, flanked by an impressive array of wines and liquors. Despite its size, there was an intimacy to it, an old-world charm that beckoned one closer. Serena loved it at once.

And they were welcomed at once. The very attractive owner, one Royce Moreno—a warlock, Serena noted—came out enthusiastically from behind the bar to greet them like VIP guests, even though the brew pub was packed.

"Hey man, good to see you!" He embraced Jared, clapping a hand on his back. "You guys eating? I've got just the right spot, if you want it."

"Yeah, man, sounds good. Royce, this is Serena."

And when Royce turned his golden eyes on her, she could sense him appraising her, in a way she'd never experienced from anyone else before. She wasn't sure if it was her imagination, but it was as if he had slipped inside her head and made quick work of reading her. Her passions and fears, despair and desires, all seemed to open up to his gentle prodding.

The weight of that piercing gaze lingered, but then Royce's face transformed into a warm smile, the previous intensity replaced with charismatic charm. "A pleasure, Serena," he said, taking her hand and placing a gentle, deliberate kiss on the back of it. "Any friend of Jared's is a friend of mine. Welcome to The Labyrinth."

"Thanks, Royce. It's an impressive place you have here."

"Thank you. Built it from the ground up three years ago and I craft all the brews myself."

Royce gestured for them to follow, leading them through a weaving path between tables filled with patrons deep in mirthful conversation. The dim lighting cast flickering shadows on the walls, and Serena could swear she saw patterns moving within them, almost evoking the feeling that the brew pub was a living entity.

They arrived at a secluded corner spot, a massive wood booth topped with soft cushions. It was intimate in spite of the raucous crowd.

"Enjoy your evening." Royce's voice had a silky tone, his gaze lingering on Serena before he returned to the bar.

As Serena's gaze wandered around The Labyrinth, she was

surprised that amidst the cacophony of laughing humans and clinking glasses, she identified more than a few witches. Their auras stood out to her, like hidden stars in a night sky. At a distant corner, a cluster of them, deep in conversation, suddenly ceased their chatter as their eyes fixed on Jared. Almost immediately, they scattered, breaking into smaller pairs, their expressions a mix of curiosity and caution.

Two beautiful witches stared over their glasses of dark red wine at the bar. One had long, blonde hair and a cold composure. The other had thick, wavy chestnut hair and wore bright lipstick that set off her olive skin. With icy glares, they looked from Serena to Jared.

"I know it's kinda loud in here tonight, but is it okay?" he asked. "We don't have to stay if it's too much."

Serena hesitated, then squeezed his hand. "No, let's stay. It's cool, and besides," she smirked, "we came for the beer, didn't we?"

Jared chuckled, the tension melting away. "That we did."

The two witches were still watching her, but Serena decided to ignore them and focus on her evening. Royce returned a few moments later, balancing a wooden tray laden with glass samplers filled with beers of varying colors and a large plate piled high with golden-brown wedges. He set them down with a flourish, the contents glinting invitingly under the ambient lighting.

"For our VIP guests," Royce began, with a cheeky grin, "a curated selection of our finest craft beers." He pointed to each one, listing the names, which ranged from 'Midnight Whisper' to 'Siren's Song' with a fondness one might reserve for their children.

"And these," he said, pointing to the wedges with an exaggerated flair, "are our world-famous jojos. A delicacy from... well, the great beyond—a.k.a. Idaho."

Serena, eyebrows raised, looked at the wedges, then to Jared, and back to Royce. "Jojos?"

Royce nodded seriously. "Ah, I see you're not from around here. Consider this an initiation."

Jared smirked, picking up a jojo. "They're just potato wedges, Serena. But 'jojo' sounds more exotic, doesn't it? And Royce's are actually really very good."

Royce winked. "Marketing, my friend. People come for the beer, stay for the jojos."

Serena laughed, picking one up and taking a cautious bite. Her eyes widened in pleasant surprise. "Wow," she mused, savoring the rich flavors. "What are these spices?"

Royce simply tapped his nose with a finger and winked again. "Trade secret." He glanced around the busy pub. "Enjoy your drinks and your... initiation. I've got to tend to the masses. Be back for your dinner order." With a nod, he retreated, leaving the two in their cozy corner.

Jared leaned in. "So, now that you've been officially initiated into the world of jojos, what's the verdict?"

Serena took another bite, chewing thoughtfully. "I think I'll need to sample a few more before I can give my official opinion."

Jared laughed, raising a beer sampler glass in a mock toast. "To new experiences and... magical potato wedges."

Serena clinked her glass against his, a smile playing on her lips. "And to—"

"Jared, good evening, sir." Two men, both tall, well-built, and dressed in flannel, stood at the end of the table. Warlocks, both of them. They nodded at Serena.

"Sorry to interrupt, miss," one warlock with rusty hair said.

A look of annoyance swept over Jared's features. "What is it, Drew?"

"I was wondering if we could have a word with you, in

private, sir? It's about the... Perceval business I told you about earlier."

"This is not a good time. I'm having dinner with...a friend."

"Yes, I'm sorry, sir. It's just that there's been a complication. It's a bit... sensitive."

Jared frowned before standing up. "I'm sorry, Serena. I'll be back in just a minute. This won't take long."

"No worries," Serena said, turning her head to watch as Drew and the other witch followed Jared to a far recess of the brew pub. As she turned back to face the table, she nearly jumped out of her skin.

The two beautiful witches were seated at the table, opposite her. Serena stifled a yelp. They fixated cool gazes on her. Serena opened her mouth to speak, but was cut off by the blonde woman.

"You're the one who opened the tea shop." It was a simple statement, not posed as a question, and Serena wasn't sure if she was looking for validation or not.

"Yep, that's me," Serena said, studying the women and trying to discern what type of power each had. She scanned for Jared in her peripheral vision. "Do you...*like* tea?"

"How can we help?" the olive-skinned woman said.

"Excuse me? Help with what?" Serena said.

Their eyes darted to the corner where Jared was still talking to the witches.

"Are you safe?" the blonde said.

"Safe from what?"

"Are you under investigation?" the olive-toned woman pressed.

"Under investigation for what? Who are you?"

"I'm Brooklyn, and this is Noora," the blonde woman said.

"I *saw* you and I was concerned," Noora said.

"Saw me where?"

"She gets visions," Brooklyn said.

"I saw you with five crows flying around your head," Noora said.

Serena inhaled sharply.

Brooklyn leaned closer. "When we spotted you with Jared here tonight, we assumed...I mean—"

"We thought you might be in some trouble with the Council," Noora said. "We heard about your teas—that they are 'blessed', you know—and we assumed that Jared..."

"He's a Lens, you know," Brooklyn said.

"And we thought maybe you needed some help tonight," Noora said. "Help getting out of here. Or a safe place to sleep tonight. Even a way out of town, if necessary."

"Oh!" Serena said, finally understanding. "Ohhhh," she said, her tone shifting. "No, I'm fine. We are just having dinner together."

The witches exchanged glances. "On purpose?" Brooklyn blurted out.

Serena giggled. "Yep. I'm perfectly safe."

"And he's okay with your teahouse?" Noora said, a look of confusion crinkling her lovely features.

"Not at first, but he seems to be coming around."

The two women stiffened, their attention pulled toward Jared's corner. Serena glanced back to see him striding across the pub toward them. The women stood to leave.

"You need to be careful," Noora hissed.

"Wait. Stop by the teahouse sometime. I'd love to brew something for you. And we could talk some more."

Noora wrapped an elegant shawl over her shoulders and nodded.

"We'll see you soon," Brooklyn added with a nod, before the two women turned and scurried away. A few seconds later,

Jared slid back into the round booth next to her. Drew trailed after him and lingered in front of the table.

"And the other issue? We—" Drew said.

"Tomorrow morning," Jared cut him off with a frown.

Drew nodded. "Yes, sir. I understand. We'll come find you tomorrow. Sorry for the interruption. Enjoy your evening, miss."

After they left, Serena leaned forward. "What was that about?"

"Well, it was something about Drew's knife finding its way into Mr. Perceval's right thigh one drunken night last week."

"What? I thought you just do land disputes and contracts?"

Flashing an indecipherable look, Jared downed the rest of his beer. "Unfortunately, most of the disputes of all kinds between witches pass through me in this town."

"So you're kinda like the judge, jury, and executioner all in one," she said with a chuckle. Serena meant it as a joke, but when he didn't laugh with her, she figured she had hit pretty close to the truth.

Flashing a tight smile he extended his hand. "Come on, how about we shoot a game of pool before dinner?"

Two hours into their date, Serena was beginning to worry Jared was growing bored with her.

She glanced around The Labyrinth as Jared checked his watch for at least the sixth time since their dinner had arrived.

It seemed to her that the date—*was this a date?*—had been going well. At least at first. When all the pool tables had been full, a witch couple insisted Jared take theirs. She and Jared chatted through appetizers and dinner, their conversation pleasant and filled with inside jokes about the places they'd gone together, and the things they had learned about each other. Copious complimentary drinks were sent to their table from other witches at the bar paying their respects, but they didn't drink irresponsibly. All and all, it should have been a lovely evening.

And yet toward the end of dinner, something in Jared's demeanor shifted. A shadow of unease draped itself across his otherwise confident facade. He started to fidget, his fingers drumming on the table or adjusting the silverware just so.

Royce caught onto it too, raising an eyebrow when he swung by their table. "Everything all right there, Jared?" he'd asked, voice threaded with genuine concern.

Jared shot him a look, a silent "not now," and Royce took the hint, nodding subtly, and disappearing.

"Do you want to head out early?" she ventured, as they finished dessert.

He hesitated, then gestured for the waiter. "One more round," he murmured.

He seemed distracted the entire walk back to the teahouse, too. When they neared her street, she sighed sharply and turned on him.

"I can make it the rest of the way on my own, thanks."

Brow furrowing, Jared halted. "What? No, come on, let me walk you home."

"Why? You've been out of it half the evening; clearly there's somewhere else you'd rather be."

Jared's face fell. "I—Serena, no, that's not true. Just let me walk you to the teahouse, and we can talk there, yeah?"

She crossed her arms, but didn't put up a fight. "Fine."

He escorted her down Bailey Street in silence, Serena scowling to herself all the way, while the space between them seemed to grow.

When they at last reached her building, she saw movement

through one of the darkened windows. Her posture went board-straight.

"Someone's inside," she hissed. Her mind was still on high alert from the crow drawing earlier in the day, and she was already forming a plan of attack in her head.

To her immense confusion, Jared simply smiled, and pulled the door open.

The moment she flipped the light on, she barked out a laugh of delighted shock. Twenty people, including her coven, Aaron, Judith, and Zoe, along with new friends and her best customers, jumped out of various hiding spots and yelled, "Surprise!" Across the far wall near the Goddess Corner hung a large, festive banner.

"Welcome to Pembrooke?" she said, reading the sign and looking up at Jared with bemused interest.

He shrugged in an approximation of innocence. "We never really gave you a proper housewarming," he explained as her friends rushed forward. "It only seemed fair. Take it as thanks, for everything you've done."

She narrowed her eyes at him.

"Fine. Take it as an apology for me being an ass, if you prefer," he said.

"I'm not apologizing for anything," Lily said, walking toward them. "And I did more work for this party than you did, Jared. Emela and I baked and everything." She embraced Serena tightly and kissed her cheek.

Serena directed her attention to the platter of somewhat homely little cupcakes on the table. "You baked these for me?" she asked.

"We might've had a bit of guidance from Judith," she admitted. "If they're inedible, you have to lie. And if they're good, say they're amazing."

Serena was beside herself, near brimming with excitement as she hugged everyone. "And if they're amazing?"

"Then I'll quit and come work for you."

At that, Emela elbowed Lily, drawing laughter from all three witches.

"Well, *I* brought the most important thing," Rowan chimed in, making her way behind the counter with several bottles. "Rena, where do you keep your wine glasses?"

"And I brought the most delicious thing," Hailey sung. "You all need to try these lobster and gouda stuffed mushrooms from Borealis. They are to die for!"

As the coven moved to raid her kitchen, Zoe approached her with a weak smile.

"Hi, Miss Rena."

"Hey, Z!" Serena replied with a grin and a big hug.

Zoe wrinkled her nose. *Virtue, she and Jared have the exact same nose.* "Dad's the only one who calls me that."

"Oh," she felt her face turn hot. "I'm sorry."

"No, you can do it, too, if you want."

She smiled softly, observing the slight glassiness of Zoe's eyes. "How are you feeling, hon?"

"Much better. Thank you, for helping Dad take care of me. He freaks out a lot when I get sick."

Jared balked at the remark, and Serena chuckled. "Well, you look great! And if you ever need my help again, just give me a call and I'll come running."

She squeaked when small arms suddenly threw themselves around her waist. Zoe hugged her tightly, and both Serena and Jared seemed to freeze in place. After a second, Serena hugged her back, gently stroking her dark curls.

"I'm glad we're friends, Miss Rena."

Serena swallowed hard, willing away growing tears. "Me too, Z."

. . .

By the end of the night, Serena felt warm from the inside out. From both wine and company. She had learned that the party had all been Jared's idea, but that he'd recruited Lily and Rowan to help put it into action.

They'd all behaved themselves at the beginning, for the most part, and less so after Judith took Zoe home, when they'd all devolved into drunken singing and dancing. Her new friends and customers left a few hours later. Rowan and Hailey left soon after, Rowan nearly unconscious and Hailey resolutely sober. Aaron and Emela's social batteries depleted at nearly the same time, and Lily was eager to follow her friend, claiming that after doing so much for the party, it was only fair that Jared be the one to clean up after.

She watched him, almost embarrassingly fondly, as he washed a glass in the empty teahouse and set it aside to dry in the rack. His sleeves were neatly rolled to the elbow, his arms shifting enticingly. There was something so quietly endearing about seeing him perform mundane tasks. She'd realized it a few days ago, watching him prepare dinner for her in his home.

"Here, I can help."

He shook his head. "We threw this party for you, Serena. Just relax, I'll take care of this."

She did as she was told, taking a seat on the extra velvet sofa that she had been storing in the kitchen hallway.

He flashed a cocky smile. "Tonight, you're the queen and I'm your humble servant."

She chuckled, leaning back into the sofa's softness. "Well, that's an image I never thought I'd see."

"What, a lawyer doing dishes?" He dunked a wine glass into the soapy water.

"No," she retorted, "a lawyer being humble."

He laughed at that, the sound echoing around the quiet kitchen. "Fair enough. But you might be surprised to learn I have many talents."

Serena leaned on the armrest, her chin resting in her hand, as she batted her eyelashes. "Oh really? Name one."

"Other than washing dishes, you mean?" He rinsed off a plate, setting it aside before meeting her gaze. "I make a mean omelette."

Serena arched an eyebrow. "I'm sorry, perhaps I misunderstood. Did you just mean to imply that we would be breakfasting together at some point?"

Jared met her eyes without missing a beat. "Brace yourself for the best breakfast of your life, Teamaster."

"We'll see about that, Counselor," Serena said, rising to dry and put away the clean dishes.

Setting down the last glass, Jared glanced at her as she busied herself storing plates and glasses. Leaning against the counter, his tall, imposing figure seemed even more substantial in the low light.

"You work too hard," he remarked, his deep voice carrying easily in the silent room.

She looked up in surprise. "You've done half the work for me. And this amazing party you all threw for me..." She paused for a moment, then added with a soft smile, "Thanks for tonight. I didn't realize how much I needed it."

Wiping his hands on a clean dish towel, he said, "What are neighbors for?" But the dark gaze that followed didn't feel neighborly at all to Serena. It felt... intimate, and doubt began to creep in about whether she should really be spending so much time with Jared. What were they doing, these two? Hating each other, sabotaging each other, then helping each other and now... seducing each other? And yet she found she couldn't stop herself. She was drawn to Jared like a star to the night's embrace.

Playfully frowning, a note of reproach in her voice, Serena said, "You know, for a neighbor, you're sorely missing from my tea shop." Stepping into the hallway, she placed two clean teacups on a narrow shelf.

"Is that a complaint I hear?" Jared said, switching off the canned overhead lights. He emerged from the darkness a second later and leaned casually against the doorframe, his face half-hidden in shadow. The dim hallway was now illuminated by only the under-cabinet lights filtering in from the dining room, and a few candles left burning near the kitchen window.

She feigned shock. "Me? Complain? I just think you're missing out on all the good stuff."

Jared's eyes raked down the length of her body as he stepped closer and she found herself cornered at the end of the short hallway.

"Oh, really?" he said. "And how good is this 'stuff' we're talking about?" His eyes burned with playfulness and unmistakeable desire.

CHAPTER 20
SERENA

"Far better than that swill they serve at Westergard and Ross," she drawled.

"Swill, huh?" He leaned closer, lips inches away from hers, his breath tinged with the scent of bourbon. "I didn't realize there was a competition."

Dizzy from his closeness, and feeling the press of the velvet loveseat against the backs of her legs, she raised her hand to rest on his arm. "Oh, believe me, Jared," Serena retorted, her voice a husky whisper, "there's no competition. My teas would have that poor excuse for coffee begging for mercy."

His chuckle was low and challenging. "Bold words, Serena. I hope you can back them up." His hand brushed a stray strand of hair behind her ear.

"Won't be a problem," she murmured.

He leaned in, his cheek grazing hers, the stubble sparking a delicious friction. His breath was warm against her ear as he playfully whispered, "In that case, I can't wait to sample these exquisite teas of yours."

Feeling her cheeks warm, she pulled back just out of reach,

her lips twitching into a flirtatious smile as her fingers moved to idly play with a button on his shirt. "Are you sure? Somehow, I think you've been avoiding them. Afraid you might like the taste too much?"

"Now why would I be scared of that?" Jared's voice dipped lower. He gently pulled her closer, his lips just brushing against hers in a tantalizing almost-kiss. "If they taste as good as you say, then maybe I would want to take my time with them. Savor them."

"So now you're a connoisseur?" She arched an eyebrow in mock challenge.

He shrugged nonchalantly, his lips still hovering over hers. "Not yet. But I've heard the brewer's pretty skilled. I'm willing to learn."

Her laughter emerged as a soft, tinkling sound. "We'll see about that, won't we?"

As his lips glided over hers, Serena's eyes fluttered closed, her heart rattling against her sternum. For a handful of moments, the world fell crushingly silent. Nothing else existed but the extraordinary now and the delicious sensation of Jared Westergard kissing her.

Then, all at once, the world buzzed to life again.

Tugging on his arms, she reeled him the rest of the way in. Jared's hand tangled into her hair as he kissed her more firmly. When he licked at the seam of her lips, she parted them with a sigh, exploring the new shared space between them. She nipped lightly at the swell of his lower lip, a thrill running down her spine as he advanced.

Their kisses became braver, more fervent, as they sunk onto the loveseat. Jared's hands caressed the curve of her hips as her calves rubbed against the plush velvet. She could scarcely hear beyond the thundering of her pulse, the rush of her blood. He ducked his head to mouth at the pale column of her throat, Serena tipping her head back and sighing as he kissed dizzying patterns against her skin.

"Do you want to come upstairs?" she whispered against his mouth, the intimacy too sweet to break.

"Are you sure?"

Serena nodded.

"Then, yes. This tiny sofa is completely inadequate for seducing you."

Laughing, she gently pushed him off, found her footing and stood. Her hand slipped into his, their fingers entwining as she led him towards the narrow staircase at the back of the teahouse. His thumb grazed against the back of her hand in gentle strokes, and the simple touch sent warmth radiating up her arm.

As Jared followed, she could feel his gaze upon her, radiating heat and causing the hairs on the back of her neck to stand on end.

At the top of the stairs, she fumbled for the door handle in the dark. After a moment, the door swung open, revealing the dimly lit space she called home. She stepped inside, pulling him with her, their fingers laced together.

The living room was filled with the gentle glow of moonlight filtering through the window. But once they'd stepped inside, Serena found herself suddenly feeling nervous, having doubts.

"I like what you've done to the place," Jared commented, letting his eyes roam around the room, taking in the cozy furniture, the stacks of ancient herb books on the coffee table, the potted plants, and the little trinkets that made the space uniquely hers.

But the centerpiece of her living room was the set of elegant French doors, now framed by cascading tendrils of ivy and fragrant jasmine. They opened onto a balcony that offered a breathtaking view of the vast, ever-changing ocean.

"Thanks," she replied, thinking back on the last time he'd been there. The apartment had been empty then, crowded only by the boxes he had helped her carry up the stairs. He'd practically accused her of being a master poisoner that day, after rooting through her plants. And tonight he was standing in nearly the same spot, trying to hide that he was watching her again, but with a look in his eyes that was altogether different.

"Can I get you something to drink? There are a lot of teas, of course, but I think I have a bottle of Cabernet in here somewhere." Her attempt at casual conversation felt strained, even to her own ears.

"Wine sounds good, thanks." Pushing open the French doors, Jared stepped out onto the balcony. Serena busied herself with digging out the wine and then scrounging through her cabinets for the three or four wine goblets she was sure she remembered unpacking.

"It's going to rain," he said when she joined him a few minutes later, handing him a goblet.

Bemused, she tilted her head upward, searching the vast canopy of stars. Only a few stray clouds marred the otherwise pristine night. It looked like a perfectly clear sky to her. The moon hung over the ocean, creating a rare night where a slice of shimmering water was visible from her perch. She set her glass on the rail and stared out in the distance.

Jared's proximity was intoxicating, making it hard for her to think straight. What was she doing? This was Jared Westergard, the one man who seemed to have the power to unravel her completely. But as she thought about it, she realized that maybe, just maybe, she wanted to be unraveled.

"Beautiful view," he murmured.

"Yeah, I really like it here." She rested her hands on the rail.

"I wasn't referring to the water," he said in a playful tone.

Her eyes flicked to him, observing the play of moonlight on his chiseled features. The gentle curve of his lips, the depth in his gaze. He was, in many ways, just like the dark ocean in the distance–deep, mysterious, and maybe a little murky. But oceans, as beautiful as they were, could be wild and unpredictable. Overpowering and dangerous.

Jared drew nearer, the warmth of his presence brushing against her back.

A big part of her wanted to turn her head and feel his lips on hers again. Intoxicate herself with the heat she'd felt in the teahouse moments before. But now the cool air was clearing her head and giving her doubts about the wisdom in what they were doing.

Perhaps Jared was picking up on her new hesitation.

"Serena, when we first met, my actions and words were inexcusable," he began. "The way I treated you, your business, and the unfair rumors I spread were all wrong. I deeply regret every threat, every sabotage, and especially the harm I brought upon your teahouse. I swear I had good intentions, but I went about things the wrong way."

"I know, Jared. You already apologized."

"Yeah, and I know words can never erase the past, but I want you to know how much I regret those choices.

"Thanks, that's—"

"Since then—"

"Oh, there's more."

"Yeah. A bit." He cleared his throat and continued. "Since then, I've come to know the strong, passionate, and resilient woman you truly are. Your dedication, spirit, and the love you have for what you do have not only changed the perspective of many, but have deeply affected me as well. I've grown to trust you, respect you, and, against all my initial judgments, care deeply for you. Whatever this... connection between us is, I want to explore it, with all honesty and vulnerability. I want to assure you of my genuine intentions now. I hope you can find it in your heart to give us, and me, a chance to discover the new paths that may lie ahead for both of us."

She glanced over her shoulder with a sly smile. "That was an impressive speech. Did you work on it long?"

Jared flashed a sheepish grin, running a hand through his hair. "A little. Actually, I cranked that out while washing the dishes downstairs. Look, Serena, scratch all that. I just wanted to say that I think you're one of the best things to ever happen to Pembrooke. And I'm kinda hoping you might become one of the best things to ever happen to me, too."

In response, Serena pulled his head toward her and planted a long kiss on his lips. His arms wrapped around her waist, pulling her back against him. Jared planted a line of searing kisses along the curve of her neck, his breath hot against her skin.

A cool wetness tickled her eyelids, then forehead, as a scattering of raindrops took Serena by surprise. Pulling away, she tilted her face upwards, letting the sprinkles kiss her cheeks and nose. What began as a sporadic, tentative drizzle quickly morphed into a light shower, each droplet an icy caress against her skin. Her arms, bared to the night, felt the bracing chill first. Goosebumps blossomed in response, spreading across her limbs and torso as the rain left silver trails, soaking into her dress and lending a sheen to her hair.

As she looked back down, Jared stood unfazed amidst the downpour. The raindrops that made her shiver seemed to be drawn to him, like loyal subjects to a monarch. As the droplets trailed down, they caught in the grooves of his collarbone and chest, glistening and emphasizing the contours of his sculpted physique. They danced around his silhouette, not simply falling upon him, but merging, seemingly becoming a part of his flesh. His eyes, usually a warm hazel, now mirrored the tempestuous depth of the ocean during a storm. Amidst the rain's embrace, he looked more deity than man, a water witch in his element, both magnificent and terrifying in his raw power.

She trembled, both at the wet cold and at the sight of him. Without warning, his powerful arms wrapped around her, lifting her off her feet as if she were a drift of cherry blossoms caught in the spring breeze. The suddenness of his actions stole her breath, a gasp escaping her lips. As Jared carried her inside, she felt the vibrations of a deep chuckle, a playful resonance echoing in his chest. With a swift move, he nudged the bedroom door open with his foot, and then firmly kicked it shut, sealing them away from the outside world and Kita, who lounged unfazed in her cozy spot in the living room.

Setting her down by the bed he took a step back and appraised her chattering teeth with a mixture of concern and frank arousal.

"You're soaked to the bone."

Swiping wet strands of hair from her face, she glanced down. Her dress was clinging provocatively to every curve of her body as drops of water slid down her décolletage. And Jared couldn't tear his eyes away.

"You are, too," she said. His dark hair shone with rainwater and his white dress shirt had turned transparent, revealing most of his toned chest. She had accidentally, and appreciatively, already glimpsed it once, before their trek into Dakyra Forest. She suddenly wanted to see it again.

"You'll catch your death," she murmured, stepping closer. Before she knew what she was doing, her fingers plucked at the buttons of his shirt. Bunching her fists around the sodden fabric, she slid it off his frame, noting a round tattoo on his upper arm.

Her hands next moved to his belt and made quick work of the buckle. His pants dropped to the floor and he stepped out of the crumpled pile. Jared's eyes had gone dark when her eyes met his.

"You need to get out of your wet clothes, too." His voice was slow and husky as he reached behind her and began to unzip the back of her dress. Serena's breath hitched when he slid the straps off her shoulders before easing the dress down to the floor.

Standing in her bra and underwear in front of Jared, she was dimly aware that she should be cold. But a heat had enveloped her body, shielding her from the dampness of her skin.

With her dress gone, his palms roamed down her sides, over her black bra, his fingertips electrifying her skin.

"I'm afraid these will have to come off, too," he said fingering the lace before cupping her breasts.

"Yes," she breathed. "They're practically ruined."

Jared reached behind her and unhooked the bra, allowing it to open, but not removing it. His hands moved to her front and slid beneath the garment, caressing her breasts as he leaned in to kiss her. The kiss went on for a long moment while he slid the straps off her shoulders and allowed the bra to fall. He inhaled sharply as his eyes scanned over her.

"Lie down." His voice was soft but belied the firmness of his request as he gestured with his chin toward the bed.

Serena took a step back and allowed herself to drop onto the bed. Jared hovered over her for a moment, his eyes slowly trailing over nearly every inch of her before he descended. Beginning with her mouth, Jared kissed his way down her body. When he reached her thighs, he divested her of her underpants, his own soon following. A hunger seemed to consume them both, one which couldn't be sated until they were pressed skin to skin, lip to lip. His heat radiated into her damp skin, removing any remaining chill from the storm. She ran her fingers down his chest, feeling the tight, coiled muscles of his abdomen.

Serena guided him to her slick cleft, gasping as he pressed against her entrance, teasing for a time, sending waves of pleasure rippling through her until she couldn't take it anymore.

Mad with desire, she clutched at his back, dampened with the sweat of their passion.

"Please, Jared," she whispered. He finally relented, sinking into her warmth and eliciting moans of pleasure from them both. They rocked together, finding their unique rhythm, until she was driven over the edge and he followed soon after.

IN THE AFTERGLOW, THEY LAY ENTWINED, A TANGLE OF LIMBS AND shared warmth amidst the silky, rumpled sheets. Serena stared up at the strange light patterns that formed on the ceiling from the windows.

"If I didn't know better," she began, "I'd think you allowed me to get rained on and soaked just so I'd have to take my clothes off."

A playful smirk played on his lips. "What? I warned you it was going to rain."

"How could anyone believe that? The skies were perfectly clear."

He arced an eyebrow. "You didn't believe me?"

"If you were so confident, why didn't you suggest we go inside?" She turned on her side and a playful smile formed on her lips. "Did you *cause* the rain?"

He chuckled softly, the sound resonating deep in his chest. "I'm a water witch, Serena, not a god."

In the dim light, her gaze dropped to the strong lines of his torso. Reaching out with a lazy finger, she traced over the tattoo on his upper arm, the inked skin a stark contrast to his tanned complexion.

"A shield?"

"*Skjoldr*, yes."

"Does it have some special meaning to you?"

"It's the symbol for the order I belong to."

She propped herself up on one elbow, her curiosity fully piqued. "What kind of order?"

"An old one. Started more than a thousand years ago."

"A Viking order?"

"Yeah," he breathed.

"Funny, you don't look much like a Viking."

He gave her a sidelong glance. "What do I look like?"

She tilted her head, pretending to study him. "Like someone who's seen more barber salons than battles."

He smirked before rolling on his side to face her. "Perhaps if you ask nicely, I'll grow out a topknot and a long, scraggly beard for you."

"I prefer your stubble." She gasped as he ducked his head, scraping his abrasive cheek against the delicate skin of her breast before gently taking it into his mouth. She sighed. "Though I must admit, you do have the conquering part down."

"Well, every Viking knows it's not the length of the beard that matters. It's how well you can swing it."

She snorted and ran her fingers through his hair. "So, are you bad knights, or good knights?"

"My answer might depend on what day you ask me. At this very moment, 'good' isn't exactly how I'd describe myself." He flashed a sinful grin as his hand slid between her thighs, reigniting the familiar, longing ache. "But in answer to your question, I'd like to think we do our part to make the world a little better."

"Oh, sweet Odin, yes, you do." Closing her eyes, Serena surrendered to the delicious sensations. Extending her hand, she returned the favor as he groaned in appreciation.

Jared sat up, extending his hands to her. "Come here." Serena crawled forward, her gaze locked with his, as she slipped her fingers into his waiting hands.

Kissing her breasts, he pulled Serena into his arms and onto his lap. Her legs straddled him, encircling his waist, as her ankles crossed behind his back. Their bodies interlocked seamlessly and, as he pulled her against his chest, they folded into each other like the intricate blossoming of a lotus bud.

Jared kissed her deeply as he cradled her against him, heart to heart, his hands tracing patterns on her bare back. The delicate flesh between her thighs pressed against his hardness, further inflaming her senses. His lips moved lower, tasting the skin at her collarbone, and sending a spiral of sensation down her spine.

"Jared," she whispered, her fingers tangling in his hair. The sound of her voice, raw and unsteady seemed to further ignite something within him.

His gaze met hers, eyes dark with desire, as he pulled her tighter against him until they became one again. Wrapped in each other's arms, they moved together, summoning forth another tidal wave of pleasure and surrendering completely to their heat and passion.

. . .

Sometime later, Serena stretched languorously, smiling with contentment. Jared's heartbeat was a steady rhythm against her temple as she rested her head against his chest.

"Sweet goddess, I need some water," Serena panted. Rising from the bed, she slipped on a silk robe and glanced back to ask Jared if he wanted anything.

A loud crash suddenly resonated from outside the teahouse, causing them to startle in alarm.

It was close by. Too close. Serena glanced down the hallway to the balcony doors, feeling a chill wind blow down the corridor. In their haste to get to the bedroom, they had left the French doors wide open.

Jared jumped up and instinctively moved in front of Serena, scanning the hall for any signs of danger before venturing out into the living room. Pulling his pants on, he peered through the open doors of the balcony before moving to the kitchen window overlooking the street below. Serena began to hear muffled voices outside.

CHAPTER 21

JARED

J ared pressed a finger to his lips to signal he had seen
something. From his obscured vantage point, he
watched as shadowy figures in dark clothing convened
in a disquieting assembly on the sidewalk below. Arrayed
in a circle, they were just silhouettes against the spectral glow
of the moon, their forms oddly distorted and elongated. One
among them, presumably their leader, stepped forward,
holding aloft a dagger that glittered under the ghostly lunar
light.

He began to chant, but was too far for Jared to make out
any of the words.

As the chant crescendoed, the other figures echoed his
words, their voices intertwining in a dissonant symphony.
Then, as if at a preordained signal, they all raised an arm
towards the night sky, their words swelling into a fevered
pitch, then abruptly ceased. The silence that followed was
chilling. Then, the figures stood and vanished from sight,
leaving behind nothing but the whisper of their ominous ritual
in the wind.

Racing down the stairs, Jared unbolted the front door and slipped outside. Turning, he pushed Serena back inside with a gentle nudge. Whatever was out there, he didn't want it to come anywhere near her. "Close and lock the door behind me. Be right back."

"No, I'm coming with you."

"Serena, stay inside," Jared whispered, a note of firm urgency threading through his words. "I may need you to call the police," he said when he saw her start to object again. "Please."

"Fine," she huffed.

His hand briefly squeezed hers in reassurance before he stepped down into the cool evening.

The Pacific air was salty, carrying the tang of the nearby ocean. Overhead, the half-moon hung like a suspended medallion in the clear sky, casting a pallid illumination over the seaside town. The street before the teahouse, usually bustling, was silent and empty. How had they disappeared so quickly?

His gaze was immediately drawn to the spot on the sidewalk where he'd seen the shadowy figures. Bending down, he spotted a scattering of black powder, glinting under the half-moon's glow. He grazed it with his fingertips; the granular texture felt rough, like rock.

After scooping a small handful of the powder, he rose and began a careful circumnavigation of the teahouse. The wind whispered through the trees bordering the property, making the branches sway and dance in the ethereal moonlight. He squinted into a thicket, the dense undergrowth obscuring any deeper insight.

Following the property line, he ventured deeper into the neighboring woods. His every sense was heightened; the crunch of his shoes against the ground sounded amplified, his heartbeat thudded in his ears. The woods, though, remained deceptively serene, protecting whatever secrets they held.

After a thorough yet fruitless examination, he circled back toward the teahouse. The comforting glow of candlelight in its windows spilled out onto the cobblestones, a beacon of warmth amidst the mysterious night. Casting one last searching look around, he stepped up to the door and rapped gently.

"All clear."

"What happened?" Serena said, throwing open the door.

"Let's go back inside," Jared said before locking the door behind him and checking the windows.

The moment the door closed behind him, Serena grabbed two steaming mugs from the counter and led him back upstairs. She set the mugs on the coffee table as Jared checked the windows again.

Serena sunk into the sofa, allowing the mugs to fill the small space with the scent of chamomile and lavender. Jared joined her a minute later.

"I thought we could both use this," she said, sliding one of the mugs toward him, their fingers brushing briefly.

Jared took a deep breath, inhaling the soothing aroma of the tea. "Thanks."

Sitting opposite him, Serena cradled her mug in her hands, letting the heat seep into her skin. "Did you see anyone out there?"

He shook his head. Grabbing an empty teacup, he emptied the powder from his fist. "I found some rock dust where they were gathered. But that was it. No sign of anyone around anywhere."

Her eyes widened a little. "Rock dust?" She glanced inside the cup. "Used in the ritual?"

He shrugged, managing a half-smile. "Maybe. But no one

in town does magic like this. So, I think it was probably just some teenagers messing around. Doesn't seem like it's anything to worry about." Truthfully, he found it more disturbing than he let on. Practitioners he knew would charge stones by the light of the moon or sun, or by using their own magic. Or they might amplify a rock's natural power by the way it was laid out in a grid or pattern. But smashing it to bits? Seemed dark and destructive. But he didn't want to worry her unnecessarily. He'd look into it in the morning.

"Okay, I hope not. Well, thanks for checking it out anyway."

"Of course." He took a long sip from his mug. "Well, Serena, I hate to admit it but you were right about one thing."

"What's that?"

"This is the best damn tea I've ever had in my entire life," he murmured, glancing down at his mug. "I'm sorry I never tried it before."

Serena rolled her eyes in mock disgust. "Flatterer."

Admittedly he probably would have lied even if it tasted like skunk piss. One look into those green eyes could make him say almost anything to please her. But this wasn't the case now and he was surprised at not only the taste, but the effect it was starting to have on him. Jared shook his head. "No, really. I already feel more...relaxed, I guess. I feel good." His worries about the intruders and the dust seemed to fade to the far recesses of his mind. He set the half-drunk mug back on the table. "I'd say you bewitched me, but you already did that long ago." He sat back and held his arms out to her.

As she snuggled against him, he felt his lids grow heavy. His arms tightened around her, pulling her closer, if that was even possible. Serena was murmuring something, but the last thing he remembered was her laying a blanket across him.

"Sleep, Serena," he whispered, his voice husky from sleep and emotion. "I'm here, and I'm not going anywhere."

Her contented sigh was the final balm on his racing heart, the last piece of the puzzle that he hadn't realized was missing. He thought he had meant to be comforting her. But as sleep claimed him, the final thoughts in his mind were of Serena, of Pembrooke, and of the unexpected comfort he had discovered in both.

CHAPTER 22
SERENA

It was a beautiful evening. The sky was slightly overcast, shrouding the moon in grey and leaving the heavens endlessly dark. Despite that, the air was warmer than usual, drifting in through open windows, and carrying with it the scent of astilbe and dahlia. Serena could practically taste a summer storm brewing in the distance. She sighed, breathing in the peace of the night.

Hailey joined her near the window, teacup held gently in her fingers. "Things seem to be going well for you," she said, and the corner of her mouth just slightly twitched into a smirk.

Serena smiled, heat rising to her face. "Yeah. Yeah, they are."

"I can see it. You're practically glowing."

"She's been walking on air ever since the party last night," Lily interjected from where she and the others sat in the Goddess Room. Serena laughed, joining Hailey as she returned to the corner room.

The room smelled sweetly of vanilla incense, chamomile

tea, and the aroma of freshly baked garlic bread. An assortment of plush pillows was scattered in the wingback chairs for comfort, as the witches gathered around the round table, each settled into their favorite spot. Serena pulled an ornate room divider in front of the doorway to the windowless Goddess Corner, to ensure full privacy, before sitting in the remaining seat.

The coven was growing. Over the past few weeks, the original five of them had brought other friends into the fold. There were ten of them now who had found each other, each witch a vibrant thread woven into the rich tapestry of their new sisterhood.

Zara, the half-Thai librarian that Serena had met at the Tinker's Trinket, was soft-spoken, but her words were always poignant and insightful. Her eyes held a mischievous glint, hinting at depths of knowledge only the oldest tomes in the library could match.

Charlotte, who had witnessed the preparation of the Amnesia Tea, was the future veterinarian with a whirlwind of boundless energy. Her love for animals was rivaled only by her passion for earth magic, a trait that often left her hinting at wanting a job at the teahouse.

Noora was the Lebanese beauty from The Labyrinth. She had an infectious laugh and a heart as warm as a Mediterranean sun. Her culinary creations, a fusion of her homeland's flavors and local ingredients, were legendary.

Noora's friend, Brooklyn, was the beautiful ice princess, her haughtiness more of a protective shield than a real character trait. Beneath her icy exterior was a woman of immense depth and emotional richness.

And then there was Alice, the newcomer from NYC, a ballerina choreographer with a grace that seemed to have been spun from moonlight itself. Her movements, even in the simplest gestures, held an effortless elegance that was pure magic.

Despite their unique backgrounds, together, they formed a beautiful mosaic, an enchanting convergence of strength, wisdom, and support.

"Well, I would love to take the credit for Serena's good mood, believe me, but I don't think it had much to do with my cupcakes." Lily leaned against the table, arching a brow in challenge. "I'm beginning to suspect that our dear friend Rena is keeping something from us."

Serena tried to laugh it off. "Are you accusing me of something?"

Lily shook her head quickly. "Nothing! Nothing."

"Good."

"It's just that you've been getting awfully cozy with Jared Westergard," Emela teased.

The flush growing in her cheeks grew hotter. "He's been turning a new leaf, that's all," she said. "I know he was an ass, but I'm not blind to the fact that he's trying to make up for things. We've become... close."

"Uh-huh. How close is 'close', exactly?" Charlotte said.

Serena had always been a rotten liar. Her face must've given her away because Brooklyn's mouth fell open.

"Serena?"

"Yes?"

Brooklyn leaned close, voice dropping low in a mockery of discretion, as if they weren't surrounded by the other members of the coven. "Is there something going on between you two?"

Serena glanced around the table, wishing once again that she could disappear. "Something may have happened between us after the party last night," she blurted out.

The news was met by eight shocked expressions.

The ninth, Rowan, laughed. "What, really?"

She swallowed hard. "Maybe twice."

A chorus of scandalized laughter followed. Charlotte had the gall to whistle provocatively. For a moment, Serena was mortified, but she quickly gave herself over to the gossip. She cast a nervous glance toward the hallway. "We, um... we kind of made out on the sofa, out there in the hall."

Alice's eyes went wide. "Serena! That's it, I'm buying you curtains."

"Well, we didn't do anything else down here!" she squeaked."Hecate's hipbones, Alice, this is a proper place of business!"

"I guess they call them loveseats for a reason," Rowan chortled.

Lily snorted. "Looks like they were right all along about those velvet sofas being sex magnets."

Another wave of laughter crested over the table, with Serena hot in the face and wearing a helpless grin.

The cackles from the ten witches bounced off the pastel walls, a comforting echo of companionship and magic that was a melody to Serena's ears.

"I still can't believe you've finally succumbed to the illustrious Mr. Westergard," Zara teased.

"Yeah, Jared?" Charlotte said. "I mean, before last night, we've only ever seen you two glare at each other... and then you secretly watch for him out the window when he's not there."

The group burst into laughter, Serena included. "I do *not* watch for him!" she protested, unable to hide her smirk.

They continued their lighthearted banter as they each took turns lighting floating candles. The candles bobbed and swayed gently in the air as the women sipped red wine and nibbled on savory finger sandwiches, crudités, and Serena's leftover homemade lemon muffins.

"Enough teasing Serena and her new loooover," Noora intervened, clapping her hands together. She raised her glass and declared, "To love! May it always surprise us!"

The women raised their glasses, the clinking sound punctuating their agreement. Alice used a bit of her magic to turn on the record player, and the room filled with the smooth jazz of Ella Fitzgerald's "At Last".

Rowan grabbed Charlotte's hand, pulling her up to dance, and within seconds, all the women were up and moving, their bodies swaying rhythmically to the music. The vibrant scene of dancing witches, floating candles, and contagious laughter was a sight to behold. Alice's ballerina instincts took over, her movements flowing and graceful, enchanting everyone around her.

The night continued well past the witching hour, with shared stories, more laughter, a few tears, some magic, and a unity that they all cherished. The Goddess Corner had become their haven, a place to celebrate their witchiness, support each other, laugh, complain, and most importantly, to be themselves.

"Look out Serena, there's a Lens in your shop!"

Serena turned in response to Rowan's warning, smiling when she saw Jared striding into the teahouse early the following morning. He nodded to her, keeping a pointless air of politeness in front of Rowan and Hailey and the few customers in the teashop.

"Am I in trouble?" she asked, bracing her hands on the counter as he approached.

"Not today. Not with me, anyway. Why, do you want to be?"

"Easy there, Loverboy," Hailey warned. "At least give us a five-minute notice before we need to make ourselves scarce and give you two some privacy."

Jared rolled his eyes, his lower lip catching in his teeth. "I'll be quick, I promise."

"That's not what Rena told us—"

"Rowan!" Serena warned, giving her a dangerous glare. She slid them further down the counter, out of earshot of the other witches, and leveled her attention on him, tilting her head in interest. "I'm assuming you're not just here to be harassed by my customers. Finally sampling the tea?"

Jared paused and smirked at their inside joke before continuing. "I'm just letting you know that I'm going out of town this weekend, that's all."

She lifted her brows. "Jared Westergard actually leaving Pembrooke? I must be dreaming."

He flashed a crooked smile. "What can I say, you've inspired me. I actually reached out to an old hiking buddy. We're going to Neahkahnie Mountain for a couple of days. Getting some fresh air and all that."

"Oh, that's great! I'm glad you're taking my advice. Just tell Judith to let me know if she needs any help looking after Zoe, okay?"

"She should get by all right. But I'll pass it on, thanks."

"Okay, well I hope you have a good time," she mumbled, a bit awkwardly.

Her heart stuttered when he leaned over the counter, pressing a kiss to her cheek. His lips ghosted near the shell of her ear, and she shivered. "I'll miss you while I'm gone," he whispered, kissing her once more before pulling away.

She tried to steady her breathing. It was embarrassing,

really, how something as simple as a peck on the cheek and a few choice words sent her mind spinning.

"Be good while I'm gone," he said, already heading for the door. "No rainforests in my office, please."

Serena smirked. "Not making any promises."

CHAPTER 23
JARED

Underneath an azure dome, Jared perched on the rocky summit of Neahkahnie Mountain. His gaze swept across the vast, green canvas of Oregon's wilderness on one side of the ridge, as tranquil and unspoiled as a Renaissance painting. The other side of the ridge was a panorama of the vast Pacific blue. His hair fluttered in the chill mountain wind, his muscles ached with the satisfying weariness that followed a hard-won ascent. This place was his sanctuary, where he escaped from the world below and its unceasing clamor. But today, it served a different purpose.

A barely perceptible noise behind him caught his attention, the whisper of a boot scraping against a rock. Jared spun around, hand on the harnessed knife at his belt. Emerging from the weathered path was a tall man with close cropped blond hair.

Ethan Thomassen, a man whose features were cut from the same hardened stone as the mountain they stood upon, walked with an otherworldly grace. His lineage descended from an ancient magic, even older than that of Jared's clan. His presence carried an aura of quiet authority, hardened by the years and many battles fought.

"Lofty heights, Westergard?" he called out, his voice resonating in the open air.

Jared gave a small smirk. "Clears the head, Thomassen." Jared approached the older man and extended his hand. Ethan pumped his hand three times as they each clasped the other's shoulder with their left hands, covering the mark of the *skjoldr*. Each had been marked with the round Viking shield after swearing fealty to the Order of Hjartator as youth.

Ethan merely nodded, taking a moment to appreciate their surroundings. His icy eyes met Jared's once more, filled with a stern readiness to address the reason behind their meeting.

Jared started, his words painting the eerie picture of the scene outside Serena's teahouse with the mysterious ritual and the black rock dust.

Ethan's brow creased, his voice a low murmur as he echoed, "Crushed black rock?" A silence fell between them as he contemplated. "Don't know of any organized group using such a thing in a ritual. But a few individuals may be a possibility. Earth witches, most likely. Would be easy for them to pulverize rock into fine powder, which could be used for magical purposes. Was it onyx, by chance?"

Jared shrugged. "Why? What's the significance of onyx?"

"Heard of a guy named Fiori?"

"Joe Fiori? Yeah. He's on the council. Why?"

"Any reason he might have it out for you?"

Jared blew out air. "Yeah. He had a thing for Willow a long time ago and always hated me for getting her. Then about a year ago, he figured out I helped the council investigate some corrupt deals and abuse of power charges he was involved with. He was reprimanded. Never forgave me for the hit to his reputation. So yeah, he and I don't exactly see eye to eye."

"He's also an earth witch. With a predilection for using onyx."

Rubbing the back of his neck, Jared sighed, his eyes scanning the distant treetops. Fiori had already paid him that nasty visit. Was it possible Fiori was trying to use the teahouse to get to him?

"This may all just be coincidental, of course. I have no intel on any recent activity in the area," Ethan said. "But I'll dig deeper."

"Thanks."

"Jared, something else troubles me." Ethan's stern expression softened into a look of concern. "This woman, this teamaster...there is talk that she is enchanting her teas. Selling them to humans out in the open."

Jared dismissed his fears with a firm shake of his head. "It's not what you think."

"I've heard rumors, and so the council might have, too. If not, it's a matter of time, I'm sure."

"She's a healer, Ethan. She's never hurt anyone."

"Will the council see it that way, Jared?" Ethan's gaze grew more intense as he turned to look at him. "And furthermore, what will they do when they find out it's been going on right underneath your nose? They'll assume you're helping her break the law, which makes you an accessory. Do you really want this complication?"

Jared held his gaze, his voice resolute. "Serena won't be a problem."

The elder knight fell silent, his gaze returning to the panorama beneath them. "She will be if you lie to protect her."

"I haven't."

"Yet."

"It won't be a problem."

"How can it be otherwise? The council will find out. The Order won't be able to protect you."

"I'm not asking it to." Jared let out a sigh. "Though if you'll recall, our allegiance is to the *people*, the witches and warlocks of the world. Not to some council."

"It's a matter of expediency to serve the council," Ethan said.

"They've made us into a glorified secret police force."

"Yet you yourself joined that very same council."

Jared paused and turned his gaze to the ocean. "It was a matter of expediency," he said, mimicking Ethan. "I get information. I get the ability to try to shape the way we are governed."

"Exactly. Same reason the Order of Hjartator allied itself with the Council decades ago, as you know." Ethan stepped toward the descending trail. He glanced over his shoulder. "We're warriors, you and me, not politicians. Look into Fiori. And be careful, Jared."

Pembroke looked better coming than going, Jared decided. Even the delicate foliage along the roadside beckoned him back home. *Just the distance, most likely.* They say that absence makes the heart grow fonder, but he hadn't exactly given himself a lot of opportunities for nostalgia lately. Too scared to look back, and nothing ahead. He'd been staring at his shoes, truth be told. Only focusing on the here and now.

And that sort of thinking was fine, for a while, but with increasing frequency Jared found himself preoccupied with 'what if's'. Thoughts that burrowed deep inside of his skull and bombarded him with endless daydreams. The kind of daydreams filled with soft pink petals, lush green leaves, long honey-colored hair, and constellations of freckles that could give any starry sky a run for its money.

Exhaling a heavy sigh, he tried to swat these thoughts away, but they clung on stubbornly. Instead, he forced his attention to the mason jar rattling in his cup holder. It was brimming with cheerful purple flowers for Serena. Oregon Irises. He couldn't say if they were any different from the common garden variety, but hell, it was the thought that counted.

What was he doing? What had he already done, allowing his feelings to overcome him like this? What would Serena think if she knew he was thinking again about shutting down her teahouse, after everything she'd done for the town? After everything that had happened between them.

Thoughts continued to drift as he drove, making his way over streams, past residential areas. Something caught his eye as he rolled past the old distillery. It had been abandoned for the better part of a decade now. The only people who ventured in these days were stupid teenagers looking for a quiet place to break things or get high.

And yet, the figures he saw making their way into the old building looked to be adults. Granted, he only caught a glimpse of them, but they both looked... familiar, in a way. He slowed to a near crawl, studying them in his rearview mirrors.

That was when it clicked. One of the men standing near the door looked like Colin Parker, the man who attacked Serena a few weeks earlier. His rage built with frightening speed, black and boiling in his gut. *That little piece of shit.* Jared had told him very plainly to get the hell out of Pembrooke. Was he deaf or just too stupid to listen?

The other man, a bald guy, looked over his shoulder, squinting at Jared's truck, now almost stalled in the center of the road. Jared released the brakes and resumed his previous pace. His thoughts remained wholly concentrated on what he'd seen, though. He was furious that Colin was still in the area, and deeply disquieted by the notion that he could try to harm Serena again. She'd fought him off last time, but that didn't make the idea of her being attacked any less horrific in his eyes.

Moreover, the other man he'd seen left a sour taste. He couldn't place it, but something about him made his stomach turn. Paranoia, perhaps. Or intuition.

On impulse, he turned onto a narrow dirt road, driving until his car was concealed by the trees. He stepped out of his car, and began to slowly trek through the brush back toward the distillery.

JARED PEERED THROUGH THE FOLIAGE AT THE BUILDING, SEARCHING for signs of life. No vehicles out front, but he could see lines of flattened grass behind the main storeroom, like someone had driven up and parked outside, recently.

He held his breath as he advanced, looking out for any movement in his periphery. Colin and his accomplice had used the front entrance, but he could see from his position that the door was fitted with a sturdy-looking padlock. Even if he could break it, he suspected that it wouldn't be particularly subtle.

Around the back, then.

He barely suppressed a sound of surprise when the silence was disturbed by abrupt squawking. A pair of crows, evidently offended by his arrival, shrieked at him before taking to the sky. Left in their wake were the remnants of a few scattered french fries, discarded in the dirt, and a single black feather. Jared took a deep breath, trying hard to shake off his apprehension.

A loud clattering sound echoed from inside the storeroom,

reverberating through the walls and making him jump again. He knew he should leave. He should go back home, report this to the higher-ups in the council, and let them handle it, like he was supposed to. But he couldn't do that. The council would just screw things up anyway. Better to take care of it now.

More sounds caught his attention. Muffled voices, perhaps? Or possibly another animal noise, distorted by the walls. He pressed his ear to the surface, trying to hear over the sound of his own heartbeat. It was no use, he couldn't parse anything of value. Not from outside, anyway.

He continued his cautious trek around the perimeter. In truth, he couldn't even say *what* he was searching for. Closure, perhaps. The sense of safety that he'd been forced to live without for far too long.

Jared didn't find that, and suspected that he wouldn't for a long while. He did, however, locate a smashed window on the side wall of the storehouse. He stood on the balls of his feet, peering into the room.

It was still mid-afternoon, and the room itself was dark, so Jared had to squint and focus to make anything out. The window opened into what looked to be a makeshift office, fitted with a table and a few chairs. The distillery's new inhabitants had cleaned, if the lack of dust and broken glass on the floor was any indication. The table was littered with books and sheets of paper, such that he could hardly see the table's surface, but the darkness and distance made it impossible for him to gather anything regarding their contents. He set his jaw, reaching into his pocket to fish for his phone so that he could use its flashlight.

CHAPTER 24
SERENA

"You okay?"

Serena glanced up, plastering a smile on her face when she noticed Aaron observing her on the other side of the counter. "What do you mean?"

He gestured to her hands. "You've been staring at your phone all day," he observed. "You're not expecting bad news, are you?"

She sighed, setting her phone face-down on the counter. "It's just Jared."

"Trouble in paradise?"

That brought a small laugh out of her. "No, no. I thought he'd be back by now. That's all."

Aaron shrugged, turning his attention back to his sketchbook. He'd set up a small still life composition, built from spare flowers, an overturned teacup, and Serena's kingfisher statue. "Maybe he is on his way."

She chewed the inside of her cheek. "He just hasn't been responding to my messages."

"It's probably not worth worrying about. Service up in the

mountains is a nightmare, you know that. Maybe his phone's not working."

She looked down at the phone, her mouth twisting slightly. "Maybe," she mumbled.

Aaron was right, most likely. Then again, Jared had been messaging her fairly regularly during the first half of his trip. Every few hours or so, usually with photos of the lush scenery for her to fawn over, including some Oregon irises she had gone crazy over. Then the messages had abruptly stopped. It shouldn't matter, she told herself. Serena wasn't the sort of girl who needed constant attention. She had her life, and Jared had his, and ordinarily that suited her just fine. In truth, she was a bit annoyed with herself for caring so much. It was just her subconscious catastrophizing, she decided. Preparing for the next surprise, especially an unpleasant one. She wasn't used to feeling comfortable, after all. There had to be a catch. There always was.

Truthfully, all the alone time was giving her too much time to think and overanalyze. Too much time to mull over the events of the past week. The painted crow, the weird teahouse visitors.

The image of the crow was starting to haunt her. The painted figure, its wings outstretched, seemed to carry a weight of meaning she couldn't yet decipher. Its sudden appearance, paired with the tea leaf reading, was too much to be coincidence. She needed answers. Was it a warning, a threat, or perhaps even a message? She considered how she could track down the artist.

The soft chime of the entrance bell snapped her out of her reverie. In the doorway stood Charlotte and Brooklyn.

"Hey, Serena," Brooklyn's voice, typically frosty, held a touch of warmth for her friend.

"Hey! The usual for you guys?" Serena asked, reaching for their preferred tea blends.

"Um, yeah I think," Charlotte replied, her eyes scanning the array of teas on display.

As Serena steeped the tea, a thought occurred to her. Charlotte was an earth witch, adept with materials and elements. Perhaps she might know something about the paint used for the crow.

"Charlotte," Serena began, pouring hot water over the tea leaves, "there's something outside I'd love to show you. I could use an earth witch's perspective."

With raised eyebrows, Charlotte nodded, her interest seemingly piqued. Serena led them outside to the tiny mural, noting the thoughtful tilt of Charlotte's head as she examined the crow, her fingers hovering over the lines.

"This looks like it was drawn with a paint pen," Charlotte mused.

Brooklyn, leaning against the wall with a detached air, chimed in. "It's not even done well. Very child-like. I don't know who or why anyone would even bother to draw that. What was the point?"

"Well, that's exactly what I'm trying to find out," Serena said. "Anything special about this paint pen? Can I narrow down where it was bought?"

"Nah, these are fairly common," Charlotte said. "You can find them in a lot of places: hardware stores, craft shops, drug stores, department stores."

"That doesn't narrow it down much," Serena said with a sigh.

"You should go talk to Zara," Brooklyn suggested. "She's got that secret stash of esoteric lit at the library. If there's any significance to this crow or who might have drawn it, she'd know."

Serena nodded."Thanks, both of you. I'll head to the library tomorrow morning."

THAT EVENING SERENA SAT ON HER BALCONY WRAPPED IN A WOOL blanket and studied the stars. The Albright Family Grimoire lay next to her on the seat. Grandma Bess would have been proud that she was reading from it again. Unfortunately, it didn't give her any new insight on crows.

To her right sat the pots of henbane and vervain, untouched since Jared had herded them onto her balcony during her move-in. She felt a pang of guilt wondering if her teahouse was slowly poisoning the community, as he'd predicted that day. She was definitely getting a lot of signs from the universe.

Perhaps she herself was like henbane. Healing at just the right dose, but harmful when given in higher amounts. Maybe she'd underestimated the effects of her magic on the town. Maybe she was pushing too much here in Pembrooke.

Maybe she was a poison.

CHAPTER 25
SERENA

The morning mist clung to the town of Pembrooke the following morning as Serena approached the public library, nestled between the town's bustling square and a quiet grove of whispering trees. She held two steaming to-go cups, one with a fragrant rose tea and the other with Zara's favorite blend of chamomile and lavender. In a small bag she had also packed some freshly baked croissants, a peace offering of sorts for the impromptu visit.

Pushing open the library door, the scent of old books and polished wood wrapped around her like a comforting embrace. Zara, with her shiny black hair pinned up and glasses perched on her nose, was already there, adjusting some books on a shelf. When she saw Serena, her eyes lit up, especially at the sight of the tea.

"You are a doll," Zara said, taking the offered cup and inhaling the aromatic steam.

Serena chuckled softly. "And these might help too," she said, pulling out the croissants.

"Queen! So you said something about crows on the phone,"

she said, fishing through the bag and taking a bite out of one of the croissants.

Serena nodded. "Yes, I've been seeing signs... and they're not good." Serena quickly explained about the reading and the painted crow.

Zara pushed back her chair and motioned for Serena to follow. She halted, took a step back to grab the bag of croissants from off the table, then continued on.

They weaved through rows of bookshelves, arriving at a heavy wooden door with a brass plate reading "Reference Room". The door creaked softly as they entered a space where time seemed to have stopped. Dust motes floated in the air, highlighted by the dim sunlight filtering in through the high windows. Desolate shelves lined with forgotten encyclopedia sets and weighty dictionaries stood as silent sentinels.

"No one ever comes in here," Zara whispered with a twinkle in her eyes. "Except me." With a sly smile, she traced her fingers over an ornate symbol etched onto her bracelet. The room shimmered, the atmosphere thickening for a heartbeat, and then everything transformed. The encyclopedias and dictionaries morphed into ancient, leather-bound historical tomes with gold inlays. Grimoires with pentacles and faded symbols, manuscripts filled with sketches of mythological creatures, and compendiums of magical lore now filled the shelves.

"Holy cow. Glamoured. Everything is hidden in plain sight," Serena breathed, her fingers grazing the spine of one of the transformed books.

"Hidden in plain sight," Zara echoed with a nod. "That's how we've always done things in Pembrooke," Zara said, her voice laced with pride.

The two witches moved to a section on magical symbols and omens. Zara retrieved a volume with an embossed pentagram on its cover, paging through the old, yellowed pages. "The five crows," she murmured, "is often seen as an omen of deceit or shadowed intentions. A warning of danger waiting in the wings."

"What about the painted crow on the teahouse?"

Together, they scoured through tomes for the better part of an hour, looking for any mention of solitary crows painted on buildings. Zara finally leaned back with a sigh. "There's nothing about painted crows here. If you've been marked, it's not by anyone using classical magic."

Serena felt a knot of frustration in her stomach. "So, what do I do now?"

"You sure it wasn't drawn by kids?"

"My intuition says no."

Zara paused, thoughtful. "Go see Noora," she finally said. "She gets visions sometimes. She may be able to see something the books can't."

"Okay, I will, love. I gotta head out and go open the teahouse now. Thanks for your help." She hugged Zara.

"Anytime. Thanks for the croissants."

"Sure, you can share the extras with your coworkers."

"Nope. Not a chance."

SERENA WATCHED THE CLOCK MORE THAN SHE SHOULD HAVE, THAT day. No message. No sign of Judith or Zoe, either. She kept her phone always nearby, like a lovesick schoolgirl. That longing irritated her even more, until she wasn't sure if she would kiss him or smack him when Jared finally did come sauntering through her door.

By nightfall, it had simmered to an ache. One that she selfishly hoped was shared. He'd told her he would miss her, while he was away. She wanted that to be true. She wanted him to think of her, to stare at the moon and find himself wanting. She felt a bit foolish for it. So desperate to cling to hope that she might well end up smothering it. But she supposed that there were worse things in the world than wanting to be adored.

But then the thought occurred to her that something bad had happened to Jared. An accident, maybe. There were countless stories of people who disappeared hiking in the mountains, never to be heard from again. Some of them fell off cliffs, some got lost until they starved to death, and some were attacked by wild animals. Jared was an amazing outdoorsman, yes, but these were the types known to take the most risks.

More than once, she caught herself glancing out her bedroom window. She observed Westergard and Ross where it sat, proud and simple and empty on the corner of Bailey Street.

Unable to sleep, she slipped on a jacket and went downstairs. She felt inexplicably restless as she stepped out into the night air. Stupid and short sighted, like a teenager sneaking out of her parents' house rather than an adult who was well within her rights to walk down her own street.

There wasn't much space for greenery outside Jared's office. Just enough for her to squeeze one plant in, but that was enough for her purposes. A small bush, blooming with pale pink camellias. A bit saccharine, perhaps, but she hoped that it would bring him some joy the next day when he returned. A cheerful pop of color, nestled near the grey. They suited each other, she thought, with a small nod.

Hecate help her, she was in love.

At her feet, blooming through a small crack in the sidewalk, a Queen Anne's Lace blossom burst into the moonlight. She smiled down at it, shining and delicate in the glow of a nearby streetlamp.

Sanctuary. Maybe so.

Serena was setting a tray of blackberry scones in the display case on the counter when she saw him. Her heart raced the moment she spied his dark curls through the window, eagerly anticipating the moment that he entered the teahouse. Instead, he made a beeline for the law office entrance after he parked, not even sparing the teahouse or the woman inside a glance.

Her heart sank.

Again, she tried to reason with herself. It didn't matter, really. Maybe he was waiting until his lunch break to stop by, so that they would have more time to talk about his trip. Maybe he had a lot of work to catch up on, after being gone. Or maybe he simply wasn't as eager to see her as she was to see him. That was fine. Either way, it was fine.

"Is everything okay, Rena? Your eye is sort of... twitching."

She glanced over at Lily, Emela nursing a steaming mug beside her. "Sorry, what was that?"

Lily turned in her seat, eyes following where Serena's gaze had been fixed. The door to the office was already shut, but his car was parked conspicuously out front. Lily chuckled. "You two are so obsessed with each other."

Serena felt her cheeks burn. She practically snapped at Lily, "I am not *obsessed* with him!"

"You are! And when you weren't obsessed with loving him, you were obsessed with hating him, which is just as bad."

She let out a weary sigh, blowing the long fringe from her face. "I just don't appreciate how hot-and-cold he's being, all right? Last week it was all 'I'll miss you, Serena, be good for me,' and now it seems he can't even spare a minute for a quick hello? Don't they say that absence makes the heart grow fonder?"

Emela shrugged, regarding her mostly empty teacup with a neutral expression. "They also say 'out of sight, out of mind'."

Lily shot her a look.

Out of sight, out of mind, then. So be it. Maybe Jared Westergard was no different than all the other men she had known, after all. She didn't spare the building across the street so much as a glance for the rest of the morning.

It didn't seem to do much for keeping him out of her mind, though.

Was she really that insecure? Why was Jared affecting her like this? It wasn't as if she'd never been the object of romance before. She'd had her share of lovers, dotted throughout the country like a trail of heartbroken breadcrumbs. She didn't ordinarily find herself wringing her hands over a man's attention, or lack thereof. Not for a long time, anyway. Then again, that might have been because it was usually Serena doing the breaking up and leaving.

But she wasn't ready to leave Pembrooke yet, not by half. Even if things didn't work out with Jared.

And based on Jared's recent behavior, that was looking more and more likely.

She jumped at the sound of the bell chiming over the door, just before lunchtime. And there he was, striding in like nothing was amiss. She hazarded a weak smile despite her swirling frustration, leaning over the counter to meet him.

"Hello, gorgeous," she said. Gods, and just like that she was flirting again?

He smiled back at her, looking pleased but oddly tired. He leaned in to press a chaste kiss to the corner of her mouth, and she couldn't find it within herself to hate the way she swooned over it.

"Good to see you made it back all right. You didn't respond to any of my texts," she elaborated, the slightest note of bitterness creeping into her tone. "I was a little worried."

He blinked slowly, nuzzling her jaw before pulling away. "I'm sorry about leaving you hanging. Something important came up on the way into town."

She studied him, unsure what seemed off in his eyes. "I guess I can forgive you. As long as you don't make a habit out of it."

She was expecting him to laugh. It felt odd when he didn't, like being turned a few degrees to the left without warning. Something was weighing on him, that much was clear.

"Or you could make it up to me by taking me out to lunch," she offered, tentatively. "Maybe something light?"

The sad smile on his face said everything, but he still mumbled, "Got a lot going on today, I'm afraid."

At least he managed to sound mostly sincere in his regret, she thought, though it mainly just succeeded in making her feel guilty for being annoyed to begin with. "Okay. I understand," she said. She didn't really, but he was making little effort to explain his sudden lack of interest.

He reached up, rubbing the back of his neck. "Yeah, I was just popping in really quickly to see you."

"Sure," she said with a tight smile. "No worries. Maybe I could see you tonight, though? I'm sure you have plenty of stories for me."

"Yeah, maybe." His eyes were on the windows, watching for something unseen. It gave her the unsettling impression that he was waiting for a disaster, one that lived just outside of her line of sight.

"Jared?"

He blinked. *Sweet goddess, he really does look exhausted. And worried.*

"Yeah?"

"Do you want me to make you some tea?" she asked. It wasn't what she really wanted to know. And it wasn't like her to beat around the bush, but something about his behavior put her on edge. "Nothing strong, I swear. Just something to take the edge off? You seem... rattled."

He shrugged it off, playing nonchalant. "I'm fine, really. Just got a lot on my mind, that's all. Give me a chance to sleep it off. I'll be fine tomorrow."

Serena chewed the inside of her cheek. "If you say so," she said, and let him go.

With a worried frown, she watched him walk back to Westergard and Ross, feeling somehow even worse than before. Yesterday, she'd only been upset with him for ignoring her. She had assumed that Jared was simply losing interest. Now, though, she felt much more concerned. She'd never seen Jared like that before, shaken and flighty, like he anticipated danger arriving at any moment. Her mind began to reel with possible scenarios, none of them good, and the anxiety it brought on sat heavy as a stone in the pit of her stomach.

Not ten minutes later, Rowan came strolling into the teahouse. She sank onto a stool, giving Serena a wide-eyed look of exasperation.

"Something for stress?" Serena guessed, though it wasn't a particularly difficult thing to puzzle out.

Rowan nodded. "The boss is all piss and vinegar today," she lamented. "Do you have a few minutes to take a break and go over and put a little smile on his face? For me?"

Serena snorted at that, the presence of a friendly face coaxing her from her downward spiral. "I tried, believe me. He gave me the cold shoulder."

"Well, how do you like that? Lot of good that vacation did him; he's been all gloom and doom since he got back yesterday."

Her brows furrowed. "Yesterday? I thought he didn't come back to work until today."

Rowan shook her head in response. "No, he was around yesterday afternoon. I asked him about his little field trip and he brushed me off. Didn't say much to anyone, really."

The dread in her gut doubled in size, the sense of foreboding weighing her down until her shoulders sagged. "He wasn't answering my messages yesterday," she confessed. "I assumed it was because he was on the road, but when I talked to him today he looked pretty distracted. I don't know what's gotten into him."

"I couldn't tell you for sure, but I'm assuming something up in the mountains must have set him off."

She shrugged, eyes drifting to the bush of pink flowers under his window. "Or he might've just needed the space to re-prioritize," she muttered. "Figure out what he wants."

"Come on, Serena. I'm sure it's not like that."

Rowan was probably right, even if the anxiety raising hairs on her arms told her otherwise. Jared seemed so out of it, and that made bad memories begin to bubble up in her mind. She'd seen that far off look before in relationships. Usually before they decided to end things. Had she misjudged the extent of his feelings and made herself foolishly vulnerable again? She wanted to kick herself for falling for a man again. Still, she would have killed to know what Jared Westergard was feeling right now.

CHAPTER 26

JARED

J ared had no earthly idea how to feel. His mind was a
jumbled mess of dark thoughts and impossible
emotions. And at the center of everything was always
Serena.

After leaving the teahouse, he had surprised himself by
making an impulsive drive to Oxport. He scarcely had the time
to spare, but he knew this was something that had to be done
in person. But now, staring down the long hallway of Fiori
headquarters, he suddenly doubted whether this journey
would prove fruitful.

Jared's footsteps echoed on the milk-colored marble floor.
Opening the door at the end of the hall, he stepped into an
expansive office, a space filled with wooden shelves and
various gemstones. Joe Fiori stood behind a massive mahogany
desk, his sharp gaze fixed on Jared as he approached.

"Jared," Joe said with a beat of hesitation, a touch of cold-
ness. "To what do I owe this unexpected pleasure?" He
gestured to a chair on the opposite side of the desk.

After sitting, Jared placed a small glass jar of black rock

dust on the desk. "I thought you might know something about this," he said.

With a look of curiosity, Joe unscrewed the lid and dumped the jar's contents onto his palm. He closed his fist around the dust. Reopening his hand a second later, he held up a reconstructed small black rock with faint, scattered white veining.

"Where'd you find it?"

"Pembrooke. At the site of a late night ritual in front of a teahouse."

"Not the brand new Velvet Teahouse?" Joe said with mocking admiration.

"The one and only."

"And why would anyone want to target an innocent tea shop?" Joe set the stone on his desk. "I work exclusively with onyx, Jared." Fiori reached over to another table, picking up a deep black stone, richer and darker than the one Jared brought. "This is onyx," he declared, placing the two stones side by side for comparison.

"And what's this?" he asked, pointing to the stone he had brought.

"Black tourmaline," Joe said, picking it up. Jared already knew this, after taking some of the dust to an earth witch buddy of his. Joe squeezed the rock in his hand and a few drops of water dripped out. "Too soft, too watery for my liking. Not something I'd ever work with."

"You know anything about it being used for rituals?"

"I have better things to do than perform petty magic in front of a teahouse, if that's what you're getting at, Jared."

"I wasn't suggesting that."

Joe inspected the stone with casual curiosity. "This little teamaster of Pembrooke have any enemies?"

"Enemies? No, why do you ask?"

He spun the stone around his fingers. "Come on, Jared, you

know black tourmaline is used in protection spellwork. So, your question *should* be, who might need protection from Serena Albright?"

"No one."

"You sure?" Setting the stone back on the desk, Joe looked up with a gleam in his eye. "Seeing as she just might be serving the oolong tea with a side of magic."

Jared stiffened. "The Velvet Teahouse is a legitimate business."

"Is it?" Fiori's eyes studied him. "Seems to me, there's more brewing there than just tea." He stretched lazily. "So maybe this teamaster of yours isn't as innocent as you think. Maybe she cooked up something that hexed someone, made them sprout wings or some bullshit. And now this person needs to reverse her magic. Or maybe someone out there is just scared as hell of her and wants protection."

"It's nothing like that."

"Maybe, maybe not." Joe shrugged. "But maybe the council needs to investigate this teahouse now."

Jared leaned forward in his chair. "What do you think I'm doing, Fiori? Watch yourself. Remember what happened last time you tried to work outside your territory."

Fiori smirked, equally unyielding. "And you remember that this crap tourmaline has nothing to do with me." He slid the stone toward Jared. "You need to tread carefully, too, Westergard. Our worlds are intertwined more than you'd like to admit."

Both men locked eyes, the air thick with tension. Jared reached across the desk and pocketed the stone.

He left Fiori headquarters irritated but satisfied. The unpleasant encounter had clarified one thing in his mind: Fiori wasn't lying. He knew nothing about the teahouse ritual. The danger lurking in Pembrooke was not coming from Fiori, but from somewhere—or someone—else entirely.

BACK AT HIS OFFICE, JARED GLARED AT HIS COMPUTER SCREEN, stabbing petulantly at the keys. Those men outside the distillery refused to leave his mind. He just couldn't shake the sense of unease. It surrounded him like a cloud, some nauseating miasma that he struggled to even breathe through.

Worse still, he had almost nothing to justify this feeling. Nothing concrete, at any rate. Just a pile of vague half-leads that only served to keep him awake at night. The papers in the distillery sparked directionless fear in the back of his skull, like an alarm sounding in a place he'd never been. Newspaper clippings surrounding Pembrooke. A magazine article about Dakrya Forest. Census data. A stack the size of a phone book of printed social media pages, belonging to about half of the town's population.

There hadn't been any sign that the men he'd seen were even still *there*, while Jared was investigating. It seemed to him like they'd left while he was approaching through the woods, probably making themselves scarce when they saw Jared driving by. Which was likely for the best, because Jared had no idea what he would have done if he'd actually been able to confront them. He suspected it would've ended violently, regardless of how irresponsible that would have been on his part.

He put his face in his hands. Seeing Colin again made him think about Serena, about how impulsive and defensive she made him feel. Unhinged, maybe, but *alive*. He needed to protect her so badly that it blocked out all common sense. He was getting way too close to her, way too fast. The worst part was that knowing it was happening didn't help him one bit. He could build up all the wherewithal he had to his name, and one look at that smile would have him melting. Damnit, he hated feeling so weak.

She could ruin him. She really could. Hell, at times he felt like she already had. She could take a crowbar and pry his ribs apart, dig past his sternum to poke and prod at the still healing, tender pieces of himself. It would be so easy, he realized. And yet he trusted her not to abuse her power. Trusted her to hold his heart in her hands, regardless of the potential danger. Still, he'd hit rock bottom before, after losing Willow. Could he survive that again? Somehow he doubted it.

He frowned out his window. A fleck of pink caught his eyes, and he peered down at the facade of the building.

Those flowers.

The same blushing flowers that Serena had manifested that night in Prometheus Cave. Unplanned, she'd said. Accidental, based on feeling alone. There was no other explanation but that Serena had planted those for him while he was gone. He smiled to himself, recalling their prior conversation. She was right, the building had needed a pop of color, after all. His heart twisted to an unfair degree, painful, as he imagined Serena manifesting those flowers with him in mind.

Without his permission, his mind conjured the image of her wearing nothing but those flowers. Tangled in that maple hair like she was the new Artemis, just passing through Pembrooke on her way to Mount Olympus.

"No one's ever parted the sea for me before," she had said. Awestruck, as if he wouldn't do it again. As if he wouldn't do it now, today, if that was what she wanted.

He dragged a hand down his face. Who was he kidding? They would never work, anyway. Serena was just so... bright. It nearly hurt to look at her, like staring at the sea on a sunny day. Lately he felt like more of a black hole.

As a kid, Jared would go camping every summer with Liam and Uncle Pete in Dakrya Forest. When night came, he would point his little flashlight straight upwards, marveling at how the beam got lost in the night sky. Maybe that was what the two of them were, at the end of the day. Serena could keep shining and shining for as long as she wanted, until her battery died, and her light would just get swallowed in his dark expanse.

They'd both be better off, the logical part of him knew, if he just cut ties with her. It was the most sensible choice. She could find someone to inspire, in the most literal sense of the word. Someone to breathe life from her lips, the way she deserved. And he would be safe, the way Prometheus Cave is safe from the sun. Not that Prometheus himself wouldn't have given everything he had for something that burned as bright as she did.

Whether he'd be able to find the strength to actually push her away still remained to be seen. Even imagining it made him feel ill. He hoped that she would be furious with him. He hoped that she would scream at him, call him an ass and chase him out of the teahouse with an army of thorns and vines. Give him as much venom as she pleased, as long as he didn't have to see her cry. Please, if there is any justice in the world, don't let him make Serena Albright cry.

Moreover, the thought of leaving her made him outright miserable. He'd grown so deeply attached to her, he couldn't bear the thought of losing her. He cared for her too much, desired her too deeply to ever let her go. Not without a fight.

His gaze was finally pulled away from the flowers outside by movement on the sidewalk. Little pink sneakers, with lights in the soles, making their eager way to the entrance of Westergard and Ross. He groaned, looking to the ceiling like a martyr in a Renaissance painting.

Zoe.

He plastered on a brave face when she entered his office. Ordinarily, that would have been easy. For some reason, though, seeing her so happy only made him feel worse today.

"Hi Dad!" she chirped, smiling at him like he could do no wrong.

"Hey, Z. What brings you here, huh? Don't tell me, you're suing somebody, right? Looking for representation?"

Zoe laughed. "No! Grandma wanted to teach Miss Rena to make creme puffs, and I wanted to come with her. But I wanted to come see you, first."

He felt her words like a knife in his gut. "Going to the teahouse again?" He grimaced. "Don't you think you spend a little bit too much time in there?"

She shook her head. "I like it there. Grandma and Miss Rena let me help them in the kitchen, and Aaron taught me how to draw a horse yesterday, and sometimes I get to pet Kita while I read."

"That does sound... nice," he conceded. "But you're on summer break now. You should be playing outside, getting dirty, making friends."

"Miss Rena is my friend," Zoe said with a frown, and Jared felt his heart split in two.

"Yeah," he said quietly. "Yeah, I know she is."

"Do you like my new hair style?" Zoe turned her head from side to side with a dramatic flourish. The sides had been braided and pulled to the top of her head with colorful ribbons.

"Oh, yes. It's very fancy, Z. It suits you."

"Miss Rena did it for me this morning before school. She said all young ladies should learn how to braid hair. She's going to show me how to do it this week. She said it's the right passage."

"A rite of passage." He smiled weakly then sniffed,

gesturing to his computer. "You go on and have fun, yeah? I've got to get back to work."

Zoe nodded, already turning for the door. "I'll tell her you said hi!" she called over her shoulder, and he gritted his teeth.

He sighed heavily once she was gone. Zoe and Serena had become so close, so quickly. Zoe looked up to her, asked about her any day that she didn't visit Serena herself, which wasn't often anymore. And Serena fawned over Zoe like she was the most precious thing she'd ever seen. Could he really say this was a merciful choice? Sure, Serena had the means to destroy him, but was severing Zoe's ties to Serena any less gruesome?

His head ached, sharp behind his eyes. He needed a drink.

CHAPTER 27
SERENA

The chime of an antique bronze bell announced Serena's arrival at Noora's beachside cottage. As she waited, a brisk sea breeze rustled the leaves of nearby trees and, from the corner of her eye, she detected movement. What looked like a fleeting shadow seemed to dart behind the neighbor's house and disappear into a grove of weathered pine trees.

Serena studied the grove for a moment, wondering if she hadn't just imagined the moving shape. After another moment, the door in front of her sprung open and she was greeted with the fragrant scent of jasmine and rose.

"Serena." Noora's voice flowed like silken honey as she planted soft kisses on each of Serena's cheeks. Her raven-black hair flowed over one shoulder and was tied back with a bright ribbon.

"Thanks for seeing me," Serena said.

"Are you kidding, gorgeous? You're welcome anytime. Come on in."

Noora's living room was a sea of crisp white walls, with

ivory sofas punctuated by pillows in teal, saffron, and amethyst. Moroccan lanterns hung from the ceiling and heavy drapes filtered the light into a warm glow. Soft, worn Persian rugs spread underfoot, and on the walls were an array of old tapestries.

Gesturing to the low table set with bowls of nuts, spicy hummus, and bread, she disappeared into the kitchen to retrieve cups for the hot tea Serena had brought.

A vibrant set of Mediterranean tiles hanging on the far wall caught Serena's eye. "These are beautiful, Noor. Have you redecorated since the last time I was here?"

Noora laughed, her almond eyes twinkling with mischief. "Guilty as charged. It's my latest find from that cute little boutique downtown. You know, the one next to that gelato place?"

"Oh, the one with the new sweet ricotta cheese flavor?" Serena mused, her eyes lighting up.

"That's the one!" Noora said, nodding. "But seriously, Serena, between you and me, I might be developing a tiny shopping addiction."

Serena chuckled. "As long as it's only 'tiny,' I think you're safe. And speaking of new things, I love your earrings. Vintage?"

Noora touched the dangling piece, smiling appreciatively. "Grandma's collection. She had amazing taste." She popped a handful of cashews in her mouth as she settled onto the sofa. "But you aren't here to talk art and fashion. So what's up? You look a bit...flustered."

Taking a seat on the opposite sofa, Serena nodded slowly before telling her about the reading and the crow painting. Scrolling to a photograph on her phone, she placed it on the table. "This appeared on the teahouse wall. And combined with the omen in my reading, I'm a little worried."

Leaning in to examine the photo, Noora's gaze deepened, the lightness momentarily overshadowed by the weight of her thoughts.

"The tea leaf reading, I agree, was an omen. But this crow painted on the teahouse, this feels like something else entirely, Serena." Noora frowned.

"Like what?" Serena felt her brow furrow.

"It feels...bad, I don't know." Noora shifted on the cushion. "I can't guarantee anything, but let me see if I can pick up something else about it." Noora studied the photograph for a minute as she eased into a cross-legged position on the sofa. Closing her eyes, she sunk into meditation. Moments stretched as she breathed deeply, and the room seemed to contract with each inhalation.

Serena leaned back, eyes roaming the artwork on the walls as she waited. She was unsure if she was imagining it, but the gentle breezes that had been playing outside began to intensify, picking up momentum after a few minutes. The windows of the cottage started to rattle.

Turning her attention back to Noora, the witch's face suddenly contorted. Noora's hands flew to her throat, her breathing became labored as if an unseen force was suffocating her. Serena rushed over, attempting to bring her friend back from whatever vision held her. Noora managed to pull herself from the depths of her trance a few seconds later, gasping for air.

"Are you okay, Noora?"

Coughing, Noora looked up with round eyes and nodded. "I'm fine. Give me a minute." She exhaled and coughed again before taking a sip of the tea. After setting the cup down, she fixed her gaze on Serena. "I saw a crow... bound in chains. Flames rising behind it, burning everything."

"A crow coming after me from out of the flames? What, like some demon crow from hell coming to get me?"

Noora coughed again, rubbing her throat. She shook her head and took another sip of tea.

"No. Not a demon crow. Serena, *you* are the crow."

Serena's heart raced. "Me? What does that mean?"

"It means you're in danger."

CHAPTER 28
JARED

J ared was on his third Dark and Stormy when a familiar presence sidled up beside him at the bar.

"You've got a lot of nerve showing up here."

Jared smirked into his glass. "It's a free country."

"So they say." A tall, lean figure fell into the stool beside him, lazily flagging Royce down for a Moscow Mule. Jared frowned to himself, observing the stubby little ponytail at the nape of the other man's neck. Well, people had always said that Liam was the better looking cousin; maybe a nice head of hair would be the final nail in that coffin. As if the firefighter's physique Liam was sporting hadn't already neatly ended that debate.

"It's been a while, man," Liam said, smiling sidelong at him. "How's it going?"

He shrugged. "I've been better."

Liam huffed at that. "I'll say. You look like shit."

"Whoever told you that your honesty was refreshing was lying to you."

He laughed, and Jared couldn't help but smile. Liam always

had a knack for putting the people around him in a better mood. Since they were kids fighting over Nana's last sugar cookie, Liam had always been the type of person to just tear it in half and share.

"I heard you went on a trip."

Jared tossed back his drink. "Somebody's got enough free time on their hands to be gossiping about *me?*"

"Believe it or not. I'm jealous, to be honest," Liam said.

"I'm sure Royce would be happy to start a rumor about you, if you asked nicely."

The other man rolled his eyes. "Not of the gossip. Jealous of the trip! Do you have any idea how long it's been since I've been on a hiking trip? I think my Old Man was still checking us for ticks."

Jared chuckled. "Not quite, unless he was checking you for ticks when you were twenty-five."

"Well, we always have been very close."

Jared huffed. "I'm sorry, all right? I'll take you next time, how about that?"

"Hey, I said I wanted to go. I didn't say I wanted to go with *you.*"

Jared just nodded, a smile tugging at the corner of his lips.

"So what's eating at you?"

"Might be quicker to tell you what isn't," Jared replied with a world-weary sigh. "Remember when the biggest problem in this town was that no one knew how to use the roundabout over on Mason Avenue?"

"They still don't, and they never will. Only difference is now Pembrooke is crawling with sketchy characters, so I pay less attention to when I get to turn."

He arched a brow. "Sketchy characters? What do you mean?"

Liam laughed it off, but it was noticeably strained. "Yeah,

man, just look at you. You're the most suspicious guy I've ever seen."

Jared narrowed his eyes. Liam was hiding something, that much was clear. That wasn't like him. That sense of unease that had been following him like a shadow reared its head again.

"Is it Zoe?" Liam asked, his hands now fiddling with an empty straw wrapper. "I ran into Aunt Judith, the other day, and she mentioned Z was sick."

He coughed. "Uh, no, she's fine now. Full recovery, thanks to the miracle brews at The Velvet Teahouse," he muttered, surprised by how upset he sounded at the mention of the shop.

"That new herbal tea shop on Bailey?"

"That's the one."

Liam nodded. "I've been meaning to make an appearance there, myself," he said. "I was at the library last week and Zara was telling me all about it. She said that she went in with a major stress migraine. Ten minutes later, walked back out feeling like she could take on the world." He frowned, shifting in his seat awkwardly. "I offered to take her there, sometime, but..."

"Let me guess," Jared interjected. "She turned you down?"

"I got a soft 'maybe'."

Jared chuckled, shaking his head in fond exasperation. "You ever going to give up on that girl?" he asked.

His answering grin bordered on mischievous. "Not anytime soon."

"I'll never understand you, you know that?"

Liam shrugged. "What can I say, I'm a romantic."

"Speaking of romance," Royce interjected with a blooming smirk as he approached, setting two fresh drinks down on the bar. "When are you planning on bringing that girl of yours back in here, Jared?"

At that, Liam's wide eyes ping-ponged between Jared and Royce. "Since when do you have a girl, Jared?"

"It's nothing, really," he muttered, running a nervous hand through his hair.

Royce scoffed. "Didn't look like nothing to me. Poor Jared was blushing like it was prom night the whole time they were here."

Jared felt heat rushing up his neck. He coughed awkwardly. "I'd really rather not get into it," he muttered. "You know me, I don't like to kiss and tell."

It was more than that, truth be told. It didn't happen often, since Serena had marked the end of a considerable dry spell, but he always avoided matters of the heart in Royce's company. Guilt, that was all it boiled down to. Royce and Jared were friends, yes, but they were family before that. Willow was Royce's older sister. And even though years had passed since her death, it felt disrespectful to even *think* about falling for someone else in the presence of her family.

"So you *have* been kissing, then?" Liam prodded. "You just aren't keen on telling."

"She was a pretty girl, too," Royce added. "Long blonde hair, nice body, great smile. Chatty, too, not that Jared seemed to mind letting her run the conversation."

Liam whistled low, clapping Jared on the back with a laugh. "Makes you wonder what else she's running," he quipped. "What's her name?"

Jared groaned, finally accepting his defeat. "Serena, okay? Her name is Serena, is that satisfactory?"

His cousin frowned. "I don't think I know any Serenas."

"She's new in town," Royce supplied.

"New girl, huh?" Liam prodded. "Look at you, Jared! How'd you meet her?"

Jared rolled his eyes. Even talking about her made him feel

elated and miserable at once. "She runs that tea shop, actually. We're neighbors."

He was expecting to be met with further questions, more light jokes at his expense. Instead, he felt the air around them shift. Liam went pale.

"What?"

Liam cleared his throat, trying to disguise his sudden discomfort. "You're dating the girl that runs The Velvet Teahouse?" he asked.

Jared narrowed his eyes. "Yeah. Is that a problem?"

"No," he replied, shaking his head quickly. "No, it's... fine. Why wouldn't it be fine?"

Damn, that boy is a horrible liar. "Liam."

Liam sighed, pulling the lime wedge from the rim of his drink and squeezing its juice into the liquid before dropping the whole thing into the cup. He spoke in a rush. "I saw a guy poking around at Kurt's the other day, that's all. He was harassing people in the parking lot. Interrogating people about that tea shop."

"He was?"

"Mmhm. Scared the shit out of this girl. The little redhead who works down at the diner—what's her name? Something with an 'H', I think. And you know I can't stand seeing a lady upset, so I told him to back off."

That frantic spark of fear worked its way up his back again. "What was he saying about the teahouse?"

Liam shrugged. "Asking if she knew anything about the owner, I think. I don't know, the girl was too upset to really explain much. I think he might've threatened her."

Royce looked up from the shot glass he'd been cleaning. "He threatened the waitress?"

"No, he threatened Serena. Seemed like he wanted to get

his hands on her, anyway. And by the looks of the guy, it couldn't have been for anything good."

"What did the guy look like?" Jared asked. Any buzz he'd been cultivating was gone, replaced with a cold cocktail of fear and fury.

Liam blinked. He seemed surprised by the intensity in Jared's body language. "I definitely hadn't seen him before, for starters. Might've followed her from wherever she lived before she came to Pembrooke, who knows? Bald head, big nose, needed a shave. I don't know."

Jared tilted his head, watching his cousin's face. Liam wouldn't meet his eyes. "You're hiding something."

"No, I'm not."

"Liam, I've known you for your entire life. I was there the day you were born."

"You were *three*."

He tried to look trustworthy. "You don't need to lie to me."

After a long moment, Liam sighed. He spoke so softly that Jared barely heard him. "He had a tattoo on his arm. Of a black bird."

All of the air left Jared's lungs at once. "You're sure?"

"Yeah. Black bird wrapped in ropes, with red flames in the background. On his left forearm."

Jared just nodded, his eyes fixed on the bar. His mind was reeling. He felt his stomach turn. The image of his encounter with Colin rose to the forefront of his mind. Standing outside the abandoned distillery, looking every bit like he had trouble in mind. That figure beside him...

"It could just be a coincidence."

He tried hard to be reasonable. "It could," he muttered. He had a sinking feeling that it wasn't.

"Someone asked me about the teahouse, too," Royce said, and both men looked up at him. "He was wearing long sleeves, so I can't say for sure that it was the same guy you saw at Kurt's, but he was very interested in the owner."

"What did you tell him?" Jared asked. He hated how his voice wavered with the question, betraying the fear he felt.

"Nothing, of course. I didn't know that was your girl, but I heard about the break-in, and the last thing she needs is more trouble, after what happened with that intruder and everything."

He tried to breathe. "That's... that's good, Royce. And you said you didn't see his arms?"

"Jared." Royce leveled a serious look at him. "You don't think this is... one of the Inkers, do you?" Jared knew Royce could pick up his fear; he was gifted in that way.

Jared's mind snapped back five years. There had been only one witness to the murder ever found, despite his tireless searching. An elderly man, who lived alone up in the mountains. It had taken Jared weeks to track him down and, by the time he managed to talk to the man, dementia had started making a wreck of the memory. But one detail stood out, perfectly preserved in Jared's mind for all these years.

"About five of them," the witness had said during brief bouts of lucidity. Five people in black robes, hauling a woman up the mountain. He'd tried to call the police, but he could tell that they didn't believe him. They'd asked him a handful of questions, barely written anything down, and left.

Jared had begged him, desperate and despairing, to search his thoughts. To reach, as deeply as he could, for details. Something, anything, that could help him find the people who killed his wife. In the end, only one useful piece of information came to mind.

Black birds. All five of them had tattoos of black birds tied in ropes inked on their arms. A symbol of the Brotherhood of the Crow's Flame, he later learned. Witches sometimes called members of the Brotherhood "Inkers" because of the tattoos.

From his research, he'd gathered that every Inker who'd killed a witch was given one of these tattoos. Worn like a badge of honor. Willow hadn't been the first kill for any of them, and he felt horribly sure that she hadn't been the last.

The Brotherhood believed in the purity of humanity and saw any form of magic as an aberration against God's creation. Inkers utilized the symbol of a crow tied in ropes to represent their cause. The crow signified the cunning and deceptive nature of witches, the ropes a means to capture them, and the flames stood as a symbol of the righteous path they believed they were treading in eradicating witches.

Jared set his jaw. "Either way, I'm not about to take any chances. Keep your ears to the ground for me, yeah? Let me know if you hear anything else that sounds suspicious."

Royce nodded. "I will."

He turned to Liam. "Same goes for you. Even if it doesn't seem worth noting, trust your gut."

"You've got it, boss. What about you? You look like you're on a mission."

Already standing, Jared made for the door. "You could say that," he called over his shoulder.

"Do you think Biscuit and Muffin will get lonely?"

Jared chuckled, ruffling her hair. "No, they'll keep each other company. They're friends, right?"

Zoe frowned, holding her favorite stuffed animal tightly. "I just don't want them to feel left out, since I'm only taking Scooter."

"It's just for a few days, Z. They'll forgive you."

After a moment, Zoe nodded, watching as he packed her socks into her suitcase.

"You and grandma are going to have so much fun," Jared told her. "I know you haven't spent much time with your Great Aunt Helen, but she is pretty cool. You won't even have time to feel homesick."

"Okay," she mumbled, squeezing Scooter once more.

He smiled, trying hard to cheer her up. "And when you get back, you can tell me about everything you got to see."

She stared up at him, her brown eyes suddenly hard. "You're not coming with us?"

He smiled sadly at Zoe, brushing her thicket of curls from her face. "Not this time, sweetie. I've got some things I need to take care of here."

"Well, can't we go visit Great Aunt Helen when you get all of your work done? So you can come, too?"

"I'm sorry," he sighed. "Really. But you've got to go without me."

Jared winced when her eyes began to well with tears. "No! I don't want to go without you!"

He dragged a weary hand down his face. "Look, we can go on a trip together before the end of the summer, okay? I promise. We can go to Sky Kingdom. Remember that amusement park down south with the spinning cups ride that you like? You can invite anyone you want."

Zoe sniffed. "Can we bring Miss Rena?"

"Sure," Jared replied, even as his chest ached horribly. "We can ask her, but I can't make any promises."

His mouth turned sour the moment the word left his lips. *Promises.* He hadn't been very good with promises, lately. Making them or keeping them.

When he turned for the door with Zoe's suitcase in hand,

236

he found his mother watching him, chewing her lip in the threshold.

"You're going to be okay, right?" he asked her. "If you need me to send someone with you—"

She held up a hand. "I'll be all right. I'm just worried about you."

"Don't be," he said, grunting as he began to haul Zoe's suitcase out to his mother's car. "Like I said, it could be nothing. But I'd rather know you two are somewhere safe, either way."

His mother sighed, watching him close her trunk. "I'll call you when we get to Portland, all right? Service isn't great up at my sister's place, but I promise I'll get a message to you."

He faltered for a moment before folding her into a hug. "Stand on the roof if you have to," he quipped, trying like hell to lighten the air.

Jared tried to pull away, but his mother held him tighter for just a moment. "Don't get hurt. Please?"

He forced a tight chuckle. "I'll do my best."

CHAPTER 29
SERENA

It was peaceful in the teahouse, that afternoon. Steady. Enough work to keep Serena's hands from being idle, to keep her wandering mind at least somewhat on task. She tried to be thankful for that. To find the easy contentment that she'd been feeling lately. It wasn't forthcoming, though, and in its absence she realized she felt worse than she did before it came. Perhaps ignorance was bliss, in this case.

Still, she found joy in small doses, just as she always had. The banana nut bread came out perfectly this morning, and Emela slept through the night with no dreams to speak of. And it was raining outside, which was good for the plants. The sound of it tapping against the sidewalk soothed her frayed nerves, and brought in passersby seeking shelter. And once they stepped inside and took a breath, they simply had to stay a while.

But regret was beginning to tug at her mind. Perhaps she had made a mistake thinking she could ever settle long term in one place. Perhaps it was just her fate in life to keep moving, a gypsy spirit at heart.

It didn't help matters to think that becoming a fried crow was on the menu if she stayed in town.

Aaron leaned on the counter, elbows braced as he watched the rain. The Queen Anne's Lace outside shook with it, ducking their heads somewhat each time a droplet tapped their petals.

"You know," he said. "You should really start serving coffee."

She lifted a brow. "Medicinal coffee?"

"Sure. Cures caffeine withdrawal."

Serena snorted, adding a spoonful of sugar to the mug of Marigold Tea and passing it to him. Smelled a little... potent, but it promoted inspiration. "I have plenty of caffeinated teas already," she argued.

"Might be good for business, that's all," Aaron said. "Plus, it might draw that boyfriend of yours in, since he seems so against drinking tea."

Serena stiffened at his words, feeling Aaron's eyes studying her.

"Don't tell me he's still giving you the cold shoulder."

She shrugged, peering through the windows at the camellias across the street. "I'm not really sure what's going on, but whatever it is, I have a bad feeling about it."

The bell above the door chimed. Another customer entered, wiping his boots on the mat before settling at the counter, dripping wet. He swiped water from his shaved head.

"Welcome to The Velvet Teahouse," Serena said, trying to inject some warmth into her tone. "What can I get started for you?"

The man didn't respond, looking around the shop with restless eyes. She wondered at first if he might be deaf, but her intuition told her otherwise. Serena cast a wary glance Aaron's way, and he shrugged.

"I'll just... get you started with a water, okay? Take your time."

Serena peered at him from the kitchen as she filled his glass, watching his body language. He drummed his fingers on the countertop, frowning hard at the crystals on the windowsill. Something about him made her anxious.

She set the water in front of him, then grabbed a detailed menu from beneath the counter. She thought she heard Kita barking in her upstairs apartment.

"That's a cool tattoo," Aaron said.

The man grunted, moving to hide his forearm from view, but Aaron leaned across the way to address him.

"Did you have it done in the area? I know a few artists, so I might know whoever did it. Is that a blackbird?"

At that, the man finally spoke, his voice low and throaty. "It's a crow."

Freezing in place, Serena tilted her head to observe the artwork. Kita was scratching at the upstairs door now, trapped inside the apartment where Serena had left her after lunch.

"Nice. Crows are very emotionally intelligent animals, you know," Serena said. She drew closer, trying to get a better look at the tattoo. "They're one of the few animals that can recognize individual human faces. The crows in Pembrooke probably know certain people, and have opinions on them. Isn't that interesting?"

Chains were criss-crossed over the crow's breast. Behind it were fire flames. Serena's heart nearly stopped. She forced herself to remain calm until she could evaluate what this man wanted.

"Sure. Very interesting." The man looked up at her, narrowing his eyes slightly. "You know, I've heard all about you, Serena Albright," he said. "People say you've got healing brews."

Her smile vanished. "Is that what they say?" Kita was growling now.

He nodded slowly. "They say they're like magic."

There was something in the way he said "magic" that made the hair on her arms rise. "Is there something you're suffering from?" she prodded. "I can try to pull something together."

"Yeah, actually," he said slowly. "I, uh, I've got a real mean cough." He punctuated his statement by clearing his throat roughly. "You got something for that?"

Serena tilted her head. His cough was clearly performative. "Sure. Give me just a second, I'll get something started."

As she fished for the proper ingredients, she heard Aaron making another brave attempt at conversation. "I've always wanted a tattoo," he said. "I want to get a crab, on my arm."

"Uh-huh."

"For my Zodiac sign, that is. I'm a Cancer."

"Mm."

"Does your tattoo mean anything, or..."

"How about you mind your business, kid," he said. There was a harsh edge to his voice, and Serena made quick work of returning to the counter.

"Your tea is brewing," she said. "It'll be just a few minutes."

"Thanks," he said, fixing her with a very tight smile. His teeth were perfectly straight, but they somehow seemed odd in his face. Like his mouth was cramped. "Say, what did you put in it, anyway?"

She tried to smile back, despite her discomfort. "Violet and anise," she replied. "They're good for respiratory health."

"Um-hmm. Anything else?"

"Are you trying to learn about herbal medicine?" Serena asked, lifting a brow.

He paused for half a breath too long before answering.

"Yeah. And you seem like an expert to me. Can you cure… pneumonia?"

She tilted her head. "I could recommend some teas for symptom management," she answered carefully. "Do you know someone with—"

"What about depression? Strep throat? Yellow Mountain Fever?"

As he spoke, his eyes never left her. She swallowed, glancing sidelong at Aaron. The artist looked every bit as uneasy as she felt. "Listen, I'm not sure what you've heard—"

"You should give me a demonstration. Show me how you do it."

"There's really nothing to show," Serena blurted, trying hard to keep her mounting anxiety from being too obvious. "I just select a blend of herbs from my stock with the right medicinal properties, and brew them like any other tea. It isn't anything special."

She walked briskly back to the kitchen, pouring his tea. He frowned hard at the cup when she set it in front of him, inhaling the steam curiously, but not moving to take a sip.

"Somebody told me that they came to your shop instead of going to the doctor last week," he said, giving her an almost threatening look. "What do you think about that?"

Her mouth turned sour. "I would never claim that my teas are a replacement for healthcare, if that's what you're implying."

He held up his palms in defense. "All I'm saying is that people all around Onyx Country are making some pretty bold claims about you." He pointed an index finger at her, showing his teeth again. "Enough to make a man curious."

"You can't control what people say, unfortunately. I stopped trying a long time ago." She didn't smile back when she spoke, just held his eyes. Didn't even blink, so he would know that she wasn't afraid.

"Show me what you really put in that tea."

"I think you should be going," Aaron interrupted, regarding him with hardened eyes. He wasn't big enough for the attempt at intimidation to hold much weight, but it seemed to make the man realize that there were other customers in the shop. Witnesses.

He sniffed sharply, pushing himself back from the counter. Serena's eyes tracked the movement, watching him shove his hand back into his coat pockets. "You'll see me again, Miss Albright," he said quietly, with a quick glance at the stairs where Kita's barks were echoing. "Very soon, you can count on that."

Serena didn't breathe until the door closed behind him. Aaron was visibly tense.

"The hell was that guy's problem?" he asked. Serena didn't respond. "You felt it too, right? He had like, really bad vibes." Aaron shivered, shaking the energy from his shoulders, and frowned at her. "Even Kita seems freaked out. Serena? You okay?"

She coughed, trying to regain her bearings. "Yeah," she said, though she was sure she didn't sound at all convincing. "Yeah, I'm fine. Just... got a bad feeling, I guess. Same as you."

It wasn't technically a lie, but it was a dramatic understatement. That man knew she was a witch, that much was obvious. And he wasn't happy about it. *He wasn't a Lens, was he?* No. Jared already told her that he wouldn't turn her in. *He wouldn't go back on his word like that, right?* And either way, that man didn't exactly exude the air of a respected council member just doing his due diligence. His presence seemed to spell chaos, not order.

"Yeah, big time. Listen, I'm going to stick around a little later than usual today, okay? I know I'm not exactly a knight in shining armor, but after what happened with that Park guy a while back... I'd just feel more comfortable knowing you had a friend here with you."

She smiled. "Thanks. You're sweet, you know that?"

"And you've always been a good friend to me," he countered. "My mother would be rolling in her grave if she knew I didn't keep an eye on you. I mean, she's alive, but she'd dig a grave and lie in it."

"I promise I'm okay, though," Serena said with a small laugh.

Aaron rolled his eyes. "I insist. Just until close and you lock the door. And if something like this happens again, call if you feel scared."

She sighed. "Aaron—"

"It doesn't have to be me," he bargained. "Call your Legal Lover, have him stay the night. I just don't like the idea of you being by yourself."

Serena could tell by the look in his eye that he wouldn't be moved on the topic. Truth be told, she was already considering calling Lily and Emela next door if she needed backup. No offense to Aaron, but having a deconstructionist and an air witch on her side would prove far more beneficial.

"Fine. If it'll make you feel better, I will call someone. Now, if it pleases Your Highness, I'm getting back to work." She rushed upstairs to open the door for Kita.

In the end, Aaron didn't need to stay. Jared burst into the teahouse two hours before closing, with something like growing horror etched into his handsome features.

Admittedly, she wasn't exactly thrilled to see him, still feeling hurt from his neglect. As his eyes locked with hers, she beckoned him back towards the kitchen. She didn't speak until they were well away from prying eyes.

"What are you doing here?" she said.

Without a word, Jared pulled her close. Pressing his forehead to hers, he closed his eyes and rested there for a long moment.

"What's wrong? What happened?" she said.

"Come home with me tonight," he said softly. "Please."

She blinked. "What? Why? I thought you didn't want Zoe to know about us yet."

He pulled away, pushing back his hair with a heavy hand. "She's not there," he said. "My mom took her to Portland; we've got family there."

"Portland? Since when? Judith never mentioned any trip."

"No, it was more of a spur-of-the-moment thing."

Serena stepped back a pace. "Tell me what's going on."

"Just say you'll come over, yeah?" he said in lieu of a reply. "Or I could stay here, if you're worried about Kita. I don't mind, but say you'll spend the night with me."

"I don't know, maybe. I promised Aaron I'd find some company. Had a really shady guy come into the shop today. It freaked both of us out."

Jared froze, and she swore the room became a few degrees cooler. "Shady, how?"

"He just seemed like bad news," she said. "He was asking a lot of questions about the teas' healing properties. And I've had a few people come in and ask these sorts of questions, but I couldn't shake the feeling that he..." she leaned closer to him, lowering her voice. "Well, that he *knew*, you know?"

"What did you tell him?" he asked.

"Nothing! I kicked him out! Well, Aaron kicked him out, but I—"

"Did he know your name? Did he threaten you? What did he look like?"

"Whoa, easy!" she said, a bit taken aback. "Nothing happened, he left. Yes, he knew my name. No, he didn't threaten me. He was a bald guy, a little heavy, with a tattoo on his arm."

Jared looked to the ceiling and swore. "Serena, I need you to listen to me. Actually heed my warning, just this once. You're not leaving this teahouse without someone going with you, is that clear?"

She glanced up in shock. "Why not?"

"Because you're in danger." His eyes darted around the store, studying the faces of the few patrons sitting at tables. "That man is a member of the Brotherhood."

She swallowed. "The witch hunting cult? You're sure?"

He nodded. "That tattoo on his arm, was it a crow tied in chains?"

She nodded.

"It's a symbol of the Inkers. You only get one if you've killed before. Killed... one of our kind."

Serena's blood ran cold. "He... he told me that he would be back," she said. "What do we do now?"

"I'll tell you what I'm going to do," Jared all but growled. "I'm not letting you out of my damned sight, and if he comes near you again, I'm going to kill him."

The conviction in his voice told her that there was no room for argument. She didn't want to try. "You can sit and wait in the Goddess Corner," she offered with a nod.

He frowned down at her. "Are you trying to lure him in?"

"Why not? You saw what I did to Colin Parker. I'll be fine."

"Serena, I can't let you get actively involved in this."

She looked up at him, her features hard and serious. "If they're coming after me, then I'm obviously already involved. Besides, these are the people that killed part of your family. That means we are both involved."

CHAPTER 30
JARED

J ared felt like a caged lion as he hid in the shadows of the
Goddess Corner.

Kita joined him, sitting at his feet and awaiting her
signal. He'd never thought of himself as a dog—or wolf—
person, but as the hours ticked by, he found himself scratching
the timber wolf behind the ears. He was grateful for her presence, he realized. She was keeping him calm and focused.
Somewhat.

His eyes followed Serena about the teahouse, tracing her
every movement, as he lurked in the shop's darkest corner. He
kept silent attention. But his mind, called to rapt alertness by
force of circumstance, was not content to watch for the visibly
suspicious alone. In fact, to his eye, every stranger seemed to be
worth observation. Each woman who hovered near the counter
a moment too long, every man who looked at Serena a bit too
closely. It was a blind, desperate sort of paranoia, one that
turned his mouth acrid and made him feel cramped in his skin.

It felt pointless to deny it anymore, the reason why he felt prepared to rip to shreds whoever touched her. To tear into them with tooth and claw. After five long years, he would finally confront Willow's killers. The rage inside him threatened to blaze into an inferno. He knew he needed to keep things under control.

Yet it wasn't only his past with the Brotherhood that threatened to send him spinning out of control, though a part of him wished that it was. Were it that simple, it might be easier to breathe. What laid at the heart of this was not just vengeance, but devotion. A territorial sort of affection, a mirror that he found displayed the best of himself at the price of at least a fraction of his sanity.

He was aware of the obvious link between Willow's and Serena's fates. How he had not been there to protect Willow. But that he'd been granted the chance for a divine do-over of sorts, the opportunity to keep Serena safe from a similar fate. And how he was afraid to admit that occasionally Willow's and Serena's faces would blur together in his dreams.

He was in love with Serena Albright. And he'd never been the sort of man to do anything by half measures. When his mind was set to a task, then it was done. So, if he was falling for her, then let him plummet. Let him stare from this empty room, challenging strangers with his gaze. From strangers onto acquaintances, until he found himself feeling jumpy when even friends approached her. Like danger could come from anywhere, at any time, in any form.

When the teahouse finally closed for the night, she made a point to leave the door unlocked, looking every bit innocent and unassuming as she cleaned the shop and prepared it for the night.

"It's rude to stare, you know." She didn't look up when she spoke, still fully focused on her own reflection in the countertop as she wiped it. He could see the smile teasing the corners of her lips.

"It's what I do, though," he replied from the darkness. "Keeping a watchful eye."

"Can I expect you to be so watchful in the future? Or can I only count on your attention by playing your damsel in distress?"

"I don't think of you like that. You know that."

She nodded at the counter. "I know."

"I respect you."

Serena snorted. "That makes one of us."

He huffed, standing from his chair with a strained grunt. He stretched his neck this way and that, Kita following him out into the teahouse proper. "If this is disrespect, then I look forward to being on the receiving end of your admiration one day."

"Hmm. Maybe someday you'll get to."

Jared moved to join her behind the counter. He watched her, the two of them coexisting in mostly comfortable silence as she went about her usual nightly tasks. His eyes traced the contours of her arms, her shoulders narrow but stronger than most, her fingers long and delicate. He felt an all too familiar urge to map the constellations that dotted her back, to kiss the shadows that were cast by her lashes.

"What if nothing happens?"

He glanced around at the dim shop. "Then I'll still stay, as long as you still want me to."

"Okay," she said, rolling her shoulders as he stepped behind her and kissed the side of her neck. "Tell you what, I have a special herbal blend I've been working on. You want to help me try it out?"

"What does it do?"

Serena smirked at him. "You'll have to try it and find out."

Jared gave her a look of interest, making his way back to the kitchen. "And what exactly does this new blend contain?"

"Go back to the pantry. There's a mason jar on the top shelf labeled 'Aphrodite'. Could you be a doll and fetch it for me?"

He laughed, not hesitating to open the pantry door. "Aphrodite. I like the sound of that one," he said. "Right away."

The pantry was a cramped, dimly lit little space lined with long metal shelves, filled to bursting with various jars, tins, and boxes. Baking ingredients along one wall, alchemical agents on the other. He peered at the top shelf, Kita nosing eagerly at a box of brown sugar on a lower shelf.

"You wouldn't happen to know if there's a step ladder in here, would you?" he asked the wolf with a cautious smile. The wolf glanced up and trotted over to the door. Jared closed it and discovered the ladder, propped up against the wall. "Thanks, Kita." He set the ladder up in front of the shelves, climbed up, and observed the jars. They were labeled with large, loopy letters.

"Geez, Kita, your mother has the worst handwriting I've ever seen."

The wolf whined and settled into a sitting position.

He plucked the Aphrodite jar from the shelf, casting a bemused look at the army of blends.

"Hey," he called out to Serena. "What's 'Wild Oats' do? Sounds interesting."

When she didn't reply, he climbed down and moved toward the door. "Serena?"

Kita was already standing. She growled, then, her hackles raised as she glared at the door.

Jared's heart stopped, the mason jar shattering on the stone floor.

CHAPTER 31
SERENA

S erena was crouched behind the counter when the door creaked open, the bell in the door frame ostensibly silenced. Rising, her head flicked toward the entrance, anticipating the man from before. She saw nothing.

The subtle scent of sage from the earlier evening's cleansing wafted around her as she strained her ears, listening.

"Serena?" Jared's voice prodded from the pantry, and she ignored him, eyes fixed on the open front door. With slow, measured steps, she moved to push it closed. She listened for signs of life in the silence between the heavy beats of her heart.

When she turned around, she yelped as the world around her seemed to pause. There was a man standing just feet from her: the Inker with the crow tattoo from earlier.

Swallowing the lump of fear that had lodged itself in her throat, she forced a brittle smile. "Sorry, we're closed for the night," she managed, trying to mask her nervousness.

His cold eyes raked over her. "I'm not a customer," he replied. As he lunged towards her, fingers reaching out to snatch her wrist, a protective rage bubbled within her.

"Neither am I," Jared's deep voice echoed through the room.

CHAPTER 32
JARED

A stocky man was holding Serena by the wrist when Jared emerged from the pantry.

The man whipped around to see Jared exiting the kitchen, with Kita following close behind. Jared closed the space between them with a few long strides.

The two of them had never met, and yet Jared knew this man better than he realized. On some level, he felt as though he would've recognized him anywhere. A sickening kind of certainty, like calling into a dark house that someone knows isn't empty.

The man with the black bird tattoo moved quicker than Jared had expected and, in the blink of an eye, he had Serena gripped in his arms, the blade of a long knife pressed to her neck. Kita, who had wrapped her jaws around Blackbird's boot backed off, understanding the danger her mistress was in. Serena struggled against him, summoning a cluster of gnarled roots from the floor. The moment they made contact with Blackbird's body, though, they withered and died.

Jared stared at him, mouth agape. Blackbird just laughed.

"You like that?" he jeered. "Your pal, Colin, told us all about your little trick with the thorns. But, you know, a while ago we found a witch who was courteous enough to whip up a quick countermeasure for such occasions." He narrowed his eyes at Jared, pressing the knife deeper into Serena's neck. Jared's eyes flickered to a thin, silver chain suspending a small black stone that was draped around the man's thick neck. "All it took was a little... firm persuasion. Black tourmaline, you ever heard of it? Wards off ill intent. With the right spell, it makes for a wonderful talisman."

"Look who's using magic now," Jared said.

"We don't defile ourselves by practicing your dark arts. But we don't have a problem borrowing your trinkets if we can use them as shields."

"Whatever you need to tell yourself. What about the little ritual you performed outside the teahouse?"

"You saw that, did you, Loverboy? Just a little ceremony we like to perform for our new marks. No magic involved, but we like to sprinkle a little black tourmaline around. Anyway, your friends from hell can't touch us with your dark magic. Not anymore."

Jared snarled. "Be careful, pal. Keep saying my people are from hell, you might just bring out the devil in me."

Blackbird cocked his head, staring him down. "You a devil, then?"

Jared took a slow step closer, eyes fixed on Serena. "From time to time."

"Jared," Serena squeaked, as the knife pushed deeper into her neck.

"I know who you are," the other man said, not paying the woman in his arms any mind. "And I remember your wife."

Fists clenched, Jared gritted his teeth.

Blackbird chuckled. "She was a fighter, that one. Nearly

clawed my buddy's eye out, if you can believe it. Funniest thing, though, she changed her tune real quick when we told her that we'd go looking for her daughter if she didn't come quietly."

A twitch of his mouth was the only thing that betrayed Jared's pain.

"She barely struggled after that. Wasn't even fun. *Almost* wasn't, anyway."

"You shut your mouth, before I shut it for you."

"How about this one, hmm?" the other man prodded, shaking Serena slightly. The action loosened his hold on her, but he was too focused on tormenting Jared to notice. "You think your new succubus will fight back? Or will she submit, like the last one?"

Whatever Blackbird was planning to say next was interrupted by the sound of Serena's elbow making contact with his stomach. He only lost his footing for a moment, but it was enough for her to slip out of his hold.

Jared lurched forward, tackling them both to the ground, before punching the Inker's face. After shoving Jared off, Blackbird jumped to his feet. Kita darted in and sunk her teeth into his leg, snarling as she yanked on it. Blackbird screamed in pain. Jared delivered another blow to the Inker's jaw. The Inker yanked his leg free, and sent a sharp kick to Jared's gut. When Jared doubled over, the man caught him by the hair and hit him once, twice, three times. Jared tasted the bright, coppery flavor of blood blooming in his mouth and spat in Blackbird's direction. Darting to the side, Jared avoided Blackbird's next lunge, but didn't see the wolf by his feet. Tripping over the animal, Jared sprawled to the ground. Blackbird was on top of him in a second, his hands wrapped tight around his neck.

A low thud sounded above him, and the man released his grip so suddenly that Jared struggled to get his bearings. On the hardwood floor at his feet, dropped a statue of a kingfisher, stained with blood.

Blackbird wobbled to his feet, holding the back of his head. Evidently realizing that he couldn't win a fight against both of them plus a wolf, he stumbled blindly towards the door. Jared chased him out into the street, his protective rage carrying him beyond any pain or exhaustion. Blackbird ducked into a nearby alley, Jared in hot pursuit, but when he came to a stop in the alleyway, the other man had vanished.

Serena followed Jared out into the street, trailing behind him with heavy bootfalls. Kita stayed glued to her side.

"He's gone," Jared breathed, air bubbling past his lips.

Her hand on his shoulder was like a balm to his frayed nerves. "Come inside. Let me fix your face."

He obeyed after a moment, trailing behind her in a haze. There was something in Serena's voice that caught his attention. A tone at once unfamiliar, but which filled him with an abstract sort of dread.

CHAPTER 33
JARED

"Stay still."

Jared flinched, anyway, when she held the disinfectant to the cut on his cheek. Blackbird must have had a ring on his finger, in addition to the tourmaline amulet, because there were two curved marks near his jawline. She dabbed at them with a cotton pad soaked in an herbal concoction, tenderly cleaning the cuts before placing a bandage over them. He shot her a crooked smile as she stood over him like a mother hen.

"Thanks."

Serena smiled weakly. Jared's face softened.

"You okay?" he asked, his voice barely a whisper.

She nodded, her gaze momentarily flicking towards his wounds before returning to meet his eyes. "Yeah. Yeah, I'm fine. He barely touched me."

He was grateful. God, was he grateful.

But her eyes broke away, fixating instead on the open balcony doors and the night beyond.

"Did you hear something?" Jared said, turning in his chair.

"Nah. Just the ocean." Serena tilted her head, her lips curving into a poignant smile. "It calms me. The sound of the waves, the endless expanse of stars. It makes everything else seem... insignificant."

He observed her for a long moment, his gaze flitting over her profile, absorbing every detail. "Yet, here I am, thinking that in the midst of this vast universe, you're the most significant thing to me."

Serena turned slowly to face him, her eyes locking with his in a gaze that bridged the silence between them. She smiled, then leaned down to press her lips against his.

In that prolonged moment, she reached out to wrap her arms around the back of his neck. He wrapped his own arms around her waist, and pulled her into his lap. They held each other for a long moment, breathing in each other's scent and taking comfort from the other. He felt her heartbeat against his, and became aware of a quiver of fear, the kind that comes with the realization of how deeply another person has burrowed into one's soul, and the vulnerability that such love entails.

A part of him ached to keep his arms around her, to offer her solace from their tumultuous night. He wanted to drown himself in her comforting presence, to shut out the harsh reality that lurked just beyond the confines of the room. There was a strange, unspoken intensity between them, and for a fleeting moment, he let himself get lost in it.

Serena pulled back slightly, and their eyes locked again, this time with an intensity that felt like it could ignite the very air around them. She caressed his cheek and leaned toward him. Her first kiss was tender, a gentle brush of lips that spoke of gratitude and relief, a silent thank you for the shared ordeal they had just survived. It was a balm to the rawness of their frayed nerves.

Then, as if driven by the undercurrent of adrenaline still coursing through their veins, she kissed him again, her second kiss deeper, more fervent and consuming, as she pulled him tighter against her. It was as though all the fear and tension from the attack were being transformed into a fierce declaration of life, of survival. Their emotions cascaded between them in an unspoken exchange, a blur of relief, fear, love, and an overwhelming desire to just be alive, there, in the moment. Jared's body came alive in a way he hadn't planned on as his hands slid up her back and then down the sides of her arms.

They surfaced for air, panting, before they drew together again, attracted as if by magnetic force. But when the third kiss erupted between them, it was frantic and fiery.

They grasped and clawed at each other, Serena running her hands underneath his shirt to stroke his chest. Jared ran his hands over her shoulders and down the front of her chest.

The straps of her tank top fell over her shoulders, the edge of her top slipping down her arm. His gaze followed the fabric as it slid lower, over the soft slope of her chest, revealing the elegant lines of her collarbones, the gentle swell of her breasts.

Exhaling a shaky breath, he felt lost in the beauty of her. The sight of her creamy bare skin under the muted light, the raw vulnerability in her eyes, stirred a fierce protectiveness in him, intertwining with the desire coursing through his veins.

"Serena..." He whispered her name like a prayer, like a promise, his lips returning to meet hers. His thumb traced the edge of the top, the small distance that separated her bare skin from the fabric.

He gently pulled her top down further, baring her to his eyes. His fingertips traced a path along her bare skin, tracing the contours of her body, as if reassuring himself that she was real. As he did, he felt the rise and fall of her chest, the hitch in her breath, the electricity sparking between them. A soft gasp escaped her lips as she watched him.

His fingers traced over her bare skin, his touch soft, almost reverent, eliciting a shiver from her. Serena was so fucking beautiful, her skin glowing in the soft light, her eyes reflecting his own desire.

He brought his hands up to gently cup her, his thumbs brushing across the centers of her breasts. His touch elicited a soft gasp from her, her breath coming faster as her body responded to him.

Leaning down, he pressed a soft kiss to the swell of her breast. Serena's hands tangled in his hair. He kissed her more fervently now, sucking gently on her nipples, making her gasp and squirm beneath him. Her breath came in ragged pants, her body arching into his touch.

The taste of her skin was intoxicating, sweet and addictive. He took his time, savoring the feel of her under him, her soft whimpers and sighs encouraging him. His lips trailed from one breast to the other, not wanting to leave any part of her untouched.

In the heat of their shared silence, Jared's hand trailed down from her waist, his fingers dancing lightly over the material of her skirt. His fingers traveled further down, reaching the hem and hitching it up. Serena bit her lip, her body tensing in anticipation.

Sliding one hand beneath the band of her panties, his touch seemed to send sparks of electricity coursing through her body. She gasped, her fingers digging into his shoulder as he explored her. His thumb brushed over her sensitivity and a low moan escaped her lips.

With growing urgency, his fingers peeled off her panties. Jared stood and lifted Serena onto the kitchen counter in one swift motion, before hiking her skirt up around her waist. Dropping to his knees, he brought his lips to the center of her pleasure between her thighs.

As his mouth connected with her core, his tongue traced a delicate path that sent a fresh wave of pleasure rippling through her. Sighing, Serena's eyes darkened, and his breath caught at the sight and sound of her. It drove him nearly mad with desire. He wanted to hear more of those sounds, wanted to see more of those expressions.

Serena rubbed his head, her body quivering in response to his explorations. Each glide of his tongue sent her spiraling closer and closer to the edge. Finding the rhythm that made her breath hitch, he continued his relentless pace.

She gasped his name, a sweet symphony to his ears, driving him on as he felt her body tense in anticipation. Her fingers threaded through his hair, pulling him closer, her hips instinctively rising to meet him.

He increased the pressure, his tongue circling the sensitive bundle of nerves that had her writhing. Her entire body tensed, a bow pulled taut before release. And then, with a cry that seemed to echo around the room, she shattered around him, her body left trembling with the aftershocks of her release.

He rose to his feet. In a swift motion, Jared rid himself of his pants, the fabric pooling around his feet. A raw desire took hold as he met her eyes, filled with a mutual need that spoke volumes.

He moved closer, the air between them charged. Serena's fingers reached out, trailing up his chest, her touch burning a path. Jared caught her hands in his, pressing them to his heart, letting her feel the erratic rhythm that her mere presence sparked in him.

Standing there, naked and vulnerable before her, he felt a powerful mix of emotions: lust, yes, but also tenderness and an overwhelming affection. This woman had seen him at his worst, had cared for him when he was injured, and still wanted him.

Bridging the gap between them, he aligned himself with her. He held her gaze as he pushed forward, sinking inside. A gasp left Serena's lips, her hands instinctively clutching his upper arms as she accommodated him.

Jared stilled for a moment, savoring the feeling of her around him. The intensity of their connection was overwhelming, causing a rush of sensation that made him groan out loud. He reveled in her tightness, her warmth, the sensation of her body yielding to his and, as he glanced up, he saw in her eyes only desire, a fierce need matching his own.

Their rhythm was slow at first, in a pace that brought mutual pleasure. He moved within her, each stroke filled with purpose and emotion. Serena responded ardently, her hips meeting his with each thrust, her breath hitching whenever he hit a particularly sensitive spot.

All thoughts of the attack, of the danger that lurked beyond the walls of Serena's teahouse, faded away. The world outside ceased to exist. All that mattered was the woman before him, the woman he was connected to in the most intimate of ways.

As he moved, his pace and intensity increased. A primal urgency possessed him, and he dimly worried if he was being too rough, though he couldn't bring himself to stop. Reassured by her raw moans of pleasure, he drove them relentlessly toward their peaks.

In the raw aftermath of the night's harrowing attack, their shared surrender to desire felt like an act of rebellion, a defiance of the violence that had tried to fracture their peace. Their bodies moved together, each touch, each caress, a protest against the fear that had sought to consume them.

It was a validation of their existence, a refusal to be robbed of the simple, profound joy of human connection. He dimly figured it was their way of coping with the swirling maelstrom of emotions—the fear, the anger, the relief—and a means of grounding themselves, both to each other, and to the very essence of life: love, desire, and pleasure.

CHAPTER 34
SERENA

In the dawn's light, the sound of keys dropping on the nightstand woke Serena from her slumber. Cracking open an eye, she turned her head as Jared sunk onto the bed next to her.

"Where'd you go?"

"Just did a quick patrol of town. No sign of our friend from last night." He sighed and kissed her cheek. "Made you an omelet."

Grinning, she reached out to stroke his cheek. "Yum. How's your face?"

"It's fine, thanks. Though I would've been screwed if you hadn't gone savage with that little kingfisher statue."

"Doubt it. Of course you wouldn't have been in danger at all if it wasn't for me." Her mouth twisted bitterly. "It wasn't heroics, it was... cleaning up my own mess."

"Serena, you didn't do anything—"

"He's going to come back, isn't he?"

He studied the floor for a few seconds. "We gave him a

pretty good scare. But if he doesn't, another member of the Brotherhood probably will. Eventually, I'm guessing."

Serena stared at her hands, the enormity of her circumstances crashing all around her. She began to rub the pads of her fingers, but it did nothing to soothe her. Her mind reeled with a swirl of feelings that had been plaguing her since the day before. Guilt, fear, sadness.

"I have to close the shop," she murmured. Throwing off the covers, she got up and started dressing.

Jared nodded, dragging a palm down his unwounded cheek. "Yeah, that sounds smart. Duck and cover for a couple of days, while we plan our next move."

She pulled a shirt over her bra, her body trembling as she started to pace about the bedroom. "No, don't you see? I can't stay here. It's not safe." She grabbed her pants off the chair.

"Come stay with me. Wait, hang on. You aren't suggesting that you should skip town, are you?" He followed her into the living room.

"They're going to come back, Jared!" she shouted as she stomped down the stairs. "And it won't just be one or two, this time. We don't know how many people are in their chapter! It could be dozens!"

Jared caught up to her in the teahouse, taking her gently by the shoulders as she began to pace again. A grayish light was seeping into the windows. "If they come back, we'll fight them off." He wanted to take her in his arms and hold her until the anxiety dissolved away.

"With *what?* You saw how our magic reacted to that black tourmaline. You and I might be able to handle ourselves all right in a fist fight, but what about someone like... like Emela? She'd be defenseless!"

"We'll figure it out," he insisted. "You and I, we can make this town safe for you again."

Serena shrugged him off, shaking her head violently as she pulled out of his grasp. "They'll come for me, and after that they'll turn their attention on you, or your family, or the other witches in town. Including Zoe." She froze in place. "The others. We have to warn the others."

"Serena, can you just calm down so we can talk about this?"

"I've put them all at risk. Lily, Emela, Rowan, Hailey, Zoe, you...you're all in danger now because of me."

Hot tears leapt to her eyes. "You were right about me all along, Jared. I was only ever trouble for everyone in Pembrooke. And I don't know how to make it right." She wiped at her eyes as she glanced around the empty teahouse, her dream now turned into a nightmare. "But I can at least start by keeping you all safe. I can't keep putting everyone at risk. I have to leave."

"Serena, listen to me."

Frowning up at him, she paused. He reached out with a gentle hand, calloused fingertips tucking her hair behind her ear before cupping her cheek.

"You..." he sighed, trying to gather his thoughts. "You can't leave Pembrooke. Z would be crushed, don't pretend you don't know that. She'll be miserable without you. Same goes for all your friends, too. Not to mention what this would do to me." He managed a small smile. "You're really going to let this town become boring again?"

She lifted her hand, pressing her palm over the back of his hand, as if to hold him in place. "I'm sorry," she said quietly. "I would stay if I could. I want to stay. I..." she swallowed thickly, choking back an incoming sob. "I stupidly thought that this could be the last time I ever had to start over. That maybe... maybe I wouldn't have to run away again."

She'd done that more times than she could count. Left

town the moment things became too intense, too stressful, too overwhelming.

At the core of Serena's retreats, beneath the layers of self-preservation, had always been a fear deeply ingrained. It was not the fear of failure, financial instability, or even the prospect of emotional heartbreak, but rather a more primal and cutting terror: the fear of abandonment.

Her flight from New York had been a preemptive escape, leaving her coven before they could abandon her to the terrifying Lenses. Her exit from Charleston wasn't solely about the threatening specter of financial instability; it was more about escaping the relationships that might crumble under the pressure of such strain, leaving her stranded in a sea of loneliness. And in Sedona, when her boyfriend unveiled a ring, her fear wasn't about the commitment, but the possibility of being left alone in the wake of a failed marriage.

Her greatest act of self-defense was perhaps distancing herself from Grace, who had opposed her decision to leave college. The thought of her mother's disapproval, the potential withdrawal of her love and support, was too much for Serena to bear. It wasn't fickleness that guided her. It was her profound fear of being abandoned, a terror that she navigated her life around, always staying one step ahead of potential heartache.

And yet for the first time, here and now, Serena didn't *want* to run away. She wanted to stay, and try to make things better. She was ready to risk heartache for a chance to be with Jared.

But when she closed her eyes, she pictured Zoe Westergard, orphaned because her father was murdered by cultists that *she'd* lured back to Pembrooke. She couldn't bear it. She didn't want to be without the friends she'd made, but she would rather the people of Pembrooke sleep safely at night than grow accustomed to a teashop of cures. It had been a lovely dream, but it was only a dream in the end.

"You don't have to run away," Jared said. "This is your home. You're supposed to be here."

She flashed a wan smile. "People leave home every day, right? Why should I be any different?"

"Then I'll come with you."

Serena froze, frowning up at the sincerity on his face. "Jared..."

"I will. Just tell me where you're going, I'll follow you. Zoe and I can start seeing the world. Just like we talked about, right?"

A few tears rolled down her face. "You're kidding, right? Your whole life is here. Your mother is here, your career is here. You told me yourself that you couldn't leave."

He opened his mouth to argue, and she placed a finger to his lips. "Think about this for a second, before you start writing checks you can't cash. I don't want you to do anything you'd regret."

Jared opened his mouth again, but paused. A stubborn flicker of hope sparked to life in her chest, but Serena made a point to crush it beneath her heel. What could he say, after all? Could he fall to his knees, begging her to stay? Ask for mercy, offer her a bribe? Tell her he loved her? Would that make her stay? It likely wouldn't; her mind was made up.

"I don't suppose there would be any point in suggesting that you could come back someday, would there?"

Serena reckoned she should have sobbed at that, but she found herself smiling. "No harm in trying, right?"

He folded her into his arms, then, holding her tightly. She sighed, closing her eyes and attempting to memorize his scent, the timber of his voice, the feel of his arms around her.

"Come back," he said, ducking his head to whisper in her

ear. "Someday, when it's the right time, come back to me. Please?"

She nuzzled against his chest. It was a tempting idea, but was it really fair for them to delude themselves? The Brotherhood had found her in a matter of months. And if she returned, they would find her again. Unless she hid herself away in Jared's house, too afraid to show her face in town. *Unable to ever brew her teas again.* It would be a half-lived life for her. And the other alternative, Jared leaving town with her, would result in a half-lived life for him. It was one thing for him to give up his own life, his own career. It was quite another to also destroy Judith and Zoe.

"Jared, I don't think we can count on..."

He stiffened, as if finally grasping the full scope of her intentions. Jared said nothing, just kissed the crown of her head.

"I just don't see how it can work between us," Serena said. "I'm sorry."

"Okay. If that's what you think is best."

She pulled back, and tilted her head upwards to capture Jared's lips. He lingered when she kissed him, unwilling to say goodbye, but she stepped back.

"You can't stay here. Not alone." Even with the pained look in his eyes, Jared was still thinking of the practical matters. "Come stay at my house. You can have the spare room if you want it."

"I won't stay here. But I'll stay with Lily and Emela until everything is packed up. It will make things easier." A selfish part of her wanted to keep him by her side until the moment she left town. But after seeing the hurt in his eyes, she knew it wouldn't be fair to ask that of him, to delay the inevitable. And keeping him around might make her falter in her resolve, change her mind about doing the right thing. No, they needed space or she surely wouldn't have the courage to do what she must do.

"Serena, can we just..."

"You should go, Jared."

With a final nod, he made for the door. She stopped him in the threshold.

"I'll miss you, Jared Westergard."

He bowed his head in acknowledgement. "I'll miss you, too, Serena. Keep the teahouse closed and the door locked tight. Don't open for anyone. I'll let word get out that you've already left town."

She nodded.

Again, he looked to be on the verge of speaking. Then he paused, sighed, and simply said, "Be safe."

"You, too."

The bell in the door jingled when he closed it behind him and, as she adjusted the Closed sign and locked the door, she watched him walk away. Serena took a deep breath. Alone again. That was familiar. She was used to being alone.

Being lonely, though, would take some adjustments.

CHAPTER 35
JARED

I f he tried hard enough—if he strained and reached far enough into his mind, until he just grazed the edges of his memories—Jared could recall the first few times he went fishing with Liam and his Uncle Pete at the lake. Neither one of them had ever been much good as fishermen back then, truth be told.

Liam had always been too impatient. Always wandering off to play in the brush and hunt for lizards. His dad would all but beg him to sit still, but he was hopeless. Gods help him, he caught more ticks than he ever did fish.

Meanwhile, Jared had the opposite problem. He would stare at the water and it would call to him, pulling him with the current until he couldn't fight it any longer. The way that it moved, quiet but insistent, with an understated sense of power. It drew him in.

The ocean had the same effect. He'd fallen in love with it, and she met him with a kind of force and aggression that Jared had never encountered before. It pulled him close and pushed him away with no care for his reaction or his desires. And he saw strength in that. He longed to contain it, but not with dams or buckets or earth. Jared wanted to hold the ocean in his hands, and for the ocean to listen.

But more than anything, Jared found himself drawn to the river, the stream, the creek. The incessant gentle flow was suggestive, lovingly coercive, almost manipulative. Its pull could be sinister or kind, he reckoned. Perhaps both at the same time.

And yet despite its fury, its raw power, water was too frequently underestimated. Subtle currents had often been confused with weak currents throughout history. Anyone who had ever waded into deceptively calm water would know the fallacy in that.

He'd been fishing the first time that his powers rose to the surface. Staring at the water, his uncle yelling at him to reel the damned line in. There was a fish on his hook, but Jared had been too lost in thought to even notice. His uncle had been worried that it would get away, and Liam was off somewhere poking worms with sticks. Jared had just panicked and frozen in place. Dropped his rod. And before he could react, the brook lurched, like it had eaten something that didn't agree with it. A moment later it spat out the fish, flopping and gasping, onto the bank.

The rest was history.

"So what happens now?"

Blinking, Jared tore his eyes away from the frothy, churning water. Dark clouds had been rolling in lately. The precious few weeks of sunlight that spelled summer in Pembrooke were already fading. The rainy season was about to begin again.

Liam was watching him with a slight frown, sandwich clutched in one hand and a beer in the other.

"I don't know," he confessed, blowing out a sharp breath.

"Keep my eyes open, I guess. Start looking over my shoulder, again. Like I always have. Like I should've been all along."

It hurt to say, and even more to feel, but it was true. He'd let himself get too comfortable. Too comfortable with life, with magic seeping into the town. Too comfortable with *her*. Now he was paying the price for all of it, in the form of sleepless nights and empty whiskey bottles. "Just hope that they don't sniff out any other witches."

"What about your girl?"

He grimaced. "She's not mine," he said after a long while. "Never was, really. I was just passing through her orbit for a season."

Liam groaned. "Come on, don't give me that crap."

Jared glared at him.

"I don't believe a word of that, man. As a matter of fact, I don't believe that *you* believe any of that, either."

"It doesn't matter," he insisted, hunching his shoulders as he watched the lure float on the gentle current. "Either way, she's going to be gone before the week is out."

Liam blinked, sitting up straight. "What, like *gone* gone? She's moving out of Pembrooke?"

He sighed heavily. "Seems that way, yeah."

"And you're just going to let her go?"

Jared frowned sidelong at the other man. "She made her decision. At the end of the day, I don't have any say in the matter. What choice do I have?"

Liam gestured as if the answer should be obvious. "You could fight for her, Jared. Be a little unreasonable, for once." He crushed his beer can in his hand for emphasis. "Stop defending what you have, and go after what you want."

"She'll be better off this way!" Jared said. "It's what she wants."

The other man scoffed. "You can't seriously expect me to

agree with you. Open your eyes! None of this is what anyone wants. The whole town loves her. *You* love her."

"I... I don't know if I—"

"Who is this better for?" Liam demanded. "Tell me."

"At least this way, everyone is safe in the end," he insisted, his voice rising over the gurgling water. "Serena gets away before anyone can hurt her, the town stops being a target, and I get to sleep at night knowing that I didn't pick my feelings over anyone's life!" He dragged a hand down his face. "It's a tough choice, Liam, but Serena made it, and I'm sticking by it. She made up her mind. What else would you have me do?"

"I'd have you tell her that you won't take no for an answer!" he said, passion flooding into his voice. "I'd have you find the sons of bitches who took Willow, and show them what happens to people who try to tear this town apart!" He rose to his feet, standing over Jared and speaking emphatically. "And then I'd have you drop on your knees and beg that girl never to leave again. She's a part of the town, man, I know you can feel it! Don't give her up! Show me some heroics. A little devotion won't kill you!"

Jared swallowed his anger at the other man's words. He was devoted. He was heroic. He didn't need to prove that to anyone, especially not Liam. He blew out a sharp breath. His voice left quiet and even. Gentle, but with a hidden threat, like a frozen lake.

"You think I don't wish that I could?" he said through clenched teeth. "But it's up to Serena, in the end. If she wants to leave, I won't stop her. I even tried to go with her. She wouldn't have me."

Liam blinked. "You... you offered to leave Pembrooke for her?"

He sighed. "I did. It was impulsive, and thoughtless, but I meant it in the moment."

"And you still won't admit that this girl matters to you?"

"It's not that simple, and you know it."

Liam opened his mouth, like he wanted to say more. Evidently he thought better of it. He sat back down, grabbed another beer, watched the water. The quiet stretched out between them for a handful of long minutes. Tense. Still, if only at the surface.

"She could come back, one day," Jared said at last. "Once things die down. She could come home. She may change her mind."

"What makes you think that she would want to?"

Jared frowned at him. "What do you mean? She told me that she didn't want to go, why wouldn't she come back?"

He shrugged. "Sure, she wants to come back *now*. I just meant that she might end up liking it, wherever she goes. She's lived lots of places, right? Maybe she'll move down to California, meet some hot new guy and shack up with him."

It ached. Even as a hypothetical, even just to hear it, it ached.

"He's got a BMW," Liam continued. "And a posh tech job. He's thirty-one and he makes mid six-figures a year."

"Stop."

"He has one of those prince names. Philip, or Charles or Henry. You think she'd be into a Henry?"

"I'm serious," Jared warned with a glare.

"And he wants an outdoor wedding, with the wildflowers and the fairy lights and everything. And—"

A stream of water shot from the river, hitting Liam squarely in the chest. Liam cast him a deeply affronted look, brandishing his now waterlogged sandwich in his face. "The hell is wrong with you!"

Jared managed a smirk. "I warned you."

"This is the good cheese, you know. From the dairy in Oxport. You can't get this at Kurt's."

"Should've thought about that."

Liam smiled sarcastically. "Thanks, I'll keep that in mind for next time," he deadpanned. He took a long drink from his beer, squinting hard at the water. "You ever planning on catching a fish?"

"Been a little too focused on birds," Jared said, thinking of the crow on Blackbird's arm. "I'm rusty when it comes to fishing."

"Maybe you could learn a little something from the birds," Liam said, gesturing to the far bank with his bottle. A kingfisher had just disturbed the water, swooping down and plucking a small fish for itself. "No hesitation, man. Instinct. You see a fish, you grab it."

Jared snorted. "Kingfishers also get their nests robbed by raccoons, if they aren't careful."

Liam joined him in laughing for a moment, and then his smile faded. He took another swig of his beer, grimacing to himself. "Shouldn't have let her go, that's all I ever meant."

Jared didn't reply. He just sat, perched on the bank, feeling miserable, and watched the water. Away in the distance, he could hear a faint rumble. The telltale sound of a gathering storm.

CHAPTER 36

SERENA

The banquet table sat lavishly adorned yet forgotten, like a Christmas tree after all the gifts have been opened. An untouched feast that was a silent testament to the turmoil of the evening. Platters brimmed with an assortment of cheeses, nuts, and colorful fruits, their vibrant hues stark against the distressed wooden table. Tender, golden-brown pastries sat on dainty porcelain plates, the delicate aroma of fresh baking wafting up from them, largely ignored.

In the middle, an unwanted cake stood proud and tall, festooned with rich, glossy frosting and crowned with delicate sugar flowers. The sweet, vanilla scent emanating from it only added to the weight of sadness. Flanking the cake were plates of uneaten sandwiches, their layers meticulously arranged, but of no interest to anyone now.

A heavy, indescribable sadness hung in the air of The Tinker's Trinket as Serena, surrounded by her coven, prepared to leave Pembrooke. The witches, usually buzzing with laughter and conversation, were now filled with a tense silence, punctuated only by occasional sniffs.

Wine glasses, filled to the brim with robust reds and crisp whites, were scattered across their round table. The wines had been chosen with care, the gleaming labels lined up beneath the soft glow of the ambient lighting. But the Merlots and Rieslings were just swirled aimlessly in the glasses, reflecting the muted light, undrunk and unappreciated.

On any other occasion, this banquet would have been a joyous indulgence, a sensory feast. Tonight, it sat as a poignant reminder of the reason for the gathering, its intended cheerfulness stark against the heavy atmosphere.

Lily was the first to break the silence. Her eyes, usually bright with cheer, were now pooled with unshed tears. "You know you don't have to go, right?" she said, her voice just above a whisper. Serena smiled tightly, clasping Lily's hand in a silent reassurance.

"We get why you think you need to leave," Emela added. "But you can always come back. Just go lay low for a while."

Hailey forced a smile. "This isn't a goodbye, Serena. This is a see-you-later. Because you *will* come back, and we'll be here waiting."

Brooklyn, who usually had an opinion on everything, was silent. Alice was fighting back tears. Charlotte wore a comforting smile, but her eyes betrayed her sorrow. Rowan was uncharacteristically quiet, her fiery spirit subdued. Zara offered no comforting words of wisdom, while Noora looked on with wide, scared eyes.

Serena took a deep breath, looking around at her friends— her *family*. "I can't risk the Brotherhood coming after you all because of me," she said, her voice steady. "I need you to all be safe."

"Serena, we're stronger together," Brooklyn said. "We can keep each other safe. We've got your back. Always."

"I know, and thank you. But I need to go."

"We'll never forget you and everything you've done for us," Lily said. "You brought us all out of the broom closet."

"And you know, you did more than just charm Jared," Rowan said. "You healed him. He was a grump, an officious ass before you came along. But with you, the man could smile again, and... it was a sight to behold." No one thankfully said aloud what Serena was thinking, that maybe Jared would stop smiling again once she left.

"And speaking of healing, let's not forget your brews, Serena," Emela said. "The people you've helped, the relief you've brought... it's been immeasurable."

Hailey nodded. "Yeah. You affected us all, Serena. You made us feel seen for the first time. You brought us out from the shadows. And for that, we are forever grateful."

"You brought us together. It's more than just a coven, we're a family," Brooklyn said.

Alice raised her glass in a toast. "To Serena, who not only transformed a town, but also the lives within it."

"Hear, hear. Serena, you changed Pembrooke, and there's no going back now," Charlotte said. "And honestly, I don't think any of us would want to."

"You've helped us find ourselves, and each other," Rowan said.

"And brought light, love, and a sense of community," Zara said.

"You *are* Pembrooke, Serena," Noora said. "And Pembrooke will never be the same."

Serena wiped her eyes as the pain of both love and loss filled her heart. The reality that she was about to walk away from this incredible group of women, and the weight of that loss began to sink in. "Promise me you will all keep the coven going," she said. "Don't let anyone tear you guys apart again."

With final hugs and tears, they all said their goodbyes and rose to leave. The room echoed with the promises of staying in touch and reassurances of reunions. Yet the weight of Serena's departure lingered, a poignant reminder of the uncertain days that lay ahead. For all of them.

The lock clicked loudly in the Tinker's Trinket's front door as Serena pulled a shawl tightly around her shoulders a bit later. Trailing behind Lily and Emela as they walked toward their apartment, Serena's gaze turned back to the shadowed silhouette of the teahouse. A weighty sorrow rooted itself deep in her chest, its tendrils spreading coldly to her trembling fingertips. She abruptly turned away, shifting her focus, as she battled the raw sob clawing its way up her throat.

CHAPTER 37

JARED

P ower could be a real bitch sometimes.

Maybe that was a bit of a harsh judgement. Power could be... temperamental. Fickle. Bitchy. Well, he'd tried.

Jared had *felt* powerful, for a while. He'd felt like he was on top of the world, right until the exact moment when she told him that she was leaving. He realized now that his mood had been hanging on the corners of sweet pink lips. Again.

Looking at him from a distance, he doubted that anyone would have pegged him as a hopeless romantic, but here he was. Was it so wrong, to need love? To thrive on the high of feeling like he belonged with someone?

His mother had once told him he was like a coconut: hard on the outside, but soft and tender once it was cracked open. It that were true, then Serena was just the opposite: soft and sweet on the outside, but at her core was an iron will.

He vividly remembered feeling utterly unstoppable, back when Willow was still alive. Maybe that was just his nostalgia taking control, to a degree. They'd had their fights, their rough patches, like any couple. But he'd still felt stronger with her influence in his life.

And then one day, she was just... gone. That was the thing about loss, he'd learned. No matter how aware of it you were, no matter how much you thought about death, you couldn't really wrap your head around it until it happened. It was a cosmic sort of horror, in that sense. Lovecraftian. One day, someone you loved would be there. They would be breathing, and laughing, and lighting up the room. And you would be better for it. And the next day, they weren't there.

It wasn't fair. He didn't lose her, she was taken from him. But what could he do?

The morning of Willow's disappearance, Jared had slept in. He'd been on a business trip to Portland. No one to answer to. He'd brewed coffee in his suite, and read a worn, old paperback in the armchair. Gone for a swim in the hotel pool. He'd taken extra time to luxuriate in the silence. In the solitude. Just sat back and listened to the muted city sounds. Reflected. And then he'd packed up his things to go home. The umbrella Willow insisted he take had gone missing, so he spent the better part of an hour searching for it. Strange, the details his mind clung to. Why on earth did he remember losing that damned umbrella? He drove home feeling untouchable, as always.

And when he walked through the front door that after-noon, instead of being greeting by his wife's usual toothy smile, he found his living room window broken, and signs of a struggle, and an empty space where the love of his life was meant to be.

Now he found himself staring over the edge of another precipice. Again, he'd fallen hard and fast. Again, he'd felt stronger whenever Serena looked his way. Again, he was losing her, albeit less painfully this time. At least he was improving, in that regard. Preventing the loss before it could happen by replacing it with a new, gentler loss. Maybe next time, he might manage to let love walk out without someone's life being on the line at all. That would be a welcome change.

This morning he had woken up before his alarm. Restless. Dread keeping him on his toes, even in his sleep. He brewed a cup of coffee and went to work early, because his house felt too empty for him to tolerate. Spent the bulk of the day trying and failing to throw himself neck-deep into his work, just begging for a distraction. Staring at the pink camellias outside his office window, promising himself that he would stop staring at them, then staring again.

At any rate, she was gone. She would be gone, anyway. Soon. He_watched her through his window all day, feeling spineless and stupid as she shoved box after box into her Robin's Egg Land Rover. He'd even gone over and helped her load some boxes. It had been awkward. And painful.

And then he went home. Having done nothing, said nothing, again. Sat down in his darkened living room, its window long since repaired, and called his mother.

She picked up after two rings. "Is everything okay?"

Jared let out a humorless laugh. "Hello to you too, ma."

"I'm sorry," she grumbled. "I'm just on edge."

Jared sat back, deflating against the couch. They needed to get a new one, but he'd never had much of a head for interior design. "It'll be over soon. Just tough it out for a couple more days."

He could almost feel her assessing him through the phone, fixing him in place with her stare. "Why do I get the feeling you've done something stupid?"

"Couldn't tell you," he replied. "I haven't, if that's any comfort."

"Then you're *about* to do something stupid?"

Jared scoffed. "Why does it have to be stupid? Haven't I earned any of your faith? You don't think you raised me better than that?"

She chuckled at him. "I raised you fine. It's the parts your father raised that keep me on my toes. Jared couldn't argue there, though he hadn't been a big part of his father's life since the divorce. Nowadays, he only saw the old man once every year or two.

He managed a smile when Zoe's voice floated through the line. A light, eager little "Can I talk to him? Please?" that made him feel a little more optimistic than before. She'd always been good at that, without even trying. Snapping him out of it, whenever he started to feel a bit too sorry for himself.

"Zoe wants to talk to you."

"Give her the phone."

There was a bit of rustling through the speaker before he heard her voice, a little muffled, like she had her finger over the microphone. "Hey dad!"

"Hey Z. You having fun with Great Aunt Helen?"

"We went to the aquarium yesterday," she answered, but she sounded tired.

"Yeah?" he prodded gently. "That sounds like an adventure. Did you see any good fish?"

"Mmhm. I saw a Mola Mola."

Jared whistled low, looking at the ceiling. "Those are the big flat ones, right?" he asked.

"That's right. They have lots of babies."

"Lots? How many is 'lots'?"

"Three hundred million," she said.

He chuckled. "Wow, that *is* a lot. I think I'm okay with one baby, myself."

That got a rise out of her. It always did. "Hey! I'm not a baby!"

"Sure, sure."

"I'm not!"

He sighed softly. "All right. You're not."

Jared looked around the empty house, moody in the low light. There were traces of Zoe and his mother everywhere. Zoe's favorite blanket, dotted with brightly colored butterflies, draped innocently over the back of the couch. The sourdough pretzels that he hated but his mother adored, sitting on the kitchen counter. Signs of himself, too. Ties he'd tugged off seconds after stepping through the door, and coffee mugs that were older than Zoe, and a shelf filled with bad fantasy novels.

There was even a sign of *her*. His chest ached. Serena had never asked him to return the kettle she'd loaned him. It was still on the counter, cheery copper shining where it lay waiting to be put to use again.

He found himself wondering what other traces she might have left, if she'd chosen to stay. How long it would take for one of her hair ties or a necklace to be left behind on his bedside table. For flowers to pop up in nearly every room. For Kita's fur to cling to the couch.

"Dad? Are you still there?"

"Yeah, I'm here," he said, bracing his forehead on his palm. "I just... I miss you, Z."

Zoe hummed. "I miss you, too."

He tried to smile. "Hey, what do you wanna do when you and grandma get back?"

There was a brief silence on Zoe's end while she puzzled that out. At last, she said, "Do you think Miss Rena would teach me to make that carrot cake with the cream cheese frosting? I think I'm ready to try it. I'm getting really good at making cookies and brownies."

Jared grimaced at that. "Listen, baby. Serena... she's not going to be here when you and Grandma get back."

"She's not?" Zoe asked. "But what about the teahouse?"

"It's closed," he said. "I'm sorry."

"When is she coming back?"

He took a slow breath. Bracing himself.

"Dad?"

"She's not coming back."

He felt her silence in his bones. It almost felt merciful when she near-whispered "W-what do you mean?"

"I mean she's leaving Pembrooke. Going to live somewhere new."

Her voice was turning thick with tears, and it tore him apart inside. "When is she leaving?"

He ran a hand down his face. "Tomorrow, I think. Maybe, first thing in the morning."

She sobbed. "I don't even get to say goodbye to her? She's just leaving?"

"I'm sorry, Pumpkin."

He was cut off by a lot of rustling and some distant tears. The next voice he heard was his mother's.

"What did you tell her?"

"Ma, can you please make sure Zoe's okay?"

"She's not," his mother snapped. "Tell me what happened."

He sighed sharply, frowning hard into the dark corner of the living room. "Serena's skipping town, I thought she should know before you two got back."

"Skipping town?" she echoed. "And you're *letting* her?"

"Has anyone in this town *met* Serena Albright? What on earth makes you think that she would listen to anything I had to say?"

"Well, what *did* you say?"

Jared swallowed. "I told her not to go, of course. She

wouldn't listen. I... I offered to go with her, too, and she still said no."

"Did you tell her that you loved her?"

The question made goosebumps rise on his skin. "I'm not going to tell her anything that I don't mean. She deserves that much."

"Honey, you've known her for less than six months, and you offered to leave home for this girl. You *love* her."

"I..."

"And that's okay," his mother added, before he could so much as form a response. "It's all right to find love again. It doesn't change anything you had in the past." She let the statement hang for a tense moment, before softly adding, "Willow would have wanted you to be happy again."

Without his permission, Jared's mind conjured images of Willow. Big brown eyes, thick dark curls, a bright, wide smile. Loving, right until the end.

"Let me ask you this: Would you have gone with her, if she'd let you?"

Freckles. Pink petals. A lopsided smirk, like she'd always been in on a joke that kept going way over Jared's head.

"I don't know. I think so. I wanted to," he said.

"Then I think you know what you need to do."

WITH A CLEARER HEAD THAN HE'D HAD IN DAYS, JARED OPENED THE heavy door of the The Labyrinth. Royce's head snapped to attention, giving him a nervous look as he approached the bar.

"I haven't heard anything," Royce told him, holding up his hands. "Not yet, anyway."

Jared nodded. "Thanks for keeping your ear to the ground, either way. That's... not why I'm here, though."

That only served to inject more worry into Royce's expression. He glanced in either direction, then indicated to Jared that he should follow.

When the office door was closed behind them, Royce rounded on him. Looked down at him with narrowed eyes. They looked so similar to Willow's eyes. "You okay, bud? You look like death warmed over."

Jared tried to look reassuring when he nodded again. "I'm okay. I mean, I think that I'm going to be okay."

It was apparent on Royce's face that he didn't believe him. "All right. I guess that's good. I was half-expecting you to tell me that you had another run in with some Inkers. What did you want to talk to me about?"

Jared took a slow breath. "I just wanted to tell you that I'm sorry, that's all."

The other man frowned. "Sorry? Sorry for what?"

"For everything," he said and, to his horror, his voice sounded thick where it left his throat. "For Willow."

Royce blinked. "That's what this is about?"

He didn't trust himself to speak, suddenly. All he could bring himself to do was nod.

"Jared," Royce sighed, in part exasperation and part sympathy. "I loved Willow, and I always will, but... well, it's been five years, man, you know? I still miss her, terribly, but at a certain point, I knew that it wasn't fair to keep myself in the past. Not fair to me or to her. I felt like if I held myself back there...ruminating, then I might grow to resent her. And I couldn't live with myself if that happened."

Jared swallowed. "Neither could I."

"It already cost me Sophia."

Jared nodded, thinking of the pretty girl—Rowan's sister, in fact—that Royce had been in love with before Willow died.

Royce fixed him with a hard look. "This is really about Serena, isn't it?"

"Yeah," he said softly. "Yeah, it is." Royce could always read him like a book.

"Look, I appreciate how much you loved Willow, how much you respect my sister's memory. And how much you value my opinion, but honestly? You shouldn't give half a shit what I think."

Jared gave a tight smile. "You know, I've never been great at ignoring what my family says," he quipped. His brows furrowed. "We are still family, right? You and me?"

"Of course we are," Royce assured him with a smile and a hug. "Now get the hell out of my bar and go find your girl."

And with that, Jared took a deep breath and made for the door. Back to the familiar roads that had been the skeleton of his childhood, heading straight for Bailey Street.

CHAPTER 38
SERENA

Serena always loved moving. It was grounding, in a way. Forced her life into perspective. No matter how big her problems felt in the moment—all the drama, the isolation, the overwhelming feeling of being lost that followed her like a shadow—every single piece of her life could be packed up into cardboard boxes and loaded into a truck. Gathered up and taken away. Out of sight, out of mind.

It wasn't as tragic as it seemed on the surface. Throughout her life, everywhere she went, people were always shockingly eager to inform her what an awful shame it was to be so transient. "Don't you wish," they always asked her. "Don't you wish that you could call somewhere home? Don't you wish that you could make some lasting connections? Don't you wish that the pieces of you didn't have to be packed up in boxes?"

They didn't understand. That was all there was to it. Transience was the nature of existence. After all, even if she stayed in Pembrooke, none of the things that she had would ever be permanent. Things died and rotted, and other things took their place. The connections Serena had made in Pembrooke weren't special, they were merely in season.

And now they weren't. It was time to pack up and find a new garden. That was just the way things were.

She descended the wooden back stairs, a box of scattered knick-knacks in her arms. The bulk of the larger furniture had already been loaded into her rented moving van, her bed notwithstanding, ready to be hauled out first thing in the morning. All that remained was to pick over the small remaining crumbs that would be stowed in her car.

The Velvet Teahouse looked bigger than it had when she first moved in, she was convinced of that fact. The Goddess Corner, empty and darkened, looked like an endless, gaping void. It couldn't be the same room, could it? The same room where they'd struggled to fit the large round table through its door? The same room that could be flooded with light by a single candle? No. That room was somewhere else. Somewhere untouched by Serena or the Brotherhood, or anything that could take it from her. And it was still cozy and warm and perfect, just waiting for her to place a tray of food on the round tabletop. It had to be.

She sighed, gathering a few crystals that had been gifted to her by Rowan and Hailey, with a wistful smile. Her eyes landed on the kingfisher statue, standing innocently near the register, and she felt an odd rush of childish indignation. That small voice that never quite grew up, stomping her foot and shouting in protest about moving again. It wasn't *fair*, she used to scream at her mother, red in the face and teary eyed. *It's not fair, it's not fair, it's just not fair.*

But Serena was old enough to know that fairness didn't matter. Leaving was for the best. She wouldn't let herself be responsible for hurting a town that had been uncharacteristically kind to her. Here, for the first time in her life, she hadn't felt like an outcast. She couldn't reward that compassion with suffering. If she did, then it would mean that everyone in the past—the ones that gave her a wide berth and ushered their children to the other side of the street when she passed—had been right all along.

So she picked up the kingfisher, took a moment to admire its beak, and placed it gently in the box with the rest of her keepsakes.

It landed right next to the framed photo of her and Zoe after they had done each other's hair. Shifting the frame in the box, Serena realized how much she was gonna miss that little girl. A nagging voice reminded her that she would never have made a good mother substitute. They'd had fun, though. The laughter they'd shared while baking, the way Zoe's fingers clumsily braided her hair, and those precious moments they'd spent talking about schoolyard bullies and crushes. Zoe considered most boys yucky at this point in her life. But Serena had pointed out that Tyler, her best bud in art class, wasn't so yucky, and Zoe had reluctantly agreed.

Serena wrapped the frame in bubble wrap to keep the glass from breaking. Another softer voice began to whisper that if she stayed, then maybe, just maybe, she would have done okay with Zoe, after all.

She nearly dropped the box when she was startled by a sharp knock at the door. Setting it on the countertop, she dusted off the front of her jeans and frowned toward the door. A foolish part of her hoped that it might be Jared, saying to hell with it all and demanding that she let him come with her, responsibility be damned.

Her hoped diminished somewhat when she heard Kita growling upstairs, but she dared to think that Kita may just be on edge from the impending move. She was smart enough to know when a long car ride was in her future, after all. As

Serena approached the door, though, the wolf made its way downstairs to the shop, snarling with her hackles raised. Serena swallowed, the air turning sour.

"W-we're closed!" she called out into the empty shop, praying that her hairs standing on end were just a by-product of her frayed nerves.

The air hung in charged silence for one second, then two. The next moment, the front door crashed open, knocked in by a great force. Serena shrieked as five men in dark robes made their way into the shop.

The five crows have come for me.

She instinctively moved to call a barrier of vines to separate them from Kita and herself, but nothing came forth. The vines sprouted, and promptly died before they could rise more than a handful of inches. So, Blackbird had shared his black tourmaline with the rest of the Brotherhood.

Kita jumped to Serena's defense, snarling wildly in anger. Serena cried out when one of the men produced a tranquilizer gun from within his robes and shot her wolf with its contents. After tussling with one of the men, Kita fell to the ground a moment later, unconscious.

A second later, Serena's thigh exploded in pain. Glancing down, she saw the black feathery dart emerging from her leg. Before she could yank it out, one of the men closed in on Serena, violence in his eyes. She feinted right, then darted to the left, trying to weave past him. He was too quick for her, though, and grabbed her tightly around her middle. Pressing one meaty hand over her mouth, he muffled her screams as she struggled.

The man cried out a moment later, pained and shocked as two more Inkers grabbed her arms.

"What happened?" one of the other robed figures asked.

The big man pulled his hand away, frowning at his bloody palm. "The bitch bit me!"

Serena craned her neck, twisting to spit red in his face before showing her teeth in a coppery smile. "You're going to regret this," she told him.

One of the men chuckled, pulling the black tourmaline amulet from around his neck and shaking it in her face. "You can't use your hexes on us this time, little witch," he taunted. "What are you going to do? Fight us?" he scoffed. "I think there's a few more of us than there are of you, sweetheart." She recognized his voice when he spoke, her lip curling in disgust. *Colin Park.* His yellow grin came into view as he pulled his hood back, vicious and victorious.

She glared at him, all fire and iron, but he was right. As much as she hated to admit it, she was at their mercy. "What are you going to do?" she challenged, lifting her chin at them defiantly. "Kill me?" She tried to harness all of the bravery left inside of her chest. She found herself wishing that there was more of it, but she was beginning to feel dizzy.

Colin just sneered at her, drawing ever closer. The last thing she felt was an incredible heaviness in her limbs, and seconds later her vision went hazy at its edges.

IT WAS THE SENSATION OF WATER ON HER CHEEK THAT ROUSED HER. A light rainfall, holding with it the promise of an incoming storm. She'd been able to feel the static in the air for days now, clinging to her skin like dread. Now the water was gentle but insistent, as it fell against her cheek. Cleansing.

The next thing she noticed was the stabbing pain her thigh. Then the splitting headache.

Serena groaned softly. She shifted, and the ground was

rough on her skin. Her mouth tasted sour, acrid with old blood and a fitful sleep. She spluttered when a boot made swift contact with her stomach. Instinctively, she moved to shield herself, only to find that her arms were bound behind her back with thick rope.

"Wake up, witch."

Her brows furrowed, the world shifting around her in a groggy, slow haze. A gloved hand yanked her upwards by her hair, gripping it in a great fistful that made tears prick at her eyes.

"I said, wake up!"

She blinked, squinting up at the figure. He refused to come into focus, but she knew that it was Blackbird.

"You..."

He frowned down at her, like she was a bug he'd found in his kitchen. "Not so tough now, are you?"

Serena fought her clumsy way to her knees, gritting her teeth at the pain that screamed throughout her body.

"Now don't try to run away," he warned her. "You're going to be feeling pretty woozy for a while. We used a sedative derived from valerian root and endymion flowers, mixed with an opioid, on you and your mutt." He sniffed. "Might've been a little extra effort, but I thought you'd appreciate the irony."

She didn't bother pretending to be impressed. Instead, she surveyed her surroundings. The five men from the teahouse, and more robed figures standing in a circle. She counted twenty in all. They were situated in a field. She could tell by the wild astilbe growing in her periphery that they were on the outskirts of town. In the distance, she could just make out the shape of a dilapidated building through the darkness. It had been a distillery once, Jared had told her in passing. The place where Jared said he had seen Colin Park, not long ago.

"Go ahead and scream, if you want," Blackbird taunted,

gesturing at the wide expanse all around them. "No one's going to hear you."

She glared up at him, but didn't scream. Didn't even speak. She wouldn't give him the satisfaction of her fear.

He hummed, shrugging it off. "Thought you would've at least tried, but if you're giving up, that's fine. Guess I've got my answer, now, eh Miss Albright? You're not a fighter, after all."

Serena cast her weary eyes in the direction of the distillery. Far off, abandoned, but just visible through the rain. Through the fog, an idea began to take shape.

She wasn't sure how far her range would go, hadn't tried to send a plant so far away before, but it was her best shot. Something easy, then. Something that came naturally to her.

"What are you going to do with me?" she asked. Her eyes flicked up to meet Blackbird's, but her focus was on the ground beneath her sore knees. There, just beyond the edge of the circle of bodies, Serena watched delicate white blossoms spring up and bob under the impact of the rain. Queen Anne's lace. Then another, just past it. Three, four, sprouting in a rough path from Serena toward the building. It took all of her energy, disoriented and sedated as she was, but she kept her mind resolutely centered on the earth.

He chuckled darkly, quickly joined by the rest of his twisted congregation. "Well, I suppose that's up to you."

She tilted her head. "How generous of you," she replied. "Then if it's all the same with you, I'd like you to let me go."

Blackbird smiled, or rather, he bared his teeth at her. "Nice try. You're funny, Serena. And you've got spirit, I'll give you that."

Serena narrowed her eyes. Blackbird may have thought it was from suspicion, or hatred. In reality it was in concentration. The flowers were beyond her line of sight, now. She wasn't even sure that they were still blooming. Despite that, she tried to draw a line in her mind all the way to the dark shape of the distillery.

"But I am giving you a choice," he elaborated. "Being released isn't an option, but you will have a say because I'm a generous man. And I hope you think about your answer, because it's the last choice you're ever going to make." With that, another robed figure stepped forward, more rope and an unlit torch in either hand.

"Tell me, Serena Albright: Would you rather be hanged, or burned?"

CHAPTER 39
JARED

W hen Jared parked outside The Velvet Teahouse, the first thing that he noticed was that the lights were still on. It was late, late enough that the entire street was dark and silent, aside from this single exception. It set him on edge. Then he saw the front door, hanging open on damaged hinges, and he was out of his car in seconds. He blew a whistle, but the guard he had covertly arranged to watch over her didn't appear.

He called her name the moment he stepped through the doorway, the once chipper bell now weakly signaling his arrival. The sound felt like a mockery of itself, and Jared's blood ran cold.

Kita was lying on the wooden floor, whining softly in a fitful sleep. He knelt beside her, petting her charcoal fur and gently checking to make sure she was all right. She was unconscious, but she seemed to be okay beyond that, as far as he could tell.

"Serena?" he called again, looking around the teahouse. A few chairs had been disturbed, but that was the extent of the damage inside. An obvious break-in, but no clear signs of a struggle. He darted up the stairs, calling for Serena again, and found her apartment completely undisturbed. They'd only been here for her, then.

He was already dialing his phone as he rushed back to his car, keys still dangling from the ignition. Liam's voice was clumsy with sleep when he picked up. "Jared?" he mumbled. "Everything okay?"

"I need backup."

Evidently his tone did wonders for dragging Liam from sleep to waking. "On it. Bring me up to speed."

"It's Serena, she's been abducted."

"Shit, you're sure?"

"Definitely. Listen, I want you to rally the troops, okay? Anyone you think would be willing to help, give 'em a ring. Including the Order."

He could almost hear the gears in Liam's head turning as he compiled a mental list. "All right. Anything else?"

He searched his mind. "You're friends with Rowan Beaumont, right?"

"Yeah, I think I've got her on my socials. Why?"

Jared nodded sharply. "Tell her to get the coven together."

"The coven? Since when is there a coven in Pembrooke? You know what, we can talk about that later. I'll sound the alarms. Where am I sending all these people, exactly?"

He frowned through his windshield, out at the rain pattering on the glass. Without even realizing it, he'd been making his way toward the edge of town, taking the same winding road he'd traveled a matter of days before. "I've got a hunch," he said, and took a turn onto an unused, pothole-ridden back road. "Out to the old distillery."

. . .

WHEN JARED ARRIVED, THE BUILDING ONCE AGAIN APPEARED VACANT, at least from the outside. Abandoned, just as it had been the last time Jared came snooping. He reached back, his fingers fumbling against the underside of the passenger seat where he had stashed a few weapons.

Once out of the car, he circled the perimeter, the rolls of approaching thunder masking his footfalls as he snuck through the wet grass, searching for the Brotherhood once more. The front entrance was still tightly locked, just like before.

Peering through the broken window showed him that the distillery was empty again. Or at least that the storeroom office was empty. Pitch black and echoing where drops of rain pattered through the wounded ceiling. He could tell that someone had been inside since the last time he'd come by. There were even more documents inside than before, as well as a large web of photos, information, and thread on the far wall. An evidence board, like something out of a crime procedural. He shone his phone's flashlight at the wall, and staring back at him was a photo of Serena Albright, alongside himself and every other witch in Pembrooke.

Jared nearly screamed into the night. They'd taken her somewhere. He tried to clear his head, to imagine where they may be going. His thoughts were cluttered, though. Turbulent, lost on his own frantic current. He felt Serena slipping from his grasp.

A flash of lightning streaked across the sky, near enough that the answering thunder rattled his teeth and set his already speeding heart pounding. It cast the area in near-blinding white light for a fraction of a second, and Jared caught a glimpse of familiar pale flowers at his feet. He fumbled for his phone, struggling to unlock it as the rainfall wet the screen. He shone the flashlight at the blossoms, studying them.

Queen Anne's Lace. A small patch of them. He was certain they hadn't been there the last time he investigated the area. He peered into the night, and his light landed on another sparse patch of flowers a few strides away. Another, further out, larger than the last. He took off into the brush, finding more and more clusters of Serena's favorite flowers until they formed a shaky, wavering, unmistakable path.

Jackpot.

He sent a quick text to Liam, then followed the trail with growing urgency, pulse rushing in a dizzying cocktail of fear and dawning hope as the path of Queen Anne's Lace became stronger, straighter, clearer. He burst through the brush and into a clearing.

And there they were. A couple dozen of them, he guessed, though he could barely make them out against the darkness of the night. The storm clouds had blocked out the moon, and they were far from any light pollution, leaving Jared to squint through the abyss in search of Serena's silhouette.

They all seemed to be congregated under a large tree near the center of the clearing, but he couldn't see exactly what they were doing from his place at the edge of the woods. There was one thing that he could see, though: the path of white flowers led straight to that tree.

The storm might have kept them from seeing any details or spotting him from a distance, but the lack of prominent foliage within the field meant that they would see him approaching from a long way off. It was possible that he could cover a decent amount of ground before they saw him, but not enough to give him any real advantage, especially outnumbered as he was. Sneaking up on them wouldn't be an option.

Well, it was either go big or go home, then. And he wasn't going home without her.

Jared sprinted along the path Serena had given him, a great

peal of thunder rolling in as he advanced on the congregation. When the first robed figure turned to look at him, he was quickly followed by the others. Once Jared had everyone's attention, he shouted into the wind.

"Let the woman go."

He saw Serena, then. Arms tied behind her back, and a noose wrapped around her neck. Not yet tightened, thank the gods. The rope remained loose, her body perched on a rickety wooden dais. She looked at him with unfocused eyes blinking slowly in disbelief.

He recognized several of the cultists, their hoods down despite the downpour surrounding them: Colin Park, an informant, infecting the town from within; Blackbird; and a few others from the investigation he'd done with the council years ago. This was probably the entire chapter, he reasoned. Their number always hovered around twenty.

"Step back, Loverboy," Blackbird said, standing resolutely between Jared and Serena. "You don't want to cross us."

"Don't I?" he replied, staring the other man in the face. "This has been a long time coming, whether you know it or not."

Another cultist moved to close in on him, but Blackbird held up a hand. He paused and appraised Jared. "Still nursing a sore spot over that witch who tried to play hero?" he prodded. "Is that what this is about? Because saving this little tree hugger won't bring back your wife."

Jared took a step closer, advancing on him with long, even strides. "You murdered my wife." His voice had gone cold. Frozen. An unnerving sort of calm. The storm was approaching. "You poisoned my home." Another step. A hush fell over the small crowd. "You took away my daughter's mother. You kidnapped the woman I love."

He stared Blackbird down, his veins nearly vibrating with unbridled emotion. "I'm not afraid of you."

Blackbird had the gall to smile. "What do you want me to say, Loverboy? You want me to tell you that I'm sorry? Your town's full of freaks and monsters, my friend." He gestured behind himself toward Serena, who was standing on shaky legs beneath the tree. The dais wobbled slightly, and her eyes went wide as she attempted to steady herself. "And Miss Albright here's one of them."

"I don't care what you think she is," he snapped. "Let her go, now!"

"And why would I do that, hmm? Her little tea parties have made everyone in Pembrooke complicit in witchcraft. She's the one that's been poisoning your town, not us!"

No one was more surprised than Jared when he began to laugh. Softly, at first, but it continued to build as the seconds passed. It was the senseless, mad confidence of a man whose only options had become death or failure.

"You think that *Serena Albright* is the biggest threat in Pembrooke?" he asked, still chuckling. "A small town botanist, who specializes in... herbal remedies? You think she's the most powerful witch that you could get your hands on?"

Blackbird shrugged. "She's got half the town under her spell. Doesn't matter what spell it is. And either way, any dead witch is a good thing, in my book. Big, small, I don't discriminate."

Oh, that was rich. Jared looked him in the eye. "Let her go, and I'll let you take me instead."

"You?" He lifted a brow. "Why would we want *you?*"

The corner of Jared's mouth lifted. He took a long, slow breath.

To someone viewing from a distance, it would have looked as though a large glass dome had just materialized around the group, the storm raging all around it but unable to enter their bubble. From within, Jared had parted the rain around them with nothing more than an exaggerated wave of his hand. Many of the cultists, who were still hiding beneath their hoods, pulled them back at that moment, staring wide-eyed at the sky.

Jared cleared his throat, and spoke a few lines of gibberish with great drama and gravity, as if it were an arcane incantation. In reality, it was nothing more than a few half-remembered fragments from a phase he'd gone through in high school, where he'd tried very hard to learn Tolkien's Elvish. It had the desired effect, all the same. As he spoke, he gathered some of the rain into a large, swirling orb that hung suspended in the air for a moment. After pausing for effect, he flung it so that it crashed just in front of two men nearest the tree, splashing onto their legs and torsos.

Any witch worth their weight in iron would be able to tell that Serena was a much more skilled and impressive spellcaster. To do what she did, with the same level of subtlety and precision, required very sophisticated techniques and intimate knowledge of, not just magic, but botany and medicine, as well. There was no doubt in Jared's mind that she was a much more powerful witch than he would ever be.

But he was surrounded by humans—not very smart ones, at that—and he'd just put on quite the show. He smirked at the congregation, releasing his spell and letting the rain resume overhead.

"There," he said, pleasantly, as if they were discussing the weather. "Was that convincing enough for you?"

CHAPTER 40
SERENA

"Stop!"

Serena's eyes locked on Jared. She swallowed, her body trembling, and spoke to the congregation, with an unwavering gaze.

"Don't... Don't listen to him. Keep me instead. I'm the one you came here for, aren't I?"

Jared took a step towards her, a few robed figures reaching out as if to stop him. He ignored them. "Serena..."

"I'm not letting you do this!" she insisted. Her eyes began to well with tears, and she tried to will them away. "I couldn't live with myself, if you sacrificed yourself for me."

His voice softened. "You have no idea how special you are, do you?"

One of the cultists grabbed him by the arms then, yanking them behind his back and binding him tightly. Evidently his display had been sufficient proof of his worth, in their eyes.

"I lost myself, Serena. I lost my heart, years ago. And you... you taught me how to love life again. How to stop living in the past, and finally move forward. You are so much more than I ever deserved."

The sob finally worked its way up her throat, spluttering helplessly into the open air. Jared just smiled reassuringly.

"Trust me, Serena."

There was a certainty in his voice, in that moment. A little spark of trademark Westergard cockiness that told her everything that she needed to know.

He was stalling.

"I do," she said, and it was the truth. "I trust you."

He nodded. "I love you."

Her mouth fell open but the words caught in her throat. Such simple words, but they were words she hadn't uttered to a man in more than ten years. Words that when last uttered had heralded the beginning of her nomadic life long ago. The world came to a halt as the Brotherhood momentarily faded from view and she was left standing alone with Jared.

Her heart lifted, despite the circumstances. Yes, she trusted him. Realized she trusted him more than anyone else. And in that moment, she understood that everyone she knew in life was going to bring her pain. The real trick was figuring out which people were worth the heartache.

"I love you, too, Jared."

Blackbird snorted dismissively. "You two are lucky that I share your flair for the dramatic," he said, coming between them and shoving Jared to the ground. He went willingly, and the side of Serena that had always been a bit too prideful for its own good lashed out, fighting against her binds.

Lip curled, Blackbird delivered a swift kick to Jared's stomach, and Serena gritted her teeth. Another kick connected with his jaw, and Jared's mouth bloomed red.

Blackbird just sniffed, staring dispassionately at the ground. "All right, Colin. Let the girl down."

"My pleasure," he said.

She expected to feel him cut the rope, or simply pull it from her neck. Instead, she let out an aborted shriek when Colin kicked away the dais, letting her fall the precious few inches that separated her from death.

Jared lurched halfway to his knees when the rope pulled taut, struggling fruitlessly. "Serena! No!"

Serena's body fought on instinct, her legs kicking blindly but finding nothing but open air. Her arms jerked despite being bound, floundering as she swung uselessly from the branch. The rope around her throat bit into her skin, crushing the air from her windpipe. Her mouth gasped, her eyes widened, as hot tears mingled with the rain.

Distantly, as though he was speaking from behind a pane of glass, she heard Blackbird say, "Why take one witch when we can have two?"

She tried to scream, but all that surfaced was a ruined wheeze. For whatever reason, her mind drifted back to the teahouse. Who would take care of Kita, when she was gone? Who would tend to her houseplants? Her vision started to go dark at its edges. The only sound was the rush of blood roaring in her ears.

She was gasping like a fish out of water when she saw the flash of metal and felt herself crash to the ground. Taking in great, hungry lungfuls of humid summer air, she felt her head rush painfully, the sensation of raindrops hitting her skin like hammers in the wake of feeling so numb. She rolled onto her back, still spluttering like she'd been drowning, and looked upward at the branch, in confusion. The dangling length of rope overhead was severed, its ends cleanly cut. A small but strong battle ax was embedded in the bark of a nearby tree.

Someone had cut through her noose.

Jared.

He was laying face down on the muddy ground now, Black-bird hovering over him. Jared was rewarded with a swift kick to the stomach for his thrown ax.

"Search him," Blackbird said. "See if he's got any more toys hiding in his clothes."

Still short of breath, Serena reflexively inched toward Jared in spite of the bindings that cut into her wrist.

"I may have underestimated you two," Blackbird began. "But I am frankly a little touched by your sense of heroism, Loverboy. And even I can appreciate a great romance when I see one. So I have a very fitting solution for you two lovebirds. Pick 'em up, boys. Bring 'em over here."

Rough hands seized her, pulling her to her feet and dragging her forward.

"Tie 'em up against this dead tree. We're gonna burn them together."

"That wasn't the deal," Jared barked. "Let her go. You'll never get a fire going big enough to burn both of us in this rain, anyway. Take me alone and I'll keep the rain away."

Serena parted her lips to speak but, before she could even try, a circle of flames rose all around them. Its appearance was met with a collective gasp, a few scattered screams. And more voices. Someone threw her back to the ground. She heard Jared bark out a laugh.

Over the commotion, she could just make out footsteps in the distance. Many, many footsteps, like a small army approaching. A pair of pale legs entered Serena's periphery, just outside the edge of the flames.

"Serena!"

"E-Emela," Serena croaked, her vocal chords burning with the effort.

"Is she okay?" More rushed footsteps. Rowan's voice followed shortly after.

"Jared? What the hell did they do to you?"

"Whatever they did, it's going to look like a slap on the wrist compared to what I'm planning," an unfamiliar male voice said. Serena didn't recognize it, but when he stepped into the light, the man, standing next to Royce, bore a faint resemblance to Jared. "Nobody hurts my family and gets away with it."

In the light of the fire, Royce's line of sight seemed to zero in on Blackbird. He advanced, Rowan quickly parting the circle of fire for him to enter. Blackbird sneered up as Royce approached, looking far too smug for a man in his position. He pulled the black tourmaline from beneath his robe. "Bring on all the fire and brimstone you want. I'm sorry to tell you, but your magic can't touch us."

Royce smiled, cracking his knuckles. "Good thing I don't need magic to beat your ass." He swung and struck Blackbird in the jaw.

"Yeah. But I'd prefer if they didn't have their little gemstones, all the same."

Serena didn't need to turn to know that voice. She watched as Blackbird's amulet, along with nearly two dozen others, lifted from their chests and sailed into the air. All at once, the chains snapped, flying toward their new center of gravity as the Inkers reached with futile hands to retrieve them. When Serena looked back, Lily and Alice were holding the necklaces aloft, with vicious smirks spread across their faces.

From the brush, she saw more figures emerge. Not witches this time, but human citizens of Pembrooke. Dozens of customers from her teahouse, there to defend *her*.

The gravity of their circumstances seemed to dawn on the Brotherhood all at once. Serena saw something like horror being born on her would-be-killers' expressions, and her mouth twisted into a weak smile.

"What are you going to do?" she asked mockingly, pushing herself to her knees as she glared at Colin. "Fight?" She forced a chuckle, and it felt like sandpaper in her throat. "There are more of us than there are of you, *sweetheart*."

One of the Inkers screamed in terror. But it might as well have been a battle cry as all hell began to break loose right after.

In an instant, Rowan opened up the circle of flames for the others. Royce tackled one of the robed men to the ground, beating him in the face with his fist, as Liam rushed toward another. The flames rose wherever the Brotherhood moved to run, keeping them trapped within the circle, while the people of Pembrooke entered, until they all moved within the enclosed, fiery wreath.

Serena tensed when she saw a glint of metal in her periphery, and a hand gripped her shoulder.

"You must be Serena," a male voice said, taking his knife to the ropes around her arms. "I'm Liam, Jared's cousin. Just relax, we've got you."

Once her binds were untied, she fought her wobbling way to her feet. Liam then moved to cut Jared free, and the moment Jared found agency, his eyes fixed on Blackbird and he disappeared in the melee.

Her attention scattered, Serena watched as Lily closed in on Colin. "You tried to kill my best friend," she said, all blood and iron. "Maybe I should hang *you*?"

Colin's feet began to rise from the ground, his hands moving to clutch at his throat. Serena took Lily by the shoulders, pulling her back.

"Stop!"

Lily rounded on her, Colin falling in a heap on the ground. "They weren't going to stop with you!" she argued. "Why should we stop?"

Serena's hand found Lily's, gripping it tightly. "This isn't you," she said softly, then sent a pointed look past the circle. The flames were dwindling; Rowan was losing her control over them. In the light, both women could see that Emela was staring wide-eyed at the violence in the circle.

"You really want to be a killer, Lily? You want Emela to be complicit?"

Lily exhaled sharply, eyes roaming around the circle. "If you don't want anyone to become a killer, you should get moving," she said, pointing near the center of the crowd.

As Serena turned, the veil of rain and darkness initially painted a frenetic tableau of figures intertwined in chaos. Yet, almost magnetically, her gaze honed onto two figures, their silhouettes marked starkly against the backdrop of the toppled dais.

Jared had Blackbird by the throat, a suspended sheet of water swirling over the man's mouth and nose. He was choking him with his bare hands, for now, but it could become an outright drowning at any moment. Royce was on the ground, wrestling with another Inker, trading blows. Liam was squared off between Aaron and another Inker, a warm flicker shifting on metal where a blade twitched in Aaron's trembling hands. In the light of the ever-faltering flames, she saw a near-animal fury in Jared's face. Unhinged, untethered, undone.

She darted across the wet, flattened grass, laying hands on Jared's tense shoulders, prying him away. Jared allowed her to pull him back, but the water over Blackbird's face remained. His face contorted, eyes bulging in panic and agony as he fought for breath.

"Jared."

Jared kicked him swiftly in the stomach, staring dispassionately at him, just as Blackbird had done to him, minutes prior.

"Jared, look at me."

He lifted his hand, outstretched fingers slowly curling into a fist. She caught him by the wrist before he could do anything, holding him desperately in a vice grip.

Jared spun to look at her, and the moment their eyes met, the savage fog seemed to blink from his eyes. He stared down at her like she was the first thing he'd ever seen. "Serena..."

"Don't let them defile you," she whispered. "I know you. I know that you don't want this." Her brows furrowed. "Do you?"

"I do, actually. They were going to kill both of us." He panted, sweat running down his forehead. Looking into her eyes, he sighed and shook his head. "Godamnit, Serena. You can't be serious."

"If we kill them all, won't they just send more? Come to get their revenge on us all? When will this end?"

She couldn't disguise her relief when she heard the sound of Blackbird spluttering, gasping for air in the grass. Jared looked around the circle, hands on hips, taking in the scene. He cleared his throat, projecting enough to get the majority's attention.

"Listen up everybody. The people of Pembrooke aren't going to go home tonight with anyone's blood on their hands," he shouted, voice steely with conviction. It took a few minutes to get everyone's attention, but the fighting had already dwindled as the overpowered Inkers had begun to accept defeat.

"We can't just let them go!" Lily protested. "We know what they're capable of!"

"Could we call the cops?" Aaron offered. "Or the... magic cops? I'm assuming there are procedures in place for this kind of thing, right?"

Jared nodded, still visibly shaking his anger off. "I could get in touch with the rest of the council, have them get involved."

"No," Serena said, eyes fixed on Blackbird's bloodied face. His nose appeared broken. "No, we can't draw any more attention to Pembrooke. There might be more chapters of the the Brotherhood in the region."

Jared sighed, exasperation creeping into his tone. "So what do you think we should do, then?"

As she searched her mind for possible answers, she looked at her friends. Her coven. Rowan. Hailey. Lily. Alice. Zara. Charlotte. Brooklyn. Noora...

The moment her eyes landed on Emela, Serena smiled.

"Bring them to the teahouse. I have an idea."

"You almost done?"

Serena didn't dare to look up from the pot. A large batch of deep blue tea bubbled away on the shop's burner, her harrowed reflection staring back at her from its surface. She stirred, frowned, reminded herself not to inhale the vapors.

"Just a minute!" she called back. From beyond the teahouse's kitchen, she could hear muffled screams. The Brotherhood's faithful, struggling in the dark.

Rowan grunted as she neared. Serena heard a thud. "Hate to rush you, babe, but is there any chance you could—*oof*—expedite the process a bit?"

She huffed. "Sure, let's play cavalier with an incredibly volatile magical substance. It'll probably be fine!"

"Well, is there anything that I could do to help?"

Her hand clenched around the ladle. Relaxed. Clenched again. "Some silence would be useful."

"*Rowan*," Jared barked behind her, and Serena felt herself smile. "Let her work, yeah? If she says it'll be a minute, then give her a minute."

"Are we sure this concoction is even going to work?" Rowan said, hovering over the pot.

Serena groaned. "It will if you let me focus."

She stared at the mixture, letting it gradually cool from its simmer. The vapors were nearly overwhelming in the cramped kitchen, intense and chemically. *Dry erase markers*, just like Lily had described. The spell would be potent. Good, she needed it to be.

Jared's request had been clear: "Make it surgical. Elegant. Make these assholes forget Pembrooke, Oregon even exists. And everyone in it. And then make them forget everything they ever knew about the Brotherhood."

"It's time," she announced, setting the spoon down. "Get ready to hold them down."

Administering the tea was the hardest part. Binding and gagging them all, dragging them back to The Velvet Teahouse, mixing and making the tea itself—those things had been tricky in their own right. But holding each Inker down, forcing them to open their mouths, to not spit out the mixture, to *swallow*, was a Herculean task. Even with backup. She'd saved the worst for last, choosing to get the lower ranked members out of the way first.

Eventually, though, only two remained.

Serena glared at Colin Park where he writhed in his chair, twisting this way and that. Aaron moved to hold him in place, but Serena shook her head.

"No. Let me."

She pulled his gag down, grabbing a fistful of his hair and yanking it until he was staring at the ceiling.

"Any last words?" she asked.

He set his jaw, struggling to look back at her. "Should've burned you."

The Amnesia Tea poured down his throat meeting little

315

resistance as he accepted his defeat. She found that it gave her more than a little satisfaction.

Releasing his head, she fixed his gag in place until the spell could take effect. She looked to Jared. He was leaning against the counter, watching the proceedings with an icy stare.

"Do you want to do the honors?" she said, gesturing to the final Inker.

Without a word, Jared pushed himself from the counter and approached Blackbird. His face was impassive, giving nothing away. Jared pulled down the gag from his blood stained face, and Blackbird snarled.

"This won't save you, you know," Blackbird said. "She's already made this whole town into a target. Revealed herself to the population. How long do you think it'll be until another chapter comes to find you?" He looked Jared up and down. "Face it, you're going to spend the rest of your damned life looking over your shoulder for me."

Jared scarcely blinked, grabbing Blackbird harshly by the jaw and magically forcing the mixture to flow into his throat.

"I'll get used to it."

Serena looked sidelong at Jared, his eyes hard on the dark road ahead of them. He'd been quiet the entire car ride. He had good reason, they both did, of course, but it still chafed at her.

They'd left Blackbird and the others with Ethan, the blond, short-haired man she had seen visit Jared's office. They had met him just outside of town, along with five other men, each mysterious in their own way. Jared would later explain they were his fellow knights, and that they would know what to do with the Inkers.

The knights had led away the Inkers, delirious and disoriented, but she knew that they would come to their senses within a matter of hours. It was an easier sentence than they deserved, but all that mattered to her was that Pembrooke would be safe.

"We don't have to talk about it," she said with a soft sigh. "But we can, if you want."

Jared took a slow breath. "It's just a lot to process," he said after a moment.

Serena nodded, not sure where to begin, either.

"Can you spend the night at my place?" she said. "I... I really don't want to be alone tonight. And I don't think that you should be, either."

He glanced at her from the corner of his eye before returning to the road. "I don't want you to be alone, either. Besides, I'll feel better if we can keep an eye on Kita. I know she seemed like she was just groggy when we got back to the teahouse, but I don't feel like taking any more chances tonight."

She tried to relax, leaning back in the passenger's seat. "That's... that's really sweet of you. Thanks."

They passed the familiar lilac sign welcoming them to Pembrooke. A cluster of astilbe stood proudly at its feet. *Good things come to those who wait.*

"Home sweet home," she muttered, nodding to the sign.

He finally looked at her properly then, lifting a brow. "Home? You're not leaving anymore, then?"

She shook her head back at him. "I never wanted to leave. I was only doing it for everyone's safety, you know that."

"I guess I just wasn't sure where you'd landed."

She smiled at him. "Looks like I'm landing here."

He nodded, taking a while to absorb the information. Serena became uncomfortable as the seconds ticked by, becoming increasingly anxious that Jared was upset with her.

"I had a whole speech prepared to make you stay, though," he finally said.

She laughed, sudden joy bubbling in her chest. Her heart flipped. "You can still give me the speech, if you want," she told him with a grin.

He waved her off. "It won't be the same now, there's no stakes."

"No, I want to hear it!"

He rolled his eyes, answering her laugh with a chuckle of his own. "It was something to the effect of, 'This town won't be the same without you, and Zoe and I would miss you terribly, and I love you too much to let you go', et cetera, et cetera. It would've been very convincing in the moment, trust me."

"Oh, I'm sure. I'm convinced right now, even. I might never leave Pembrooke again."

He sighed, his face softening as her laughter died off. "I meant it though, Serena. What I said out there. I love you."

She leaned across the car, pressing a kiss to his cheek before resting her head on his shoulder. "I know. I meant it, too. I love, you, too, Jared."

CHAPTER 41
SERENA

Mabon festivities heralded the official start of autumn for the witches of Pembrooke. With it, the trees began shedding their leaves, turning the Weeping Woods into a plush red carpet. The chill in the air brought a rosy hue to meandering cheeks and noses, and kingfishers prepared to migrate for the winter. Best of all, the dropping temperatures made the people of Pembrooke crave a piping hot cup of tea, to warm their bones as much as their stomachs.

Jared Westergard's car turned onto Harbor Street, windows cracked so that Kita could poke her nose outside and take in the fresh air. As if she hadn't already had enough of it today.

"You're way off base," he said, as Serena turned to laugh at him from the passenger seat.

"You think so?" Serena said.

Jared gave her a playful look. "Absolutely."

"Well, what fruit do *you* think you'd be?" she prodded.

He shrugged, parking the car near the end of Bailey Street. "I don't know, but not a blackberry."

Serena opened the back door, quickly clipping Kita's leash on with a ruffle of her fur. "You just remind me of a blackberry, that's all."

He furrowed his brows. Zoe was quick to take his hand as the three of them set off down the street and, without thinking, Serena moved to take Zoe's other hand.

"Explain your reasoning to me."

She snorted. "I used to hate blackberries."

"Right, very flattering," he deadpanned, but cracked a smile. "And how do you feel about them now?"

She smirked at him. "I could take 'em or leave 'em."

Jared laughed.

"Well, I think you'd be a coconut," Zoe chirped.

Serena agreed with a grin. "Sure, since his skull's so thick."

He rolled his eyes at her. "Well, what would you be?"

Serena hummed in thought. "Zoe would be a strawberry."

"Naturally."

"I don't think it's fair to have to pick my own," Serena pouted, and Jared huffed in false exasperation.

"I think you'd be a peach," he declared, making a point to look her up and down with obvious appreciation. "A ripe, Georgia peach."

Serena felt herself blushing, and she nudged him with her elbow, giving him a pointed signal to behave himself.

He simply responded by darting close to kiss her temple. It softened her, in spite of herself. It had been a beautiful day, after all. A morning of hiking through Dakrya Forest, a picnic lunch at the Left Eye River Basin, and she was looking forward to an afternoon hard at work. Reaping what she sowed. It was a simple life, maybe, but it was hers.

Kita must've detected an irresistible smell on the far end of the sidewalk, because she suddenly veered in front of Jared, causing him to trip over her lead. Serena reached out to steady him, holding him upright by his arm.

"Sorry," she said, trying to urge Kita back to the path.

"Serena, just take her off the leash."

She frowned up at him. "Are you trying to get us a ticket?"

He shrugged, crouching down to release Kita. "Rules are meant to be broken, right?" he teased, face shifting to a grimace almost immediately. "Uh, don't repeat that, Z."

"Whatever you say, Dad."

When he stood, Kita trotted off into the brush, eagerly nosing her way through the plants.

"Dad, she's running away!" Zoe shouted, pointing toward the wolf.

"She's not running away," Jared assured her, watching as Kita investigated the scent, then circled back around and rejoined the group. "She just needs to be allowed to explore. You need to trust that she'll come back."

Serena smiled up at him, retrieving his hand and squeezing it reassuringly. "She knows to come back, she always does. We're her family, after all."

They slowed as they approached the teahouse, its cheerful purple sign greeting them from outside. Serena felt a sudden tug at her arm, and when she looked over at Jared, she realized that he'd stopped walking.

He cleared his throat a bit awkwardly. "Hey, Zoe, why don't you go ahead and take Kita inside, yeah? I wanna talk to Serena for a second."

It didn't take more convincing than that. Zoe sped into the teahouse, leading Kita inside with her.

When the door fell shut, she gave him a curious look. "Everything okay?"

"Serena," he started, running a hand through his dark waves, "I spoke to the council."

Serena's heart skipped a beat. She took a deep breath, her mind preparing for the worst. "And?"

Jared stepped closer, enveloping her in the warm scent of amber and spice. "They're willing to let you keep the teahouse open."

Her eyes widened, relief and surprise evident. "Really? Even after everything?"

He nodded, his fingers tracing a pattern on the back of her hand. "I told them how accepting the people of Pembrooke have been of your magic. I convinced them that Pembrooke could serve as... an experiment of sorts."

"An experiment?" She arched an eyebrow.

"Yes. To see if our world can coexist with the mundane. To witness if magic can be practiced in the open, in front of ordinary humans, without causing chaos."

Serena's heart raced. The weight she'd been carrying for weeks, fearing the closure of her haven, began to lift. "Jared, I don't know what to say. Or how to thank you."

He smiled, a genuine, heartwarming curve of his lips. "You don't have to. This is as much about the future of our community as it is about your teahouse. If Pembrooke works, it could be the blueprint for how we live out in the open everywhere."

She leaned into him, feeling the steady beat of his heart. "Yeah, it's a good start."

He wrapped an arm around her, pulling her close. "It's a new beginning. So yeah, everything's very, very good," he murmured, before dipping his head into the space between them.

Serena smiled into his kiss, lifting a hand to hold his cheek. His arm slipped around her waist, tugging their bodies flush. She sighed, parting her lips.

She pulled back in shock when a sharp thudding sounded next to her. It was Rowan, knocking on the window from inside the teahouse. She gestured pointedly at the rest of the shop interior, indicating that everyone inside could see them.

"Still need to get those curtains," he whispered to her with a breathy laugh. She pushed him away in fond annoyance, her cheeks burning.

"Come on," she said. "I want to show you the changes I made inside."

Rowan whistled at her the moment she walked through the door, only making her face burn hotter. "Look out," she teased. "It's Pembrooke's hottest couple!"

Jared ignored her as he gazed around the teahouse, immediately noticing the striking transformation. Serena had replaced her original, elegant esthetic with something that felt old-world and cozy. Gone were the straightforward teas with suggestive names hinting at their magical properties. Instead, an array of vibrantly colored dried herbs and flowers now resided in glass jars that lined the shelves behind the counter. The vibe was reminiscent of a vintage apothecary, bringing a touch of whimsy to the place. Strategically placed dried plants adorned the walls, their faded hues contrasting beautifully with the more modern décor. Potted fruit trees dotted the floor in strategic locations.

His eyes roamed over to the menu board where she hoped he noted another change. Instead of listing teas by the ailments they could alleviate, each blend was now named for its primary ingredients. 'Lavender Dreams', 'Rosemary Reverie', and 'Hibiscus Sunrise' were just a few of the poetic names that now graced the menu.

Seeing his attentive gaze, Serena stepped closer. "The real magic doesn't need to be loud or ostentatious. It's more about embracing the tea's foundation." She gestured at the jars behind her. "These herbs and flowers, they're more than just plants. They're a testament to nature's magic. And by focusing on them, I can still weave my enchantments into them, just more covertly. Hidden in plain sight."

Jared, taking in her words, looked around once more, appreciating the elegance of the changes. "Hidden in plain sight," he murmured, echoing her earlier sentiment.

"Exactly. A humble herbal teahouse. No more hinting at the magic, but not denying it either."

"I like it." He reached out, gently squeezing her hand. "You've found a beautiful balance, Serena. This feels right."

"Oh good, you two are finally here." Judith appeared behind the counter, restocking the display cabinet with fresh lemon pound cake and apple walnut cookies.

"Sorry for running late," Serena said, quickly washing her hands at the sink. "Did I miss anything important?"

"Sheila Patterson, that nice girl who runs the rec center on Hitchcock Avenue called. She injured her elbow this morning. She wanted to know if you could whip something up for her, before she came all the way out here."

Serena nodded, shrugging her way out of her jacket and looping her apron around her neck. "Of course, but I wrote down a recipe for the anti-inflammatory tea; it should be in the book. We're calling it Gingermint Tea now. All the ingredients are already fully enchanted and it just needs to be brewed."

Judith shrugged helplessly. "I know, I know. But she said it had to be made by you. I told her it would be ready in an hour."

Flashing a sympathetic smile, Serena began to gather the ingredients. She supposed Judith hadn't been working in the teahouse for quite long enough to garner a reputation. But by New Year's, Serena felt confident that people would be happy to be served by Judith as well, rather than Serena alone. For now, though...

"Superstitious, then," Lily mused, her elbows propped on

the counter. "Although, I bet you could send a cup brewed by Judith her way and she wouldn't know the difference."

Aaron chuckled. "I think she would probably notice when her arm didn't actually feel any different."

"Maybe, but it all tastes the same."

Serena rolled her eyes, nudging Lily from across the counter. "Don't you have work to be doing?"

"Emela's keeping an eye on the shop." She leaned closer, lowering her voice. "Hey, do you think Royce would save us a table in the back on Saturday? Enzo's back in town and I want to take him out for our anniversary."

"I can get you guys a table at Borealis Saturday night," Hailey said, after bursting through the front door. "Why go to a brew pub when you can have fine French cuisine?"

"I can't afford you," Lily said. "Too spendy."

Jared strode around the counter, then, summoning some water from a nearby pitcher and bringing it effortlessly to a rolling boil. "I'll give Royce a call for you," he said. "Oh, and congratulations on the anniversary."

"And congratulations to Emela, too. When is her book coming out?" Aaron asked. "I want the first signed copy."

"She's supposed to hear back from the publisher tomorrow afternoon," Lily replied. "And I'm first in line for the autographs. I've had dibs for years now."

"Hey, I talked to all the other ladies and we have finally decided on a day," Hailey said. "Seems the coven will be meeting every Thursday evening, starting next week."

"And don't forget we're celebrating Mabon tomorrow night," Serena said, hoisting a basket onto the counter. "Judith and I have been busy gathering all these spuds for the big potato bake."

"Hey, let's do a bonfire on the beach!" Rowan said. "We can

roast them down there. I'll bring the fire." She laughed maniacally.

The bell over the door chimed, and Serena took a centering breath, smiling brightly as she turned to welcome the next customer. To her surprise, Alice rushed across the floor, panting, her pretty face reddened.

"Hey, Alice. What's up?"

Alice dropped her hands heavily on the counter and grimaced, looking up through a fringe of long lashes.

"Ghosts," the witch said with a deep sigh. "Have you got anything to help me deal with ghosts?"

FREE ROMANTIC FANTASY NOVELLA!

TWO WARLOCKS, ONE DEADLY RIVALRY,
AND THE WOMAN WHO COULD DESTROY
THEM BOTH.

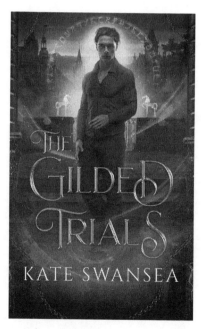

www.kateswansea.com

Download your free copy of The Gilded Trials when you subscribe to my newsletter to stay up to date on New Releases, Giveaways, and Exclusive Content. Go to kateswansea.com.

Vivian and Hayden descend from old, prominent witch families. Their engagement has been prearranged since before she was born, in a union meant to merge their powerful families.

When a magic tournament is announced to replace one of Black Lake Falls' prestigious Protectors, it draws alchemists from all corners of the world, including the enigmatic but handsome Jack.

Hayden and Jack find themselves locked in a fierce rivalry, contending not only for the prestigious title of the town warden, but also for the affections of Vivian.

Forced to choose between duty and passion, Vivian uncovers startling dark secrets about both Jack and Hayden. In a story where unwise choices have deadly consequences, she soon learns she may just have the power to destroy them both.

Also by Kate Swansea

THE PARAVAL SERIES

Midlife Alchemy

Midlife Incantations

Midlife Shadows

THE VELVET TEAHOUSE WITCHES

A Sip of Magic

www.kateswansea.com

THE PARAVAL SERIES

BOOK 1: MIDLIFE ALCHEMY

Part paranormal fantasy adventure, part romance, this is the tale of a fabulous, forty-something witch who is finally coming into her power. Because it's never too late.

Elise Clair has just sent her youngest off to college and is looking forward to returning to her career and fixing her broken marriage. But the fates have other plans in store for her. After her husband cheats on her and derails her career plans, she's disappointed in how life turned out.

Maybe even a little angry.

When she starts accidentally turning dental mirrors into machetes at work, she knows it's time for a little get-away.

What she ends up doing is packing up and moving across

the country, after receiving a mysterious job offer in Washington state that sounds too good to pass up.

She has a second chance to create a new life for herself and do what she wants for a change.

She's expecting a fairy tale alpine village and lots of skiing.

What she gets is a town crawling with witches and rebel vampires.

And a gorgeous general and his minotaur partner.

Oh, and a gate that leads to hell.

She'll need to resurrect her long-abandoned magic to discover the town's secrets, and how they may even unlock her own family secrets.

Act Two of her life may turn out to be even better than Act One. If she can survive it.

Made in the USA
Monee, IL
14 September 2024

65760909R10196